The Stargazey

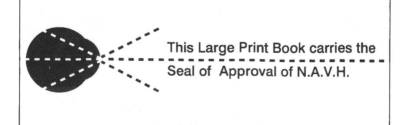

This Large Print Book carries the
Seal of Approval of N.A.V.H.

The Stargazey

A Richard Jury Mystery

Martha Grimes

Thorndike Press • Thorndike, Maine

Copyright © 1998 by Martha Grimes

Published in 1999 by arrangement with
Henry Holt & Company, Inc.

Thorndike Large Print ® Basic Series.

The tree indicium is a trademark of Thorndike Press.

The text of this Large Print edition is unabridged.
Other aspects of the book may vary from the original edition.

Set in 16 pt. Plantin.

Printed in the United States on permanent paper.

Library of Congress Cataloging in Publication Data

Grimes, Martha.
    The stargazey : a Richard Jury mystery / Martha Grimes.
       p.   cm.
    ISBN 0-7862-1788-X (lg. print : hc : alk. paper)
    ISBN 0-7862-1789-8 (lg. print : sc : alk. paper)
    1. Jury, Richard (Fictitious character) — Fiction.
  2. Police — England — Fiction. 3. Large type books.
  I. Title.
    [PS3557.R48998S7   1999]
    813'.54—dc21   98-51094

To Travis and Kent
and Roanoke —
stargazers all.
April 25, 1998

Far in the pillared dark
Thrush music went —
Almost like a call to come in
To the dark and lament.

But no, I was out for stars:
I would not come in.
I meant not even if asked,
And I hadn't been.

> — ROBERT FROST,
> FROM "COME IN"

PROLOGUE

St. Petersburg
February

The snow looked blue in the dusk, its fresh fall an untrodden path leading into the dense fog that shrouded the Palace Square and the Alexander Column. Ice encased the tall trees on the edge of Nevsky Prospekt, along which cars picked their way, braving the winter gloom. Snow falling on snow muffled the shuddering gunfire sounds of the Neva's ice surface splitting and cracking, as the wide river fought itself free of January's thick ice. From this height, she could see St. Petersburg's snow-topped roofs, the drums and domes of St. Isaac's, the ice-sheathed bridges. She loved St. Petersburg's bridges almost as much as London's. Between the time she had entered and left the museum, it had snowed again. A layer of ice as thin as lace had crackled delicately underfoot as she'd walked across the flat roof of the restaurant.

At least the blade-sharp wind had

stopped, thank God. Like pendant smoke, her breath hung before her, as if it were crystallizing in the frigid air. Her hands were frozen in gloves that were as thin as her breath, more like a layer of black ice than leather. Anything heavier would have made it impossible to handle the rifle.

The rifle was fitted with a telescopic lens and a night scope. She had used it many times but hadn't expected to use it this evening. This evening she had to improvise, something she disliked doing, not because she hadn't the wit for it but because planning should always be impeccable, and hers was usually flawless.

But this afternoon there had been a flaw. She had made certain the rest room was empty but had forgotten the janitress, who came in while she was standing at the sink dismantling the walker. It was this woman for whom she was now waiting. She had watched them all, the staff, and the building, for weeks. She had recognized the cleaning woman when she'd come into the rest room with her rags and bucket. But tonight schedules were upset because no one had been allowed to leave until the police had asked their questions.

Since her Russian was bad and her French was excellent, she had presented her French papers. Her fabricated identity — *Cybil Odéon, Paris, 6ᵉ Arrond., blvd. St.-Germain* — was one of several. What were the Petersburg police to do but wave off this old, half-deaf French pensioner who couldn't get around without a walker? And who hadn't been clear about what had happened because her glasses were so thick-lensed that her eyes looked drowned behind them, strands of hair trapped in the stems like seaweed.

The staff had been trickling out, one, two at a time. No sign yet of the cleaning lady. She jammed her hands down in her sheepskin-lined pockets, just to warm them for a moment; otherwise she wouldn't be able to hold the gun. Now she picked it up again, sighted down its barrel at the statues on the parapets of the Winter Palace. She moved the rifle a little to the left until she saw the Alexander Column. The angel on its top floated on icy wings. The column itself was perfectly balanced, supported by its own weight. She had read this somewhere and liked it. *Supported by its own weight:* a study in splendid isolation.

That was how she felt now. She would have preferred the isolation not be a freezing one, but personal discomfort bothered her only insofar as it kept her from performing. She had trained herself to withstand any discomfort that could come along, discomforts of either body or mind. The mind was more difficult, being limitless. She raised her eyes for a moment to look up at the stars. In the course of her studies, she had read that what fueled the stars was the merging of atoms. Fusion science. What fascinated her was the notion that the amount of energy in was the amount of energy out. There was an equation: $Q=1$. And this, she had to imagine, was perfect balance, like that of the Alexander Column. Perfect balance was what she was after; it was all she was after. She wanted to get to that point where nothing resonated, where the past could not pretend to shape itself into the present, where planes had clear, sharp edges to which nothing clung. People didn't come into it; they weren't part of the equation. What relationships she'd had had been brief and in her control, though her partners didn't seem aware of this. It was astonishing how easily people were hoodwinked, how easily — even eagerly — led.

$Q=1$. She would have made a good physicist if she hadn't been deflected in her studies and instead become a killer.

People were trickling out, one by one, finally released from being questioned — by museum security, by state security, by city police, probably none of whom had coordinated efforts with the others. There seemed no end to the permutations of police authority sent to plague the Russian citizen. One could scarcely blame police, though, considering what had just gone missing. A few men, a few women, all leaving through the main entrance only to be stopped again by the guards standing outside of the entrance doors.

She sighted the distant doors of the museum through the scope. The cleaning staff came out this way. In the lavatory, the janitress's glance had swept over her — the old French lady with the walker — without seeming to register. It was hard to tell with these Russians, with their decades of training emotions not to reach their faces. She had always admired that trait. If she knew the Russian temperament, the janitress would need to think about what she'd seen. Probably, she would not have rushed into the room where police were questioning people. The woman would leave, go back to the flat she no doubt shared with a dozen others, and start thinking about it.

It was too cold to keep to one position; she had to put the gun down, to blow on her hands, to stomp her feet, to pivot her head on her neck, and, in doing so, to look again at the darkened sky. Night fell, weighted with stars. She felt a great affinity with the stars, with their detachment, their distant, icy indifference.

Again she retrieved the rifle, sighted through the scope. The door opened; the old janitress appeared, carrying a bag and wound about in a black scarf as close as a shroud. She got the woman in her cross-hairs and squeezed the trigger and felt the rush. It was her reward, the rush. Like a black bird, the woman fell into the powdery snow, sending up puffs like white exhaust. She stood up, looking off towards the scene. It was snowing again. Through it, she watched the tiny crowd collect, the guards at the museum doors, the few people within the grounds. She imagined them distraught, imagined them with arms flung up and out, the tiny black figures rushing through snowflakes falling slowly, dreamily, rushing toward the fallen woman as if drawn there by enchantment. Death woke in her long-slumbering scenes of a childhood she could not place — snow, fields, mountains — which sank again as quickly as they'd arisen.

She dismantled the rifle, as she had the

walker, and put the stock in her backpack, the barrel in the long case. She retraced her steps across the crackling ice, left the roof, and descended the several flights back to the restaurant.

She returned to the table she had left twenty minutes before. The room had grown noisy, filling up in this early dinner hour. Her vodka glass had been refilled; she had asked the waiter to do this before she'd left the table. He had smiled hugely, nodded.

When he returned to her table, he nodded towards the case across the other chair and asked her if she played the flute in the Philharmonic. No, she smiled and said, the oboe. Then she ordered bream stuffed with kasha and, for dessert, *blinicki* with jam.

When he'd gone off, she looked at the oboe case a little sadly and wished she were more musically inclined.

1

London
November

Saturday night. It was not a night to be spending alone, riding a bus. When he was a teenager at the comprehensive, Saturday night without a girl, without a date, without at least your mates to raise hell with, Saturday night alone would have been shameful. One wouldn't want to be seen alone on a Saturday night. . . . *Who are you kidding? That was never your life, Jury, not yours.*

There had been an errand to run in South Kensington, and he had taken the underground from Islington. Once out of the South Ken station, he had boarded a Fulham Road bus. It had been a long time since he'd seen this part of London, though it was where he'd lived for part of his childhood, that part he could still call "childhood." It had been a long time since he'd been on any bus at all. The conductor gave him one of those vaguely suspicious looks that conductors are trained up on, and Jury took the short flight of steps to the upper deck more quickly than was advisable for even agile youth, and he was a long way from that now. Up there the only other passengers were a boy and girl who couldn't keep their hands off each other; an old lady sleeping, chin on chest; and a dark-haired man in a tuxedo. Strange way for him to travel. Jury wondered where the party was. He was almost glad for his circumscribed life — no black-tie dinners, no champagne picnics at Ascot. No, for him it was work, home, the local.

Little shops lined both sides of the Fulham Road, expensive little shops, like the swank kitchen outfitters, Smallbone. Who, he wondered, had a Smallbone kitchen? He had never seen one. Fusty little electrical shops, an Oddbins, then the inevitable espresso bar that appeared to be replacing the caffs. Sad, that. High-priced grocers, high-windowed dress shops, windows blank but for one or two oddly angled and headless mannequins in mushroom-colored, loose-waisted clothes. A brace of antique shops, small and elegant, their facades looking as if they'd been stamped on Roman coins.

Jury had wanted to sit right in the front row where the wide window gave an unobstructed view of the street, as if one were hanging over it in midair. But those seats had been commandeered by a couple of teenagers with fade haircuts and a boom box, mercifully turned down. He had taken a seat near the back, wanting to distance himself.

He had always liked the street at night. When he was a uniform, he'd always chosen late duty. He had liked walking past shut-up shops, peering down dimly lit alleys. Perhaps night was just a good place to hide — any alley, any doorway.

For several years now, he'd been thinking of leaving London or transferring to one of the provincial police forces, such as Exeter. Macalvie would love to have him in Exeter. Or Yorkshire, up there in the snowy North Yorkshire moors. Or Stratford-upon-Avon. Sam Lasko would like nothing better. As it was, Jury worked often enough on Lasko's cases. Stratford. That made him wonder where Jenny Kennington was. She had left months ago, after her trial. He was still trying to understand what had gone wrong between him and Jenny, why there had been that mutual lack of trust. He had been so certain, at one time, they'd stick. He wondered as he had before, about his problems with women. Well, one could hardly refer to death as a "problem." Jane Holdsworth . . . Helen Minton . . . Molly Singer . . . Nell Healey. He should have been able to rescue Nell, at least. . . . *Rescue.* That was an odd way of thinking about it. Not only odd but arrogant. Hadn't Jenny described him as a man who wanted "to pull women from burning buildings"?

He looked out the window at a small clutch of people standing in front of a shop that sold furs. Or would do, if the demonstrators would get away from the door. What were they doing here at night when the place was closed? They carried placards with terrible pictures on them of animals imprisoned in lab cages or caught in leg-hold traps. (Jury thought those traps had been outlawed.) People had to walk around the group and could not avoid the signs.

The bus left the animal activists behind.

He was thinking his life was like this bus ride, then thinking, How mawkish, how maudlin. But it was the aimlessness of the ride; he didn't even know where it was going. Putney, probably; it was a number 14. At the next stop it pulled in behind another 14 and there was a bus in front of that one, too. He couldn't see the number, though. There was a fair queue of people; they'd been waiting a long time. He wondered at that law of bus scheduling that had three identical buses piling up at a stop. Why did it happen? You waited for damned ever, and then along came three. Sergeant Wiggins would probably have an answer. He did to most things, though seldom a convincing one. Jury smiled.

Passengers came clattering up the stairs, and two of them rustled their packages into the seat behind him. Two women, one apparently American, for she was going on at length to her British friend about Thanksgiving. Would she be home in time to make all of the preparations? She spoke of her far-reaching family — the relatives who always came from out of state to join her immediate family, which sounded huge to begin with. Parents, grandparents, aunts, uncles, children, babies. Last Thanksgiving (she told her friend, whose contribution to this was an occasional "Uhm," "My," "You don't say?"), they'd had twenty-three people at the table. She described the dinner — the turkey, the vegetables, the breads, pies, cakes — and it sounded to Jury like something going on in a medieval banquet hall.

The woman seemed besotted with the

holiday. Why? Why would anyone want to prepare such an enormous meal for so many people? His idea of a holiday was to go to sleep, to read, to go to the Angel and have an extra pint. Several extra pints. Her voice rose and fell amidst the flotsam of other voices, the subdued conversation, the blanketed noises coming from the Fulham Road. He wished she would be quiet. He was tired of her. He imagined her friend was too.

Jury closed his eyes, rested his chin on the palm of his hand. Finally, the two women rose, the American making a big fuss over gathering up her parcels and umbrella. Still talking, she followed her friend down the stairs to the lower deck.

He was sitting on the left and could see the passengers get off. It was the Chelsea and Westminster Hospital stop and he was momentarily distracted, wondering if this was the hospital in which he was born. There were a dozen or so people getting off, most of them women, so that he could only guess at which the American was. The tall one, he decided, the one with the most parcels and with a very couture look about her — well-tailored coat, shoes in the new heavy-heeled style. Yes, he decided, it was definitely she; she turned to a small,

19

dowdy woman and talked to her as they walked along.

Finished with the American, Jury glanced across the road where several people were coming out of a pub called the Stargazey. He liked the name and thought he'd seen it before. He wondered if there was more than one Stargazey. The bus still idled at the stop, a minute early in its schedule perhaps, while Jury watched a blond woman in a sumptuously sleek dark fur coat crossing the road. He lost sight of her and then regained it when she came from around the front of the bus and boarded. In the fleeting seconds he had taken an impression of her; she was very blond, attractive. He hadn't gotten a good enough look at her face to tell just how attractive. The bus hove itself away from the curb, trundling along the Fulham Road.

An airy scent of perfume floated past him, and he looked up to see the blond woman taking a seat several rows up. He was delighted that he could sit here and stare at her, even if it was only at her back. But occasionally, within the next eight or ten minutes, she would turn to look out and down and he caught a glimpse of her profile. Shoulder-length hair pulled back, so light you could see the moon through it,

20

a profile with that fragility which only the very fair-skinned seem to achieve. They rode that way for perhaps ten minutes, he studying her back, her hair, her profile when she turned it to the window.

Just before the bus stopped opposite the Fulham Broadway underground station, she rose and swayed as she walked up the aisle. He wanted to look her full in the face, but in the way that people do who feel they'll be found out, he didn't risk even a glance. She walked on by.

He thought she might be going into the station, but she didn't; she simply walked on in the direction the bus was headed. Would have headed, had it not been for the snarl of cars and buses where two principal arteries came together, and neither of them big enough to accommodate the traffic. The bus wasn't making any progress. It was one of those inevitable traffic tie-ups where the flow of cars, lorries, and buses vied with roadworks to see which could create greater havoc. One could walk faster, which was probably why the woman in the fur coat had left the bus.

The bus pulled away again and found an untrafficked stretch of road, which it shot down for two blocks while she fell behind. Jury strained to watch her, but a Sainsbury lorry eclipsed his view. Then she came into view again, having gained the time the bus had lost stopping for a red light, a zebra crossing, and another traffic snarl. Her hair, shoulder length and abundant, was fastened at her neck with a silver clip that glittered above the dark pelts of the coat. Where on earth could a woman like this, wearing a coat like that, be walking? She should have been passing below him in a Jaguar or BMW, together, perhaps, with the man in the tux. Then the bus sped away for another fifty yards, passing a pub called the Sporting Rat and a few cafes, all trying for the Paris left-bank look, all with cafe chairs and tables set about on the pavement, even in November. The blond woman caught up again when the bus had to stop at a zebra crossing for two very old people, one with a walker, the other, looking as if he should have one, doing his best to assist her. Probably man and wife, probably had been for a hundred years. Jury wondered about that; it must surely be like a second skin, must surely be like an attachment that had always existed.

Jury watched the progress of the woman in the fur coat, thinking, in a rather romantic way, of the bus as the boat that follows the long-distance swimmer, keeping a little away but there in case of crisis, cramp, or potential drowning.

At the next stop, the romancing couple across the aisle rose and clattered down the stairs, followed by the man in the tux. The party must be here. Jury could see them jump off before the bus had stopped completely, could see the conductor hanging on to the pole, looking up and down. He was surprised, then, to see her board the bus again, across from a pub called the Rat and Parrot — Fulham seemed big on rats. She was preceded by a mother and a surly-looking child, the boy straining back against the mother's hand. The mum took his arm and shook it as if he were a piece of clothing she was trying to get the wrinkles out of. The boy bellowed. The bus pulled out into much thinner traffic.

She did not come up to the top deck.

He watched passengers get off at the next two stops. Then, at the third — Fulham Palace Road — he saw her get off again.

Jury rose quickly and maneuvered, bus-drunk, down the semicircle of steps wondering why more people didn't go hurtling down them, given the sudden stops and starts. Then he jumped off in the same way he'd disapproved of the others doing it.

It took him less than a minute to get to the street she'd turned in on, called Bishops Avenue. It surprised him to find he was going in the direction of Fulham Palace. It was past nine and had been dark for several hours. It surprised him far more, though, that he was following her. He kept well behind her, walking past some tennis courts, part of a park complex.

She stopped in front of the high iron gates that were the entrance to the palace grounds, diaphanous light from a nearby lamp silvering the dark fur.

Falling back, he stopped too. What on earth was she doing here? (What on earth was *he?*) He would have thought the palace grounds closed at this hour, yet he saw her go in through the gates, which were still open. When he covered the twenty or thirty feet to the entrance, she was gone. He could see nothing but murky blackness beyond. The lamp pooled weak light on the ground. For some moments, Jury stood, wondering why he didn't walk in. But he didn't. He just stood there. *Like a great twit.* He knew it was always much safer to decry one's actions than it was to understand them. At any rate, he stood there beneath the lamp, decrying.

That she and her mission were absolutely none of his business was not, he was sure, what stopped him. It certainly hadn't stopped him from coming this far. What, then? He paced back and forth before the black mouth of the iron entrance to the palace grounds.

Jury was dying for a cigarette, but he hadn't smoked for nearly a year now (ten months, anyway). Smokers these days had to huddle in the entrances of office buildings, exposed to wind and rain, taking furtive jabs at their cigarettes, the outcasts, the cast-outs. Society would not share its office with them. Jury did not need society to cast him out, only Sergeant Wiggins.

He then suddenly realized that what he felt was just that: cast out. But from what and by whom?

2

The next day was Sunday, and Jury decided to catch up on his life. He opened his bills, glanced at them, tossed them in the desk drawer. There was one personal letter, this from Melrose Plant, which he set aside for later reading. Then he opened the Sunday paper he'd nicked from in front of Stan Keeler's door upstairs. Stan wasn't there; he often wasn't. Carole-anne and Mrs. Wassermann fed Stan's dog, Stone, and Jury took him for walks, or Carole-anne did. Occasionally, they took Stone for a walk together.

He finished the paper, along with a cup of tea and some toast.

Having thus caught up on his life in Islington, he thought he'd go out. He would go to a museum, the Tate, perhaps. Museums were what one "did" on a Sunday, at least before the pubs opened. He hesitated. One part of himself cautioned the other part against doing the Tate; better to go somewhere else — the V and A, perhaps, or to Trafalgar Square and the National Gallery. But he still wound up taking a bus along the Embankment, getting off at the Tate, and trudging up the wide white stairs, all the while telling himself this might not be a good idea.

Stopping off in the Tate Gallery had, in the quite recent past, had rather dramatic consequences. Early in the year, in January, he had wound up in the States, in Baltimore. A short while later, a couple of weeks, he had wound up in Santa Fe, New Mexico. The Tate was a chancy venue, especially the gallery housing the pre-Raphaelites.

Which is where he went, of course, and stood in front of the Chatterton painting, where he always ended up standing (wondering if the painting was sentimental, not caring if it was), and let the memories take hold. Perhaps he thought there was the possibility of exorcism in all of this. Maybe, but he didn't know.

He spoke to no one for the whole day, beyond the mere request for a pint of this, a half pint of that. Jury rarely went pub-crawling, usually confining himself to the Angel, in Islington, or one of the places in St. James's near New Scotland Yard.

Almost without conscious intent, he worked his way, via bus and tube, to the Fulham Road. It ran parallel to the King's

Road, and if he stayed on this last bus (the number 14), which went to Putney Bridge, he would be at Fulham Palace again. No, he would not do this, he told himself, and left the bus at the Chelsea and Westminster Hospital for the pub on the corner. It was a compromise move, he decided. He had kept himself from going to Fulham Palace.

Under its black and gold sign, the Stargazey looked quite promising and not in the least scruffy. Before he went in for a pint, he stopped at a newsagent's and bought a fresh Sunday paper to take back for Stan, in case Stan were suddenly to return, which he often did. The pub was handsome, well appointed. He was not sure whether this was actually Chelsea or Fulham and decided it must be right on the border. Fulham had come a long way over the last thirty years towards gentrification. It was no longer "foul Fulham" (as a friend of his on the force had christened it). It seemed almost flowery, somehow; it seemed blooming. Certainly it had all the indicators that it was an area where the chattering classes would flourish: property values zinging upwards, cappuccino bars, pricey boutiques and antiques, fancy grocers who "dressed" their windows in arrangements of fruit and foie gras.

Islington had gone the same way, only sooner. The terraced house where he had a flat would probably bring at least a quarter million pounds these days. It seemed to be a prime topic of conversation in the Angel, property values, and those people with their cell phones were probably estate agents. They walked up and down outside of the pub, cell phones glued to their ears, the "pavement prancers."

But at the same time, areas in a long slide downwards had slid more. The fabric of life for many was still worn thin. The divergence between upper and lower became more noticeable; the fraying of a seam had become a rip, and Tony Blair would do sod-all to stitch it up. He sighed, opened Stan's fresh paper, and read the sections he hadn't read in his flat.

The pub was crowded and smoky and filled with the familiar air of Sunday desperation. Sundays had less structure. The paper, the pub; that was about it. Jury shoved his glass to the back of the bar, caught the bartender's eye, and signaled for a refill. Then he slit the envelope of Melrose Plant's letter. Two pages in Plant's elegant script on thick, creamy paper that took the ink so beautifully the pages looked engraved. Old stationery, which still bore a crest and his old titles. The crest was left, but the titles were x'd out. Jury laughed all the way through it. The usual "nothing" was happening in Northants, but if there were ever a man who, like Nature, could fill a vacuum, it was Melrose Plant. He could fill in a black hole; he could void a universal void. Jury laughed again and returned the letter to his pocket. He would answer it when he got back to his flat.

When he looked up he saw the woman who worked behind the bar remove a bottle of whisky and wipe it and then return it to the shelf. She did the same thing with the next bottle, wiping it carefully and returning it to its place. Apparently, she would do this all along the length of the shelves until stopped by somebody wanting a drink, or the telephone, or something else claiming her attention. Jury watched this for some moments, her taking such great care in her handling of the bottles, especially the cognac, the Rémy Martin. She smiled as she did this, and Jury smiled, watching. It seemed such a loving wiping-down of the bottles, and she seemed to take such pride in her handiwork. She appeared to be a gentle person, one who would not turn men's heads but who was softly pretty.

He was sitting at the end of the bar by one of the wooden pillars where a few postcards were tacked up, one of which he peered at closely. Half of the front pictured a pub called the Stargazey, although not this one. He read the small print. It was in Cornwall, one of those little perpendicular villages that let you slide down to the sea but make it hell to walk up. Maybe he'd been there and seen the name. On the other half of the card was depicted a strange-looking fish pie, perhaps the pub's specialty.

"Can I ask you something, love?" Jury said to the woman dusting the bottles.

She turned with a questioning smile.

"Do you sell these postcards here? I'd really like to have one of these." He pointed to the card he'd been examining.

She squinted at it and said, "We did do, yes. Just let me have a look here. . . ." She opened first one drawer and then another, beneath the bar, and triumphantly held up the card. "It's the last one, aren't you the lucky winner!"

It was Jury's first real smile that day; she was so uncommonly delighted with this humble treasure. Too easily made glad, thought Jury. Wasn't that what the Duke of Ferrara had said of his ill-fated duchess?

"Here." She slid it across the bar. "You just have it."

"Thank you, but I'd be glad to pay —"

"No. I can't remember anyone ever asking for one before. Most people don't notice little things like this. You miss a lot in life if you don't notice little things." She returned to her task (though, for her, bottle wiping seemed more a vocation) and took down and ran the cloth over a bottle of Sapphire gin.

Jury said, "I don't think I've ever seen any pub take so much trouble over its stock, either."

She blushed. "Oh, me. I guess it's just silly — and he sure don't like it." Here she shot a glance toward the bartender or manager or owner. "But these bottles I think are quite lovely, standing there against the glass. Just look at this one." She held up the gin bottle for Jury's examination. "Did you ever see such a blue? It's so pretty —"

"Kitty, come along here," called the bartender.

Kitty blushed, returned the Sapphire gin to its place, and breathed good-bye to Jury.

He drank off his pint, took a pen from an

inside pocket, and wrote on the message side of the card, *Ten pounds says you can't find the recipe.* He supposed that sound deep in his throat was a chortle, or a chuckle.

Jury put some money on the bar to pay for his last pint and left the pub. Outside he looked for a pillar-box, couldn't find one, and was about to cross the street when he saw the number 14 bus that would be heading for the South Ken tube stop coming along a short distance off on the pub side of the street. He hurried along and joined the short queue. The bus pulled in and he boarded. When he sat down, he looked at the card again, laughed again. That was the second one of the day.

He looked out of the window, viewing again the places he'd viewed on his way to the pub. What he wanted to do, of course, was to go in the other direction to Fulham Palace. It was almost a need, a yearning whose source he couldn't put a finger on. He felt caught up in the drift of the tides or the pull of the moon (neither of which, he reminded himself, were currently present). Still, there was a feeling of inevitability, of fate.

He hated thinking in these terms, given he didn't at all believe in any sort of preordained scheme of things. Nevertheless, just for the hell of it, he searched around in Stan's paper, finally found the horoscope column. His horoscope importuned him to "refuse to be drawn in, no matter how alluring the prospect."

Hell. Okay, he'd refused, hadn't he? He hadn't gone back. She wasn't his business.

That was Sunday.

3

Sergeant Alfred Wiggins was talking (nasally), not as if he'd caught a cold but as if he'd invented them. His comments were cold-proprietary: "They seem to take me different than other people: like yourself now, you can shake them right off, go about your business, they don't hang round you" — as if colds didn't fancy Jury — "like they do me. This one" — Wiggnins swiped a tissue back and forth under his nose for emphasis — "it's been sent to plague me, it being November, and as you know, 'A cold in November will last through December'; they're hell to get rid of."

Surely, he just made that up about December, thought Jury, but he refused to be sucked into Wiggins's versifying, which was a lot worse than Wiggins's prose. Over the cold- and flu-ridden years, Wiggins's drone had become, on the other hand, almost soothing, a counterpoint of woodwind to the brassy trumpeting of Chief Superintendent Racer and his ill-tempered dispatches, one of which Jury was now drowsing over, flipped back in his swivel rocker, arms crossed over his chest. Without looking up from the memo, he asked, "Seen a doctor, Wiggins?" and yawned.

Wiggins put on an almost hurt expression. "You don't find me running to them with every little ache and pain. Not like some."

The sergeant's look seemed to suggest Jury was a raging hypochondriac, always hauling himself off to doctors and emergency rooms. Yet Jury couldn't even recall the last time he'd been to one. He let this pass and concentrated on the little bottles Wiggins had lined up on his desk, the tops of which he was unscrewing. He extracted a dropper from some clear liquid, leaned back, and brought it to his eyes.

"You missed."

Wiggins batted his eyelids a few times to distribute whatever it was and frowned. "Missed?"

"You got them in your eyes instead of your nose."

"Very funny, ha-ha. They're eyedrops, obviously."

Wiggins always thought his ha-ha's were a big put-down. To make up for his ha-ha remark, Jury asked, "Listen: how's Nurse

— or Miss — Lillywhite?" He'd forgotten the first name of Wiggins's lady friend. He didn't know why he'd been under the impression the love of Lillywhite should have cured Wiggins, since no mortal hand could possibly do that.

"Fine, just fine. Went off to Portugal to see a friend."

As Wiggins didn't seem at all put out by this, Jury assumed the friend was a female. He set aside the memo and went back to reading that morning's newspaper, which he'd taken from Stan Keeler's doorstep after going in and feeding Stone, who, he knew, would later be collected by Mrs. Wassermann and taken to her basement apartment.

Suddenly, he brought his chair down, hard. An item on an inside page had caught him unawares: Hammersmith and Fulham police force were asking anyone who might have been in the vicinity of Fulham Palace on the Saturday night between the hours of six and midnight to come forward with whatever information they might have regarding a woman found shot at Fulham Palace.

"What's the matter, sir? Look like you've seen a ghost."

"Maybe I have." Jury did not think he'd

ever have to answer the request for "anybody who has any information regarding." He dialed the number given for the Fulham police.

It was clear the police wanted somebody to identify her. Difficult in the absence of a picture or any details that might single her out. Except — at least for Jury — the detail of the fur coat. The coat and where she'd been found: Fulham Palace.

When a policeman came on the line, he told him why he was calling and asked for the investigating officer. The police constable said he could take down the details first. Jury told him what his own role had been — not without some embarrassment — ending with, "I didn't go in."

"You followed her all that way and then dropped her." It was not even a question, more of a judgment.

Jury squeezed his eyes shut as if light were the source of his discomfort. "Listen, I'd suggest that you not take such a hostile attitude if you want people to cooperate."

The constable was glib. "Surely you understand that we have to screen out —"

Jury cut him off. "What's your name?"

"Chance."

Jury hated to take advantage of that. He switched to: "Who's in charge of this case?"

"Detective Inspector Ronald Chilten."

"Well, put me through to him." Chilten. The name sounded familiar. After various connecting noises, Jury was asked to hold. He put his hand over the receiver and asked Wiggins, "You remember a Chilten with Hammersmith and Fulham? Didn't we work together on something?"

Wiggins stopped stirring his small cauldron long enough to reach for his Rolodex. "Fulham, Fulham. Here it is. Chilten, Ron. That was that nasty case, the domestic out in the North Road."

"All domestics are nasty. Now I remember him. Shrewd fellow."

" 'Too shrewd by half,' I believe is what you said. 'Likes to keep you hanging' is also what you said."

Jury definitely remembered the "keep you hanging" part of Chilten's nature. He went back to the phone and a voice that held some authority and answered to Detective Inspector Chilten's name. "I've got some —" It was only then that Jury realized how absurd his information would sound. Too late now. "I don't know if you remember that case we worked on —"

"Sure I remember."

"It's about this Fulham Palace thing." Jury paused. Chilten waited, not helping.

"You identified her yet?"

Chilten let Jury wait for an answer, as Jury knew he would. "No. No handbag, no identifying marks — nothing much to put in the paper except some morgue shots, which I might just do if I can't shake anything loose."

"She was shot — the gun found?"

"No."

"What range?"

"Over six feet, under twelve. Close, you know, there's the residue pattern."

"You're putting time of death between six and midnight?"

There was another silence. Chilten had a habit of keeping a direct answer back or making an obscure comment that forced you to ask a question. "We're hoping to shave some more time off that when the pathologist finishes."

"I can shave some off for you. Make it after nine, not six. I saw her outside of Fulham Palace." Jury thought he heard something overturn or hit the floor. A great thud. For a change, he had surprised Chilten.

"*Saw her?* You know this woman, then?"

"No. I only saw her walking along the Fulham Road."

"Tell me."

Jury did. From the time he picked her out, boarding the bus outside of the Chelsea and Westminster Hospital, to his following her on Bishops Avenue to the gates.

"Why did you stop there if you were shadowing her? Why didn't you go in?"

Jury sighed. He'd dreaded the inevitable question. "I wasn't 'shadowing' her. And I don't know why I didn't go in."

There was a lengthy silence. Chilten was good at deploying silences. Jury felt like hitting him.

Finally, Chilten merely asked, "What were you doing on a number fourteen bus?"

Exasperated that now his own movements would be under scrutiny, he said, "That's not important. I mean, not relevant." He sighed, thinking of how often he'd heard a suspect being questioned say that.

Chilten seemed to be questioning Jury's evaluation of relevance. Then he said, "Are we sure we've got the same woman?" Chilten was eating as he talked; Jury recognized the sound, having listened so many times to Sergeant Wiggins medicating himself with black biscuits on the other end of a phone. As if reading his mind, Chilten

41

said, "Didn't have any breakfast so I got a couple jam doughnuts. So how do we know?"

"I'll describe her: Very pale blonde, somewhere around five-seven, five-eight, as best I could judge. Very good-looking, hardly any makeup, maybe none. Then there was the coat. Long and dark — mink, if I had to guess."

"Sable. Okay, it's probably the same one. Traffic must've been weird if you could keep her in view all the way to Fulham Palace Road. That's a hell of a walk."

"As I said, she reboarded and rode."

Chilten chewed awhile. "This is very weird behavior."

Jury didn't know whether he was talking about Jury's or the woman's. Both, probably. He gave Chilten a moment to digest this information, along with his jam doughnut. Jury was hoping for an invitation; met with Chilten's silence on that point, Jury invited himself. "Look, I'm not trying to muck up your turf, but I would really like to have a look at the mise-en-scène."

"Holy Christ. What the hell's that?"

Jury blushed, glad Chilten wasn't there to see it. For some reason, he had hesitated over saying "murder scene" and had used

42

the fancy phrase instead. Yes, it sounded affected. "I might be able to help; I mean, I might be able to add something. Or not." Jury shrugged, as if Chilten were present to see how he tossed this off.

"I seem to remember locking horns with you a few years back, in one of your I'm-not-trying-to-muck-up-your-turf moods."

Jury gave a short bark of laughter. "Lock horns? *Me?* You must he thinking about my sergeant. His name's Wiggins." Jury looked across at Wiggins, who, hearing his name, stopped his ablutions and stared. Jury gave Wiggins a can-I-help-this-unreasoning-goon? shrug. "So what do you say, Roy?"

"Ronnie, not Roy."

Jury smiled. He'd done that deliberately. "Sorry." He waited.

"If you wanna come to Fulham this afternoon, you can have a dekko at your mise-en-scène. Meet me at the palace gates." He added a salting of sarcasm. "You must know where it is."

"The herb garden. It says she was found there, in a patch of lavender." Jury frowned at the ironic benignity of the scene. The mise-en-scène. He smiled.

"Yeah, well, Linda Pink might give you an argument there."

Chilten gave information the way others

43

did blood, a drop at a time. Jury stopped himself from asking the obvious question — Who's Linda Pink? — and, instead, said smoothly, "We'll see you in an hour, Roy, and thanks." He hung up and muttered, "Linda-bloody-Pink."

Wiggins raised his eyebrows. "Who's Linda Pink?"

"We may never know." Jury sat back, allowing himself, if only for a few moments, to be stunned, to be enveloped in sadness. "I should have gone in."

"Pardon me, sir? Gone in where?"

Jury didn't answer. Instead, he rose. "Come on, Wiggins. Chop-chop."

With great and grave reluctance, Wiggins stood too, downed whatever the putrid stuff was in the glass, and asked, "Are you sure, sir? Aren't you afraid I'll lock horns again, me?"

Jury shoved his arms in his raincoat. "Never. You'd never make the same mistake twice."

4

The thing about Detective Inspector Ronald Chiltcn was this: He loved to cloak mystery in mystery. If there was no mystery to hand, Chilten stirred up an atmosphere, an ambience — indeed, his own little mise-en-scène — that would keep the other person in suspense. He could do it over a three-car pileup or the color of a hair ribbon found at the scene or the number and nature of the books a teenager was carrying home from school when he was mugged. If he could keep you in suspense when there was no real suspense to be had, God knows he could do it over a body found in the Fulham Palace grounds. Jury had begun grinding his teeth ever since the telephone call less than an hour ago. He called upon his store of seemingly bottomless patience, reminding himself that Chilten was a very good cop.

That their destination was an herb garden had a most salutary effect on Sergeant Wiggins, washing away, as one of his tinctures literally might, all of that "locked-horns" business and rendering him an agreeable companion.

The three policemen — Jury, Wiggins, and DI Ronald Chilten — were walking through the grounds of Fulham Palace. They passed a boundary of holm oak trees and a silver lime; passed cedar, chestnut, maple, walnut, an enormous California redwood — a world of trees Jury couldn't put names to. It was Chilten who pointed them out, which surprised Jury, as he wouldn't have expected the man to have a horticultural or aesthetic bent. "Beautiful prospect, isn't it?" he said, stopping to gaze upwards at the tiered branches of a holm oak. "It's a wonder more people don't know about these grounds, considering how much we love our gardens. There must be more different kinds of trees in these few acres than anywhere else in the British Isles."

They continued walking, Jury looking back at the rather severe Georgian facade of the palace, recalling from some garbled history he had heard as a boy that all bishops at one time were said to live in "palaces," so the term was merely a euphemism for "house." "When did they stop using it as a residence?"

"The bishops? Seventies, maybe."

"But it's being used."

"The borough rents it out as offices."

"Fulham does?"

"Hammersmith and Fulham, yeah." They had reached a brick wall that Jury assumed must enclose the gardens. Chilten said something to one of two uniformed policeman who appeared to be on guard. They nodded.

With a curt nod toward an indentation in the brick wall, Wiggins said, "Bee bole."

Jury waited for further comment, but the sergeant said nothing. Wiggins and Chilten, thought Jury, should get on like a house afire.

What was most vivid was the enormous quiet of the place. London might have been dissolving around them; no traffic noises, no shouts and cries reached the little herb garden, walled in within the outer wall of the rest of the gardens.

Jury looked at the brown vines, imagining the spring when veils of wisteria would shiver in the breeze, undulating along the long fence to their left. On their right was a ruined greenhouse, a vinery, a grape arbor, given the look of the hardy vines that still ran within it, now with its roof caved in. It was a pity, Jury thought, that a place like this couldn't get funded by the government when one saw so much money wasted. The old story.

In the center of this walled garden was a large tear-shaped bed, sectioned off into small allotments for various herbs, now dry and overgrown. It was shaped like an eighteenth-century knot garden. There were patches of thyme, rosemary, lavender, and a dozen others, which he could tell apart only with the help of the museum map.

Wiggins looked down at the weedy, brown, and blighted winter aspect of the garden as if he were visiting the graves of the dead. He made his mournful way around the center plot, bound round by the bright yellow POLICE DO NOT CROSS tape, which was used to keep a murder site in as pristine condition as humanly possible.

Wiggins was in his element, not because this was police work but because it was herb work. "Feverfew, that stuff is." He pointed to the first section within the plot. "I don't believe I've ever seen that, I mean outside the shelves of my homeopathic medicine shop."

The wreckage of the *Titanic* wouldn't have called forth greater awe. Jury consulted the map. "Lavender." He nodded toward a section beside the feverfew. "That where you found her?" He watched Chilten pause to take out a pack of Chiclets.

Chilten held the pause long enough to put the gum in his mouth and crunch it around, as if even the Chiclet was part and parcel of the overall mystery. Finally, he nodded. "That's it. Face up in the lavender." He stepped back, backed up to the wisteria vines. "From about here, we figure, given the trajectory." He moved back to the lavender patch. "She was found Saturday night before midnight. That's when the *caretaker* said he saw her. But you saw her as early as nine, nine-thirty."

Jury waited. Nothing. "Who found her? The caretaker?"

Another piece of gum went into Chilten's mouth. He chewed. "Uh-huh. Or he reported it to Fulham HQ, anyway, says *he* found her around midnight."

It was Wiggins who helped out, filling in. "You mean, it sounds like the caretaker *didn't* actually find her?"

"Well, he did and he didn't." Chilten smiled slightly as he went on chewing.

Jury wanted to chew nails.

"Did and didn't, sir? What's that mean?"

"It was Linda Pink the caretaker said actually *found* her."

Ah, thought Jury. Finally got around to Linda Pink. In name only. He sighed. "Look, Ron. You know we don't know who Linda Pink is, so why not enlighten us?" Having to ask the direct question, that was the price you paid for getting information out of Chilten.

"Oh. Didn't I tell you? Linda Pink lives out there, along Bishops Park Road. She comes over here all the time, according to the caretaker. Day and night. Miss Pink found the body, *she* says, around seven-thirty, seven-forty-five. But she didn't tell anybody about it. Not until this morning, when she found the caretaker in the porter's lodge having a cuppa. Said she saw in the paper about finding the woman in the herb garden. My guess is, she probably wouldn't have said anything even then, except she wanted to be disputatious." Chilten slid Jury a look. He stopped talking, studied the crime-scene tape.

Jury waited. He was good at waiting.

It was Wiggins who couldn't stand it. "Disputatious? I don't understand."

"Linda Pink claims she found her in the lad's-love, not the lavender. But the caretaker is sure it was the lavender."

Jury frowned. "Lad's-love? What —"

Wiggins helped. "It's an herb for nervous problems."

"Never mind what it's for. Where?" He looked down at the patch of lavender.

"Right here," said Chilten, shoving the toe of his brown shoe into a wild and weedy dry patch that looked just like the patches on either side of it. "That's lad's-love." He shrugged. "Hard to tell the difference."

"Then," said Jury, "it's simple, isn't it? The caretaker would know one patch of herbs from another. Miss Pink is mistaken."

"Yeah?" Chilten lit a cigarette. He still chewed his gum. "Tell that to Miss Pink."

"You don't mind if I talk to her?"

"Delighted. She's ten."

Jury blinked, looked at Wiggins, who looked rueful. And as if mood were an herb indicator, he looked round for it, the rue. "Ron. This dead woman was found by a *kid?*"

"Mmm-hmm." Chilten trebled the sound, and with obvious pleasure, as he exhaled a thin stream of smoke and watched Jury's expression.

For once, Jury didn't give a bloody damn if someone else got to smoke and he didn't. As Chilten puffed away, Jury said, with mock sweetness, "Whenever you're ready, Ron."

"Oh? Thought I told you: Linda lives over on Bishops Park Road" — he watched Wiggins taking notes; gave him the number, added — "with her aunt. Great-aunt, rather. It's the aunt who owns the place, obviously. Name of Dresser." He gave out a few more details (gratis), and Wiggins parked his pencil inside his small notebook. "And that fur coat, you might be surprised to hear."

There was a definite period after "to hear." No pause, no cough, sneeze, or sudden interruption by Chilten's pager or cell phone. "To hear *what*, damn it?" Jury tried not to come down too heavily on the "damn it."

Chilten raised his eyebrows. "I didn't tell you? The coat was Mona Dresser's."

Jury's mouth opened, shut. "You're talking about this Linda Pink's *aunt?*"

"*Mmm*-hmm." Another cigarette was popped from his pack. "It's a long story, Jury."

Jury set his teeth, managed a synthetic smile. "I'm in the long-story business, Ronnie."

Wiggins's mood was becoming infected by all of this having to hang upon Chilten's answers. "I expect you could brief it up for us, Mr. Chilten," he said, a bit sharpish, as he got out his notebook, preparatory to being briefed.

"Okay. The fur coat belonged originally to Ms. Dresser. She passed it along to her stepdaughter, Olivia, who later sold it through one of those — what d'ya call 'em? — ah, consignment shops. How it got out of the shop onto the back of the dead woman, that's anybody's guess."

"But we're not," said Wiggins, seeing Chilten was through, "in the anybody's-guess business. Do you think we could see the body?"

"Let's go." Chilten looked from Jury to Wiggins as if they'd been holding him up, stopping here.

It had always astonished Jury how medical examiners, attendants — all those who worked there — could give the impression they felt completely at home in a police morgue. Perhaps they did, and why not? It was theirs, and they liked it. He understood that a postmortem might present a challenge to a medical examiner, but the debonair way in which MEs could tick off body organs and their condition made him blink. The Fulham doctor, a woman, named them almost fondly, as she might have done the dolls lined up on her bed when she was little.

He hadn't been present at this postmortem where Chilten had done the honors. Fortunately, Sergeant Wiggins hadn't been, either. As far as Jury could remember, Wiggins had attended a postmortem once and once only. Had it been that fateful event that started the sergeant on his supposed long decline into quirky health?

The room was cold and coldly fitted out: white enamel paint, stainless steel, glare of lights. The attendant had, following Chilten's earlier call, removed the body to one of the stainless-steel tables, draped in a sheet. He pulled it back at Chilten's nod.

A dead face does not look like a living one. That might be an obvious statement, but most people ignored it. A dead face is one from which all attachment has flown.

Jury looked, nodded, said yes, that was the woman, and the attendant started to cover her face. Jury stayed his hand, pulled the sheet back. For a lengthy period that had Chilten shuffling his feet, Jury looked down at her: the long neck, blond hair escaping the clip that held it, the now strangely complexioned face, the very emptiness of which could of course be playing tricks. But he didn't think so. Perhaps it was the nose.

Jury shook his head. "It's not her."

As he drew the covering back over her face, the attendant clearly didn't care one way or another if it was "her."

But Chilten rocked back on his heels. "What? Your description — blond, beautiful, height, weight, Fulham Palace, *sable coat.* Jesus. How can it not be her?"

Jury looked at Chilten. "I don't know."

What bothered Jury almost more than the dead woman's not being the one they thought she must be was the relief he felt that the woman on the morgue slab was not, indeed, her.

5

The only dark parlor Jury had seen that could compete with Mona Dresser's was Melrose's aunt's. Mona Dresser's house, though much larger than Lady Ardry's, gave the impression of cocoonlike climensions, the result of little light and a lot of stuffing — in furniture, cushions, birds, and the odd beast that had seen the ministrations of a taxidermist. (Somebody loved to hunt, thought Jury.) Even had the long velvet curtains puddling the floor been all the way open, the large room would still have been ill-lit, for the house was poorly situated to catch the sun. Several lamps of ruby glass and stained glass burned low, and the fire in the grate had simmered down to ashy coals. There were two oil portraits on opposite walls, one of Mona Dresser herself (looking remarkably as she did now) and one of an imposing-looking man in a long black cloak. There was a hush to everything that reminded him of the quiet around Fulham Palace but made him think even more of the quiet that pervades a theater just before the curtain rises. Yes, it was all quite theatrical. Yet he didn't assume this was an effect striven for by Mona Dresser herself.

She could not make out his identity card (she had told him when she met him at the front door) because she hadn't her spectacles. "So if you're the Fulham Flasher, I expect I'm at your mercy. Come in, come in." The sweeping gesture with the arm and the impatience of the tone suggested Jury had been stubbornly refusing to move from the doorstep all day.

She was a woman in her late seventies with frizzed and flyaway gray hair and small dark eyes, and if she was not exactly fat she was very well padded. Like the house, she herself bore a resemblance to Lady Ardry; Jury hoped it ended with these physical details. This day she wore an amplitude of flower-sprigged black lawn, setting off a long pearl necklace and a dangling pince-nez that she could very well have used to see his card (preferring instead to make the quip), a black lace scarf, and trainers. It was a combination Jury found irresistible.

As she made another sweeping gesture, this time pushing a big ginger cat off a horsehair chair, Jury surprised himself by saying, as he sat down, "My mother loved your movies."

She had picked up a ball of blue yarn (at which the cat looked greedily) and was winding it when Jury said this. Her smile was one of purest delight. "Well, thank you!"

"She really did. I was a little kid, only three or four, but I can remember how she'd put on her black straw pillbox, poke a hat pin into it, and say, 'Well, Richie, I'm off to see Mona,' and then set off for a cinema in the Fulham Road. Or maybe down to Leicester Square. She thought you were wonderful, talked about you as if you were family."

Mona Dresser blinked several times, made a covert swipe at her nose with a lace handkerchief taken from her sleeve, and cleared her throat. "It's very nice of you to tell me that. Back then, yes, that was my heyday. The war and all." Her eyes looked off towards the portrait of the black-cloaked figure. "My late husband was killed in the war. Dear old Clive." The handkerchief made its surreptitious appearance again. Then she said, brusquely, "Well, here we're both being nostalgic, and I know you've come about that Fulham Palace business. I expect you want to talk to Linda. And then there's the coat." She sighed.

"Yes to all three of those, Ms. Dresser." Jury smiled.

"Mona. After all, your mother thought of me as family."

The smile she flashed at him told Jury right then and there why his mum and most of England had been besotted with Mona Dresser. She might be old and almost homely, but a lot of younger actors would have killed for such a smile. It tugged at you and reeled you in.

"I can't tell you any more than I did that Fulham policeman — what was his name?"

"Detective Inspector Chilten."

"What a bossy man. He acted as if he were the real owner of that coat to the point I wouldn't have been surprised if he'd come in wearing it. I can't tell you any more."

"No, but tell me again. Something, some detail, might have gone missing; things almost always do."

"I gave it to my stepdaughter, Olivia. How it got from Olivia onto the back of a stranger, I'm sorry, but I've no idea. Have you talked to them, the Fabricants? They live not very far from here in Chelsea. But Olivia's not one of them." Mona had picked up a sheet of pleated paper, her homemade fan, Jury supposed, as he watched her fluttering it. "She's my husband's daughter by his first wife. Clive's daughter." She sighed, saying his name. "I wonder if your mother ever saw us together."

"You mean your husband was an actor?"

She laughed. "Oh, my God, I'm glad Clive didn't hear you say that! Definitely an actor. Quite brilliant, far better than I ever was. We did several plays together. It's how I met him, you see. We did quite a bit of Restoration comedy together. *She Stoops to Conquer* was our favorite. We were wonderful; we were Squire Hardcastle and Mrs. Hardcastle. We toured: Paris, Vienna. We even went to Russia, to Stalingrad. No, it was Volgograd by then. Krushchev renaming things, you know." She picked up the ball of yarn that the ginger cat had been mauling. "Really, Horace."

Horace gave her one of those slow-blinking looks that cats do when they want you to feel the full thrust of their indifference. The cat then leapt up on the couch to have a wash.

"But going back to the coat. I should think," Mona went on, continuing to advise Jury, "you'd be checking into other things. What about her other clothes? Ostensibly, she was wearing something under

60

the coat? Or was she naked? There would be labels, perhaps laundry marks, things like that. It was easy enough to trace the coat, apparently. It had my initials in it: M.D. I was cast in several thrillers — you know, police, detectives, hugger-mugger, and all that."

Horace made a grab for the yarn and she swatted his head with it. He slid from the couch and made a dignified exit to the rear.

Mona sighed heavily, put her hand on her slanted bosom, said, "Or do you expect the answer to come up and bite you on the nose? I mean, with all of the equipment you people have, all of this sophisticated forensics machinery and all of your experts, it's hard to believe you can't even come up with the poor woman's *name*. Fibers, DNA, fingerprints . . ." Mona shook her head, as if police incompetence were entirely too much for her.

Jury was about to make a reply when there came a thunderous crash from the dark innards of the house. A crash, remnants of sound, a silence.

Mona hove herself partway off the sofa, then sat back down, heavily. "Oh, why bother investigating? It happens all the time." Jury rose as if to investigate himself, and she added, "But I expect, you being a detective, it's in your blood. Well, go on, go on." She flipped her hand at him a few times. "In there's the dining room, and the kitchen's just beyond." She called to Jury's retreating back as he went through the door, "Why don't you put the kettle on, while you're out there?"

What had caused the racket in the dining room was clear; a wooden screen, quite elaborately carved and painted in a complicated oriental fashion, had fallen over. There was also a mahogany table overturned. The table, however, had not fallen by accident but had been placed so, for behind its top were lined up every doll and figurine imaginable, from big to Lilliputian. The tiny ones might have been kidnapped from one of those little Christmas dioramas: carolers, tiny skaters on a mirror pond, kids on sleds. The table was apparently serving as a protective screen for this assortment of possible refugees; whoever had done this might have attempted to move the screen so that it served a similar purpose. War, no doubt. A Lego set was messed about on the floor and a bridge partly constructed between the table and the bottom rung of a chair over which (he imagined) the refugees would flood. Jury returned the screen to its vertical position but left the table until he received further orders from the front.

The kitchen, by contrast, was neat as a pin. It was large and light, the house's western side being in a better position to catch the afternoon sunlight. There was a big garden out there, too. A bit wild, but Jury liked such gardens. He picked up an electric kettle, filled it, returned it to its base, and flicked it on. Then he went back to the living room, where Mona Dresser had found her cigarettes and lit one. At times, Jury thought the whole world smoked. He told Mona what his investigation of the dining room had turned up.

She sighed and said, "It's Linda. I'm too old to chase around after her. She's always getting up to things."

"But where is she?"

"Who knows? She'll appear when it suits her."

"Inspector Chilten says she's your niece."

"Does he really? She's my great-grand-niece, actually. Her mother died very young and — oh, it's too long a story, and hardly interesting to you. She'll be in here in a minute, acting as if nothing had happened. Just wait, now."

He was to take this literally, apparently, and sat back, as Mona did, and with no other sound but the quiet ticking of a longcase clock somewhere, they waited.

Within two or three minutes, the little girl came strolling in, preceded by the cat, Horace, both of them looking as if they'd never mauled yarn or furniture in their lives.

Jury imagined it wasn't easy to call up that expression of total witless astonishment on the face of Linda Pink, but call it up he had. She had prepared a persona for her Aunt Mona, but it didn't necessarily encompass this new person.

Her expression changed completely in just the time it took her aunt to turn and say to her, "Linda, what have you been doing?"

"Nothing."

Jury wanted to laugh. The answer, the one shared by all the world's children: nothing, *nada,* no, *non, nein* — a multicultural denial.

"Nothing? With that infernal racket we've been hearing? Here I've had to send this gentleman — who is a *detective,* Linda, and I hope the significance of that is not lost on you — here's a *policeman* come from *Scotland Yard,* gone into the back of the house to investigate, so you'd better look smart or you'll land up in the nick." Mona gave the girl's ear a little tug.

Leaning over the arm of the sofa, Linda said, "I told that other policeman she was lying in the *lad's-love*. That's where she was, not the *lavender.*" She began the minor gymnastics that children do to take your attention away from substance so you'll concentrate on style. A sort of sleight of hand, it was. Linda crossed her arms above her head and started turning.

Jury watched her for a moment. Then he said, "Humph."

She stopped in a flurry of turns; she frowned. The high drama of her lad's-love discovery surely rated more than a *humph.* "Well, *I* saw her first. Before *they* did." Doubtfully, she considered Jury's unchanging expression. Now she had moved to the arm of his chair. "I guess you can't tell the difference between lad's-love and lavender. Either."

"Sure I can. Lad's-love's good for nervous disorders." For once, he was grateful for Wiggins's encyclopedic knowledge of herbs. "Lavender's for headaches or muscle pain. Right?"

Linda considered. "Sometimes."

Jury ignored that qualifier. "But this

time of year they both look like bunches of brown stalks and twigs. Even side by side you can hardly tell."

"*I* can. I go to that herb garden all the time." She moved closer. "Do you know what bee boles are, then?"

He should have asked when he had the chance. "Still, it was dark, wasn't it?"

Mona was yanking her ball of yarn from the clutches of Horace. She said, "It's no good, Mr. Jury. She *does* know that garden like the palm of her hand. She's always over there at the palace, though I tell her not to after dark. Now, I thought Harry was to take you to that film. The Dalmatian one."

"He went home."

"But he was to stay to supper, too."

"He got irritable."

Jury mentally rehearsed a few scenarios that accounted for Harry's irritability and wished Mona Dresser hadn't changed the subject.

"But Harry's such a lamb, and he's so patient."

Now Linda was flapping her forearms so that the elbows met over her face, thereby allowing her to cast looks at Jury that were not designed to bring him comfort but to gauge the limits of his knowl-

66

edge and see how he was taking all of this. "Well, he's not. He's . . . really . . . determined . . ." (the jig she was doing was making her breathless) "and . . . he's . . . stubborn."

Had she picked up these terms only that morning, or had they been prominent in young Harry's vocabulary?

"Anyway . . . all . . . that . . . noise . . . was . . . Horace's . . . fault." Her words bounced with her as she skipped from foot to foot.

Both her aunt and Horace looked at her in disbelief. "Horace? Oh, don't be daft; Horace couldn't cause all that racket."

Now with the villain firmly in mind, Linda disagreed. "He jumped on Harry and made Harry fall against the table, and it turned over. Then he jumped onto the screen and it fell over, too."

"Stay still." Mona grabbed at the belt of her overalls. They were light blue, and she wore them over a white T-shirt. She too was wearing trainers, but with no socks.

The kettle screamed and Linda ran from the room, calling back she'd make the tea.

Mona said, "I know it's difficult taking the word of a child, Superintendent, but if she says that's what she saw —" She shrugged.

"Not difficult for me, actually. But then I'm not Fulham police; I didn't discover the body. But let's talk about Linda for a moment. Why didn't she tell anyone? Why didn't she raise a shout when she found this woman? Must have scared her to death."

"Probably. So there's your answer, isn't it?"

"That she was too frightened to do anything?"

"First of all, she *did* do something; she ran for the caretaker — she knows him, probably thinks he's her friend. But he wasn't around, was he? I mean, he was around, yes, but she couldn't find him. Fulham Palace has only one full-time, and the poor man can't be everywhere at once. When she couldn't find him, she ran home. Here."

"Why didn't she then tell *you?*"

"I wasn't here either. I was out to dinner. Only the cook was here. You're going to ask, Why didn't she tell *her?* That question I can't answer, Mr. Jury."

"But you came home. She could have said something then."

"I'm surprised a man in your line would expect people to behave rationally." Mona smiled her unforgettable smile to let him know she was not remonstrating, just surprised.

Jury felt somewhat stupid, said so. "I spoke before I thought. You're right, of course. Only Linda would know why she acted in the way she did."

"And she *did* finally talk to the police, didn't she? When she found out the story in the paper was wrong."

Jury grinned. "That would get Linda up and running, I expect."

Mona slapped the cushions of the sofa, sending up sunlit motes of dust. "Well, I'm for a few lashings of whisky, the devil with the tea; how about you? Or is all that rot about police drinking on the job really true? Anyway it really isn't your job, so what? It's that Fulham policeman's, isn't it?" She finished this off as she was making for a Victorian washstand that served as a drinks table over in a dark corner near the longcase clock.

"You're right. Yes, I'd love a drop of whisky." Clinking and rattling went on as Mona set about getting the drinks, and Jury asked, "The sable coat?"

"Oh, that again. I gave it to Olivia, who, apparently, put it in a consignment shop after a few months." Mona shrugged. "Poor girl needed the money, I guess. I can't understand why Olivia lives with the Fabricants — she's so different. Perhaps they have her there as a sort of antidote to Pansy."

"Pansy?"

"Sebastian Fabricant's daughter. She's thirteen."

Mona went on racking up the family members like billiard cues. "Olivia, she's the best of the lot. Quite nice, really. My husband's daughter by his first marriage — did I tell you that? — came rather late in the day, when he was over forty. Olivia would be — oh, early forties, I think. Divorced her husband years ago, very unsatisfactory marriage, and now she lives with the Fabricants. They're my relations by marriage. The boys, Sebastian and Nicholas — half brothers, they are — have an art gallery in Mayfair. Do very well, I understand. Their mother — well, you must meet their mother. She was Clive's second wife. I never knew the first, but if Olivia is like her, I daresay she was a sweet woman. I would not call Ilona sweet. Awesome, but not sweet. I've no idea what Sebastian's father was like — Sebastian is Ilona's son by her first marriage. The father, Michel, was shot by the Cheka secret police as a conspirator; this was right after Stalin came to power. He was innocent, of course, but then weren't they all?"

She stopped in her pouring and turned to Jury.

"I mean that literally; I'm not being cynical. Was there ever a bloodier regime than Stalin's? Convenient, isn't it, if you want to raze the houses and dachas of wealthy families? Accuse them of something, anything, and just get them out of the way. The government confiscated everything Ilona's family had: money, silver, even the piano. And their art. They had a great many paintings."

She put a drink in Jury's hand.

"Clive seemed to be a man of catholic tastes when it came to women. God knows, the man wasn't always marrying *his* mother; either that, or Mum must have been a very peculiar specimen." Mona set her drink down, picked up the paper again, and fanned herself.

"Are there just the two of you in the house all the time?"

"No, there's my cook, Edna, and a little maid, Janie. The Linda brigade. Between the three of us, we can usually track her down. Oh, don't let Linda fool you, Superintendent. She appears to be obdurate, but in reality she's quite malleable."

Jury nodded, as if agreeing, but as far as he was concerned this was one instance when appearance and reality met like long-lost brothers, and malleability didn't come into it. But he thought Linda's comings and goings might be too problematic for safety.

"You think she's mistaken, I imagine, about seeing the body in a different place."

"Not necessarily. Both Linda and Fulham police might be right. It was some time between Linda's being in the garden and the caretaker. Five hours, about, if the caretaker fixes the time he saw her at midnight."

"Oh, I see. Time enough for the woman to get up and move from the lad's-love."

Jury smiled. "Not precisely. She had help."

"But then the killer must have come back. Is that what you think?"

"Quite possibly."

Mona Dresser had picked up her empty glass and was peering into it as if the liquid there had vanished magically. She shook her head and rose again. "I need another lashing of this. Do you, dear man?"

"Lash away." He held out his glass.

6

The house in Chelsea was Georgian, red brick and white pilasters and a brass door knocker in the shape of a fish. Jury lifted this and let it fall a couple of times. There was also a white porcelain push for a doorbell, which he tried when the brass fish brought no sound of steps advancing. No one answered, but the open window on the ground floor and the car — a Jaguar — parked in the gravel drive suggested someone was there.

He walked down the short flight of stairs to peer over a lacy wrought-iron fence. It was nearly obscured by white shrub roses, but there were a few places where the shrubbery had thinned, through which Jury could see a large garden of beds and borders, hedges and paths. He could see a woman, her head hidden by a canvas hat, kneeling near a yew tree and plying some garden tool. He called to her.

Her head came up and then she rose to her feet, tipping back the hat and wiping her forehead with the sleeve of her shirt. It was an outsize shirt, much too big, but one of those garments people sometimes favor for a putter round the garden. As she walked towards him, his assessment of her looks changed. Dark hair and middle age became red highlights and a complexion that might have been the envy of the unpruned roses lolling over a hedge as high as Jury's shoulder. Her skin was luminous and pale pink along the cheekbones.

Jury showed her his ID, and after an "Oh, my" and a raised eyebrow she smiled and unhooked a gate in the fence that opened onto the steps. She did not introduce herself, either simply forgetting to or assuming he knew who she was, he being, after all, the police. And her inviting him in without asking him beforehand to elaborate upon his business suggested her upbringing had made a point of good manners. She apologized for not hearing the bell.

"I was digging. Bulbs take so much work. I'm digging eight inches, but you have to, don't you? Or they'll be blind."

Jury had no idea what she meant. Blind? "I'm no gardener."

"You're smart. Sometimes, I wish I lived in one of those arid desert states, like Arizona, where things seem to grow by default. Cactus, and so forth."

The interior of the house had that cool, shadowy, understated look Jury associated with wealth. It seemed drowsy with money: a huge, worn oriental rug lay over travertine marble in the large foyer. The decoration was rich without being ostentatious. A large oil portrait of some dead relation — much decorated in war, by the look of it — faced another oil of a breathtakingly beautiful woman in black velvet and pearls that reminded Jury of the one in Melrose Plant's dining room. "Your mother?" asked Jury.

"Oh, my no. That's Ilona. Ilona Kuraukov. My father's second wife, but she kept her first husband's name, I think trying to honor him, as his life and death were so wretched, poor man. That was painted, of course, years ago, when they lived in St. Petersburg." She held out her hand. "I'm sorry. I forgot to introduce myself: Olivia Inge."

She pulled back one of the two pocket doors and showed him into a living room, the room with the open window. Creamy light reflected off the white wall, the burnished dark wood, the Adam ceiling, which was edged with an extremely ornate molding, but one that didn't interfere with what seemed the room's pale placidity. French doors led out to the back garden, where he saw part of a lily pond, a shaded walk, a tree trunk edged in cyclamen. There was also what looked like a knot garden outlined in box hedging. He commented on its similarity to the one in Fulham Palace.

"It's about that dead woman I expect you've come, isn't it? The one wearing my coat?" He took the seat she gestured towards, a deep wing chair. She said, "I'd like a drink, how about you?"

Jury smiled. One couldn't say the Fabricants were stingy with their liquor. "I've just had one with your —" Should he say stepmother? The relationships in this family were complicated. "With Miss Dresser."

She laughed. "I expect you needed one. Now you can have one with me." She smiled at him. Jury was surprised by the deep sense of intimacy this conveyed, although he was sure it wasn't a conscious attempt on her part. But she seemed such a restful person to be around that he stretched out his legs, settled back, and said, "What I'd like is some soda water, if you have it."

After she'd fixed the drinks, handed him the soda water, and sat down in a comfort-

76

able-looking chair, she said, "So you talked with Mona. She was a fabulous actress."

Jury sat forward. "Yes. My mother would go over and over again to see the same film."

"But did you ever see them *together?* Mona and Clive?"

"Your father, right?"

She nodded. "He was especially good in Restoration comedy and the Noel Coward type of play. The comedy of manners, that was his thing."

Jury sat back, remembering why he was here. "This woman found —"

"Haven't you discovered who she was yet?"

"No. She had no identification; there was nothing. Except for the initials on the lining of the coat."

"You discovered it was Mona's. I mean, Mona's originally."

Jury nodded. "You told Detective Inspector Chilten that you'd taken it to one of those consignment shops. To have them sell it."

"Yes. Well, I needed some money and, anyway, I finally decided one doesn't want to wear fur these days, not with all of the activists and the protests. I turned it over to this shop in the Brompton Road. That was some time ago. I don't know if the place is still there."

"It's still there."

She raised an eyebrow in question. "Well, then, why —"

"— am I talking to you instead of the shop?"

"Yes. I mean, I don't mind, understand. But as that shop was the last place it can be traced to —"

"Their records came to a dead end. The person paid cash. It must have been quite a lot."

"Yes, it —" Olivia was interrupted by the sound of a car pulling up in the drive, one that sounded like a sporty, pricey one. Olivia half rose from her seat and peered over Jury's head. "That'll be Seb," she said, reseating herself. "Sebastian Fabricant. If you want to talk with him . . . ?"

The man who came in through the French doors was tall and on the thin side, middle-aged but still good-looking, looks Jury put down to good bone structure. When Olivia introduced them, Sebastian Fabricant thrust out his hand and, that done, asked Olivia for a drink. As she rose to get it, he sank into the sofa with a sigh of relief.

"Bad day, Seb?" she asked.

"You know. The fucking gallery." He turned to Jury. "I have a gallery in Mayfair." He raised his eyebrows in a signal that the location must convey what a headache that was.

But it conveyed nothing to Jury. "Sounds upscale-quiet to me. You're talking to someone who spends most of his time downscale-noisy, messing about in North London."

"Not at the moment, however." Sebastian raised his eyebrows again, the only part of him that questioned Jury's presence. Even this question appeared rhetorical, however.

"No." Jury smiled. It interested him how much the people in this family found his presence amongst them just another part of the daily reckoning of events, part of the furniture of living, more or less.

Sebastian thanked Olivia for the whisky, raised the glass slightly to Jury, toasting nothing, and drank. "That's better. North London is probably a hell of a lot more interesting." He took a Marlboro before he dropped the pack on the table (thus dashing Jury's hopes the house was a smoke-free zone) and tortured Jury with the *click click click* of the flint in his gold cigarette lighter. Finally, he found a flame, got the thing going, inhaled and exhaled, and sat back with a sigh of supreme comfort. Jury hadn't had a cigarette in ten months. He gave himself a little ego rub by saying, when Sebastian offered him the pack, "I stopped." He hoped this sounded somewhat more casual and less sanctimonious than he felt in the saying of it.

Sebastian gave the standard answer, "Lord, I wish I could," and went right back to blowing smoke rings, whose upward progress Jury watched intently. Then he looked at Jury and said, "Oh, sorry. Nearly forgot you were a policeman."

So much for the ego rub. "That's okay. A lot of people do."

Said Olivia, "You should feel flattered."

Jury did not know why. "As you probably assumed, we were just talking about the woman found at Fulham Palace."

"Ah! The wayward sable, yes?"

"More the wayward woman, really. We still haven't identified her."

"Oh," was all Sebastian had to offer. He slumped even farther back in his chair and, as Jury had done, stretched out his legs. He was over six feet, as tall as Jury. Then he added, politely interested, "It is peculiar, I'll grant you that."

Jury wondered what Sebastian Fabricant wouldn't grant him. "Mona Dresser's coat is really all we've got at the moment."

"Well," said Seb, studying the ceiling molding, "it wasn't robbery, was it? Though I can't imagine anyone intending robbery prowling the grounds of Fulham Palace." He grinned at Jury. He projected a sort of clubby conviviality, as if this place were where they met for drinks most days.

"No. Miss Dresser gave the coat to you —" He had turned to Olivia.

"And I took it to the consignment shop."

Said Sebastian, "Not the most lucrative way of selling it. As I told Libby."

Jury imagined that Seb had told Libby several times. Indeed, he imagined Sebastian told her a lot of things several times. The condescending brother — or half brother. Clive Fabricant had been married three times, after all.

She gave no sign of resenting this. "I didn't want to advertise a sable coat in the *Times*. I'd've got more for it, but we also might have got more than we bargained for."

"Libby thinks someone might have called and come round, feigning interest, to get inside a house where people could afford sable coats and have themselves a quick look round to see what else we could afford. She didn't want to take the chance." He gave a little bark of laughter, dismissing Olivia's concern.

"She's right. There'd have been more than a chance, too. Almost a certainty."

Olivia's face flushed with something like pleasure that someone was defending her. She took a sip of her whisky, asked them if they wanted more.

"Aye, aye," said Seb, holding out his glass.

"More water?" she asked Jury.

"No, I'm fine, thanks." He drew the police photograph out of his pocket and handed it to Sebastian. "Do you recognize her?"

Sebastian looked at it, shook his head. Olivia turned from the drinks cabinet and, still holding the decanter of whisky, came to look over his shoulder. "Never seen her before," said Sebastian, handing back the picture.

"Mrs. Inge?" Jury looked at Olivia.

She turned and shook her head too. "No. I've never seen her."

"We went all over this with that other detective. And why would Scotland Yard be investigating it anyway?"

Jury smiled. "We're just part of the Metropolitan Police Force. I know you've been over this ground, perhaps more than once. I guess I'm hoping — in the retelling, something surprising often turns up —"

He was stopped by the entrance of a young girl that caused Olivia a startled moment, which was soon smoothed over and an introduction made. "This is Seb's daughter, Pansy."

Pansy Fabricant could conveniently be grouped among surprising things that might just "turn up." She was the most worldly-looking child (if child was the word) he had ever seen. It wasn't simply that she looked older; it was that she looked at Jury out of eyes that seemed to be, but probably weren't, lit by experience. If not by now, definitely later. Her hair was long and lit up, as if it might ignite and send off sparks; it wasn't precisely blond but seemed more a color intrinsic to Pansy herself, as if it had come into being with her. She was wearing an ice-blue dress with a currently fashionable empire waist, made of some shimmery material that flashed when the light hit it. It went with the hair.

She gave Jury a murmured "hello" and a small smile. The smile stayed in place as she stood beside the arm of the sofa, hovering over her father without his actually claiming her attention. He leaned back his head and looked up at her, placing a hand on her forearm. In this gesture it was clear to Jury that Pansy had her father under control. The arm was braced against the back of the sofa, her head bent slightly towards her shoulder. In this pose she looked at Jury in the way an appraiser might study a picture, assessing its worth.

Worth for what? he wondered, reminded himself that Pansy was — what? Mona Dresser had told him fourteen. Or was it thirteen?

There was nothing at all in her face that expressed discomfort upon finding a detective in their midst. Jury thought her chief venture in life lay in making others react to her. God knows she was good-looking enough for a child (and one had to keep reminding oneself of the fact) to cause a reaction without further effort. But Pansy was willing to make that effort in the gaze she had turned on Jury. Pansy wanted more than mere attention; she wanted intrigue and secret-sharing; she might even have wanted tragedy, as long as it wasn't hers.

He looked beyond the French window into a wintry twilight. The temperature inside seemed to have dropped, and what had been pale sunlight was now like a skin of ice spilling across the rug. He could make out the formulaic neatness of the knot garden: the pond, the box hedge. From deep in the garden, a flock of starlings flew upwards, forming a wing of darkness. This awakened in Jury an old panic that rose in him like the flighting birds. The room had become oppressive in its silence.

He wished Wiggins were here to ladle out some common sense as anodyne to Jury's overactive imagination. And all these thoughts had passed through his mind in scarcely more than the time between the raising of her father's glass of whisky and the setting it down again. Now, Jury simply picked up the photograph and handed it to her.

Sebastian started to say, "Pansy wouldn't know —" A look from Jury stopped him. He shrugged.

He could not tell from her face whether there was recognition or not; her apparent desire for drama made her hold the picture a few seconds too long for someone who was looking at a perfect stranger. Something slick in the expression, practiced and artful, avoided committing her to one line or another of response. Finally, she shook her head.

Olivia asked to see the photo again and, when she had it, said, "She was extremely pretty." She looked up at Jury, as if to see whether he shared her sadness over the waste of this pretty woman.

He did, or thought he did. Whoever was responsible for Pansy's self-centeredness, it wasn't her aunt. Olivia, he thought, would be generous with her solicitude and her sympathy. And whatever else she was, she was genuinely trying to help. "I wonder if Nick or Ralph — ?"

"*Rafe,*" said Pansy, coolly. She was studying her nails. "It's Rafe, not Ralph."

Jury was a little surprised that when she finally contributed something, it was a banal something, since she had been putting so much effort into the appearance of sophistication.

Olivia smiled at this upbraiding. "Oh, that's always seemed a bit affected to me."

"That's how he prefers it, Aunt Olivia. It's *his* name, after all." She told Jury that Rafe was a painter and was having a show at the Fabricant Gallery. "It's very experimental, his work, isn't it, Daddy?" Her pronunciation of the name was precise to the point of edginess.

"Very. You should visit the gallery, Superintendent. Rafe's done some terrific stuff. Abstract, minimalist. Do you like that sort?" Seb's smile was condescending.

"I'm still trying to figure out the Impressionists." Jury's smile was genuine.

Pansy, sensing she had lost control of the room, was walking about it now, trying various venues at which to come to rest: the fireplace, the long windows that faced the street, a satinwood inlaid side chair beneath an interesting still life of a musical instrument Jury couldn't name.

"Nick and Ralph, excuse me" — Olivia gave the name the preferred pronunciation — "went over to this shop in the Brompton Road to collect the money. The shop keeps thirty percent. That seems only right, since they've got the work of selling the clothes."

"Nick's going there — that won't tell you anything, Libby," said Seb unhelpfully, as he rattled the melted-down ice cubes in his glass.

"We don't know what will or won't help," said Olivia tartly. "I expect if the police only investigated what they were sure of, fewer murders would be solved."

"Fewer are," said Seb, good-naturedly enough.

Jury was about to laugh as they turned towards the sound of the tires of another car pulling up on the gravel. (Three cars, at least, for the Fabricant family.) A door slammed, then another. Voices, laughter.

"It must be Nick and Ilona," said Olivia.

The French doors opened again, and the man whom Jury presumed to be Sebastian's brother — or half brother, he supposed — stepped into the living room.

"Here's the other half of the gallery," said Sebastian. "Nicholas is the social side; me, I'm the business side, the buying end." This seemed to put brother Nicholas on a decidedly lower plane, but that was probably where Seb thought he belonged.

Pansy, who had been moving about, came to rest beside Nick; she lifted his arm and draped it over her shoulder possessively. He gave the shoulder a little squeeze.

Nicholas Fabricant was younger than Sebastian, by some ten years, and handsomer. His face had the straight classic lines one finds on old coins. His streaked blond hair was cut short at the sides but long on top, and straight, so that it had a way of falling charmingly across his forehead and eyes, causing him often to scrape it back. The heavy Aran sweater and rumpled gray slacks added to the youthful look.

No one else about to bother, Olivia again did the introducing, adding, "Superintendent Jury is here about that woman found dead at Fulham Palace."

Nicholas smiled, shrugged. "Police have already —"

Jury finished for him, "— been here. Yes, I know."

He passed the police photo to Nicholas, who gave it a glancing look, shook his head. "Never seen her."

"Would you mind looking at it more closely, Mr. Fabricant?"

He looked. His verdict was the same: no. Nick handed it back.

Seb asked, "Where's Ilona? Did she come with you?"

"She went round by the front door. She's talking to Hedda —"

This was cut off by the door's opening again and another of the Fabricants walking in.

"Hello, Mum," said Seb, getting up and taking advantage of the movement to go to the cabinet and fix himself another drink. Jury rose also; rather, he felt pulled from his chair: The woman did not look like anyone's mum. She was outrageously beautiful, the thirty-years-older version of the woman in the painting in the foyer. But the passing years had barely scratched her surface. She must have been in her seventies if she was Seb's mother, but her carriage hadn't in it a hint of the bent posture that often comes with advancing years. She was very tall and slim. He knew now where Pansy had got her unusual pale hair. Her grandmother's shimmered white-gold, the color of the pale sunlight that had recently escaped him but that now shone again across the floor. No wonder the men in the family were so damned good-looking. Yet Olivia, whose mother she wasn't, shared something of that high-cheekboned look. Ilona's lipstick was blatantly young and red, a color startling against her ivory skin. She wore a long-sleeved black dress, one sleeve caped, with the end of the cape slanting up across the breast, its end caught near the shoulder. It was fastened by a massive diamond pin. One didn't have to inspect it closely to see it wasn't costume jewelry.

She said, "Don't call me by that absurd appellation, please." She said this dismissively, not looking at Sebastian but at Jury. She had a pronounced Eastern European accent. Russian, she must be, recalling what both Mona Dresser and Olivia had said.

"Police again, eh? I am Ilona Kuraukov. Mum." Her slight smile was ironic. "I use my first husband's name; meaning no disrespect to Nikolai's father. I feel . . ."

But whatever she felt, she wasn't saying. She still had not sat down and apparently did not intend to. Standing up was perhaps one of the ways she exerted her matriarchal authority.

With three generations of Fabricants before him, Jury felt oddly vulnerable, unshielded, disarmed. Ilona was especially disarming. Notorious for it, he'd bet.

She looked round the room, at all of them. "Are we all here now?" It was as if Jury, or she herself, had with some effort rounded up the Fabricants. And it did seem almost as if the meetings were staged, one character entering at a time, saying a line or two. Was it good theater? her ironic smile asked.

As Olivia had done, Ilona took some time studying the photograph of the dead woman. First she held it nearly at arm's length (to accommodate her imperfect eyesight), then resorted to a pair of small gold-rimmed spectacles, which she perched on the end of her nose. (It was the nose that Nicholas had been fortunate enough to inherit.) "Almost." She handed the photo back to Jury.

"I'm sorry, Madame Kuraukov. Almost?"

"Well, I *almost* recognize her. But I don't." She shrugged, held out her palms.

"What is it that looks familiar?"

"That is the problem. I don't know, Inspector."

Jury pocketed the photo, smiled. "It's Superintendent, actually." Ordinarily, he didn't bother to correct the mistake, realizing that "inspector" was merely a generic term to most people, covering any policeman who wasn't "constable." But the Fabricants were too damned blasé and condescending to allow him to let the demotion stand.

"Ah," said Ilona, inclining her head in lack of apology. He doubted she apologized for very much. "Did you see Mona Dresser? You would, of course, the coat having belonged to her. It is a lovely coat. I know Russian sable. I own one."

Olivia turned to Nicholas. "Nicholas, you remember going to collect the money for the sable coat? The shop in the Old Brompton Road?"

"Yes, of course." He looked at Jury. "Why?"

"I thought the shop assistant, or whoever you talked to, might have said something that would help us find her, something that might identify the buyer," Jury said.

"It might have been a different person," said Olivia.

Jury nodded. "Did the shop assistant say anything, Mr. Fabricant?"

Nick gave the impression he was thinking this over. "No. Except she did remark on how quickly it sold. They hadn't had it very long; it had been in the window only a day. Surprising, she said, considering how much money was involved." He scraped back the hair that had fallen across his forehead.

"You didn't tell me that, Nicholas," said Olivia.

He shrugged. "Didn't think it was important."

"Nikolai," Pansy said, rising again to the challenge of names, "not Nicholas."

Jury thought Pansy might even have called him "Superintendent," given half a chance.

Sebastian said, "Nick likes to claim his Russian provenance, you could say."

"Like the coat," said Ilona Kuraukov.

Nicholas looked embarrassed. "Oh, it's only a joke."

Ilona raised her eyebrows theatrically. "I don't thank you for *that,* my dear!" She said to Jury, at the same time fixing a cigarette into a long ebony holder, "You know, Superintendent Jury, this business of the sable — it's a very slender thread you've got hold of."

"I don't know, Madame Kuraukov. After all, it led me to you." He smiled.

She stopped in the lighting of the cigarette, looking stunned by both the smile and the compliment. At least, she took it as a compliment. Probably she did most things. She seemed born to deserve them.

Jury rose and handed Sebastian his card, took Sebastian's and his brother's in return. He looked at all of them, at the strangely united front they presented — despite what internecine battles might go on between them — said good-bye to Olivia (who had risen to go with him) and that he could see himself out, and left.

7

"The fish are arranged, whole, to break through the crust, the dead eyes staring upwards." Melrose Plant stole a covert glance over the top of the cookery book. He knew she would say it was disgusting and that he was making it up.

Said Agatha, "That is absolutely disgusting."

(Right.)

"No one would eat that. You're making it up."

(Right again.)

"It's right here, word for word" (although he himself had added the garnish of "dead" fish eyes). He tapped the book. "Starry-gazey Pie. That's what they call it."

She was marmalading another scone. "Instead of spending your time sitting around all day trying to think up nonsense to fool me with, you would do better to attend to that neglected garden" — she poked her head forward in the direction of Ardry End's extensive grounds — "and do some planting. You hired that Momaday person, remember, and all he does is wander about."

Melrose put the book between the chair arm and himself and took up his own cup. "Well, wander around is all *I* do — except when I'm sitting around — so it's a comfort to have someone to wander with, if only in dreams."

"I don't know what you're talking about. I'm only telling you for —"

(Your own good.)

"— your own good, Melrose."

(Right again.)

Agatha's threat never to speak to him again (after the dog and chamber-pot affair) had, unfortunately, not been carried out. How he wished he were back in the little courtroom listening to Marshall Trueblood's excellent defense of Ada Crisp. *That* had been an unexpected treat! Agatha had dragged poor Miss Crisp up before the magistrates, not only citing the secondhand furniture shop for displaying wares on the pavement (tables, chairs, and chamber pots), thereby endangering life and limb, but also accusing Ada Crisp's little terrier of attacking her when Agatha went belly-up. Marshall Trueblood, having appointed himself as attorney for the defense, made mincemeat of Agatha's solicitor's arguments. For once he wished Agatha would drag somebody else into court. Perhaps he could get her to sue *him*. Well, he'd have to drop dead first, he supposed; then she could contest the will. Only he wouldn't be around to see it.

He picked up Jury's postcard and inserted it as a bookmark in the old cookery book. He had set his man Ruthven the task of looking up the recipe Jury was betting him ten pounds he couldn't find. Ruthven (who had been a part of the Ardry-Plant staff for what seemed a hundred years) would, of course, get the ten pounds.

Agatha stopped reading snippets of Melrose's *Telegraph* aloud to him long enough to marmalade a scone and pick up his *Country* magazine, which she held at arm's length (what, he wondered, were her bifocals doing for her?). Now she was reading an article about the museum theft some months ago.

"— *the hitherto undiscovered painting by Marc Chagall only recently acquired by the Hermitage and believed to have been painted before he fled to Paris in the early twenties. The painting, titled* Wingless, Wingless Angels, *is the only Chagall in the museum. It is believed to have been part of the spoil seized from the homes of the wealthy during the revolution.*

"Cut right out of the frame on the wall of the Hermitage. Look at it." Agatha turned the magazine for a moment toward Melrose, then back again. "What an absurd picture. It's got people all floating around, and there's even a cat. Can't imagine what the man must be thinking of. All this modern art is just too much for me. Give me a nice Rubens."

"Yes, well, that's probably what the thief said: 'Give me a nice Chagall.'"

"I wouldn't give tuppence for them — these paintings that are nothing but little squiggles of paint or great big squares —"

"Are you referring to Mr. Pollock and Mr. Rothko?"

"What difference does it make? A painting should be *of* something, shouldn't it?"

"I daresay Mr. Pollock and Mr. Rothko think theirs *are*." Why was he contributing to this inane exchange? He had only himself to blame for its continuance.

"It's valued at nearly a quarter of a million, it says here." Agatha gave the magazine a little slap, as if spanking it for its headstrongness.

"The Chagall? Hmm. That's not really much for taking such chances, is it?"

"*You* should talk!"

Melrose looked up, surprised. But why should he be surprised? Any attempt at an ordinary conversational exchange was doomed with Agatha. "*I* should talk? Sorry, I don't get your drift." The painter Chagall inspired Melrose to do a bit of artwork of his own. He picked up a pencil and started drawing little fish heads, making the eyes big and blank.

"It's fine for those of us who have money —"

(Agatha not being among the "us.")

"— to speak of a sum such as that as *not much.*"

Melrose ignored her and drew a scalloped line all around to represent the pie. "You exaggerate my personal worth. I've told Martha to employ a number of cuts in our menus. We're having fish pie for Sunday dinner."

She was now drawing the local paper out of her voluminous bag, having done with the bigger issues of life as reported in the national papers. Melrose noted that she was awash in papers this morning; usually she depended upon her own stop-press reporting. As if it had fleas, she shook out the *Sidbury Star*. "There's this horoscope rant that Diane Demorney's on."

Melrose rather liked the notion of a horoscope *rant*. Of course, Diane Demorney ranting about anything (even including the proportion of vermouth to vodka in her martini) was difficult to envision. She was much too languid. "Well, her horoscopes have livened the paper up considerably." If one could breathe life into mummy remains. "To call it ranting is overdoing it, I think."

Agatha slapped the paper a few times. "Listen to this; it's Pisces:

> *"As somebody once said, 'To every man there is a season,' and you've had yours. Get up, get out, get it together. Instead of constantly effing and blinding about the way the world treats you, consider the way you treat the world, to paraphrase John F. Kennedy. As the Moon transits Neptune there could be trouble, so don't go making it for yourself: Stop whining!"*

"You don't think that's good advice? I'd take it to heart, if that were my sign." Melrose said this absently, as he sat back and compared his sketching of fishes with the fishes on Jury's postcard. Pretty good.

Perhaps he did have a calling after all. Not art, but making fish pies. He held his drawing out for her to feast her eyes on, as he was pretty certain she wouldn't want to feast her mouth on it.

Agatha stopped in the process of her own rant to put a dollop of thick cream on her scone. "What were you saying about Sunday dinner? What fish pie? It sounds absolutely dreadful."

"Starry-gazey pie. I saw Martha just this morning, cleaning the little fish. It's one of her specialties." He decided to poke another fish head through the crust. He wished he had some coloring pencils.

In a tone of abject disgust, she said, "Melrose —"

(Don't be ridiculous.)

"— don't be ridiculous."

(Right again.)

8

In Shoe Lane, to which Melrose had repaired after Agatha polished off the plates, the scented air told him he was nearing the cottage of Miss Alice Broadstairs. As usual, she was gardening, while her oafish gray cat, Desperado, loafed on top of one of the stone pillars rather ostentatiously set on both sides of her short paved walk. Melrose had several times tried to excite this cat, but he couldn't. Neither could Mindy nor Miss Crisp's Jack Russell (of chamber-pot fame). Miss Broadstairs, however, was eminently excitable, even when no one was trying. Excitement seemed to be bred into her marrow, for she was a fluttery, breathy woman, thin and dry as the leaves she trod underfoot. She and Lavinia Vine were always taking home the blue and gold ribbons from the annual Sidbury flower show.

"One can't start too early, Mr. Plant!" she called, referring to this spring extravaganza, and came to talk to him over her neatly trimmed hedge.

As far as Melrose was concerned, one

needn't start at all. But he smiled his encouragement in a most friendly manner. Her voice was low and her look secretive: lips crimped together, hydrangea-colored eyes darting left and right, as if probing the empty lane for flower thieves. "I'm forcing sweet peas."

Melrose blinked at this unexciting news, uncertain how to respond, "To do what?"

Alice Broadstairs seemed to think this the funniest thing in the world and laughed and laughed. "I've a new one; it's quite the loveliest pink you can imagine."

She vanished from his view — *poof!* — as if she'd suddenly fainted under too heady a sweet-pea scent or had an attack of the vapors (which is the way he thought of it; couldn't help himself, Miss Broadstairs seeming more likely to succumb to a nineteenth-century complaint), and Melrose tried to see over the hedge, when — *poof!* — here she was back again, brandishing a coral-colored sweet pea.

"Oh!" he said. "Well, that's quite beautiful. Yes, a beautiful color."

"It's from my little greenhouse. I've a nice little plot of them." Here she vanished again and again was back within a moment, this time with a sky-blue sweet pea. "This one, Mr. Plant, was not wholly successful. I was trying for a more vibrant shade of blue. But have it, won't you?" She thrust it towards him.

Apparently, he was to be the recipient of one of her laboratory failures, in the way of Dr. Frankenstein bestowing upon him a poorly functioning hand. "Why . . . thank you, Miss Broadstairs." The flower was too large for his buttonhole, but he stuck the stem through it anyway and carried on.

The Wrenn's Nest Book Shoppe occupied a corner next to Ada Crisp's second-hand furniture shop and across the street from the Jack and Hammer. Theo Wrenn Browne, the owner, competed only with Melrose's aunt for the title of the village's highest-ranking troublemaker.

Having been bested in his attempts to drive Ada Crisp into either bankruptcy or a nervous breakdown, his current campaign was to shut down Long Piddleton's small library by supplying the reading public with an opportunity to get new books hot off the publisher's press. Miss Twinny, the local librarian, who might just lose her job over this, could not get them half as fast. Browne had been expanding this service over the years. And to get the non-book-buying people in, he had put in a large periodicals section, even a table and chairs, to make it appear that he welcomed the casual reader (which he didn't), a water cooler, and a candy rack. Melrose asked him when they could expect the slot machines.

The only person Browne hated more than Melrose Plant was Marshall Trueblood. Both of them had, between them, everything in the world that Browne wanted: land, money, titles, looks, exquisite taste, high wit, and goodwill. Although the man had no control over the first four qualities, he could have done something about the last ones, but they were things Browne had kept hidden behind something resembling the brick wall cemented in place by Poe's Montresor. He was vulgar; he was banal; he was mean; he was ostentatious even to the point of having added an "e" to his name (thinking that might separate him from the workaday Browns).

The little boy whom Theo Wrenn Browne was chastising over the counter looked to be no more than three or four. This dusty urchin had apparently been sent on the errand of returning a book to Browne's "lending library." Browne was bedeviling him with the news that his rental book was overdue, not by days but *over six months!* Didn't he understand that it had been a brand-new book and people had waited for it? The book in question looked familiar to Melrose, who had gone over to scour the magazine rack for astrology offerings.

He looked towards the counter, squinting up the title. . . . Yes! It was *Patrick, the Painted Pig*, the very book young Sally had got a dressing-down for a few months before. Melrose stood back and listened to Browne scold this luckless child, younger than Sally, who must be her brother Bub. The boy was pale and small, with stick-thin arms and legs. Melrose had kindling wood in better shape.

"And here's a torn page" — Theo Wrenn Browne rattled it — "and here's a stain that looks like fingerpaints . . . well! You can see it's damaged and you'll just have to pay for it. Tell your mum it's twelve pounds fifty; that's what another will cost me." He snapped the book shut. Bub, already as white as rice paper, went whiter still.

Melrose (who thought God was in his heaven for once) plucked a magazine and picked a candy bar from the candy rack, then stepped up to the counter with the KitKat and the good news. "Pardon me for interrupting, Mr. Browne. I'll have one of these, I think, and this magazine." Melrose put the money on the counter for the magazine and the candy, which he unwrapped and carefully bit a piece from, before handing the candy to Bub, who looked like he needed a shot of caffeine in the circumstances. "Problem with one of your rental books, is it?"

Browne looked as if he could spit. His voice full of venom, he said, "I can't have my books come back torn and smudged all over."

"No, I expect not." Melrose looked the book over for identifying marks, found several he clearly remembered from young Sally's debacle with *Patrick, the Painted Pig*, and said, the taste of the words more delicious than chocolate on the tongue, "Only, this book" — Melrose held it up and tilted it back and forth — "this book doesn't belong to *you*, Mr. Browne." Melrose could scarcely remember when he'd been more tempted to jump up and click his heels. But he kept his feet on the floor.

"It most certainly does. Here's my library card in back." He flipped the book to the back cover, where he'd placed a pocket to hold the lending record.

"Oh, yes, it was yours *once. Originally*

yours. But have you forgotten, when Sally brought it back several months ago — also, alas, late — that I purchased it from you and gave it to *her?*"

Browne opened his mouth, closed it, opened it, stood speechless. Finally, he said, "Well, but then why is young Bub here bringing it back?"

Young Bub, however, was no longer "here." The moment he'd seen that an adult was at hand to take up the cudgel, he'd departed on greased feet.

"I'll hazard a guess: Mum found it, had no idea anyone had actually bought and paid for it, and, as Bub happened to be there to take the flak, hurriedly sent him round with it. Only a guess, of course, but does it matter?"

Theo Wrenn Browne clearly thought it mattered. His complexion was mottling from misty gray to pale umber to a flush of pink as his blood rose like a sunrise over the Norfolk Broads. "Well. That whole family's careless as can be. The mum doesn't teach those kids manners any better than a mongoose!"

Melrose thought for a moment about mongooses while Theo Wrenn Browne punched his computer, entering the price of Melrose's magazine and reminding him, with a leer, that he'd als̶ ̶taken a KitKat, as if this would leave Melrose with no recourse but to stand on the corner with a begging bowl. He fingered and fingered the computer — it simply amazed Melrose that the machine supposed to take the pain out of all sorts of niggling jobs took more time to perform a simple one than it would have taken Bub to do by hand ten times over. The computer sent its morsel of information to the printer and the printer spit it out, a receipt as long as Magna Carta.

Seeking revenge, Browne looked at the magazine and said, "I wouldn't have thought you'd have much interest in this." He shook out a brown bag, placed the lowly (and garishly colored) astrology magazine in it, and added, "I'd've expected you to take Caesar's line." He looked at Melrose with his crimped little smile.

Melrose didn't know what he was talking about.

"Well, my goodness, Mr. Plant, a *well-read* person such as *yourself*, you should know *that:* 'The fault, dear Brutus, is not in the stars, but in ourselves, that we are underlings.' That's sound advice, now, ain't it?"

Melrose shrugged as he picked up the

bag. "I wouldn't know, not being an underling."

He whistled a tuneless tune and crossed the street to the Jack and Hammer, which would be open by now. Long Piddleton had not gotten around to keeping London hours and probably never would. The pub kept to the old eleven o'clock opening; it was now nearly noon, and Melrose felt the need of a preprandial Old Peculiar.

Dick Scroggs was, as usual, reading the local paper. As he watched the level of Old Peculiar rise in the glass, Scroggs told Melrose that it was "disgraceful" what that Browne fellow was doing to the library's business and therefore to Miss Twinny, the librarian.

"I mean, she's at our little library forty years, ain't she? Well, they've been looking for a reason to close it down and that Browne's given 'em one." Dick frowned over Melrose's half pint of dark brew and went on. I mean, that job's her *life*, innit? Oh, sure, she'll get her pension — if *anyone's* going to get a pension, these days; you never know, do you? — but it ain't the money with Miss Twinny."

Melrose wondered how Dick, who had never mentioned the woman from one year's end to the next, had got on such friendly terms with Miss Twinny, ever since a so-called editorial had appeared in the Sidbury paper calling for "library reform." It had probably been ghost-written by Theo Wrenn Browne.

Dick set the glass before him, and Melrose said, "And a small glass of water, please."

Dick frowned. "For what?"

"For my sweet pea." Dick eyed him as if Melrose were touched by the sun, slapped down a shot glass, and measured water into it. Melrose thanked him and walked to his favorite table, the one with the window seat looking out over the street. The window was crossed by vines of climbing white roses, brown-edged from November cold, which ran rampant over the pub's facade and had lately threatened to throttle the mechanism of the Jack and Hammer's sign: a wooden figure up high in a turquoise jacket, who, upon the hour, would stiffly raise and lower his hammer to a forge, simulating strikes of the clock. The hammer was raised halfway now, frozen in space as if Jack and everyone down here were held prisoner in some doomed village.

The door opened, ushering in Diane

Demorney and a current of cold air made colder owing to its proximity to Diane. Her arctic impression was much augmented by her white skin and her white clothes. She always wore white or black and was always as perfectly groomed as a Derby winner, not a shank of her black razor-cut hair out of place, not a wrinkle in her dress, not an unpolished nail or shoe. Melrose always had the impression that Diane's Art Deco angularity was carved out of the surrounding air, leaving everything beyond it, by contrast, slapdash and slipshod. Melrose always had the impulse to tidy up any space she walked through.

Unfortunately, this sharpness of outline did not extend to her mind. Diane's thoughts settled like murky sediment in a dark tarn, stirred occasionally into life by someone's tossing into it a bit of juicy and mendacious gossip. It amazed Melrose that people actually thought her marvelously intelligent. As often happens, such people equated intelligence with knowledge, and Diane did know things. Strange things. To offset her sluggish thinking, she had taught herself a single, usually arcane fact about every topic imaginable — or at least every topic that was likely to come up in the boozy environs of drinks parties. Since she chose obscure facts — ███ as the writer Stendhal fainting in th█ █resence of great art — it was assumed she knew everything else about the man, when she couldn't even tell you a book that he'd written. Now she was into stargazing, and the interesting thing was that what she was writing was — well, interesting.

Melrose stood and drew out a chair for her. She always took such small attentions as her due.

Referring to a column of print, Dick said, "This 'Seein' Stars' is quite rich this week, Miss Demorney."

"Oh, good," said Diane, with a total lack of enthusiasm, as she plugged a cigarette into a six-inch ivory holder. She accepted Melrose's light, then called over to Dick Scroggs, still bent over his paper. "The usual over here, if you don't mind. I shouldn't have to ask you twice, should I?"

Dick took umbrage. "Twice? You only just came in, you only just asked. That's once."

"I had to ask you yesterday, didn't I?"

Diane's preference was buffalo grass vodka, which she herself supplied. Yet she still paid him full price for the drink. No one would call Diane stingy. Next to Melrose and Marshall Trueblood, she was the biggest ██████ibutor to the Long Piddleton Save-██r-Library Fund.

"And I'll have another half pint, when you get around to it, thanks, Dick."

"Why do you always get *half* pints, Melrose? It only means bobbing up and down for refills."

"I like to bob."

Dick had come with Diane's martini — handicapped at twelve-to-one — and brought the *Sidbury Star* with him. Before he collected Melrose's glass, he opened it to "Seeing Stars" and asked, "Now, what sign were you born under, Lord Ardry?"

"The Jack and Hammer." Melrose held up his glass.

Diane said, "Capricorn."

Melrose frowned. "How did you know? Besides writing horoscopes, or what passes for them, have you become psychic too? Do Capricornian emanations pulse from my being? Do I have all those queer manifestations of Capricornianism, such as drinking half pints instead of pints?"

Diane just looked at him. "You told me your birthday."

"Oh. My drink, Dick?" Melrose held out his glass.

"It's the sign of the Goat," finished off Diane.

"Oh, ha. In case I'd forgotten?"

Paying no attention to the glass Melrose thrust toward him, Dick attended only to Melrose's zodiacal sign. "Just you listen, Lord Ardry —"

Melrose had given up his titles, but some people seemed determined to give them back. He could not break Dick Scroggs of the "my lord" habit and had given up trying.

"This week you had better be extremely careful! With the Moon transiting Aries, your sex life is even more defunct than usual. You depend entirely too much on time, tides, and the stars to sort out your problems, especially your cold-footed approach to the opposite sex.

"Get a life."

Dick thought this was extremely risible and added (never the one to know on which side his bread was buttered), "Oh, you got him right, there, Miss Demorney." Then he collected Melrose's glass and, still chortling, went back to his beer pulls and optics.

" 'Get a life'? Why does that strike me as something a bona fide astrologer would *not* say?"

"Because most of them refuse to upset

115

people" — a thing Diane would never hesitate to do, if it got her a soupçon of what she called "amusement." She, who had always been languor's handmaiden, had taken over the horoscope column of the *Sidbury Star.* In the classified section of that paper (where she had been scanning the Personals in hopes of securing *WM, tall, ageless, loves travel, good food, spending money*), she had come upon a job offer to replace the woman who was retiring and leaving her column — "Seeing Stars" — in need of a writer. *Experience . . . wisdom . . .* ability *to relate to others.* None of this deterred her from applying, of course. But she made a gross error: she was under the impression the column's heading meant that the journalist would spend her time in the company of celebrities — film folk, theater-and-music folk, savvy politicians, and artists.

She was hired on the spot, for who could possibly resist the soignée, cool-spoken, richly garbed, beautiful Diane? When she finally found out the column was to be written by the astrology consultant (herself), she gave it a whirl anyway, lacking anything better to do.

Diane's prognostications were always downers, ranging from the dour to the diabolical. There was no room for the glad tidings of the usual daily horoscope column: no inheritances, handsome strangers, promotions, cures, new jobs, money — none of that. The news was always bad. That or the reader had to put up with being preached at. And yet people appeared to like this approach. Melrose had heard circulation had increased a good twenty percent after Diane had "come on board."

"I thought you'd like that," said Diane, rinsing her olive in vodka. "I wrote it just for you."

Melrose was about to tell her that star signs were not a just-for-you thing, when the door opened and another stiff wind shoved in Marshall Trueblood, as if the natural world didn't want him in it; yet in his customary vibrant colors he resembled Alice Broadstairs's garden. What could one call that shirt but periwinkle purple? That tie but sweet-pea pink? And that muted windowpane Armani sports coat: Could it be anything but love-in-a-mist blue?

Trueblood was in one of his Campari-and-lime moods, which is what he told Dick to bring him. Campari went with boredom and desuetude. He yawned, then asked, "Do you think I should go up to

Oxford and read law? Perhaps that's what I'm meant to be — a barrister." He'd been making these noises ever since his brilliant chamber-pot defense. "Yes, perhaps the law is really my destiny after all, and all these years I've been messing about with antiques." He plucked the sweet pea from the shot glass and held it against his coat. "It just matches." He plunged it back in its water and sighed. "Thank you, Dick." Dick Scroggs had set his drink before him.

Diane looked shocked when Trueblood mentioned "reading" and "Oxford." "Surely you're not serious! It would be masses of work, wouldn't it, Melrose? It could take you a whole year, maybe even more, shut away in that gray tomb of a school with nothing but those screaming spires driving you mad."

" 'Dreaming' spires, Diane," said Melrose.

"Well, you've found your proper work, Diane," said Trueblood. "That column of yours is extremely entertaining."

"*Work?* I hope not. I hope I've managed to purge it of *work,* for heaven's sake!"

"By not knowing anything about astrology, yes," said Melrose, still smarting from his weekly dose of Capricorn.

"Naturally. But writing horoscopes isn't the job I *applied* for, if you recall. If that's what the job turned out to be, it's no fault of mine. And it's been done quite well without going to some school to *read* something." She turned to Trueblood. "Really, Marshall, don't even consider it. I'm almost sorry I wrote that nice little horoscope for you."

"You never write a nice one for anybody, Diane. That's what makes it good."

"Well, I do once in a while." She turned round and called to Dick. "Dick, just read that little bit of horoscope under Aquarius, would you?"

"Glad to," said Dick, happy to be called on to perform. He snapped the paper straight and stood with the authority of a jury foreman to read:

"We all know that Aquarians are true individualists! What is less well known is their extremely charitable nature. This will be demonstrated —"

Trueblood interrupted. "Charitable nature? Well, it's less well known because I haven't bloody got one."

Diane shushed him. "Dick, go on."

"Right." Dick cleared his throat.

"— will be demonstrated this very week as the Moon passes through one of the rings of Saturn and you take delivery on a number of objets d'art —"

"Wait a minute! Whoa!" Trueblood declared. "Are you referring to delivery of that possibly Ming-dynasty urn you're slobbering after? You think you'll get it on the cheap, then? Ha! Not a bloody chance, Diane."

"Good heavens, Marshall, horoscopes can't be *that* specific, or else how can one appeal to the masses?"

"And just how many masses are taking delivery on objets d'art today?"

Unruffled, Diane ran a hand over her dark hair, to smooth what was already as smooth as glass and black as her heart, and said, "What I really meant was not exactly *d'art* but more like goods and furniture. For instance, there's Ada Crisp, right over there." She pointed her cigarette holder toward the window. "And there's Theo, don't forget."

There was a lorry sitting outside of the Wrenn's Nest. "Those are books, not art."

Diane said, "Speak of the devil."

"I'm not sure the devil would thank you," said Trueblood, observing Browne

120

across the street on the pavement with the lorry driver. "Bring me another Campari, Mr. Scroggs, and a glass of ice water to pour over my head."

Theo Wrenn Browne swept across the street with his tie over his shoulder (arranged there, Melrose was certain, by his hand and not the wind), looking both ways as if heavy traffic on the High Street was synchronized to get him from both directions. All Melrose saw was a boy on a bicycle. But Theo wanted everybody to think he lived on the edge.

He came in, barked his drink order to Dick Scroggs, and walked over to their table. Lately, he'd been shaving only two or three times a week because he thought the days-old stubble made him look as if he'd just been modeling shirts for *Elle*. All the two-day growth made him look like was as if he'd been sleeping rough.

As he sat down, Diane said, "We were just talking about this crazy idea of yours to shut down the library." Diane took her arguments wherever she could get them.

"Crazy? There's nothing crazy about it, I assure you. Don't forget it's *our* money that pays the Twine woman's salary."

"Twinny," said Trueblood. "If you're

going to ruin her life, at least get her name right."

"You're so dramatic," said Browne. "The woman's on the verge of retirement anyway."

"She wouldn't be if you weren't acting as lending library for twenty p per day."

"If people are willing to pay it —"

"You've an advantage over the library," Trueblood went on, "because you get the best-sellers straight off the printing press and Una Twinny has to wait until whatever she gets goes through channels and clears the Sidbury library and the Northants library system. So by the time Una gets these books, you've already rented them to half of Long Piddleton and taken away her business."

Theo nodded to Dick as Dick set down his single malt whisky and Trueblood's Campari and ice water. "I'm performing a public service —"

"Oh, bosh," said Melrose. "I could understand it if you were competing with another bookshop. But you don't have a Dillon's or a Waterstone's next door."

"Just what's in this for you, Theo, old sweat?" asked Trueblood. "Why this agitation to close the poor two-room library and lose Una Twinny's job for her?"

"Absolutely nothing. I'm merely trying to save the taxpayers money."

"Completely altruistic motive, is it?"

Theo, never popular in the first place, realized his popularity was taking a further plunge. He tossed his remaining whisky down his throat and rose. "I'm taking delivery on some books. Got to go." He wheeled out as he'd wheeled in.

"We could privatize; that's the direction the country's going anyway," said Melrose.

"There's got to be some marketing, some PR. Get Twinny to sell lottery tickets? Rent videos? . . . Drink?" Trueblood asked Diane.

"You can't dispense alcohol in a library," said Diane. "Unfortunately."

"No, no, old girl. I'm asking, Do you want another drink?"

Melrose brought his fist down on the table and jumped his glass. "That's it! I've got it! A coffee bar: espresso, cappuccino. Like they do in those great big bookstores in the States. I'm surprised Browne hasn't come up with that for *his* place."

Trueblood, his refill forgotten, turned this over in his mind while firing up a jade-green Sobranie. "You know, that's rather interesting, old sweat. I say, it just might work. There's that second room Una

Twinny uses for storage, but there's not much to store so it might just accommodate the coffee bar. I could get my hands on one of those espresso machines. Then there's a fridge; that'd be easy. Furnishings — counter, stools, tables, and chairs, which, in all of the sales I come across, would be easily found. I can bear the cost of a lot of it; it'll be dirt cheap. You bear the cost of the supplies — coffee, milk, biscuits. And I'd bet anything Betty Ball would contribute scones, croissants, whatever. Una Twinny is a good friend of Betty's."

"But who'd run it? Who'd do the coffees? Miss Twinny wouldn't have time."

"The library is only open three days a week." Trueblood waved the difficulty away. "Someone in the village could do it. . . ." He looked at Diane.

Who looked back.

Trueblood went on. "Well, someone will. Of course! Vivian, she's just the person!"

"She's in Venice," said Melrose.

"*Now* she is. But she'll be back soon."

"If they're not out dragging the Grand Canal for her." This was Diane's happy thought. "I tried to tell her before she left not to go. Neptune's transiting her solar house."

"That's bad?" asked Melrose.

"Dreadful. Anyway," Diane went on, brushing a bit of ash from her white sleeve, "if nothing happens she'll be back next week. Friday or Saturday. "

"Her horoscope says?"

Diane rolled her eyes at Melrose's obtuseness. "No, that's what *she* said. The stars can't track every little detail, after all."

"No?" said Trueblood. "They're certainly tracking my objets d'art. Now: our coffee bar. We'll need a cat or a dog."

"A cat? Why in hell do we need a cat or a dog? To make the cappuccino?"

"Every library has something four-legged, old sweat. They're to lie around and look content." Trueblood sucked a piece of ice. "We could just borrow one from the village. What about Desperado?" The Broadstairs cat was always mauling the other village cats.

"Desperado? Are you joking?" said Melrose. "He'd eat everything in sight, besides wrestling us to the ground doing it. He'll check out all the weight-lifting books."

Trueblood said, "Anyway, that's just a detail."

"What if it's against the law or something? I mean, don't library systems have rules about what their branches can do?"

Trueblood wedged down in his chair, shot out his legs, looked at the ceiling. "You know, I might just have to go back to the law if something stupid like that comes up."

Diane rolled her eyes. "Oh, *please* don't go on about that again. Listening to both of you is exhausting me. Dick!" She waved her stemmed and rink-sized martini glass in Scroggs's direction.

He was bent over his paper again and didn't look up. "Sorry, Miss Demorney. We're out of vodka."

Diane wheeled round in her chair. "Out of luck," "out on a limb," "out of time," "out of countenance," "out of her mind": These were all concepts she could relate to. "Out of vodka" was not one of them. She started taking things from her big leather purse: lipstick, compact, receipts, pen, small velvet bag —

"What's in there?" Melrose asked, pushing at the velvet with his forefinger.

"My pearls."

— notebook, leather gloves, three key rings, *smack* down on the table.

"Why are you carrying them around? Do they need to be mended or what?"

Her head bent over the bag, she said, "No. Because they're very valuable and I don't want to leave them at home." The items went on: nail polish, two handkerchiefs, gun, silver pencil —

Trueblood lurched forward. "Good lord, Diane. That's a gun!"

She said nothing but continued to plunder the seemingly bottomless purse. Another lipstick, a book of stamps —

"Well? *Well?*" Melrose insisted. "Why are you packing a gun around?"

"Because I'm carrying my pearls and for protection. Ah, here." Out came two miniature bottles of vodka, which she set side by side, smiled at, and called to Dick to come and get.

"Since when have you had a gun, Diane?" Melrose poked at it tentatively. It was small, probably a two-two, and pearl-handled.

She plugged another cigarette into her holder and waggled it towards them, one or the other, to light.

"Protection? Since when do we villagers need protection?" asked Trueblood. "You mean you know how to fire the damned thing?"

"Obviously. I've taken to carrying it round with me since I got into journalism.

That and my pager." She waggled a small black object. "You know, reporting can be dangerous."

"You write *horoscopes,* for God's sake!"

"Not the ones people want to hear. Light?" she asked, pointing to her cigarette.

Trueblood fired up a match. "Why in hell do you need a pager?"

"So people can get in *touch,* obviously. Emergencies, that sort of thing."

Melrose looked at the ceiling. "A zodiac emergency. I've heard of those."

"She's not going to marry him," said Diane.

"Who?" Melrose frowned.

"Vivian. Isn't that who we were talking about?"

"Count Dracula?" said Trueblood. "Do vampires have star signs?"

9

If Long Piddleton had tracks, Melrose Plant knew that Plague Alley would be on the wrong side of them. Or perhaps the "wrong side" would be the row of almshouses inhabited by the Withersby clan. Almshouses in these times were considered "quaint" and snapped up by Londoners to throw money at in costly renovations. But Northampton was not in the Chelsea belt, so Long Piddleton's almshouses were allowed to go to rack and ruin. The Preservation Society would be deeply pleased to know the houses were pretty much still put to their original use.

It was in Plague Alley that Agatha lived, in a darkling cottage that also might be called quaint, as it met most of the criteria. The windows were small, leaded, and obscured by the overhanging thatch, which had loosened from the roof. Light was thrifty here; the parlor was steeped in darkness. Melrose called it the Twilight Zone.

He was employing himself (while his aunt made tea) by picking out objects;

from his ability to do so, or not, he could conclude whether he needed his glasses changed. Over there on a rusty floor stand meant for a birdcage sat the stuffed owl whose burning copper eyes were enhanced by the darkness. He had often wondered how E. A. Poe would have fared if the owl had been the poet's inspiration. Indeed, Poe might have found Agatha's cottage on the whole quite to his liking. There were the items sitting on the mantel over the fireplace: candlesticks, a pair of pottery shepherdesses, a Limoges knockoff — no, wait, perhaps not an imitation but the real thing, one of the Countess of Caverness's real Limoges figurines. The Countess, Lady Marjorie, his mother. Melrose had discovered quite a few of the Ardry End collection here in Plague Alley. He could go to the mantel and look, but he did not feel like prying his way out of the over-stuffed chair he was wedged into.

He heard rattlings and clangings going on in the kitchen — Agatha organizing the tea. Her brute of a cat swayed in, an odd-looking creature that always seemed to have something wrong with one or more of its limbs. It sidled up to Melrose, stood there staring, then jumped up on one of the chairs and lay down. It had the queerest, most colorless eyes, which glowed like silver discs in the dark. Trueblood might consider him a candidate for the coffee bar, if worst came to worst.

"Melrose!"

"Yes?" He had always disliked the practice of people shouting through rooms.

"Oh, never mind." The exasperated tone suggested Agatha had been beseeching him for hours to do something, only to meet with his cold refusal.

"All right, I won't."

She came, stoutly lugging a tea service that could also have been the Countess's. The unreadable, intertwined initials could have stood for anything: Marjorie, Countess of Caverness; Lady Agatha Ardry; Dead Mouse in Pot.

"Here, permit me to help you, dear Aunt."

"Never mind." She muscled him out of the way. "You always do it wrong."

Could one pour tea *wrong?*

She clattered cups and saucers and cake plate around, stopping to inspect the silver creamer and complain that Mrs. Oilings hadn't polished it properly. "I don't know why I bother with that woman. She's not worth half what I pay her."

"Thank you," said Melrose, accepting a

cup of tea that he was quite sure was being presented in one of his mother's Crown Derby cups. "I don't know, I rather think the Oilings woman is perfect for this cottage."

Agatha regarded him suspiciously. "Why?"

"Whenever I see her she's always leaning on a broom, puffing a Gitane, thinking dark thoughts. Goes with the owl." Mrs. Oilings, he fancied, wove cobwebs wherever she stood.

"Talking nonsense, as usual. I must say I was surprised to see you."

"Why? You're always seeing me." Melrose hesitated over taking a rock cake from the plate and thought it would be as safe as anything. "I just wanted to tell you I'm going up to London."

"What do you mean?"

Melrose thought it had been fairly clear, so he repeated it. "I'm going up to London."

"Very well. I could do with a day at Harrods."

But could Harrods? "You may come along, if you don't mind sitting in the back on a stack of old quilts."

"Back of what?"

"We're going in Trueblood's van." He

knew she'd refuse. She would forego Paradise if it meant driving there with Trueblood. "There's to be a big catalog sale at Sotheby's, and he needs the van to bring back what he buys."

"I've no intention of going anywhere with Marshall Trueblood." She thought for a moment. "But as long as you're going to Sotheby's sale, you might pick me up a fall-front desk."

Melrose looked round at the great lumps of furniture that, from what he could see, covered every inch of floor space. "Where were you thinking of putting it, in the front garden?"

She looked ceilingward. "Upstairs, in my bedroom. I need a writing desk to take care of my correspondence."

"But a fall-front? That's a *secrétaire à abattant,* and they're quite large. Tall, especially, with bookcases and such. Why don't you settle for some little Queen Anne thing, or even a writing table?" Why he was helping her furnish this cottage with, it appeared, the spoils of Ardry End, he couldn't imagine.

"Because a writing table doesn't have shelves and drawers and little nooks and things, that's why."

"Anything in a catalog sale is going to be

quite dear, you know."

She flapped her hand as if to say money was no object, which it wasn't, as long as it wasn't hers. "I'll reimburse you."

"I doubt very much Trueblood would want to give over space in his van to a piece that size."

"Why on earth are you going to London?"

Melrose thought for a moment and finally came up with: "To see Mr. Beaton. You know, my tailor."

She was astonished. "You only just saw him in February. "

"Well, that's why: I must go back for a final fitting."

"It's taken him all that time to throw together a suit?"

"Isn't that rather like saying Pissarro threw together a lot of blurry little strokes? Mr. Beaton takes his time, he's a perfectionist, and have I ever been in a hurry? Tailors such as Beaton are rare birds, these days, and much in demand. Then I mean to drop in at my club." Melrose took a bite of cold toast.

"Club? What club?"

He was, apparently, full of surprises. "The club my father and my uncle — you remember Uncle Robert? — belonged to.

And their father before them. And their fathers' fathers —"

"Oh, *do* stop. Robert belonged to no London club."

Robert had been too smart to tell her where he was going. Unlike Melrose.

She asked, "Which one is it? White's? Boodle's?"

"No. Boring's."

She shook her head. "Never heard of it."

Which should put paid to Boring's. "It's very exclusive."

Agatha made a dismissive noise. "Those men's clubs. Prehistoric, they are, the way they still don't admit women."

"Yes, I expect that is one of the criteria for a men's club."

"Well, it's totally behind the times."

"I should think that a virtue, myself. Anyway, I've never understood this feminine objection to the exclusivity of men's clubs. It's perfectly all right with me if women want to start up a women's club that I can't get into."

"That's not the point."

"But why isn't it?"

"*Mel*-rose, it's the idea behind it; a man's club is *symbolic*."

"All I can see it's symbolic of is an organization that doesn't admit women into its smoke-and-brandy-snifter environs."

"Precisely."

"Precisely *what?*" Why was he arguing with her? "That's not a symbol, Auntie, that's a fact. It's an organization that doesn't admit —"

"Oh, stop being tiresome."

"And perhaps I'll drop in on Superintendent Jury." *That* would irritate her!

"What? You can't simply drop in at New Scotland Yard! Anyway, he'll be much too busy to lollygag around with you."

"Oh, I don't know. Jury's always good for a lollygag or two. We'll have a meal at Brown's; we usually do when I'm in London." Brown's had always been his favorite hotel, probably because it was where his mother had taken him as a child for a treat when she went to London. A treat for both of them, she would say. His mother had never been condescending to children; it had been one of her charms. . . .

Melrose felt a sudden pain and set down his cup.

He had put in the call to New Scotland Yard and was waiting for a return call while he sat in his living room, trying to adjust his eyes to the light. After Agatha's cottage, it was almost blinding.

The old dog Mindy slept in front of the fireplace, in which a low, comfortable fire burned. He sat there with a glass of sherry debating Mindy's age. Twelve? Thirteen? Ninety? Hard to say, since he hadn't known how old she was when he had found her left behind at the old Man with a Load of Mischief. So she might be fourteen or fifteen. Even older. Occasionally, someone would suggest that Mindy be put down. (Melrose loathed that evasion.) Why? he would ask. To put her out of her misery.

What misery?

Ruthven swanned in with the telephone on its long cord. Melrose had never had an extension put in the living room, since he would then have no excuse for leaving the room if Agatha was around.

"Is it Superintendent Jury?"

"No, sir. It's Miss Demorney."

Why was she calling? "Diane. Hullo."

"I was sitting here thinking that if you and Marshall were going up to London tomorrow, I might just tootle along, Melrose."

"There's not really room for a tootle, Diane. Trueblood's taking his van and there's only the front seat; he might have a jump seat, but I don't remember."

"It's a *van,* Melrose. He transports *furniture,* doesn't he? So there'd be oceans of room in the back for a comfy chair. I can bring along my cold box and we can have drinks."

Melrose frowned. "I don't think we should have a rave-up on the road. Not with you with a gun in your bag."

Her sigh was huge. "Oh, don't be such a fossil, Melrose. Anyway, the only one who shouldn't drink *is* the driver. Which certainly isn't going to be me. But I'd be happy to pay for the petrol."

He slid down in his chair and looked at the ceiling molding. "Why do you want to go to London anyway?"

"To go to Paris, of course."

"Why?"

"Does one need a reason for *Paris?*"

He saw her point. "Well, it's Trueblood's van and Trueblood's comfy chair, not mine, so you'll have to ask him."

"He doesn't answer his telephone." She was sulky.

"He's obviously out somewhere. Did you try the shop?"

"Marshall shouldn't be going out, not with" paper rattled — "not with his Venus in transit. Incidentally, do you know what hour of the day Richard Jury was born? I might have given him wrong information."

Should he attempt to work out this conundrum? "I don't even know what *year* he was born: 1888? What wrong information?"

"Umm."

That did for her answer. She was probably inhaling whatever she kept around the house.

"Are you going to see him when you're in London?" she asked.

"Jury? I expect so. I put in a call to him just a little while ago. He may he trying to call back."

"I wonder he's never got married. Nor have you."

"How did we get from the comfy chair to Jury's and my matrimonial status?"

"Of course, having been married four times myself, I can tell you it's a good thing to have an understanding right from the start that you'll leave one another alone."

Melrose took the receiver from his ear and looked at it. Then he said, "Diane, doesn't that rather defeat the purpose?"

"What purpose? Look, I'm afraid I'm going to have to ring off now; my pager's beeping. 'Bye."

The instant she hung up, the telephone

rang, and Melrose snatched it up. "Ardry End here."

"New Scotland Yard here," said Jury. "Your line's been busy."

"I've just been having a talk with Diane Demorney. She wants to know the hour you were born. Did you know she has a gun? Did you know she was writing up horoscopes for a Sidbury rag? It's really wonderful; wait a minute." There was a paper at his feet, and Melrose messed it about until he found the right page. "Okay, what's your sign?"

"Leo. Why does Diane have a gun, in God's name? How'd she get it?"

"Listen, this is your 'Seeing Stars' for today: *Brooding won't solve anything. Instead of moping about the house —*"

"The flat."

"*— about the flat, you should be contacting friends, have a meal together. Get out, get going, get a life.* She's always telling us that: Get a life."

Jury laughed. "How does she expect to win readers?"

"What I just read is mild. You should hear some of them. I think she's taking the opportunity to deliver trenchant messages to her acquaintance."

"Anyway, she got mine right. And here I

am, getting a life."

"And here you are, having a meal with me."

"Delighted, but where?"

"London." He told Jury about the trip.

"My social calendar may have room."

"Good, do you have a favorite spot?"

"Yes. In my easy chair eating takeaway Tandoori."

"Listen, why don't we dine at Brown's?"

"Fine with me. That where you're staying?"

"No. At my club."

A brief silence ensued; then Jury asked, "Your *club?*"

Melrose sighed. Was everyone going to take that *your club* tack? "Yes. It's in Mayfair. Wait a minute, and I'll give you the number."

"You belong to one of those men's clubs?"

"Why is that so awful? I'm not out shooting orphans, for heaven's sake."

"It's so bloody unlike you is why."

"Why is it so unlike me to sit around in an armchair drinking port and reading the *Times?* What do you think I do all day, march off to work the early shift at the canning factory?"

"They're so elitist. Purveyors of such

anachronistic ways of life. Totally out of it."

"You sound like Agatha." *That* should shut him up! "They're merely places where you can sit and read a paper and have a drink."

"Go to Leicester Square and sit on a bench. The only difference being you'd be having your drink out of a brown paper bag in the company of a lot of other brown paper bags."

"How funny."

"I've known you over a decade, and never once have I heard you mention your club. When's the last time you were there?"

Melrose thought for a moment. "It was with my father."

"Your father's been dead for twenty years. You haven't been to this place in twenty years?"

"Actually, longer than that. When I went with my father I was pretty small."

"How do you even know it's still in Mayfair?"

"Places like that are always there."

"Would they still have you on roll call?"

"Of *course*. Probably you only get struck from the list if you do something criminal."

"How's the food?"

142

"Oh, you know. Clubby. Roast beef, roast lamb, fish. Boiled potatoes. Pudding. Treacle tart. That kind of thing."

"Hmm. I'd rather dine there. So you'll be in Mayfair. That'll be convenient."

"Convenient for what?"

"There's an art gallery I'd like you to visit."

Melrose was suspicious. "Oh? Why?"

Jury did not answer, except to say, "I'll tell you what's been going on when I see you. Give me the rest of the address. What's the name of this club, anyway?"

"Boring's."

"That sounds about right."

10

Wiggins opened a fresh pack of black biscuits and talked about television.

"It's much the best thing I've seen in years. Have you?"

Jury had been lost in his own thoughts. "Have I what?"

"Seen this American program on the telly. It's called *Homicide: Life on the Street*. It's set in Baltimore, which is one of the reasons we'd especially enjoy it. I mean, having been there and all."

"I was thinking more along the lines of something set in Fulham, Wiggins, if you don't mind. Having been there and all."

"Oh, sorry, sir." Wiggins then relayed to Jury the information he'd obtained about the offices rented out by the council: "Couple of insurance companies, small architectural firm, a priest, Father Charles Noailles — who I haven't spoken to yet because he's in France; he's writing a book on the Bishops of London — and a Captain Bread who runs the Siddons Trust. Had a bit of luck there, sir. The Siddons Trust is a fund for elderly seamen, set up by an old naval officer named Siddons, administered now by one of those elderly seamen it was set up for; he's the one I talked with. It was hard keeping him on course, the way he liked to talk about himself and the sea; it was all like a travelogue." Wiggins sniggered. "I learned more about the Paradise Isles than one would care to know. Did you know that the puffin population —"

Jury interrupted the travelogue. "What's the name of this elderly seaman?"

"Captain Neville Bread. That's spelled B-R-E-A-D, but it's pronounced with a long *e*. He gets most annoyed if it's said wrong."

"I'll send Pansy along to keep it straight."

"Pardon?"

Jury waved a hand. "Just a little joke. Go on."

"It's up to Bread to decide what worthy retired seagoing bloke — his words, those are — should get some of the money." Wiggins munched his black biscuit and continued the history of the Siddons Trust.

Why didn't someone set up a similar fund for elderly detectives? "So where's the bit of luck?"

"Sir?" Wiggins looked puzzled.

Jury sighed. Had the world gone deaf and literal? "You said there was a bit of luck connected with this trust."

"Oh, sorry. Yes. Well, Captain Bread was working in the office that night. He left a little after nine, locked up, and went to the car park — not the big one across from the entrance but the small one that skirts one side of the palace, up past the museum —"

"I know where it is," said Jury, closing his eyes.

"He was unlocking his car door when he saw her."

"*Saw* her?"

Wiggins nodded. "That's right."

"Well? Go on!" Jury motioned with his hands like someone urging on a runner or an engine.

"He's pretty sure it was her, this woman described in the paper. Said it was sometime after nine he saw her. He says he got a clear look at her — of course, it was the coat; he couldn't mistake that sable coat. He was about to ring up Fulham police after he saw the paper, and then I turned up."

Jury was silent, waiting. When Wiggins simply kept eating the biscuit, he asked, "*And?*"

"Well, then Captain Bread got in his car and left through the main gates."

"But — didn't he think it strange, her wandering around, a stranger in a sable coat, in the grounds of Fulham Palace?" When the telephone rang, Jury ignored it.

"Yes, of course he did."

The "bit of luck" had been little enough; this Captain Bread was merely confirming what Jury already knew.

The phone rang, Wiggins answered. "The guv'nor wants to see you, sir."

The guv'nor was, as usual, rampaging.

Chief Superintendent Racer picked up a stack of files and slammed them down again, as if all this paperwork were Jury's fault. "Three cases handed me on a platter this morning; take your pick. . . . No, better yet, you can handle all of them."

"Thanks. All at the same time?"

Racer ignored that. "One up in Northumberland, one in Cornwall, one in Armagh."

"Armagh? That's in Northern Ireland!"

"I bloody well know where Armagh is, Jury."

"What else would it be but political? 'Murder' and 'Northern Ireland' strike me as redundant, doesn't it you?"

"Shadow warfare doesn't stop serial kill-
ers. They can exist side by side with the
mercenaries. That bloody country. Get
your skates on and clear up whatever
you're doing. Which brings us to your total
lack of action in the Danny Wu business.
That so-called restaurateur in Soho,"
Racer added with contempt.

Jury said, tiredly, "It should be the Drug
Squad's party. That murder last month
can't be linked to Wu."

Racer looked at him, frowning. "Where's
that beast, anyway?"

Jury was confused. "Danny Wu? I
wouldn't call him —"

"No, no, no." Racer looked as if he could
spit nails. "The bloody *cat*." Nodding
toward the outer office and Fiona, he
added, "She's hiding him somewhere, I
know it."

Jury shrugged. The cat Cyril, of course,
would take precedence in CS Racer's mind
over Armagh and Danny Wu. The cat was
the bane of his existence. In another year
or so, if they were lucky, the cat would
drive him over the edge. They could all
only hope.

Jury left Racer's office.

"Now here's an interesting item, sir,"

Wiggins said, lowering the paper to see how fury was taking things and deciding it was all right. "PET PSYCHIC PULLS PLUG ON FIDO'S THOUGHTS. That's the headline. Listen:

"Miss Imogen Loy, formerly manicurist at the Mile End branch of Hair Today, is now doing animal therapy full time. 'I discovered I had this power, see, to communicate with dogs and cats and thought I might as well go into the business of treating them, you know, like a psychologist, or something.' Animal Friends Pleasure Park employs Miss boy as a consultant, and she says she is also on call at other places. She says, 'We're all of us tapped into other people's brain waves; we just don't know it.'

" 'What gives you the unique ability to read an animal's mind?' we asked.

" 'Oh, I never said it was unique, did I? If everyone would just sit down with Scrappy or Ginger and tune in, they'd find out a lot of things. Thing is, you have to apply yourself; you have to keep it up and not be discouraged when your pet walks away. Remember, they — our pets — have spent all their time, years and years, being mentally ignored, so they might balk at the beginning. So just because the animal appears to be the same, that doesn't mean you haven't reached him.'

" 'So you deal mostly with behavior problems, is that correct?'

" 'That's correct, yes. If Kitty refuses to use her litter box or Spot won't fetch in the paper — that kind of thing's what I deal with.'

"Asked what she charged for the service, Miss Loy said in the thirty-to-fifty-pound range. That's for an hour. It depends on the seriousness of the problem. For phone consultations, it's lower because 'I don't have to actually go to the place, which saves on petrol.'

"Asked how a telephone 'reading' works, Miss Loy said, 'Oh, it's easy: the owner just holds the receiver to his pet's ear, and I talk to him or her. Cat or dog.' How does she know if the animal has absorbed what she's said? 'Well, of course, you can't tell by just looking, as they appear pretty much the same. But you'll know when Kitty starts using the litter box again.'

"Is this effect immediate? 'Not usually. Usually, it takes some days or even weeks. It's best to be patient.' "

Wiggins folded the paper. "But if you're patient, the problem will go away without any mind reading, won't it?" He asked this in all seriousness.

"Let me have that, will you? Not the paper, just that page." Jury pulled his jacket from the chair, stuffed the folded page in an inside pocket, pulled his coat from the tottering coat tree, and told Wiggins he was going out for lunch.

Which he was drinking, sitting in the pub on the Fulham Road.

It was the pub she had come out of when he had first seen her, and it was back to the pub in the Fulham Road that he went. It was Wednesday morning, and it was the fourth time he'd been here since the Monday. Since Monday afternoon, when he'd gone to Fulham Palace with Chilten.

And why did he think the woman he'd seen on the bus would revisit the Stargazey, when on that Saturday night she might have been simply walking along the pavement, come from anywhere in London, and on the spur of the moment stopped in here for a drink? Why did he think she'd come back?

For the simple reason that there wasn't anywhere else he could go to look for her. And there might never be. Eventually, the identity of the dead woman would be discovered; possibly not, but in most cases unknown victims became known. And if that were true, then there'd be more to go on — maybe.

It was Kitty he wanted to see. She was in Brighton, but she'd be back. He'd shown the police photograph to everyone who worked in the Stargazey, but no one was sure. Kitty, though, was different. *You miss a lot in life if you don't notice little things.* Kitty noticed little things, like the light falling on the Sapphire gin bottle. If she'd been in here, Kitty might remember.

The lack of a history, of his failure to find out who she was, was the source of deepest frustration for him. It added to Jury's sense of remorse. Anyone would tell him he had nothing to feel remorseful about; he was being irrational. Yes, he knew that, or thought he did. It didn't help, though. Leaning against the bar, ordering up a pint of lager, Jury wondered if he could simply spirit her up, like a genie out of a bottle.

He was not very hopeful; it was all so nebulous, any connection between the dead woman and the Fabricants, the only one being Mona Dresser's sable coat. No, as everyone was fond of telling him, it wasn't much to go on.

There was a fair-sized lunchtime crowd eating sandwiches and salads. Jury wasn't hungry. He was, however, tired, and when he saw three people leaving a small table, he claimed it, giving away an extra chair to a table of four that hadn't enough seating.

Once seated, all four people took out cigarettes, matches, and lighters and set about the tantalizing ritual of lighting up. This was the thanks he got for giving them his two chairs? He could not help it; his eye traveled up the thin thread of lavender smoke coming from the redhead's cigarette. It intertwined with that wafting upwards from the blonde's until finally blending with the smoke ceiling drifting overhead.

Jury sighed, opened the tabloid paper he'd picked up, and looked for that day's horoscope. Diane Demorney had called him for the sole (she claimed) purpose of informing him he was a Leo, and with the moon "transiting your sign" he'd better change his diet. Needed to drink less caffeine, more juice. Jury had interrupted to suggest this was really Sergeant Wiggins's horoscope she was doing. She gave him a bunch of advice and rang off.

There is every reason to suspect the business transaction so long in abeyance will come to fruition if you are just careful was what was in the works, according to this paper's horoscope. Nice to know, thought Jury. Then, seeing two young women looking about longingly for a seat, he folded the paper, rose, and indicated they could have the table. They acted as relieved as if they'd been lost in the desert.

Tired, thirsty . . . mirage. . . . Ah!

11

Trueblood had contrived to stop three times within the seventy-odd miles to London. This rest-stop side of Trueblood was one Melrose had never seen before and showed him to be somewhat egalitarian. *That* had been a surprise. Of course the egalitarianism had been considerably tempered by Trueblood's mirth at being "among them" but not "of them." *Doesn't it make you feel wonderful that you're not a lorry driver?*

Trueblood was one of those people who enjoyed little horrors because he didn't have to put up with them. Doors marked with an X in the plague years would probably have put him in a merry mood, so long as he wasn't behind one. He and Joanna Lewes enjoyed reading bad books for the pleasurable discussions they could have about their badness. Bad books, bad films, bad plays. Anything except bad food. This delight in badness derived at least in part from knowing one could, at any time, close the book, get up and leave the film. Just walk out. The experience appeared to be intensely liberating.

Melrose was reminded of all this when he stepped through the heavy door of Boring's, where the silence was broken by the ticking of a longcase clock and the whisper of the porter's shoes as he appeared to glide toward Melrose in the manner of a hovercraft, floating just above the carpet. It was so silent, Melrose would have imagined the place to be empty had he not seen, through a large archway flanked by several potted palms, a half dozen members in leather armchairs reading or drinking or both.

"You are a member, sir," said the old man, with a low and ingratiating voice whose tone did not suggest alternatives. One would not be so idiotic as to set foot in Boring's if one were *not* a member. The old man's failure to recognize Melrose — as he couldn't have done — did nothing to change this assumption.

Melrose handed him one of the cards he had disinterred from a dusty cubbyhole and mumbled something about "family" and "father" and "Earl of Caverness." "You might remember I rang up yesterday, don't know who I spoke with."

"Ah, yes, yes. You spoke with young Higgins. Yes, we have you down for three nights; is that correct?"

"Yes. If it's a day or two longer, I trust you can accommodate me?"

"Certainly, sir. If you'd please step this way?"

He followed the old porter to a mahogany front desk. The man raised the flap and went behind it; he then dragged over an enormous book, which he consulted. "Higgins made a note of it . . . ah, here we are. Lord Ardry, is it?"

Melrose nodded. That was one of several titles Melrose had relinquished years before. Yet Ardry and Caverness came in handy as the dickens sometimes. With a flourish, he signed the book, which had been turned his way for that purpose. The porter produced a key that might have opened Napoleon's cell on Elba. "Look, if you can have someone take this bag to my room, I'd appreciate it. I think I'll just go in the lounge and have a drink."

"Our Members' Room. Certainly. I'll just have young Higgins take it up for you. I'm Budding, sir, should you need anything."

Melrose thought young Higgins seemed to be doing all the work.

In the Members' Room, two fireplaces were blazing, pleasant in the November chill. But Melrose imagined they had as much to do with ambience as cold. It would always be a little cold in here, he thought. The room was much as he'd imagined it: groupings of leather club and wing chairs around low tables, some of them drawn a little closer to the fireplaces; chesterfield sofas, a half dozen of them, arranged back-to-back down the center of the room. All the furniture was covered in a soft, fine-grained leather in autumnal shades of brown and dark green, wonderfully worn, as if a soft-gloved hand spent all its time rubbing and polishing.

There were perhaps a half dozen elderly men sitting around in what might have been a post-luncheon haze. The only sounds were the crackling of the flames and of newspaper pages being turned. He could not see all of these gentlemen, only, in some cases, a shoe or a shoulder around the back of a chair and a hand holding a paper. These were the men who, had they not had money and privilege to call their own, would have wound up in one of those lodges or manor houses adapted to the comfort of "retired gentlefolk." Growing old is hell, Melrose thought. He wondered if their daughters or sons or family members in hope of inheritance ever visited them. Of course, he knew he was really wondering if anyone would visit him if he found himself in the same way.

Thus, feeling comfortably sorry for himself, Melrose selected a wing chair beside the fireplace on the other side of which two old gentlemen dozed. He wondered if smoking was permitted. He reflected that the last couple of decades of giving over to no-smoking rooms would have had precious little effect upon Boring's, if indeed Boring's had ever heard there were such rooms. Without another thought, Melrose took out his cigarette case from which he removed a cigarette, closed the case with a satisfied little *click*, and lighted it with his old Zippo.

He signaled to a white-jacked young man, presumably another porter — Young Higgins, perhaps? — and the boy moved immediately to his side. Question asked and answered as to what Melrose would like. He'd like a double whisky.

This transaction awakened the two old members who were seated on the other side of the fireplace, both of whom looked to be in their late seventies or even their eighties, both dressed in tweeds and stiff white collars, one possessed of a monocle, which dropped from his eye as he came huffing awake; the other having a little pocket watch that he took out, checked, and absently wound as his gaze fastened on Melrose's face.

Melrose said, almost gaily, "Afternoon."

One of them leaned forward a bit, making guttural sounds: "Uh . . . wuh . . . eh. . . ."

Talk, Melrose reflected, was not something entered into lightly at Boring's. One had to warm up first.

The other one did not attempt speech but looked out from under his wild white eyebrows with blistering blue eyes, their intensity perhaps arising merely from the fact they were set in a face lined and furrowed and old.

Melrose carried on for all three of them as he put out his hand. "Name's Plant . . . Lord Ardry, actually. How'ja do?"

Ready, apparently, to join in, the white-browed one said, "Ah . . . yes. Well . . . I'm Major Champs" — he leaned forward and adjusted his eyeglasses, probably to get a better grip on Melrose — "and this is Colonel Neame." He gestured toward his friend. "That's *Champs* with a soft *Ch* if you don't mind. New, aren't you?" asked the major, winding his pocket watch. "Don't recall ever seeing you in here before."

"I am. This was my father's club, you see." Melrose hadn't the least idea of what they were supposed to see from this announcement, but they apparently did, for they both made sounds of affirmation and understanding.

"And where from?"

"Northants, actually. Little village outside of Northampton."

"Really? What'd'ya think of that, Neame?"

Colonel Neame made some *oh-ho-ho* sounds — simulating laughter, perhaps? — and started in making digging gestures with his arms. Melrose watched this and wondered what it meant. Nothing, probably.

"Northants! Northampton hasn't much to recommend it as a city."

Melrose smiled. "It's a cut above Sheffield, let's give it that."

Major Champs gave a braying laugh and slapped the colonel on the arm. "Hear that, Joss?"

People must really be hurting for humor around here, if they thought that remark was funny.

After Champs quieted down, Melrose asked, "Well, gentlemen, may I offer you another of what you're drinking?" An empty glass sat before each of them.

They were back to their indecipherable *ups, nums,* and *ehs,* sprinkled here and there with a *dashed, don't mind, good, trouble,* during which Melrose signaled Young Higgins again, and he came like a shot. Melrose certainly couldn't give the service bad marks. He ordered another round and the porter dashed off.

"Tell me, gentlemen, would you recommend the food here?"

Again, they lost Melrose in their labyrinthine answer, comparing notes on the lack of success of the leg of lamb on the night previous but finally arriving at a compromise. Said the major, "Sometimes yes, sometimes no. Soup's good, though."

"Windsor soup . . . quite tasty," added Colonel Neame. "Yes, I did miss a spot of good Windsor soup when things got rough."

Melrose wondered if *major* and *colonel* were literal ranks meaning wartime service or were figures of speech, complimentary tags indicating their stations in life. Rather like life peerages bestowed by the monarchy in gratitude for having done (in many cases) sod-all. He sometimes thought it a pity the United States hadn't the practice of parceling out peerages instead of taking the sometimes ruinous course of doling out high government offices to make good on campaign promises. So much better a baronet than a booby.

No, these two old men were probably the real thing, but whether they were the right real thing remained to be seen. Was the *major* one of those "scarlet majors at the base" of Siegfried Sassoon? Or had he seen action? "So, gentlemen, where did you see service?" Military men usually liked recounting their experiences.

Muttering several unintelligible phrases before he actually launched into conversation, Major Champs said, "Colonel Neame here was one of the Dam Busters; you remember them, don't you? No, before your time, I expect. Crackerjack outfit, that was, eh, Joss? Looked in the jaws of death every day, every hour. Good men." He regarded Colonel Neame, who did not reply but positioned his monocle in his eye socket and seemed to look at Melrose as if wondering if he was a worthy repository of this account. Then the monocle came out again and dangled near his lap, as he looked down and laced his fingers.

Major Champs continued. "I was with the Eighth in Africa with Montgomery, you know. At El Alamein. Later on, at Arnhem, trying to secure a bridge —"

" 'A bridge too far,' " said Melrose. This was making him feel a little ashamed, as the nearest he had ever come to dying was death-by-ennui over tea with Agatha.

"Right. Right." Major Champs shook his white head. "Yes, that was something."

But his tone suggested it was something best forgotten.

He went on, and all the while he was talking, Neame fiddled with his monocle, taking it out, putting it in. Once having positioned it in the eye socket, Neame would scowl, as if he'd been forced to look at a scene especially foul, whence he would lift an eyebrow and the monocle would drop out again. Then he would look down, lacing and unlacing his fingers, as Champs went on about the skirmishes, the strategies, the gains and the losses.

Melrose listened to Major Champs and watched Colonel Neame and felt even more abashed that he had seen nothing of the landscape Neame was painting. Dunkirk. Anzio. Arnhem. Nagasaki. And Melrose's only contribution had been that puerile remark about "a bridge too far."

". . . and after Joss here got the Victoria Cross —"

Melrose just slid down farther in his wing chair. My God. The Victoria Cross.

"— he was mustered out and went to Bletchley Park. You know about the work they were doing there."

It was Melrose who was muttering now. Bletchley, Bletchley. It was on the tip of his tongue.

"Decrypters. Code breakers. Breaking the Germans' Enigma code. Oh, my, that was something! They say it shortened the war by at least a year. Can you imagine how many lives were saved?"

Melrose asked, "Is your background mathematics, then, Colonel?"

Neame nodded. "Umm."

"He was teaching at Oxford in 'thirty-nine. Joined up right away. As did I. After V-E Day I found myself in Burma. The war wasn't over for us. They said it would be another year or more. But Hiroshima happened. And that was the end" — Champs looked at Melrose out of those burning blue eyes — "of war as romance."

Joss Neame laughed heartily. "War as romance. Oh, Christ. *War as romance!* Right you are there."

12

"You saw her all the way down the Fulham Road?" Melrose put down his spoon. They were eating Windsor soup in Boring's dining room.

Jury nodded. "All the way to the gates of the palace grounds." He looked round the softly lit, walnut-paneled dining room. "I followed her." Jury had already filled Melrose Plant in, but he lingered over this.

Melrose cocked his head, waiting.

Jury sighed. "Yes, I know it sounds weird." He looked at his soup, no longer hungry.

"Did I say it sounded weird? Go on."

To have something to do, Jury spooned up some of the dark brown soup. It matched the dining room, he thought. He also thought — for the hundredth time — that he couldn't explain himself. So he tried to. "I . . . expect I was fascinated by her behavior. Or her looks, don't forget her looks. That sable coat. What" — he looked up from the soup to his friend — "was she doing, anyway, getting on and off the bus?

And why was she going into the palace grounds at that time?"

"And you worked out that —"

"I haven't worked out a bloody thing, except the woman they found wasn't the woman I saw."

"You don't know —"

"I don't know the identity of either woman. Chilten, of course, thinks I'm wrong; thinks, probably, that I'd make a lousy witness." Jury smiled.

Melrose said, "Perhaps you didn't want to."

Jury frowned. "Didn't want to know?"

Melrose gave a slight shrug and bent his head to his soup.

They sat in silence, soup finished, until their dinners appeared, carried forth by a waiter so old his skin looked translucent. This was (Melrose had been surprised to discover) Young Higgins, and not the fleet-footed porter who had served him in the Members' Room. The old waiter set their plates before them. Lamb and a silver dish of new potatoes, carrots, peas.

"You win the lamb round."

They had flipped a coin. Melrose had guessed some kind of chop. Yes, the menu was pretty much what the major had predicted. Thinking of him and Colonel

Neame, Melrose diverted the talk from Fulham to the war. "Were you evacuated? I mean, you were a child, and they did evacuate children, didn't they?"

"I was very small," answered Jury thoughtfully. "I was taken with some cousins to the country. Cheshire, it might have been. Warwickshire, somewhere around there. The cousin who lives now in Newcastle, she was older than I and remembers more. She's told me all sorts of stories about the family we had to live with, how crowded together we were, how tough it was. But we managed; we had to."

Melrose was not sure he was up to this, another set of wartime reminiscences, another recounting of stoicism. He had ultimately been so saddened by Major Champs and Colonel Neame he had gone up to his room to lie on the bed and stare up at the ceiling.

"We'd nothing to play with, no toys, so we were left purely to our imaginations. . . ."

Maybe it was worse than combat: kiddies making do with playing in the rubble and using broken broom handles as rugby sticks. Tales of doughty tots confusing enemy ships by flashing mirrors from the shore or putting shortwave radios out of commission. Melrose shook himself free of these fantasies. But Jury was merely talking about his little cousins and how they cared sod-all for the war effort; still, it brought out something good in them.

". . . What we did was —"

Best friend or not, if you tell me a story of hope and glory, I'll turn my bowl over on your head.

"Are you listening to me?"

Melrose jerked himself free of his meditation on war. "What? Of course, every word."

"Uh-huh. Well, let's get to what I want you to do. I want you to go to this gallery and say a lot of shrewd things."

"Pardon me, but you always seem to think I'm shrewd about things I am not shrewd about. Painting is one of them."

Jury went on as if Melrose hadn't spoken. "The owners are two brothers named Sebastian and Nicholas Fabricant. 'Nikolai' is actually what he's put on his card. His mother's Russian, and that's really his birth name. The painter's Ralph Rees but uses our other pronunciation, Rafe."

"Oh, dear. That is the correct British way, I suppose. Have you seen his work?"

"No. I wonder if they have some more

rolls." Jury craned his neck. "Where'd our waiter go?"

"To get triple-bypass surgery, probably. Why haven't you been to this gallery?"

"Too much police presence, especially since there's not anything at all to link these people to the dead woman other than Mona Dresser and her fur coat. Precious little, hardly enough to warrant police harassment. No, I don't want these people on their guard."

"What makes you think they'll be *off* their guard around me? I walk in and look over the paintings and then ask them about the night of November fifteenth?"

"Not like that, no. Not until you get to know them better."

Melrose was suspicious. "What do you mean?"

"Well, they'll probably invite you out for a drink. After you buy a painting or two."

"Buy? You mean not only am I to put myself in harm's way, I'm to pay for the privilege? How clever of you to think this up."

Jury shrugged. "How else will you have an excuse to hang around? If you buy something, then they'll be happy to see you come back and will — I'd lay my pittance of a wage on it — invite you for a

170

drink, even to dinner, even to dinner at their house. Then you'll be able to have a look at all of them."

"*If* they invite me to dinner."

"Of course they will."

"Am I so irresistible?"

"No. But you're a source of financial gain for them and of ego gratification for the artist."

"And just how big will their financial gain be?"

"I can't say. But considering the gallery's in Mayfair, home of pricey hotels, swank restaurants, Jaguar and Roller showrooms" — Jury looked around — "and exclusive men's clubs, I expect we're looking at something in the thousands."

"What do you mean *we? I'm* the one looking at it. Helping out Scotland Yard is expensive. I'm not Robin Hood."

Jury went on, ignoring this. "Just don't sit around making things up the way you usually do. And after you get yourself in good with the Fabricants and their resident painter, I might just have you go along to talk with Mona Dresser."

"Mona Dresser. That name seems to ring a bell. Where have I heard it?"

"She was an actress. A great comedienne."

"Of *course*. My mother was a huge fan —"

"Yours too!" Jury smiled. "So was mine. I bet they would have liked each other, your mum and mine."

Melrose nodded but said nothing. For a few moments they ate in silence. Then Melrose asked, "What do you mean I shouldn't make things up the way I usually do?"

"You know, like the antiques appraiser. Talking about Turkey rugs and so on."

"Well, how else was I going to convince people?"

Jury smiled. "All I'm saying is, don't start in on some baroque tale about your years in Paris and art school and countless hours spent at the Musée d'Orsay studying the Impressionists. That's all. Look, why are we arguing about this?"

"Well, we're not *arguing*. You said I make up baroque tales about things. So do you."

Jury looked surprised. "*Moi?* Never. I don't have the imagination to do it."

"No? What about Jimmy Poole?"

Jury frowned. "Who?"

Melrose pointed a finger. "You see, *you see?* It was such a lie you can't even remember the name! Jimmy Poole was your fictitious little childhood friend who stole

172

things and whom you told Emily Louise Perk all about!"

Jury sat back, shaking his head. "*Good lord!* Emily Perk — that was a decade ago. How can you still remember?"

"Accomplished liars always remember. It's time for our sweet." Melrose had taken a coin from his pocket and flipped it now.

"Heads," said Jury.

It came up heads. Melrose said, "Okay, you get first choice."

"I say . . . treacle tart."

"And I say some kind of pudding."

As if they had suspended all thought of murder and war, the two sat quietly until Young Higgins approached with the tray. He removed their plates to a side table and set dishes of pudding and custard before them with a trembling hand.

Melrose said, "I win, it's Spotted Dick!"

Jury shook his head. "You don't win. You never said Spotted Dick."

"We didn't establish any rules. And you should have objected when I said 'some kind of.' You can't object now."

Jury took out his billfold, thumbed out a tenner, slapped it down. "You're a stickler for details."

"I should think you would be too, you being a policeman." Melrose held the ten-pound note up toward the light of a wall sconce, snapped it.

"Oh, very funny," said Jury, slapping down the hand that held the note.

"One can't be too careful, can one?" Melrose folded the note and pocketed it. "Let's assume these people at the gallery —"

"Fabricant. Sebastian and Nicholas. They're the owners of record, although I'd be surprised if Mum hasn't chipped in a few quid. I get the impression she has the money. I also get the impression she's extremely clever. Smarter than her sons. She's in her seventies, but she's a handsome woman. Doesn't show her age."

Melrose spooned custard over a bite of pudding. "Well, there are some people, some women, who seem to flower in their seventies." He ate the bite of pudding. "Look at Agatha."

Jury laughed. "Talk about flowering."

13

By ten o'clock the following morning, Melrose was standing outside of the Fabricant Gallery, admiring the painting — a single painting, made more effective by its not having to share the limelight. That is, Melrose *appeared* to be admiring it, since the picture had blessed little about it to admire. It looked like a poor Picasso spin-off, body parts roving all over the canvas instead of being collected into one (or perhaps two) ordinary-looking people.

The gallery was located down a short street in the Shepherd Market section of Mayfair in W1, one of the more expensive areas of London. It was here that wealthy tourists ganged together to take on London shopping and West End theater.

A door buzzer loud enough to broadcast a prison break sawed on Melrose's aching head (he shouldn't have helped put away that second bottle of Château Boring — the cheap thrills of cheap wine!), but the headache calmed down when there was a *click* and he was able to enter the quieter environs of a smallish room that served as a foyer, dimly lit. Through a white archway, he saw a long hall. The gallery was larger than it appeared to be from the outside.

No one came forward immediately to attend to him, for which he was just as glad. The carpeting and lack of custom were responsible for the hush that descended when he was in the presence of Art. He would not, however, faint (he hoped) as poor Stendhal had done after viewing too much of it.

The deep honey-colored carpet permitted someone to materialize eerily at his shoulder with no warning. "May I help you?"

Startled, Melrose jumped. "Oh, how do you do? Didn't hear you come up. I'm just having a look round." He was speaking to an extraordinarily handsome, youngish man with coloring much like the carpet. Honey-colored hair and amber eyes in a handsome, high-cheekboned face, with a hardy build but an effete manner, which Melrose imagined the man might have cultivated because he was an art dealer. His hooded eyes and sleepy smile gave him a dreamy quality that set him apart from the pragmatic and utilitarian.

And he was pleasant enough. "Well, we're delighted you came in. Take all the time you like." He waved a lithesome hand. The "we" in this case smacked of the Royal, as there was no one else backing him up here.

There appeared to be two rooms on the left in which the art was displayed, with a hall leading back past a large desk where the money changed hands. A computer sat there. The paintings hanging against the off-white walls were of quite different "schools" (whatever that meant) or influences or genres. Here was a still life of dew-beaded pears and apples. He had never had much feeling for still lifes, unless it was food that made his mouth water. He moved on to the next one, also a still life, but of flowers, a bowl of peonies; they too had beads of water clinging to their petals. Both paintings were arty and unrealistic, which seemed weird, since they were completely representational. But the only way those fruits and that flower could look as if they'd just sat out in a dew-filled early morning would be to have done just that. And obviously arranged on a cobalt blue platter or a mahogany table, that was impossible. Why was he bothering to sort all this out, for God's sake? And why didn't

177

anyone ever paint a still life of a glass of port or a tumbler of whisky or a Diane Demorney martini? There was a challenge! It was Melrose's belief that martinis were beloved because of their aesthetic appeal: the clear lake-water look of the gin or vodka in the fragile, thin-stemmed glass, with a green olive bobbing in its depths or a curled sliver of lemon peel drifting on its surface. . . .

"Do you like this one, then?"

Melrose jumped again at the sudden appearance of the young man.

"You seem quite struck, quite smitten!"

"Oh. But one does, doesn't one?" That meant nothing, of course, but this gallery person would accede to just about anything, living as he did in the cradle of ambiguity.

The handsome dealer shoved his hands into the pockets of his wheat-colored deconstructed jacket (whose soft Italian lines Trueblood would gladly kill for) and cocked his head. "Umm. Yes, I expect you're right."

Right? About what? It occurred to Melrose that they could hang about here all day trading meaningless words. "Are you Mr. Fabricant? I mean, as in the gallery's name?"

178

"Right. I'm one of two. My brother and I are co-owners. I'm Nikolai Fabricant. How do you do?" He thrust out his hand.

Melrose shook it and introduced himself — or what used to be himself — and handed the man his card. Nikolai (whom Melrose had already decided to call "Nick" at the earliest opportunity) Fabricant took it, looked at it deeply, mouthed a title or two, before he looked up, clearly savoring Melrose's presence. No matter what egalitarian beliefs people gave lip-service to, Britain could not erase (or eschew) class consciousness. Melrose said, with an apologetic brush at commonality, "It takes me rather a long time to view a painting." Oh, how pretentious! What a snob! Yes!

But Fabricant was all for it. "As well you should. I wish more were like you. I'll let you alone." Melrose smiled and nodded, and, as the other man slipped away over the quiet carpet, he turned to contemplation of a flagrant and amateurish J. M. W. Turner imitation: Venice's Grand Canal at either sunrise or sunset. The light in this work appeared gratuitous, seemed to explode at the end of the canal, in some poor, poor attempt to Turner-ize light. Still, it saddened Melrose, for it reminded him of Vivian's absence.

He moved on to the next painting, which he assumed had been done by the artist who had painted the one in the window. The only difference he could detect was in the rearrangement of body parts. The eye in the forehead here was drifting at the bottom. Ye gods, he hoped this artist's were not the paintings he was supposed to purchase! He went closer to read the identifying card: no, the name of the artist wasn't Ralph Rees but Carol Brick. Carol had named her work *Afternoon in the Forest*, and the brothers Fabricant were asking two thousand quid for it. Melrose could hardly contain his shock and struck his palm against his head as if he would clear his eye and mind of this nonsense and come up with a more reasonable figure say, twenty quid. *Afternoon in the Forest?* Carol, surely you got your little name cards mixed up, or the gallery people did. Now he felt challenged to see something woodsy in it, but try as he might he couldn't see a tree either in the body parts or in the bright, banal colors. That small purple thing could be a glass of port and that brown oblong a half pint. She should rename it *Afternoon in the Jack and Hammer.*

He moved along. Once again he reared back, but for an entirely different reason:

he had come upon what looked like an honest-to-God genuine painting. It was a small work, a scene from which it was hard to look away. Indeed, Melrose couldn't look away, though he wanted to, for it was unbearably sad: two women, dressed in dark gray, one old, one young, standing on a rocky shelf by the sea in what (given the light and water) seemed to be a calm that followed a tremendous storm. There was sea wreckage. The women were facing one another, or would have been had their heads not been bowed. The colors were astonishing. How much variance there could be in gray and brown had never occurred to him. He moved up to look at this card, hoping it might be Ralph's: no, again. It was called *The Storm*, and the artist was —

Beatrice Slocum.

Melrose stepped back a few paces, thinking surely his eyes had deceived him. Beatrice Slocum? It must be "his" Beatrice Slocum; how many could there be who were also painters?

He was simply stunned. She who had loved J.M.W., which was how she referred to Turner. He looked from *The Storm* to the Venetian scene and thought how very odd that the Venice painting was so clearly derivative and hers wasn't, not for all of her looking at J. M. W. Turner's paintings in the Tate.

He shook his head. Bea Slocum. White Ellie. Ash the Flash. He'd discovered she "painted" but had no idea she could turn out a work that was superior to anything he'd seen so far. He hadn't seen Rees's paintings, but they'd have to be damned good to beat *The Storm*, which was selling for — he went to the card again — a measly five hundred quid. Only five hundred, while the dreadful preceding ones were being sold for thousands?

The shadow of Mr. Fabricant seemed to hover back in another room. He called it over.

"Found one you liked?"

"For starters, this one."

"Ah, Slocum. Sweet little thing, isn't it?" Nicholas Fabricant cheerily agreed.

Melrose wanted to send a right to his jaw. How condescending could one be? He defended the painting. "I wouldn't say *that* about it. It's much too powerful. And I have a question: Why is this one going for only five hundred when some of these others, which do not appeal to me at all, and are not — you'll forgive me — nearly as good, why are they going for five times the amount?"

"Ah. Well, you know, it's supply and demand." Fabricant peered more closely at the Slocum painting, a puzzled look on his handsome face, a look of *Could-I-have-missed-something?*

"Yes, I realize that. But that's only putting my question in another way. *Why* would there be a demand for this Brick person's work, or that sentimental and derivative depiction of Venice, over something like this?"

"Um. Carol Brick is extremely popular," he said, still not answering.

"So is my dog, but that doesn't mean he can paint."

Nicholas Fabricant was beginning to get defensive. "Well, you know, a painting appeals or doesn't appeal."

That about covered the whole shebang, thought Melrose. Art dealers were like horoscopes — excepting, of course, Diane's — something nice for everyone.

"The *critics* seem to like Brick's work," added Nicholas, bolstering the gallery's position.

Critics? Melrose merely nodded. It was obvious he wasn't going to get a sensible answer: possibly, Fabricant didn't know himself; he wasn't, after all, responsible for public taste. Melrose had got so caught up in the two gray-garbed women, he had forgotten why he was here. He didn't think he wanted to ask about Ralph Rees; that would make it appear he'd come deliberately to see his work, and he wanted his coming here to seem accidental and spontaneous. "I'd like to keep looking round, if you don't mind."

"Mind? I should think not." Fabricant laughed. "Take your time. I'll just get this ready for you. You'd like to have me deliver it somewhere?"

"No, no. I'll take it with me."

Nicholas took the painting down, carefully, and started off. "I wonder if you'd be interested . . . we're still doing a show here, a number of paintings by Ralph Rees. I wonder if you'd like to see them?"

Touchdown. Goal. Or whatever you say. "I'm afraid I don't know his work."

"He's just breaking out. The show's got some rave reviews. It's back there" — Nicholas gestured with his head — "in the other room. We had it out in this room, the front room, when it opened two weeks ago. We've just moved it."

"Yes, of course, I'd enjoy seeing it."

"Fine. Follow me."

Melrose followed him down the short hall where the desk and computer were located. Nicholas turned, still holding Bea Slocum's painting. "In here. I would like to know what you think."

"All right. Thanks."

When he walked into the room and took a quick look round, his stomach sank and every last drop of adrenaline went with it. On three walls were hung five paintings. And, except for a variance in size, they were all the same. Literally.

Again, Nicholas came up behind him, having divested himself of *The Storm*. Apparently, he just had to be in on Melrose's reaction.

Too bad for him. "These paintings," said Melrose, "are white. All of them."

Nicholas did not pick up on the reproachful tone, he being so eager to show the work off. "Yes, remarkable, isn't it? The most original collection we've had in some time."

Melrose was a pretty good liar (he did have to agree with Jury on this score), but he wondered if he'd be able to do it in this case. How in hell was he going to work up the enthusiasm he'd need to buy one of these white rectangles? The only thing different about them was their size. Except, he saw in the last one (No. 5, it was labeled), a thin black line down in a corner and barely visible. It looked more as if Bub or Sally had defaced it, in giggling enthusiasm, than it did the artist's attempt to — to what? What on earth was the asking price? He was afraid to look.

Nicholas misinterpreted Melrose's slack-mouthed look as one that Balboa, perhaps, might have given upon finding the Pacific. Wonder. Delight. Discovery.

Horror. Hands behind his back, Melrose was moving from one to another, not trying to see what the gallery folk saw in all of this (for there was nothing to see) but trying to work out what he could say. He was right to have been fearful of the prices, too. Not one of them under a thousand pounds, and one he had passed had been three thousand. How had they arrived at these variations? Who was kidding bloody whom?

Nicholas mistook Melrose's stunned look for appreciation, for one struck speechless in the face of brilliance.

Well, he was half right: Melrose was struck speechless. He could not in any way, shape, or form imagine anyone's admiring this lot, could not imagine a painter seriously turning it out or a gallery who would hang it on its walls. On each identifying card was written a name and a number.

The numbers varied; the name didn't: *Siberian Snow: Five Ways of Seeing.*

Nicholas Fabricant said, "It's possible we've found another Ryman or even Rothko."

It was worse than Agatha. Blind Auntie he could forgive, but not this gallery owner, this art maven. Melrose squeezed his eyes shut, appalled at this coupling. Although he had never understood Rothko, right now he felt like making a pilgrimage to the Museum of Modern Art to bow down before his paintings in return for hearing him thus maligned. But he had to swallow the various ripostes clamoring for expression; he had, after all, been given the charge of buying one of old Ralph's paintings, so he would have to muster his courage. Jury had never seen them; otherwise, Melrose would never have forgiven him.

Nicholas, standing by his elbow, said, "*Siberian Snow.* That's the series."

It was true he was good at dissembling, but —

He had a small epiphany. Diane Demorney was a champion of all things white. Her house was white, her living room was completely white — furniture, objets d'art, cushions — her cat was white, her car was white: all white. Indeed, Diane had a white painting above her white marble mantel: it was a painting as white as the whitest of Ralph's; hell, maybe it *was* Ralph's.

For as he'd been looking at them, Melrose had noticed, besides that damned twig thing, a slight gradation of pigment emerge in the narrow border of the fifth. He could just see the white becoming cream, becoming bone. Meaningless nuances, he decided.

Diane, at least, knew white when she saw it.

"I have a friend —" Melrose stopped to savor this announcement. It had, predictably, the effect upon Nicholas Fabricant of making him breathless with expectation.

"Yes?" Nicholas prompted.

"— who would *adore* this work. But, I wonder. . . ."

Again, Nicholas prompted. "Yes?"

"What would be the effect, if it's a series, of the removal of one? I mean, wouldn't it spoil utterly the effect of the whole? By the same token, wouldn't one painting by itself misconstrue the meaning of the whole?" He should shoot himself for playing along. But he loved the way Fabricant was running his thumb back and forth across his brow in puzzlement, as if this hadn't occurred to him.

Melrose went on. "Perhaps one should simply take the entire series." *And pigs might fly!* Ah, well, he should not be cruel to the poor fellow.

Nicholas was saved from answering by the appearance of a second man gliding across the carpet. You couldn't hear a person bearing down on you in this place.

The young man eagerly introduced his brother. It was clear that Sebastian Fabricant was delighted (and as expectant as his younger brother) to hear the "Lord Ardry" part of the introduction.

"Lord Ardry wonders about removing a painting from the series." Nicholas repeated what Melrose had said.

"Ah," said Sebastian, unruffled. "No, for each one is self-contained. Each has its own integrity. Each one —"

Is bloody *white,* Melrose wanted to scream.

"— speaks separately."

What Melrose couldn't decide, though, was whether they themselves believed in what they were saying or whether the whole thing was a hoax or something. He came down on the side of their believing it; no one could say what Sebastian had said without laughing.

"Well, then, I'll have one," said Melrose, as if he were standing with a fruit vendor choosing a banana. He'd sooner have been.

"Which one, Lord Ardry?" asked Nicholas.

The question was redundant as far as Lord Ardry was concerned. He was about to say, Number five, but there was that twig. It was beginning to obsess him. He decided to let price be his guide and chose the mid-priced two-thousand-pound one: Number four.

"Excellent choice," said Sebastian.

How did Melrose know he'd say just that? "But a difficult choice, Mr. Fabricant. Difficult." That was true enough.

"It's an interesting technique Rees uses. He uses a thin sort of sandpaper to overlay the canvas. Gives it that rough texture. I see you also are taking the Slocum."

But what a relief to express true enthusiasm. "She's remarkable."

"We're trying her out."

Melrose wanted to say *white of you* but refrained. "I hope you've another to put in its place."

Sebastian laughed. "He didn't paint several of the same kind."

He didn't? You could have fooled me! Melrose said, "I don't mean him, I mean her. I mean Beatrice Slocum."

Nicholas said, as he stood now with the big white painting, "Yes, we've two or three more of hers in the back. Would you want this delivered to — ?"

Melrose gave him Boring's address. "It's a gift for a friend." (Diane's lucky day.) What Melrose couldn't understand was, having bought the Beatrice Slocum and having shown further interest, the brothers Fabricant didn't immediately go and trot out every painting they had of hers. If Ralph had any more white ones lying around, he bet they'd be off in a flash to get those. They were clustered round the desk in the short hallway now, and Melrose had his checkbook out. "Do you suppose I could see the other Slocum paintings? If they're handy?"

Sebastian Fabricant frowned slightly, as if he couldn't understand the request. "Well, yes, I expect so. Nicholas?" Just then, the telephone bleated its effete gallery tone, and Sebastian answered it and Nick went off towards the rear.

Nick, it appeared, was general dogsbody. Was that his punishment for being younger brother? Melrose wondered how the spoils here were divided up. There had been no more custom since he'd come in over an hour ago, but, of course, this wasn't Marks & Spencer. To shop in this place would require serious money. And how was he to endear himself to them to the extent he would be taken to the family bosom? What would it take to get on the matey side of these two, the why-don't-you-come-for-dinner side? Then Melrose remembered Ralph. While he was in the middle of this fresh idea, Sebastian was putting down the receiver and Nicholas was coming towards them, carrying Bea's other paintings.

Melrose knew, even before they were set in front of him, that he'd buy them. If anyone deserved a leg up, it was Bea Slocum. Yet buying both would leave that blank space on the wall, so he decided on one. And as soon as he saw the smaller of the two, he knew which one that would be. It was a scene of a London street, a North London street, and Melrose recognized it even before Nicholas read from the card taped to the back:

"This one's called *Catchcoach Street*. Nice, no?" Nicholas was peering over the top as if he could view it upside-down.

Melrose smiled. How much better could it get? "Nice," was all he said. Although she hadn't particularized this little bank of row houses, she had painted the pub at the end of them, the Anodyne Necklace, and he would swear those kiddies with their hoops and balls — or were they rocks and hatchets? — were of the family Cripps. Whatever one might call the ambience of Catchcoach Street, Bea had nailed it: run-down houses behind gardens one tried to tend but which still withered. The amiable squalor, the Dickensian lucklessness of Catchcoach Street. He smiled. "This one I'll take with me, I think. Perhaps you could send the other round to my club with the — ah, *Siberian Snow*." Bea's was only three hundred, and it could have gone ten rounds with any other painting in the place — except for the other Slocum.

He made out his check, and it was a considerable sum to have change hands. Despite the waste of two thousand on the Rees painting, Melrose was only too happy to spend it. It was worth it just to see that Bea Slocum was succeeding. He felt she would have been succeeding more if more of her pictures had been hanging there. Why was this? he wondered again.

Melrose tore off his check and handed it to Sebastian, as Nicholas placed a square of cardboard on top of Bea's painting and then wrapped it up in brown paper.

"Look," said Sebastian, "it's getting on for lunchtime. Why don't we find a bite to eat?"

"Thanks, I'd be delighted! Do you have your favorite place?"

"We'll go to the Running Footman. Just up there a ways."

The Running Footman! Memories, memories. With *Catchcoach Street* under his arm, Melrose felt comforted; he had no idea why he should feel so. Perhaps it was so seldom demonstrated that justice was abroad in the world; that the deserving did get rewarded. He patted his brown-paper-wrapped painting and thought that whatever ills he might have to suffer at the hands of the Fabricants, it would have been worth it.

14

Leaning against the bar, ordering up a half pint of lager, Jury was beginning to feel like a regular. How many times had he been here at this point? A half dozen, surely. The clock on the wall in the Stargazey said four-thirty. He wondered how Plant was getting along in the gallery. He was not very hopeful; as everyone was fond of telling him, there wasn't much to go on. Kitty, who'd been out for a couple of days, still hadn't returned. Jury shoved his glass towards the bartender.

Behind the bar was a long mirror, and when he looked in it he saw a blond woman in a black coat making her way through the crowd towards the door. He wondered if he was drunk on only a pint of lager, for he had a queer feeling of seasickness, watching her walk, as if the pub had turned into the Fulham Road and she was once again walking the pavement and he was on the bus, following her. Her transit through the room was only a matter of seconds, with Jury holding his fresh lager up, transfixed. Then he pulled himself together, dropped some coins on the bar, and moved quickly to the street.

Out in the waning light and a gauzy rain that felt like cobwebs on his face, Jury looked up and down the Fulham Road, saw nothing, went to the corner; still no sign of her. But there was no sign of a departing bus, either, so she must be somewhere; either that or she'd jumped into a cab.

And then he saw the black coat, the pale hair some distance off at the nearest bus stop, with a bus just coming. He could not make it to that stop in time, but if he ran he could get to the one farther up. He broke into a jog and got to the stop just after the bus, which still idled by the curb.

She was not sitting on the lower level, so he hopped up the steps to the upper level and sat down several rows behind her. The only other passengers up here were a group of teenagers in uniforms, late from school, probably.

They meandered through South Ken and Brompton and Knightsbridge; he watched to see if she showed signs of getting up. Harrod's was in this block of buildings; rather, Harrod's *was* this block of buildings. No. The bus joined the procession of buses making their way to Hyde Park and Piccadilly.

Why he hadn't simply gone to the front and sat down beside her and produced his identification, he didn't know. One part of him told the other part, Well, he didn't want to embarrass her. Embarrass how? The teenagers wouldn't care if the conductor came through and announced the next stop was Red Square. It took more than a lone policeman to get their attention.

So, why? He hated to admit that he didn't know, really, what to do. He had grounds for detaining her, for taking her in. Reasonable grounds. She had been at the scene. He went over and over this as the bus made its way around Piccadilly Circus.

She got up.

Jury looked out of the window and saw the bus was traveling up Shaftsbury Avenue, and, after she'd descended the stairs, he did too, waiting halfway down until the bus stopped. He jumped off just as the bus moved away from the curb.

A number of theaters lined one side of Shaftsbury Avenue, so perhaps that was her objective. It was too early for the evening's performance; perhaps she'd come to buy tickets, though in this computerized age it was hard to believe someone would make a trip simply to purchase tickets.

She was on the other side of the street, going through the doors of the Lyric, where an American play had just opened. He didn't enter the lobby but waited just outside the glass doors while she transacted her business. In a few moments, it was done and she was returning things to her bag; the tickets she inspected as she walked slowly towards the doors beyond which Jury stood, and which she now pushed open, unseeingly, for her eyes were on the tickets.

"Madam."

She started, took an involuntary step backward, bumped into the door. "What?"

Jury had his identification ready, held it out. "Superintendent Jury, CID. I'm with New Scotland Yard."

She seemed to be utterly horrified, a reaction Jury had seen more than once, usually on the faces of the innocent. Some of them thought he had come to accuse them; some, that he had come to inform them. In neither case was it a happy meeting.

"If you could just spare me a few moments to talk?" Closer now, he could see that her eyes were hazel, changeable in the changing light. She was wearing makeup this evening, a coppery shade of lipstick, very light brown eyeshadow.

"Talk? I'm sorry, but — why would I — ?"

She shook her head, and her pale blond hair, which was not pulled back this time, swirled as if they were dancing and he had just spun her away.

It was different from the dead woman's hair only in the shade of its blondness, its sheer luminosity. Which meant it was altogether different, only it might take a long time looking at it to see that. Jury had been a long time looking.

That disbelieving look he was getting — he could see he was in for a time. "There's an investigation going on, and I was hoping you could help us with our inquiries. I've reason to believe you might be able to."

"What reason?"

It had started to rain again, or perhaps it had never stopped; it was the sort of rain one gets used to and hardly notices. "Look, there's the St. James pub right over the road. Would you have a drink with me?"

"I didn't know policemen did that — bought drinks for people 'helping with inquiries.' " Her smile was a little sly. "You really say that, do you?"

At least he was hearing a hint of humor. "I don't, not usually."

"You're sure you are a policeman?"

"I'm sure."

She seemed to be taking the measure of his smile. "All right, then, why not?"

The pub looked invitingly warm and intimate, windows showing bronze light through smoke, the smoke of endless cigarettes.

The St. James was fairly large, with a long oval bar and tables sitting in pools of shadow or, at the rear, actual darkness; Jury took one better lit, then went up to the bar. He could see her out of the corner of his eye, and she seemed calm and unsuspicious. He set the pint of lager and half of Guinness down on the small damp table and, after seating himself, said, "Let's begin with your name."

This surprised her. "You don't know it?"

"No. I'll explain in a moment." But the point wasn't his explanation; it was hers.

"It's McBride. Kate."

"And you live — ?" Jury had his small notebook out.

"South Ken. In Redcliffe Gardens. It's on the edge of Fulham. Would you please tell me what this is about?"

"If you've been reading the papers, you know about a woman who was shot in the grounds of Fulham Palace?"

"Yes, I saw something about it. It struck me as strange, bizarre. But what —"

"You frequent a pub in the Fulham Road called the Stargazey?"

She frowned, even more perplexedly. "I've been there, yes. Did this woman — ?"

"And do you recall going there on the night in question?" He was retreating behind this stiff formality.

By now, she had her chin planted firmly between her fists, eyes leveled at him as if she had just discovered he was fascinating. "What night *is* in question?"

"The night of November fifteenth. On the Saturday."

"No."

"You weren't there, at the pub?"

"No. I mean, I don't recall."

"It's less than a week ago. Could you try?"

She seemed quite sincerely to be trying as she sat back and squinted at the ceiling. "Let me think. It was the evening a friend of mine called about a dinner party . . . and then I had dinner. . . . Later I had tea with an elderly lady who lives upstairs. . . . Yes, it was Saturday. Last week."

"But you don't remember going to the pub?"

She shrugged. "I might've. The Stargazey is quite near my flat. It wouldn't have been until later, though."

"Later?"

"Oh, around ten, I expect."

"And then?"

"I would have gone home."

"You didn't board a bus?"

She shook her head. "I didn't, no."

Jury let a few seconds pass. He said, "Somebody who looks enough like you to be your twin *did* board a bus outside of the Stargazey and ride down the Fulham Road."

"Then that's who you should be talking to, the someone who looks like me." She had removed her black coat and adjusted the neck of her pearl-gray suit. Its cut was elegant, Jury thought.

Jury smiled a trifle grimly. "Yes. Well, the point is, it *was* you, Ms. McBride."

"I shot this woman and then ran off?"

"I hadn't got that far in my mind yet."

She opened her mouth, but it was as if she'd come only on empty air. Her hand went into her leather bag, felt around, came out with a cigarette case. The hand was slight and fine, thin-skinned, the fingers long and almost delicate. The case was silver, fine too. The great settler and mind-clearer, a smoke. Jury felt an awful longing.

She did not open the case, though. She said, "To be as certain as you are that I was on some Fulham Road bus, you'd need an awfully dependable eyewitness. You have one?"

"Yes. Me."

The effect of this was to turn her fine ivory complexion chalk white, thin across the bones. It was the first indication that this conversation *was* affecting her. Her posture shifted; she bent slightly, as if she were a reed in the wind. But her expression didn't shift at all. It was perfectly composed, as fixed as the marble face of a statue.

Jury wondered if she'd trained herself not to react.

"You're mistaken." She said this flatly, without any inflection.

"Do you own a fur coat? A sable, a mink?"

She laughed. "Good lord, no. Is that what whoever you saw was wearing? It certainly wasn't I, Superintendent. Look," she said earnestly. "You've simply made a mistake. A glimpse of someone on a bus, or getting on or off a bus; it would be easy enough —"

"It was more than a glimpse. You got off the bus —"

"*She* got off the bus. Why are you so set on discarding the obvious explanation for one so unlikely?"

"Because it isn't unlikely."

"Then what in God's name is your theory?" She turned the silver case over and over in her hand.

"I don't have a theory. But the fact you were there certainly needs looking into."

"If I *was* there — which I wasn't — what would it mean? That I shot her because she looked like me?"

"I've no idea what the motive for the shooting was."

Jury could see in her movements now her intention to leave.

She said, "I expect this is the point at which I say I need a solicitor."

He said nothing, watching her stow her cigarette case and lighter in the leather bag. As she moved, the light that had fallen across her pale hair spilled like water over the shoulder of her gray silk suit.

She gathered up her coat and said, "Well, I'm leaving, Superintendent. You know where I live. Indeed" — here she held up the ticket she had just purchased — "you know where I'll be this evening. Good night."

Jury rose as she did. "You might expect we'll be in touch with you. Or the Fulham police will."

Her look told him nothing that she was thinking, as if he were a blank wall.

Jury watched her move through the crowd and the smoke and watched the door swing shut behind her. He did not know what he'd expected, only that he was hugely disappointed.

He did the only thing he could do: had another drink and watched the smoke weave upwards, collecting over the heads of the people at the bar.

Less than an hour later found Jury at Fulham Police Headquarters.

Ron Chilten would have been surprised by Jury's encounter with this woman, had the Fulham police not turned up the victim's identity just that afternoon. "Nancy Pastis, that's the dead woman's name. We're running it through records."

"How'd you find her?"

"A little lady by the name of Verna — no, Vera." Chilten thumbed up a couple of papers. "Vera Landseer lives in the same building and recognized the photo in the paper, or thought she did. Got a flat in Mayfair — Shepherd Market — in the same building as Ms. Pastis's. That's what we've got so far. I've got two of my men going over the flat now. Sharing it with C Division. Milderd, you know him?"

"Slightly."

Chilten leaned his chair back on two legs, rubbed at the ankle hooked over the other knee. "I'll admit I thought you were wrong about the woman you saw on the bus. At first, remember, you identified the dead woman as the one you followed, so I figured —" Chilten shrugged.

"Now we know there were two of them. Nancy Pastis, Kate McBride."

"Yes. But the one you saw still could have been the victim. Otherwise, Kate McBride, if it's Kate McBride you saw. . . . Why was she wearing the Pastis woman's coat? Unless there are also two sables in the picture."

"The McBride woman had to have switched coats."

Chilten looked down at the darned place in his sock. "Sometimes the most obvious explanation —"

"Don't do the Holmes quote on me."

Chilten shrugged again. "Okay, but then

why take off her coat and dress the dead woman in it?"

"Good question."

Chilten brought the chair down with a thud. "Jury, eyewitnesses are, more times than not, wrong."

"I guess I'd know that, having questioned so many wrong ones."

15

"It was the same woman," said Jury.

At a little after nine o'clock, dinner at Boring's was winding down, or at least the half dozen diners spotted about at tables seemed to be dozing over their cheese and biscuits.

Jury was drinking coffee and Melrose was drinking a superior whisky and wondering if he was drunk. He and the Fabricants had downed several drinks at the Running Footman that afternoon. Now here he was, listening to Jury claim the dead walked in the Fulham Road. He said it sounded like a genteel version of a John Carpenter film.

"I didn't say the dead walked; pay attention," Jury said, a bit testily. "She looks like the woman found at Fulham Palace is what I said."

The two of them were sitting in front of the fire in the same wing chairs Colonel Neame and Major Champs had occupied. Melrose was beginning to feel right at home in Boring's. Crusty, almost; almost giving those mumbled responses of Champs or Neame to Jury and the ancient porter. He upended his glass for the last morsel of whisky, the "moiety" he had instructed Higgins to bring him. What was left now was the very dew this excellent whisky advertised itself as being soft as.

Jury sat back, a little depleted from the day's activity. "At least you haven't told me I'm hallucinating. Which is what Chilten did: 'This whole business, it's got right up your nose, Jury.' What a strange metaphor." He sipped his coffee and pronounced it cold.

Melrose signaled Young Higgins, who steered in their direction and took the order for another whisky and another coffee. Melrose wanted a cigarette badly but felt it would be gracious of him not to light up. It would be, but he took out the cigarettes anyway. Jury had often said he didn't want people abstaining from smoking just because he'd stopped. Said it made him feel like a funeral parlor. All of that suspended animation, that artificial hush, that dying-to-be-gone-before-last-orders.

"All right, then," Melrose went on, as he watched a wizened old gentleman lever himself up from the depths of one of the leather sofas. "The two women are either related — twins, even — or they're look-alikes. Well, that's obvious. Doppelgangers."

Jury nodded.

"Let me review the scene: she — the woman you saw that night — leaves this Stargazey pub, boards the bus, rides it for ten minutes or so, then disembarks at — where?"

"Fulham Broadway. Roughly a mile from Fulham Palace, or rather the palace grounds."

Melrose nodded. "And you observe her walking. She gets on yet *again,* and the bus then arrives at the intersection with Fulham Palace Road. Whereupon she gets off again and you leave the bus and follow her on foot to Fulham Palace. How far was that?"

"A short distance. No more than a five-minute walk."

"You see her go through the gates." When Jury nodded, Melrose repeated it. "You *did* see her go through the gates?"

"Yes. The gates weren't closed. Apparently, they're open nearly all the time."

"Thus far the only question this raises, aside from your behavior —" Melrose smiled.

"Thanks."

"— is why she walked when she could just as easily have ridden. First possibility: She wasn't sure where Fulham Palace was and got off at the wrong place. Second possibility: She changed her mind about something and left the bus, changed her mind again, and reboarded."

"Third possibility: She wanted to be remembered. I mean, she wanted the *victim* to be remembered."

They were silent for a moment.

Melrose said, "The woman on the bus and the dead woman aren't the same person. There's not one but two women. Anyone who might have come forward to help police with their inquiries, as you say, would have said, 'Yes, that's her, that's the one I saw walking along the Fulham Road. *I remember the coat.*' No one would ever have known there were two women. Right?"

They both contemplated the fire. Then Jury turned the conversation back to the Fabricant Gallery. Melrose told him about Rees's series of vacuous paintings labeled *Siberian Snow.*

"That whole display is simply too awful. Nicholas might see genius there, but then he's Ralph Rees's special friend, I think. His significant other. Love is blind. But

Sebastian, he's certainly shrewd enough about painting." Melrose shrugged. "It's fishy."

"I imagine a lot of people thought Jackson Pollock was fishy at first. It could simply be taste." At Melrose's dubious look, Jury said, "So how do you account for this fishiness?"

"I don't know. How does one flummox the art world?"

"Easily?" Jury shrugged.

"But here's a surprise: Guess who else they're representing? Beatrice Slocum."

"You're joking!"

"Her painting was hanging right there between two awful ones."

"I thought it was *her* old significant other, Gabe Merchant, who was the painter."

"So did I. So did everyone. I did, before I had dinner with her —" Melrose hadn't mentioned this before and was sorry he had now.

"Dinner? Where?"

"Bethnal Green. It was when you went rushing off to Santa Fe." Melrose glanced over to see if Jury was smiling in some supercilious fashion. He wasn't, but then he never did. "She talked about her painting, called it her 'blue period.' Not, however, like Picasso's. Said she was depressed, but depressed with no talent." Melrose laughed. "You wouldn't think it to either look at or listen to her, but she's extremely modest, or maybe" — Melrose thought this to be true — "being very good at what she does, she doesn't have to showcase her talent. Like you." This prettily framed compliment Melrose meant to get him off the hook about Beatrice Slocum.

Of course, it didn't. "She was on the list, as I recall."

Melrose feigned ignorance. "What list?"

"The one you were making at Ardry End, with the names of all the women you knew who you said would make convincing witnesses."

Good lord, didn't the man ever forget anything? "Oh, that. Anyway, they had two other paintings of hers stuck in the back among the ones they keep in reserve. One's a painting of Catchcoach Street. That brings back old times, old memories, doesn't it?"

"Not really. Since we saw the whole lot of them, the Crippses, only this past February."

"I had no idea you were so literal."

Jury smiled.

"It occurs to me" — Melrose placed his

drink on the piecrust table between their chairs and sat forward — "Beatrice must know something about the gallery and Ralph and the two brothers. I called her before you came, but she wasn't in. I'll try again tomorrow."

"Try the Crippses. She spends a lot of time there."

"I will. But just what are we trying to find out?"

"I don't know."

"That's helpful. Look" — Melrose spoke with some earnestness — "the only tangible thing connecting the Fabricant family and the Dresser person with your mystery woman, or women, is this sable coat."

Jury nodded, looking sleepily at the fire.

"That sounds extremely ten—"

"Tenuous. Yes. I often hear that word." He yawned.

"What will your Fulham CID man do?"

"Drag her in for questioning, which he may already have done." Jury looked at his watch. "I'd better call him."

"Since you told her you saw her, we couldn't spring it on her that there was a witness, could we?" Chilten's tone was acerbic.

Fulham police had picked her up earlier,

at her flat in Redcliffe Gardens. Chilten told Jury she had stopped in Soho for dinner and hadn't got home until after eight. She was, understandably, shocked.

"And she has an alibi, Jury. She was having a cuppa with the old lady upstairs."

Jury thought about that. "You checked it yet?"

"I'm sending someone now."

"She was on that bus at nine o'clock, Ronnie."

"The *victim* might have been on that bus, Jury. McBride insists you were wrong."

"I'm not wrong, Ronnie. What's this old lady's name?"

Chilten turned away from the phone and said something to somebody. "Laidlaw. A flat on the first floor, right above McBride's."

"Do you mind if we talk to her, this Mrs. Laidlaw?"

"Suit yourself."

"What about the McBride woman's flat?"

"You got a subpoena? Neither have I, yet. Kate McBride lives a pretty quiet life. Widowed. No family, except for some in-laws, relations of a husband who she never sees; they live in the States — 'upstate New York' is what she said. She doesn't work; she doesn't need to because the husband left her provided for. Not rich, but enough to live on. He was with the embassy, and they lived for several years in Paris." He shrugged. "That's the lot. She wants to talk to you."

Something gripped him. It felt almost like fear. "Why?"

"Well, Jury, she didn't favor me with that information. Can you get down here in the A.M. tomorrow?"

"Yes." He thought for a moment, then asked, "Why didn't she come forth when that photo was published?"

"Probably thought it would implicate her. The thing is, it hangs more and more on you, Jury. You're the one who places her at the scene." There was a rustle of papers on Chilten's end. "The only one," Chilten added. "You're pretty positive that it wasn't the victim herself you saw."

Jury hesitated. "I hear a question in that. I am pretty positive."

"No room for doubt?"

Jury sighed. "There's always room for doubt."

Chilten gave a small explosive grunt. "You sure as hell aren't making any. Look, R.J., we can't hold her for effing ever, not without charging her. And we've got sod-all for reasonable grounds."

Jury smiled. "Oh, I don't know, Ronnie. You've got *me*."

Chilten made a noise deep in his throat and rang off.

16

Phyllida Laidlaw invited them into her kitchen at the Redcliffe Gardens mansion house, saying, "I've just put the kettle on, so we can have tea in a few moments." The smile on the ninety-year-old face was dreamy, as if Jury and Wiggins had walked into her fantasy.

Wiggins sat himself down on a wooden chair and lost no time in dispensing advice. "Maybe you should look into those new electric kettles. Plastic, mine is, and it boils the water three times faster."

"Really? But I don't like plastic. And the metal ones are so expensive."

Jury, hoping to force Wiggins off the information highway, said, "Mrs. Laidlaw, you know Kate McBride?"

"Oh, my, yes. The other policemen asked me about her. They could have told you and saved you all the trouble. But I don't mean I'm not delighted to have your company." The kettle screamed, as if to give the lie to Wiggins's "three times faster" comment.

Wiggins put a hand on her shoulder when she started to get up and said he'd fix the tea.

"I'm afraid I've only tea bags — there, in that tin box. And the sugar's in the cupboard. Milk in the fridge." That crucial step taken, she folded her hands in her lap and looked at Jury from wash-blue eyes, indicating he could get on with whatever trivial thing he was there for.

"Mrs. McBride had tea with you on the Saturday night. Do you recall what time it was that she was here?"

"Well, it was just before *Homicide*."

"I beg your pardon?"

Wiggins filled him in as he doused tea bags with water. "Remember? I told you about it. You haven't seen it. We just started getting it over here. It's real, like."

"Oh, it certainly is — only one spoonful for me, thank you. They've got such *interesting* characters. That wonderful black lieutenant."

Wiggins set down the three mugs for them. "G."

Both Jury and Mrs. Laidlaw looked at him.

"G, that's what they call the lieutenant."

"We don't have biscuits," said Mrs. Laidlaw reproachfully.

"Right. I'll have 'em in a tic." As if he'd stocked the cupboards himself, he drew out a package of Rich Tea Biscuits, put some on a plate.

"And that's how you're determining the time, Mrs. Laidlaw?"

She looked at him as if he were throwing spanners in the works, interrupting sense with senselessness. Wiggins stirred his tea and looked at him in much the same way.

Jury cleared his throat. "Kate McBride, Mrs. Laidlaw. She was here while this television program —"

"*Homicide*."

"*Homicide*."

They said it simultaneously, Mrs. Laidlaw looking pleased as punch that at least one of England's finest was keeping up with daily events.

"Right. So when did Mrs. McBride leave?" Jury's eyes were searching the room.

"Oh, nine-twenty-ish. Just before nine-thirty. I'd missed most of *Homicide* by then —"

"I missed it too."

Jury glared. Wiggins shut up.

"— so I just watched this silly quiz program I can't tell you the first *thing* about, so if I have to account for my time, well . . ."

220

She raised her hands and shrugged slightly. Her smile was almost beatific.

Jury smiled too. "No, your movements seem quite believable. There's just one thing I'm wondering about. When Mrs. McBride visited, did you have tea here in the kitchen?"

"Yes. I always do have it in here."

"I notice you don't wear a wristwatch, and I don't see a clock. How did you know your program was on?"

"She had one. A wristwatch, I mean. That's how I knew it was after nine. She told me."

When the WPC brought her into the interview room at Fulham HQ, Jury was sitting at the table still wearing his raincoat. That, he supposed, gave the impression of a man who wasn't going to stop here for very long. He didn't know whether or not it was the impression he wanted to give. He only knew that Kate McBride threw him.

She looked exactly the same as when he had seen her on Shaftsbury Avenue in the St. James — same suit, same hairstyle — but she would, of course, since Chilten had picked her up last night, had waited outside her flat in a car until she returned.

Chilten had, of course, already questioned her, together with another of his men, and had her testimony on tape. She had not requested a solicitor be present. She had been so certain of her immediate release that she hadn't felt she needed one.

Kate McBride sat down on one of the uncomfortable folding chairs opposite Jury and said, "I appreciate your coming."

The voice was the same, too. It didn't waver; it was not tight with anxiety; it gave none of the signs of anything but confidence that all of this was some dreadful mistake, easily cleared up if she could simply tell the right person where the mistake lay. Jury was, apparently, the right person.

He did not remark on her "appreciation." He inclined his head slightly in response. Then he asked, "Why did you want to see me?"

Kate McBride didn't answer immediately. She spent a few moments taking in the room that he'd have thought would be, by now, quite familiar to her. It was hardly a place one would want to commit to memory, anyway. Then she said, "Would you tell me what you saw — what you thought you saw — on that Saturday night?"

"I did tell you."

"You saw me in the Fulham Road boarding a bus. The one you were on."

"Yes."

"And?"

If she thought his going over it again would help, he would comply. "About ten minutes later, at the Fulham Broadway tube station, you got off and started walking. Perhaps because of the traffic tie-ups; you may have thought you could get where you were going more quickly on foot. The bus was in stop-go traffic for another ten minutes, at least, because of the daytime roadworks. Later, when the bus stopped opposite a pub called the Rat-and-something, you reboarded. At Fulham Palace Road, you got off and headed for Fulham Palace."

She waited. When Jury didn't continue, she said, "You followed her."

"I followed you." He smiled slightly.

Oddly, she didn't mention her neighbor, did not take up the alibi. Was she so sure of her ground she didn't need to?

She said, "Are you certain it wasn't the coat I was supposedly wearing that made you mistake me for — her?"

"No."

"You're so positive."

Jury's eyes cut away for a moment, which was a mistake. He felt he was already on the defensive.

She took advantage of this heartbeat of hesitation and said, "You're not, are you?"

"Is this why you wanted to talk to me? To tell me I'm not positive about what I saw?"

"No. But I don't see how what you say happened makes any sense."

"It doesn't. It's my aim to make sense out of it."

There was a pause. He watched a band of sallow light play across her hair.

She said, "I didn't kill this woman."

"Oh, but I didn't say you *did*. You might have had some reason for going there — though it's a strange place to rendezvous after dark. Also, a strange place to be followed to."

"To be followed to?"

Jury shrugged. "I thought of that as a possibility. Your behavior might suggest someone who's trying to throw someone else off the scent."

Her short gasp of laughter suggested this was really too outlandish of him. "You've quite an imagination."

"Not really. I'm quite an unimaginative sod. But pretty obviously, being a detective, I'd want to find reasons for your actions. As I said, why would anyone go to a place like Fulham Palace at night? Not many tourists make their way there, even during the day. It's one of London's best-kept secrets, I've heard." When she didn't comment, he said, "You live alone? No one to corroborate your story? Your husband?"

"Is dead. Michael died of leukemia. He was only forty."

"I'm very sorry."

She went on as if she hadn't heard him. "He was from Norfolk, the Norfolk Broads. He was partly American; his mother was. I thought he might want to come back, but he wanted to die in Paris. He adored Paris." She smiled at some distant vista. "He could get drunk on Paris. From our window we could look down at night on the streetlamps on the rue Servandoni, and Michael — but I'm rambling. Sorry." She put her hand on her forehead as if to hold back the memories.

"No. Go on."

She went on, describing the cafes where they would sit for hours in the boulevard Saint-Germain and Saint-Michel; the walks and flowers in the Luxembourg Gardens and the Tuileries; the wet look of the cobblestones of the rue Servandoni and the Ile Saint-Louis; Pont-neuf in the fog; the great avenues of light such as the Champs-Elysées.

The voice had a visceral effect on Jury; it seemed to seep into his muscles and calm him like a drug.

"We lived there for seven years, in Saint-Germain-des-Prés. Michael had a government post, undersecretary, and we were well provided for after he died. Michael himself, I mean his family, had money, and so we were comfortably off, though by no means rich. If he had to die, I'm only glad he died before what happened to Sophie." She stopped, looked away. There was nothing to see but the blank wall.

"Sophie?"

She nodded. "Our daughter. She was born soon after we got to Paris. I don't know which of the three of us Michael loved more: me Sophie, or Paris." Her smile was a trifle wicked now. "I sometimes think it was Paris. But he adored Sophie." Again, she fell silent. Jury could hear someone, Chilten probably, talking beyond the door and, now, opening it.

"You said something happened to Sophie. What?"

Kate stood up as the door opened and said, "She vanished."

She turned towards the woman police constable and Ron Chilten. The policewoman led her out.

"Your timing is impeccable," said Jury to Chilten, as he looked at the passport Chilten had just handed him. They were standing in the corridor outside the interview room. "Why do these photos always make a person look like a corpse?"

"This one *is* a corpse. Nancy Pastis."

"Sorry." He looked at the face, its unsmiling, noncommittal expression; its high brow, with the hair pulled slickly back. He remembered what Plant had said: *Doppelgangers.*

Chilten looked at him. "Easy to mistake one for the other. Anyone might."

"Then I'm not anyone, Ronnie." Jury flipped from the front to the visa entries. "This only goes back three years: Argentina, France, Denmark, Russia. But it stops nearly a year ago. I mean, according to this, Ms. Pastis hadn't been doing any traveling for ten months."

"So? Maybe she got tired of it." He nodded towards the room in which Jury had lately sat with Kate McBride. "Get anything useful out of her?"

Jury shook his head. "Embellishment on what you already know: husband with embassy in Paris; lived in Paris for seven years; had a daughter. Did you know she disappeared?"

Chilten frowned. "She didn't tell me about it. What happened?"

"I was about to find out when you walked in." The door to the room he had just left was open; he looked at the chair where she had sat, studied the barren, spindly tree beyond the window. "I'll be back."

17

A bored police constable stood guard at the entrance to the elegant old building on Curzon Street. He nodded at Jury's and Wiggins's IDs and told them to go in, that the flat was on the second floor and there was an elevator. It was one of those ancient birdcage elevators, painted gold, that rattled to a stop on the second floor.

There was no crime-scene tape; the flat hadn't been sealed against entry; still, Jury was surprised there was no policeman by Nancy Pastis's door, too.

The flat was a little on the small side, if one were to judge by square footage. Living room, one bedroom, bath, and kitchen. But Jury found that it gave the impression of spaciousness. The ceilings were very high and the molding — painted white, like the walls — was beautiful. Jury and Wiggins started in the living room, two walls of which were given over to floor-to-ceiling bookcases; there was a library ladder for reaching the higher shelves, which were, like the lower ones, full. Books had been stacked in front of the shelves, waiting for a place. Other books would have to leave to accommodate them. These were clearly books that were being read; this wasn't for show.

All the furnishings appeared to be antiques except for a slick-lined off-white sofa and a deep-seated slipcovered armchair, the sofa probably an Italian design but the chair, good old English parlor. Beneath these pieces was an oriental rug whose background color was a larkspur blue. There was a heavy rolltop desk with a fragile-looking gilt chair — French, Jury imagined — pulled up to it. A bulbous glass-fronted cabinet housed porcelain of Sèvres and Limoges. Everywhere were lamps of varying styles and heights.

The impact of all these different styles was one immediately pleasing to the eye, perhaps because the impression given was that each piece had been chosen separately because the owner liked it, rather than as part of a collection or an attempt to orchestrate the room as a whole. By being artless, the effect was artful, yet nothing a decorator would have achieved.

Paintings crowded the other two walls of the living room, and, while Wiggins went about opening drawers and assessing the small accouterments of a life, Jury indulged himself by gazing at the paintings. As far as he could tell, they were all originals or, at least, superior reproductions. One smallish painting was of the Cornwall coast drenched in light. Jury knew it was Cornwall only because it was titled *St. Ives*. The slant of light gave the little town an unearthly glow and stippled the sea with radiance. The largest painting was quite dazzling, a modern study of an inlet or marina covered with small craft, fishing and sailing boats. Nancy Pastis seemed to prefer seascapes, or at least water; there were lagoons, lakes, ocean views, rivers. Another painting looked like a view of St. Petersburg and its famous river; Jury tried to call up the name. Whatever it was, it was beautiful. The smallest of the paintings was equally dazzling, a miniaturist rendition of a black sand beach and a turquoise sea caught at sunset — or was it sunrise? Jury would never make a painter, he decided, if he couldn't tell the difference. The little painting was alive with light.

He went into the bedroom, a fairly somber room with heavy draperies and bedspread but extremely neat, as the living room was. Wiggins came in behind him

231

and made for the dressing table and the bureau, the chest of drawers.

The kitchen was a wonder of a place, containing probably every modern cooking tool on the market: espresso machine, Cuisinart, pasta maker, copper pots slung on a circular copper bar that hung from the ceiling, and a quite incredible (and shiny) industrial-restaurant-sized cooker. Eight burners, and you could stuff an ox in the oven. Someone took cooking very seriously here, as seriously as reading and painting.

Of the some dozen cookbooks on a Spanish-tiled counter surface, two were French, one was German. Jury pulled them out, leafed through them long enough to tell they had indeed been handled and that Nancy Pastis spoke more than English. Her passport told them she traveled frequently. Frequently and seriously, he thought.

As he was returning to the living room, he heard voices in the hall, male and female. Wiggins had opened the door upon an elderly lady and the constable Jury assumed Chilten had posted here. Upon seeing Jury, the police constable turned brick-red, a flush that could have had a charcoal fire going.

"Oh. Sorry, sir. I was just . . . I was only gone for five minutes."

Mildly, Jury reprimanded him. "In five minutes, any sort of riffraff could get in here. As you see." Jury smiled.

The elderly lady came to his rescue. "It was *entirely* my fault. The constable here was kindly helping me move a table, and I offered him a cup of tea. Are you family? I'm so sorry."

Jury smiled, wondering how innocent the life a person lived if she could mistake two cops for anything but cops.

Wiggins told her no, not family, and produced his identification. "New Scotland Yard, madam." The words themselves sounded stiff, but Wiggins always managed to make identifying himself — or them — sound like a neighbor walking his dog. He sounded completely friendly.

Jury (the dog) stepped up and, with a smile, produced his identity card, told the constable to stay by the door, and invited her into the room. "Are you Mrs. Landseer?"

"Vera Landseer, that's right. I live next door." In her hands was a fine linen handkerchief, which she was kneading.

She was smartly attired in an acid green suit — a color very nearly chartreuse —

with a jet brooch pinned to the collar and a strand of real pearls. She had the fine, papery skin of some old people, skin that looks talcumed. She gave off a woodsy perfume scent and her gray hair was exceptionally well styled, probably by Toni and Guy up the street.

"You were a friend of Nancy Pastis. You helped the Fulham police —"

"Yes. I wasn't a real friend, though, I'm afraid." Vera Landseer's troubled eyes suggested that she should have done better, and now she'd never have the chance. "I've been in her flat two or three times. She invited me in to have tea one afternoon. It's quite beautiful, isn't it? What will happen to all of this? The books, the art?"

Jury shook his head. "I don't really know. When we discover some relation or other, perhaps that person can take care of it."

Vera Landseer looked past them at the paintings on the far wall. "I always had the queer feeling there wasn't anyone. You know, wasn't any relation. I've no idea why, but there must be a reason for that impression, wouldn't you agree?"

Jury smiled again, nodding. He liked the way her mind worked. "When you had tea with her, you had conversation. Perhaps she said something then."

She stood quite still to think about this. Then she said, "I mentioned my family as living in Kent. She said hers had been living on the Continent for the last ten years of their lives. So obviously the immediate family was dead. She wasn't married — well, that's fairly obvious too: I mean, given this." Her arm swept to take in the room. "She talked a little about her travels; I think that particular weekend she'd just got back from" — Vera Landseer pinched her forehead, as if that might bring up the name — "Ireland, Northern Ireland. Armagh, I think she said." She laid her narrow hand with its tissue-thin skin against her throat and played with the pearls round her neck.

"The flat is extremely neat, especially for being as full of furniture and books as it is," said Jury. "I've never been in one so — immaculate."

"Yes. It always was, the few times I've ever seen it. So very orderly." Vera Landseer fidgeted with the strand of pearls. "Well, I've an engagement. If you'll excuse me?"

Jury held out his card to her. "If you think of anything that might be helpful, Ms. Landseer, I'd be most grateful if you'd give me a call."

She studied the card and looked at him as if searching for a match or his identity. "Yes. Certainly. Well, good-bye." And she set off down the hall toward the birdcage elevator.

"I'm glad Vera came in," said Wiggins. It took him no time at all to get onto a first-name basis with witnesses, victims, and perps. "I'll tell you, it was kind of spooking me."

"What was?" The gold elevator stuttered to a stop.

"The lack of stuff."

" 'Stuff'?" Jury laughed. "Place is full of 'stuff.' "

"No, I mean little personal stuff: the lack of mail, the lack of photos, the lack of snapshots. I know Nancy did a lot of traveling, but a person accumulates things, I know I do. Is there anyone alive who can throw out *everything* he's finished with? There weren't any documents or photos stuck in shoeboxes on the top shelves of closets."

"Chilten's men probably took some things away." But Jury recalled Chilten had said that, except for the passport, bank statement, and a couple of bills, they came away with zilch. Jury thought he'd been speaking figuratively, but perhaps Chilten meant it literally. In any event, the upshot was a big nothing. Jury said, "I agree; it's odd."

Wiggins shook his head. "No. If Vera hadn't come in here — well, I was beginning to feel we were hunting a ghost."

The bright neon-blue sign of the Starrdust shot cometlike across the narrow building in Covent Garden. Villains dealt with for the moment, homeopathy and *Homicide* temporarily dealt with, Wiggins was ready for his own life on the street.

The Starrdust was Wiggins's favorite venue, probably in all of London. Afterwards, they could chase Racer's wild goose to Soho and the restaurant owned by Danny Wu. *Duck*, thought Jury, telling himself a little joke, *not goose — Racer's wild duck chase*. Wu's served the best duck in London.

Wiggins parked the police-issue Ford illegally on the opposite side of the street, and they got out and walked across the cobbles. They stopped outside the shop window, sharing the pavement with a half dozen kiddies who were hypnotized by the Starrdust's big window. Something was always going on; the scene changed without notice. The window dressers, Meg and Joy, who were Andrew Starr's shop assistants, had a friend who was some kind of electrical engineer and devised all manner of pulleys and moving parts and mechanical tracks to animate their scenes. The three of them had probably produced the best window in London; Harrods and Selfridges couldn't begin to compete.

Today the scene was a night wood. Off to the left, two small children were moving along a path, when, suddenly, a witch with raised arms and clawlike fingers popped jerkily from behind a tree. The moon brightened, the stars glittered harder, and out of his cave came Merlin in his coned hat and star-drenched coat to hammer on the witch with his miter until she disappeared. Then the wood grew darker as several forest creatures came out of hiding. Finally, the scene was so dark that eyes and stars hung in the little window theater until the whole thing went black as coal.

Everything about the Starrdust seemed to be the work of invisible hands.

"Mister, tell me how they done that," demanded one tiny girl, who might have been the understudy for a bisque doll herself. She gazed up at Jury with her hands on top of her head as if it might blow off in the wind that was coming down Flower Street.

"The Wizard, that's who does it. Merlin. The one in the tall hat."

The look she gave him was of the long-suffering variety. "*Mis*-ter." She rolled her eyes as if to say he should know better and spun away like a leaf carried off by the breeze.

It was a wonder, Jury had to agree, though he thought the "how-they-did-it" was less important than the "why."

The "why" of this venture lay in a deep part of the mind of Andrew Starr. He was the Merlin-in-the-wood, orchestrating these doings without doing them himself. Right now, he was leaning over an old hunt table that served as his shop desk. Atop it sat a computer and a cash register and, at the moment, something Andrew had spread out in front of him: a horoscope, most likely. Andrew was a serious astrologer and had a dedicated following, from housewives to media personalities. He was hellishly expensive, but no one bickered about the price, for he was amazingly prescient.

The shop seemed to exist in a perpetual gloaming, shadowy and darker the farther one moved toward the rear. Wiggins immediately went in the back, where the children usually collected by the Horror-Scope, a kind of Wendy house from which issued squeals of delight and fright.

Jury stopped as he always did to admire the second ceiling, the one Meg and Joy and their engineer had devised as an absolute marvel of night sky, with a moon that could wax and wane, stars and planets that could brighten and dim. Behind each planet was a light that lightened or darkened, however the timer was set, so that as Venus grew dark, Mercury dazzled. Stars, moon, all the planets of the zodiac appearing and disappearing. It was wonderful, and all courtesy of Meg, Joy, and the engineer. And the mind of Andrew Starr.

The shop was quite truly out of this world, including the music: old, scratchy songs that came from ancient records collected by the owner over the years. Hoagy Carmichael's rendition of "Stardust" was a staple, as was Glenn Miller's "Moonlight Serenade." Jury stood gazing at the ceiling, listening to a piano's waterfall of notes, trying to place the song. It was one of those tunes that maddened as it called up memories, for you knew it but couldn't come up with it and also knew it would sadden you if you did.

" 'Stella by Starlight,' " said Andrew, looking up from his work and smiling.

And mind reading, thought Jury. He was convinced that Andrew Starr had some sixth or even seventh sense. If there was such a thing as a dreamy businessman, Starr was its paradigm. He had shown his shrewd business sense when he'd hired Meg and Joy, had realized before they did anything that their near fairy-tale presence would be marvelous for business. They were unrelated by blood but twins of fortune. Meg and Joy appeared to spring out like Merlin to chase away your troubles. They were hovering right now by the Horror-Scope, a structure the size of a small room with a low ceiling from which emanated the sounds of bad weather, a sky lanced by lightning, eerie sounds, and "phenomena" (at least, that was what Wiggins called it), and you had to pay your twenty pence to find out just what constituted this wonder. Jury had never treated himself to the inside of the Horror-Scope, and Wiggins refused to tell him about it.

One of the "phenomena," and one he knew well, was Jury's upstairs neighbor, Carole-anne Palutski. This particular phenomenon with its amethyst eyes and red-gold hair came streaming toward him now in clouds of pink and salmon chiffon and a lot of tiny bells wrapped around her somewhere, probably the ankles. A silver lamé turban crushed down her abundant red-gold hair, making little curl splashes around her face. It made Jury think of a pretty little girl in a Dutch painting. She was carrying a small plate that held a big slice of coconut gâteau, which could fatten the air through which it moved, but not Carole-anne herself.

"Super!" she called, in a tone of embrace, both welcoming and wondering where he'd been all her life, despite their having shared bowls of Weetabix just that morning. Then she remembered he'd stood her up for their pub date. "Come to get your palm read?" Palmistry was "Madame Zostra's" forte, together with messages from the dead who managed to laser their way into her crystal ball. "Because if you have, you needn't bother. It'll be the same."

"No, that wasn't my intention. But are you telling me one palm-read is good for a lifetime?"

"Yours is." She mashed her fork into cake crumbs.

If he was looking for her to find long trips and love affairs in his palm, forget it.

Jury wondered why he seemed to be surrounded by people who were not in the
least bothered by ambiguity: Carole-anne,
Wiggins, Mrs. Wassermann. Even the cat
Cyril appeared to have a tighter grasp on
the iffiness of things than these people.

"Well, love, I hate to disillusion you, but
there are things going on in my love life
not accounted for by your hasty palm reading back in January." Why in heaven's
name did he remember it had been in January? he wondered. This increased his irritation no end. Lord knows it wasn't a
fortune that would stick in the mind,
largely because it was so absent of incident. Why did he recall it? It could only be
that Carole-anne herself was more vivid
than anything anybody could invent.

"Love life? Whoever said you had one?"
She stuffed another bite of cake in her
mouth and said around it, "Nah me, ahm
sure." She set her plate on the counter and
said, "I only just came out to get the cordless." She reached beneath the counter and
brought out the telephone, adding, "I've
got to call Stan." She gave Jury a snooty
look. "We've an engagement." Carole-anne
had a way of using Stan Keeler to measure
Jury's jealousy quotient.

"Going to Berlin, are we?"

"I'm *sor*-ry?" She cocked her head as if listening to Jury were a trial, he being a blabber of meaningless syllables.

"Stan's in Berlin doing his gig thing."

One thing Jury marveled at was Carole-anne's ability to process information lightning-quick. Without missing a beat, she said, "I didn't say we were going *out*. We fixed up when I was to *call* him is what I meant."

"Ah. Well, as regards my own love life, may I qualify things by saying just because you don't predict one doesn't mean there isn't one."

Andrew was enjoying this exchange. "That rather defeats the entire purpose of predicting, doesn't it, Superintendent?" His smile was happy and on Carole-anne's side. Andrew didn't believe for a minute that she could see any farther into the future than her next manicure. Andrew was well aware of Carole-anne's limitations as a spiritualist, but he always championed her and any causes she might espouse.

Any clouding of Carole-anne's brow cleared when her boss said this. "So, what d'you want?"

"To do something for me."

She tried not to look pleased when Jury handed over the page from the *Mirror* he'd had stashed in his pocket. "What is it?" Carole-anne forked up another bite of cake.

"Just read this —" adding, when she gave him her put-upon look, "when you get a free moment. Then we'll talk."

Haughtily raising her chin, she said, "Suit yourself," and took off for her silken tent, both cake and cordless forgotten.

Drowsy laughter floated towards them from the Horror-Scope. Wiggins was still back there. "Wiggins!"

All sound was momentarily suspended, Wiggins and the other kids not wanting to be called back to the daily round of clocks and seasons.

Only the promise of a meal at Danny Wu's could galvanize him into exiting from the Starrdust. "Wiggins," Jury called again, "are you ready for Danny Wu's?"

First Wiggins's face appeared round the door of the Horror-Scope and then the whole of him, coming down the darkling aisle. As was the case with Carole-anne, it was difficult for him not to don the cloak of martyrdom.

"I've been ready all this time, sir. Only waiting on you."

Ruiyi — the name of Danny's restaurant

— was, according to his customers, food reviewers, and, most important, his own countrymen, the best restaurant in Soho. Jury and Wiggins were delighted that this was true because the ongoing investigation of Mr. Wu's alleged sideline — drugs, now bodies — had the two of them sitting at one of Danny Wu's tables a couple of times a month.

This investigation would ordinarily be handled by the Drug Squad (obviously, what those people were there for) had not Chief Superintendent Racer insisted that Jury take it. Jury only worked homicides, but that had never bothered Racer. Now that a body had been added to the drug mix, Racer was even more rabid about Danny Wu.

Danny Wu was an elegant, soft-spoken, Italian-suited man in his early forties who looked more Eurasian than Chinese. He was himself Cantonese, born in Guangdong province, later gone to Beijing. When his mother — who had raised him by herself — had realized how dreadful the place was and how difficult to get out of, she had risked her life a half dozen times to take him either to Hong Kong or Shenzhen or back to Guangdong. His mother had come from a long line of patrician landowners and had been very beautiful in the way that truly courageous people can be beautiful. And she, Jury was sure, had been. One only had to look at the face of Danny himself to know that. He had seen her picture, too. But Danny had never known his father, "so he could have been," said Danny, "you know, one of you knobby-nosed lot."

"Not with your nose, guy," Jury had said, laughing.

Well-born but poor, Danny had taken any job he could get and had wound up washing dishes in a Shenzhen hotel. Fascinated with the way the cooks' knives could slice a whole head of cabbage in almost less time than it took to say the word, he had worked his way to vegetable cook and then to sous-chef at the age of nineteen, after which he had braved the barbed wire that kept Shenzhen separated from Hong Kong. Five years were spent as head chef in a Hong Kong hotel before he came to London. As top chef in one of London's best restaurants, he had made enough money to buy real estate, and from these proceeds he'd bought up this valuable corner site in Soho and opened his own place. He had named it Ruiyi, after his mother.

All of this dedicated cookery work had been interrupted over the years by spells of work on a snake farm and some industrial espionage in Shenzhen. ("It's easier getting the Crown Jewels out of the Tower than a Barbie doll out of Mattel, Inc.")

Jury had decided that Danny Wu was the greatest liar since Homer. "How much of him do you believe?" Wiggins had once asked. "Only the snakes and the mother," Jury had answered, then corrected himself: "Only the mother." That Danny spoke the truth about his mother was as evident to Jury as the rain flying against the windows, an un-English rain, a rain that spelled overrunning rivers or flash flooding somewhere.

Whenever Jury and Wiggins showed up here, they were moved in as smoothly as the little figures on the electric rail in the Starrdust's window. If police could keep Wu under surveillance as well as Danny managed to keep them, any drug trafficking would have been discovered long ago. A magician couldn't have cleared a table-top quicker than it was done for Jury and Wiggins.

"Please," said the venerable old waiter, bobbing and smiling as he swept his arm over a table that Jury could have sworn had been fully occupied only moments before. The waiter pulled out both chairs and motioned for them to sit. They sat. Jury looked across the small room at the queue on which they'd brought up the end and got stony stares in return. He could hardly blame them. One always had to queue up at Ruiyi.

Menus were handed them and the waiter pointed out the specials of the day. Jury always took a special, but he still liked to read the menu. Wiggins grew absolutely rapt looking at it; it appeared to be a source of nourishment in itself, or fascination.

"Superintendent!" Danny Wu always brought his own particular ambience with him; he saturated the heavy, smoky air around him with a cool and silky friendliness that Jury had never been certain was real. He wore tailor-made shirts and designer suits. Jury could usually distinguish an Armani; otherwise, he was uneducated when it came to such clothes. Wiggins had made the point that Danny Wu could make anything, no matter how humble its origins, look like Armani or Stegna but had added they'd never know, since Danny Wu didn't wear things of humble origin.

This was certainly true tonight. His

French-cuffed buttercream-colored shirt was worn with an astonishing purple tie and silk square tucked in the pocket; his suit was a deconstructed silk-wool blend of such a chocolate brown that it almost looked black. Jury thought of the sable coat.

"Hello, Danny. Business is booming, as usual. You should expand."

"Ah! That's as banal an idea as I've heard today."

Wiggins sniggered behind the menu he was still exhaustively reading. He always read the menu this way, even though it didn't change except for the chef's suggestions of the day.

"Anyway, thanks for the table. That's what I meant, I expect."

"You're perfectly welcome, as always. Consider this and the many other evenings you've whiled away in here one bribe after another."

Jury laughed. "Have we been on you about the Limehouse business?"

"Yes, *we* have. You know, what fascinates me is that when you have a murder in Limehouse — or Docklands, as it's called now — you go for a Chinese gentleman such as I. I mean, is Scotland Yard still back there in the days of the opium dens, the easy murders, the fog, the wharves, the rats —"

"I'm ready to order if you are, sir." Not opium, not rats, would take Wiggins's mind off the menu. He was spreading his napkin in his lap, getting down to the real business at hand.

Danny Wu said, "If I were you, Sergeant, I'd order the crispy-fried whole fish with brown sauce. Especially if your sinuses are playing you up."

Wiggins hadn't said a word about his sinuses, *yet* —

They were halfway through their dinner when Wiggins brought up the priest. "Noailles. I meant to tell you. He's back from Paris." Wiggins doused his rice with more soy sauce.

"You've got my attention, Wiggins. And?"

"I called again, to see if he was back, asked him if he had seen anything on the Saturday night. No, he said. *But* —" He stopped to fork up some sauce-doused rice.

Jury stared at him, willing him to stop eating. It didn't work. Wiggins was angling his fish off the bone as if he had a rod in his hands. Jury sighed. *"But?"*

"He saw the bit in the paper about a

woman helping police with their inquiries. He knew someone of that name in Paris, he said. At least he thought he had. He knew a Michael McBride and thought his wife's name was Kate. Could be a coincidence, of course. Anyway, I told him we'd pop round this evening and see him, and he said fine."

Jury was about to remonstrate that they could have popped round when they'd been at the Starrdust or, certainly, sitting here eating. But he preferred to act. He got up, unhooked his jacket from the back of his chair, and said, "Come on."

"*Sir!* We haven't finished our dinner!"

"We can come back. Danny'll still be open. Chop-chop, Wiggins!"

Reluctantly, Wiggins began to get out of his chair. "I'm really not supposed to take exercise right after I eat, sir. It hinders —"

Jury walked around and hooked a finger in Wiggins's collar, bringing them as face-to-face as they were ever likely to get. "I'll carry you all the way to Fulham, if I have to."

18

Although it was crowded with dark and heavy furniture — medieval, Jury thought — the room had a vaporous quality, the air infused with a combination of sweet smells, confusing yet familiar. Jury had breathed deeply of it, thinking one doesn't forget, even after long absence, the bitter perfume of the censer, the musky odor of drying flowers, camphor, and candle wax. Jury's absence had been long. When was the last time he'd gone to church? Years ago, and even then it had been in the service of a case he was working on.

It looked as if Father Charles Noailles had gone to some trouble to make the room homelike or, possibly, churchlike. On the wall behind the priest hung a stylized wooden Madonna, her blue cowl rubbed back to the original wood. She was as long and thin as a Modigliani sculpture. Jury was always in awe of the transporting peace-fulness in the expression of these figures.

Father Noailles was a tall man in his late forties with a manner practiced to put others at ease. When they arrived, he'd been standing by the window, which gave out onto the wide lawn in the front of the palace. This window overlooked the abundant trees planted there and eastward, towards the walled garden. Beneath the window was a chest, like an old seaman's chest, the wood burnt in some of the seams. For a moment, Jury wondered what seas Noailles might have crossed and what fires he'd been through. Probably, he'd picked it up for a few quid on the Portobello Road. That's where he could have come by the chest of drawers against the wall, worm-eaten oak that sat on the none-too-level floor. Something white — a book of matches or a squared piece of paper — was fixed under one of the fat round feet of the chest. There was even a narrow iron bed covered with a gray blanket against the same wall. Perhaps the most interesting object was a telescope fixed on its stand, pointed upwards at the window, trained on the sky.

"You really inhabit this office, don't you?" Fearing that sounded smug, Jury added, "I wish my own office were a little more habitable." He laughed. His of lice was plenty habitable; Wiggins had seen to that.

And Wiggins gave him a stare, not wanting to take verbal issue, that seemed to say, Well, what do you want? We've got our tea-making kit, and even a small sink, and just about any pill or powder you might need for your headaches or insomnia. Except crabbiness — we haven't got one for that. Wiggins sniffed, as if he had said this aloud and hoped the superintendent would take it to heart.

"I don't actually live here," said Charles Noailles, "although it looks as if I did. Please sit down, won't you? Here, this chair is good." He folded a stack of papers and quarterlies into his arms and dumped them on a table against the wall, already full enough to make the stack tilt.

Jury took this seat, old scratched and much-rubbed oxblood leather, worn but comfortable. He sank into it and found it surprisingly comfortable. "You're an astronomer, Father?"

Noailles seemed almost glad of the Scotland Yard intrusion, as if this released him from some wearisome occupation. "Amateur, strictly amateur."

Wiggins was making a circuit of the room, appraising a chair here, a bisque figure there, looking at this and that (as if he were searching for clues, which he wasn't). Jury knew he was making his way to the telescope, which he thereupon appropriated. He did this with all the stealth of a cat closing on a dish of cream.

"What about you, Sergeant Wiggins," said Noailles, "are you an amateur stargazer?"

"Oh, yes. When I was younger, you'd never find me far from a telescope."

Jury contemplated the ceiling for a moment, as if he were in a planetarium, as Wiggins made a brief circuit of the heavens. Finished, Wiggins announced, "There's a lot to be said for it." His tone was sententious.

"For what?" asked Jury.

"Why, for the night sky, the constellations, the moon —"

"Thank you, Wiggins. You don't have to tell us what's in it. We know at least that much." With a smile for Noailles, Jury said, "We didn't really come here to look at the stars, Father." Glancing around at the tiers of books and spilled papers, Jury apologized for interrupting him, as he was obviously very busy.

Noailles held up his hands. "Please, don't apologize. I'd sooner do almost anything than this writing."

"Are you referring to your book, sir?"

Wiggins, true to the Wiggins health regimen, sat down in a hard-backed chair and took out his notebook.

"*Lives of the Bishops*, I'm calling it. The Fulham Palace bishops, that is. It's really a history of the palace. I guess I had the idea that the palace itself would be a good environment to work in. You know — inspirational."

Jury smiled. "And has it proved to be so?"

"No, of course not. No more and no less than writing on a bench in Montparnasse or Leicester Square. It doesn't really make any difference, does it, what surroundings you're in?"

Sagely, Wiggins nodded. "I've certainly found that to be true."

Jury blinked, once again wondering about his sergeant's many avocations. "How long have you had this office, Father?"

"Nearly a year. But I'm sure you didn't come here to discuss my writing."

Jury smiled again. "That's not what I was doing." Wiggins was opening his mouth to do just that, and Jury cut him off, saying, "You told my sergeant here that you know, or knew, Kate McBride."

"Possibly. I knew a Michael and Kate

McBride in Paris. At least, I knew *him*. Michael was with the British Embassy."

Jury waited. "Go on."

"Actually, I met them in Aruba."

Jury nodded. Noailles was getting off the track, but Jury believed in letting witnesses tell a story as they wanted to.

"It was on one of those magnificent beaches that scalloped the entire island, pinkish-white sand and narrow; it looked like a string of pearls. They were having a brief holiday, and when we discovered we both lived in Paris in the Sixth Arrondissement, we took it as Fate bringing us together, or at least Michael did. Anyway, we got to talking. It was good conversation, you know, the kind that doesn't bother with the standard questions: What do you do? and What do *you* do? That's why, I suppose, when they met me for dinner in the hotel, they might have felt they'd been duped."

Jury wondered. "Duped?"

"To find out I what I was. I was wearing my collar, see." He pointed at his neck, where no collar was tonight, as if to initiate the two policemen into the mysterious habits of the priesthood. "I hadn't been, obviously, at the beach."

"This made a difference to them?"

"Oh, I don't think so. Well, I know it didn't in the case of Michael. But his wife was never a talker to begin with. So I don't know about her."

"You got to know him but not her?"

"That's right. I don't think Kate was awfully knowable, anyway."

Jury thought this a queer thing for a priest to say but smiled at his saying it.

"As I said, it was really her husband I knew. My church was in Saint-Germain-des-Prés. Saint-Sulpice. They lived near there, had a flat just off the rue de Vaugirard in rue . . ." Noailles frowned, trying to bring it back.

"The rue Servandoni?"

"Ah, yes." Noailles registered surprise that the police would know this but said nothing. "That was it. Michael sometimes attended matins, quite early in the morning. He struck me as rather devout." Noailles paused awhile, scenes of Paris perhaps turning in his mind like pages in a book of photos.

"Yes?" Jury cued him to continue.

"Oh. Sorry. I was just thinking of Saint-Germain. I loved being in Paris. I told you I didn't really know her, I'd only really been together with her when the three of us first met, and after that I'd see her from time to time with Michael."

"Tell me anything you remember about her. On Aruba, for instance. I imagine that was the longest you were around her?"

"Yes." Noailles drew his hand over his chin, reflecting. "I do remember that big sun hat she wore. It had an enormous brim. It made an aisle of shade wherever she walked."

Jury thought he seemed to be taking pleasure in the memory of Kate McBride and wondered. All he said was, "Go on."

"Honestly, Superintendent, there's nothing to be going on *with*." His hand made a gesture of waving away smoke. "As I said, she kept herself to herself." He paused.

"Were you here this past Saturday night?"

Noailles fumbled a bit with his answer. "Yes. I left for Paris on Sunday. I'm here most of the time, really. Most nights or evenings. It was evening, wasn't it, when this woman was murdered?"

"Somewhere between six and around ten. You were here all evening, then?"

"Yes. It was one of the nights I slept here, actually." Noailles got up, moved about the room, rubbed his shoulders as if they ached.

Jury watched him. "When you saw the

photos of the dead woman, were you surprised?"

"You mean, did I think it was Kate? I thought I recognized her, yes."

Jury said to Wiggins, "Have you got the morgue shot?"

"Oh. Yes, sir." Wiggins drew a picture from a big raincoat pocket, passed it to Noailles.

He frowned over it. "It does look like Kate McBride . . . but not quite." His eyes narrowed, as if a squint might help him identify her. But he shook his head. "I never really saw her that much to be sure." Noailles returned the photo.

"What about the other offices here? Did you see anyone else?"

"No — yes, I did see old Bread. Captain Bread, he calls himself. He was still here. He often is. Rather fanatical about this trust for seamen he runs."

"Do you know any of the other people who're letting offices?"

"A little. Enough to say good morning, good evening to, yes. But not much more than that."

Jury paused. "She didn't come to see you then?"

At first, the priest seemed not to grasp Jury's meaning. When he had, he paled, whether from anxiety or anger, Jury didn't know. "I've told you, Superintendent. I've told you what happened." His tone was cold.

Now Noailles was on the defensive, and it was doubtful he'd get any more out of him. Jury tried to recoup by saying it was merely a routine question. "We truly appreciate your coming forward." He rose. "We'll leave you to your work."

Wiggins rose too, seemingly reluctant to leave the far-flung planets.

At the door, Jury paused and turned. "What about the little girl? The McBrides' daughter. Did you know her?"

The priest shook his head. "No. Only him, Michael. He didn't talk about her, but of course there's no reason their children would have come into the conversation. It was his spiritual dilemma we talked about, not his family. Anyway, as I said, I didn't know his wife —"

"— very well." Jury finished it for him, smiled, and they left.

19

Ralph Rees was not exactly what Melrose expected; he didn't put on the painterly ennui that often goes with absence of talent. He was dressed for the stereotype, though — black turtleneck sweater under a cream wool jacket with drooping shoulders and sleeves turned up a couple of times — and he rather cultivated the stereotypical artistic look: thinnish, a little peaked, with hair not quite to his shoulders and the nervous habit of shaking it back off his face.

There was, however, no question about his being glad to meet Melrose; in his enthusiasm for this British aristocrat, he crushed Melrose's hand between both of his. He was quite overcome with delight that the gallery had sold one of his paintings, more so that a customer had been able to appreciate it.

"The series gets a blank look from some people."

Including me, thought Melrose. But Ralph Rees seemed, in saying what he did, utterly ingenuous, and Melrose began to warm towards him, lackluster painter that he was. Ralph Rees appeared to have all the enthusiasm for his own work that a four- or five-year-old would have as he rushed to Mum with his latest finger-painted tree or house. Melrose wondered, then, and asked, "You've probably done other sorts of work, Mr. Rees?"

"Call me Ralph. I pronounce it 'Rafe,' in the old way. Whichever." A smile beamed in Melrose's direction.

"Right. I was saying you no doubt have done other kinds of painting."

"Oh, yes. But, you know, derivative stuff."

Sebastian put in: "Portraits and Venetian canals and the Swiss Alps." He discounted Rees's past efforts with a dismissive smile.

"Really? I've always had a liking for a portrait, and certainly J. M. W. Turner was never afraid of paintings of Venice being labeled derivative." He was grateful for the whisky in his hand that Olivia had seen he got immediately, and with a rather merry look that suggested it might be the only way to get through this dinner.

They laughed in different ways. Rees was sincere and Olivia appreciative. The Fabricant brothers were less so.

It was at this point that the living room

door slid back and Ilona Kuraukov entered. Melrose knew it was she; it could be no one else, not from Jury's description. Nicholas and Sebastian both greeted her as "Mum." She was far from Melrose's idea of one. She looked rather as if she should be displayed on one of those Art Deco posters with a wolfhound at her side and a Pernod in her hand.

It seemed only reasonable that she should be wearing mink — or was it sable? — (which Nicholas was now helping her out of). Underneath it was a dove-gray dress of some soft material that draped easily across bosom and hips and made her eyes (that might be gray-blue) grayer. Her pale hair was pulled back in a French twist, a hairdo Melrose hadn't seen in some time, but Ilona Kuraukov could easily revive the fashion. And models would have killed for those cheekbones. It was very hard to imagine that Sebastian was her son; how could she be old enough? In her late sixties, even her early seventies? She might be as old as Agatha! How he wished he could take a couple of Polaroids back. *Now, dear Aunt, how old would you say my friend Ilona Kuraukov is?*

After the coat came the drink — vodka that had apparently been kept as frozen as an ice floe, the bottle shoved down in the ice. She took this straight from Seb (as she called him) and sat down by Nikolai (as she called *him*) and patted his knee. Then she sat back with her drink and took her time apologizing for her lateness. When she plugged a cigarette into an ornate holder, Melrose was up in a flash to light it. Her eyes regarded him through a curl of smoke.

He sat down again and, not wanting the subject of Rees's paintings to drop while they turned to other and more banal topics, said, "We've been talking about art. About Mr. Rees's — Ralph's" — Melrose inclined his head politely toward Rees — "*Snow* series."

"Ah, yes." Ilona Kuraukov nodded. "Quite different, quite a — how do you say it? — departure! Yes."

Melrose was interested in this departure. That is, he was interested in talking more about the art Ralph Rees was departing *from*. He was about to say something to this effect when the door opened again and a young girl entered: Pansy, the last of their household.

Melrose wondered if late appearances were Pansy's stock-in-trade, arriving late and last, thereby dramatizing her entrance and herself, though she hardly needed to. She was, in her own way, as dazzling in her youth as Ilona was in her age. The girl was her granddaughter. Melrose wondered which of them resented this relationship the most. He could imagine competition among these people was fairly intense, if not absolutely insane.

And now here was Pansy, quite prepared to astound any newcomer but being out-shone by Melrose himself, who was a new-comer with a title. Yes, Pansy was gorgeous, a floral centerpiece, but Melrose was the guy the whole table had been set for, the one with the money, the titles, the land, and the privilege. She seemed not to know whether to disdain all that or try to get her hands on it. This amused him. Pansy would have to make an effort, which, he thought, might be uncharted territory for her. It amused him also, watching her size him up. Jury had said she was thirteen or fourteen, but she looked several crucial years older: seventeen or eighteen, perhaps. When she sat down on the end of the sofa nearest the fireplace, hence nearest him, she did so with a regal bearing she must have copied from her grandmama. Then she looked up at him and asked if he had horses on his land in Northamptonshire.

"No. There's only the house; there are no outbuildings, paddock, or anything of that nature."

"It's what I loathe about London, its not being country," she said, pleating her white silk skirt between her fingers and sounding as if she loathed every inch of the place. She looked around the room, challenging them to disagree.

Here was beauty unsullied by a shred of intelligence. "Yes, I've noticed that about London. Well, you'd find Ardry End pretty uncountrified, too, without horses and sharing the loathsome London aspect, so you'd better not come." He smiled brilliantly.

Had she missed something? Her eyes were wide with uncertainty and surprise, as if some invitation had been extended and she not made part of it. "I —"

Melrose simply cut across her. He had business to attend to, and it didn't include humoring a girl too much taken with herself anyway. "You mentioned Ralph's departure," he said to Ilona. "Is it the portrait-and-Venice thing he's departing from?"

Ilona regarded him coolly over the cigarette in the long black holder. His presence in their — or was it her? — house appeared questionable to her. "You're interested in the *Siberian Snow* series, then?"

Ralph Rees explained. "Madame Kuraukov, Lord Ardry —"

"Please call me Melrose. All of that 'lord' stuff gets to be boring."

"— Melrose here bought one of the paintings."

The holder in her hand stopped in midair. "But that's — quite marvelous." Then she inhaled and asked, "Which one?"

"Number four." He hoped he hadn't made it sound like a doubledecker bus. But he couldn't imagine anyone but the artist and the gallery owners taking those canvases seriously.

"Mum paints," said Nicholas. "Or did, once upon a time. Very good, her stuff was, too. Why'd you stop?" It seemed just to have occurred to him to ask.

Ilona gave a little laugh. "Don't be silly, Nicky."

He accepted that as an answer.

Then Olivia said, "I'm afraid I'm the odd man out here. Forgive me, Ralph, but I honestly liked your landscapes. *And* your portraits. Mona's — that one especially. I don't understand this new white progression of yours."

Melrose wanted to cheer.

Ralph Rees was perfectly good-humored. "It's not for me to say, Libby. I count only as one more critic of the work."

Oh, hell, Melrose thought. Rees was into that "new criticism" that made such a splash several decades ago. Empson, I. A. Richards — the textual purists who counted a writer's life as wholly separate, or other than, the work he produced. Melrose had always thought that literary stance an exquisite piece of hocus-pocus. Anyway, if Ralph Rees didn't know what the hell he was doing, that made three of them, including Olivia.

He wondered about her position in this household. She might be at a serious disadvantage if she was Clive Fabricant's daughter. A half sister by Fabricant's first wife probably would not be overly popular. But then he had no idea what was at stake. She would be a steadying influence on Pansy (who gave Melrose the impression of being completely unmanageable), if Pansy were amenable to such an influence, which he doubted.

He laughed (somewhat superciliously). "But you certainly had some inspiration for painting those five canvases. So you must have *some* understanding of your own work. Critics are, after all, permitted their opinions." (No, they weren't. That's why they were critics.) "And, anyway, am I correct in thinking your *Snow* series can't be articulated? I mean, it doesn't lend itself to analysis and interpretation." What in hell was he talking about? If you had money you could say anything and nobody gave a damn. And why had the new criticism popped up in his thoughts? Empson — well, he was always hovering, but Richards? Good lord, he hadn't thought of him in a hundred years, not since that last course he'd taught in the Romantic poets. He laid it on. "It's completely visceral, a metaphor for emptiness. I liked your" — here he turned to Olivia — "seeing it as a 'white progression.' Though I myself look at it as more of a regression." *Blah, blah, blah, blah.* How could they listen? The idle rich, minting coins with their mouths.

At this magic moment a middle-aged woman in an apron entered the room to whisper to Madame Kuraukov that dinner was ready. She was thinnish and of a mousy-brown plainness that made her fade right into the wallpaper, or the shadows, whatever was around to blend with. She

271

seemed quite shy, for as Ilona said, "Thank you, Hedda," the woman turned and left the room without having made eye contact with anyone.

Melrose supposed what he was doing was allowing himself to register on their minds as a transcendent bore. This was a disguise that had suggested itself the more he rattled on. It occurred to him that the crotchety pair of Neame and Champs would never excite suspicion, would never raise questions in other people's minds — *Ah-ha! What are they up to?* — unless one saw the skull beneath the skin of those two.

Rees, of course, would not think Melrose boring at all. Far from it. To him, Melrose would be a fount of wisdom because he was talking about Rees's work. And, not surprisingly, it was Ralph who prompted him to continue as they all sat down to dinner in a jumble and got bibbed up.

"As I said, I get this feeling, it's like a fist in the solar plexus" — here Melrose demonstrated by hitting himself — "that the entire series is more than the sum of its parts."

Rees nodded eagerly. "To take them all in at one gulp, that's what you should do. That's why I'm so grateful to Seb and Nick for giving me a place to hang all of them."

Ilona said, from the bottom of the table (Sebastian was sitting at the top) "It must be gratifying to you, Ralph — all this enthusiasm. Please remember I insist on buying one for myself. I told you that."

This rather surprised Melrose. She couldn't actually *admire* these white paintings. He asked her, smiling, "Which one?"

In the smile Ilona returned, and in the tiny inclination of the head — as if conceding a point — Melrose thought there to be more than a glimmer of irony, as if she recognized his question as a repetition of her own. "Oh" — she waved his question away — "I haven't decided yet."

Melrose made no comment on the puzzling nature of this way of regarding art. But he was concentrating now on what looked like an excellent poussin being handed round by the colorless Hedda. She seemed to have been banished to some fairy tale in which she would vanish if looked upon too openly and directly. Her existence depended upon her invisibility. Well, if the excellence of the chicken matched that of the soup, he was in for a treat. And when he tasted one of the carmelized new potatoes, he only hoped that no one would be silly enough to stare at Hedda and make her disappear in a puff of smoke. People could kill for such cooking.

"You'd better, Mother. They're going like hotcakes!"

Both the cliché and the voice in which Sebastian uttered it were so resoundingly hollow that it struck Melrose for the first time that he was not enthusiastic after all about the *Snow* paintings. Nor did Melrose understand the actual content of what he'd said. Had more of the paintings been sold than the one to him? he asked.

Nicholas answered, "Two of them, perhaps. More than one person is interested, and we're very hopeful." He smiled warmly at Ralph.

Before he said anything, Melrose allowed the morsel of roast young chicken to melt in his mouth. He took a sip of the wine, and it and the chicken converged in an ambrosial meeting of flavors. He thought Hedda went unappreciated, for no one was remarking on this wonderful food. Being careful not to look at the cook (who had brought in some hot rolls and was passing them), he said, "This chicken is more inspired than your painting, Ralph. If there were four more ways of cooking it, we'd none of us need art." He kept his eyes on his plate, smiling. And from somewhere came a giggle. He looked up, only to see the door to the kitchen swing a little in a ghostly encounter.

Olivia did remark that Hedda was a marvelous cook. She hoped they weren't taking the woman for granted; they should get someone to help her, at least to do the serving. "Several of our friends have tried —" Just then, the cook came back through the swinging door to go into the living room. Olivia stopped talking until she was out of the room, then continued in a whisper. "Our friends have tried to steal her away from us with offers of much larger salaries."

"Oh?" Heartily he declared, "Well, they can't be friends, and they can't have enough money." That was properly vulgar, he thought, for a title.

Predictably, they all chuckled. Wasn't it dreadful that social convention demand they all put up with the crude, the vapid, the vulgar, and — worst of all — the boring? He felt like reciting aloud the poem that was going through his head: *My wife and I have asked a crowd of craps/To dine with us. . . .* Melrose smiled. . . . Philip Larkin. *There* was someone who knew the dreadful prospect of cocktail parties and dinners.

But he was doubly frustrated because he could find no opening at all to bring the talk around to the Fulham Palace murder. Then he saw, though the archway into the living room, Hedda folding Ilona's coat over her arm, probably preparatory to putting it away in some cupboard. If she would only cross through the far end of the dining room . . . ah! She was!

Ilona saw her too. "Hedda, just leave that out, will you?"

A weak "Yes, madam" came from the hallway.

"Fur is not popular these days, is it?" She said this on an almost challenging note, in case there were any hunt saboteurs among the dinner guests.

Melrose very much doubted animal-rights activists could influence Ilona Kuraukov in any way. He took advantage of the incident. "That's a very handsome fur, Madame Kuraukov. Mink, is it? Sable?"

"Sable. It was given me by my late husband." Here she colored slightly, as if everyone, including Melrose, also knew of Mona Dresser's sable, and that Clive Fabricant was handing out furs right and left.

Unfortunately, Melrose couldn't be that knowledgeable, couldn't have read about

the coat on the dead woman having belonged to Fabricant's last wife — Mona
Dresser — for the newspaper accounts had
made no such disclosure. He was left,
then, with an oblique maneuver. "Every
time I see a fur coat these days" — ye
gods, that was clumsy enough! — "I can't
help thinking about that queer murder.
Did you read about it? The woman found
in the grounds of Fulham Palace?" To
Melrose, it seemed they all should be able
to see right through him: that he was a
mole, planted here in their house by
police. But he plodded on; there was no
way he could reintroduce it more skillfully.
"We're near Fulham here, aren't we? Is
this South Ken?"

"Chelsea." A hint of disbelief that
anyone could confuse the three.

"Oh. Well, I expect such news leaks
across the border, doesn't it?" He wasn't
sure, hut he thought Olivia was looking at
him with slightly narrowed eyes. She had
stopped eating and was resting her chin on
her palm, looking at him. "Every time I
think of sable" — seldom enough — "I remember that film *Gorky Park*. Did you see
it?"

Pansy, who had said next to nothing and
eaten next to nothing and had simply kept

277

turning her fork over and over, said, "I saw it on video. I thought it was awfully dull."

"It was all that snow and those sables I remember. Lee Marvin, what an unappreciated actor."

"He was awfully *old,* wouldn't you say?" Pansy said.

Hell, in attempting to bore them all again he saw the talk was going towards something entirely different and he'd have to snatch it back. "Old? He was only fifty or so, wasn't he?"

Pansy shrugged and looked away. "That's what I mean."

"He was certainly a commanding presence, standing there in the snow with a gun in his hand. Was she shot? I can't remember."

"Was who?" Sebastian frowned.

"The woman at Fulham Palace."

"Yes," said Nicholas, looking uncomfortable. "We've had police here all —"

"Nikolai," said Ilona, reprovingly, trying to shut him up. But he'd already mentioned the magic word.

"Police? Good God! Whatever for?" Melrose feigned astonishment.

Pansy announced that she "went absolutely spastic." Sebastian gave Nicholas a dirty look for introducing the subject.

It was Olivia who calmly told him the reason. "It was the coat, you see. Actually, it was mine."

Melrose gasped. *"Yours?"* He looked around the table as if he couldn't believe what he'd heard and would someone please explain.

Ilona Kuraukov looked as if she'd rather shoot him than inform him.

"You're joking!" He kept it up.

Olivia took a sip of wine, regarded him over the rim of her glass, and with a rueful shake of her head, said, "No. It's quite true. It wasn't my coat originally. It belonged to Daddy's last wife, Mona Dresser. She had it for years and scarcely ever wore it and finally just gave it to me."

Melrose said the name over. "Mona Dresser, Mona Dresser. Why does that name sound familiar?"

"Because she used to be a film star," said Nicholas. "Quite famous in the 'forties and 'fifties."

"Of course," said Melrose. "So she gave the coat to you?"

"And after a while — well, I'm not really too fond of fur. So I put it in a consignment shop. A little place in the Brompton Road."

She showed signs of wavering, so

Melrose prompted her. "Yes?"

Olivia shrugged. It was rather a shivery shrug. "They sold it. Presumably to this woman." Olivia smiled wanly.

Ilona put in, "It's all ghastly, but there it is." Her tone was an attempt to be dismissive but strain underlaid it.

"I wonder you didn't put it with Christie's or Sotheby's," said Melrose irrelevantly. "After all, the coat had been Mona Dresser's."

"Yes, you're right."

Melrose thought his interest in this sable venture might seem a bit too pointed, so he backed off and brought on the pedant, Lord Ardry. "Christie's do quite well. I've put some of my own objets d'art under the hammer there." He laughed affectedly. "A *bureau du roi* that fetched quite a handsome price." And he went on in the most tedious detail about the bureau, the blanket chest, the bonheur du jour (all of these belonging to his friend Max Owen, in Lincolnshire, where he had done a passable impression of an antiques appraiser earlier that year).

Pansy made no effort to hide her boredom, Sebastian took a covert glance at his watch, and Ilona studied her fine hands. Nicholas filled up the wineglasses. Only

Olivia and Ralph were listening. If he wanted to be invited here again, he had better not bore them to death, so he stopped. He did not revert to the sable coat, however. He would leave immediately after consuming this delicious-looking lemon mousse that had been set before him by Hedda. It was frozen and sitting in a raspberry cassis.

"This mousse is exceptional," said Melrose.

"One of our favorites," said Sebastian, who had broken out a Sauternes to go with it.

"And that chicken! But where does your cook come by lavender flowers? I can't recall ever having anything laced with lavender."

Olivia said, "There's an herb garden out behind the house."

Pansy still played with her fork and yawned. "That's where they found her. In the lavender." When all eyes turned to her, she looked a trifle disgusted, as if only she had been taking the trouble to follow the dinner-table conversation. "The *dead* woman. At Fulham *Palace*."

20

Somnolence settled over Melrose Plant like a cloak as he sat the following morning in one of the club's wing chairs, digesting his full English breakfast and ruminating over the next job Jury had given him: to visit Mona Dresser and her niece, Linda Pink.

Having decided to pay his visit that afternoon, he then set about reading the arts section of the *Times*. His eyelids did not want to cooperate in this venture, and his dozy brain went along with this mutiny and he drifted off.

He was torn from sleep a few minutes later by a rant coming from behind another newspaper, where a member was declaiming, "Rubbish, rubbish, rubbish, rubbish," in a voice not unlike Lear's as he wandered across the vasty moors of both the stage and his mind. Melrose sat, waiting for the final "rubbish."

"Rubbish!" The paper came down from in front of the face of a member in the sixty-to-eighty age range Melrose had come to expect. This face, however, was far livelier than those of most of the members. He addressed Melrose without preamble.

"Have you read the so-called 'arts' section? You have the *Times* there." This was said in an accusatory manner, suggesting that if he had that paper, he had damned well better have read it.

"Ah. Actually, I just seemed to doze off before I got to . . ." Under the dark cloud of the man's countenance, the jutting gray rock of his eyebrows, Melrose felt excuses were unacceptable.

This gentleman shook his head slowly. "That's the trouble with you young men. No sticking power. I'll read it to you." He snapped the paper once or twice to let it know which was master, which was slave, and read: *"The startling exhibit of Charlie Chambers.* Sounds more like a tap dancer than a painter.

> *"Chambers begins with his representational portraits, carries us through his neo-classical nude period, and ends with a post-Abstract Realism that distorts vision through the use of acrylics, fingerpaints, and, most astonishing of all, multicolored Gummy Bears."*

The paper came down again like a lead balloon. "What do you think of that?"

Oh, art, art, art. . . . Now Melrose felt like Lear. "I'd say it's rubbish!"

If the old man thought his nose was being tweaked, he didn't seem to care. "You agree, then. I saw this so-called exhibit of 'neo-classical nudes,' and I'd sooner visit a frozen meat locker. I left before I acted on my impulse to go out for a can of spray paint. My name's Pitt, incidentally. Simeon Pitt."

"Mr. Pitt, happy to meet you." Melrose thrust his hand across the open space between them. "Melrose Plant." He could not bear to trot out the titles again. "That bad, was it?" He warmed almost immediately to Mr. Pitt and wondered what comment this made on his own tolerance level. Was it zero?

"*That bad* does not begin to describe it. I'd be giving the so-called artist too much credit by calling his work 'anarchic' or 'counter-art' or something like 'post-Warholian.' Christ, even Warhol — whom I dislike, only not so much — had some sort of idea — exploiting consumerism — of what he was doing. This one" — and here he balled up the paper as if he'd crumple the whole newspaper world — "has about

284

as much notion of paint as a two-year-old would. This Chambers fellow couldn't paint a cow if it posed for him in a field of sheep. And now we've got old Phinny Fogg lauding the damned exhibit to the skies. It's a disgrace." He tossed the crumpled ball of paper towards the big fireplace. "Rubbish!" Then he sat back and his eyes made a slow circuit of the room, as if to see whether his act had cleared the air at all. "I'm having a whisky. Want one? Or is it too early for you?"

"Is it ever too early?" Melrose was enjoying his companion; it was a conversation begun *in medias res,* a style of presentation he'd always liked, the style of which White Ellie Cripps was mistress, for it meant that small talk had already been dispensed with, given that the conversation began in the middle, and in the middle of something the speaker had feelings about.

Mr. Pitt laughed a laugh that sounded something like a drowning man desperately grabbing at air, a kind of sucking in and snorting out. "Good man! Whisky? Or something else for you?" He raised two fingers and beckoned to Young Higgins, who nodded and started his infinite journey to the center of the room, as if it were the Outer Hebrides where they sat.

"Whisky's fine." Melrose took the lull in the talk (which he imagined wouldn't last long) to consult his copy of the arts section. Apparently, this Phineas Fogg really was the art critic for the *Times*. . . . Well, Melrose should have gathered that. The exhibition in question was at a small gallery, and the artist this Charlie Chambers fellow. Melrose had never heard of him, but that was hardly a blight on Mr. Chambers's career.

Young Higgins made it and took the order and clarified one or two confusing issues about the drink.

Whisky and soda on its way, Mr. Pitt settled in to make mincemeat of old Phinny Fogg's artistic pretensions. "This exhibit that Fogg finds so *sublimely*" — he checked the column again — "no, so *beatifically* beautiful —" Pitt shook his head and closed his eyes. "Has there been any artist since Turner you can say that about?"

"You mean J. M. W. Turner?"

Simeon Pitt cocked his head. "How many Turners are there?"

Melrose smiled. How refreshing. Mr. Pitt was not one to allow place to rhetorical questions. "Only the one, I think." He thought of Bea Slocum. "I wonder —"

★ ★ ★

"Words can only hint at the bottomless despondency one feels looking at the so-called art of this Chambers fellow. He stands for so much one loathes on the current art scene." Pitt's fingers drummed on the arm of his chair. By the round, cherubic look of him and the thin veil of whitened hair that covered his otherwise bald pate, Simeon Pitt looked to be in his late sixties, at least. He acted more like sixteen, as if nothing took place in his life that did not require physical emphasis. "He's getting all this adulation now, as a result of *this*." He picked up the arts page and shook it as if he might be able to shake it free of the redoubtable Fogg's words. "People will swarm to his exhibit and talk him up because they've been told he's good, while a really deserving fellow has to scrabble for pennies to buy paints."

Melrose smiled. "I was getting the impression there *were* no really deserving fellows."

"Untrue, untrue! They are few and far between, mind you. We're lucky to see one come along once in a decade. Ah, here comes Higgins."

Whenever Young Higgins crossed the room with a tray, Melrose had the impression of an elderly bat boy. The contents of the soda syphon sloshed and the glasses slid and rattled, but in general the tray was brought safely home.

"Thank you, sir," said Pitt, signing the ticket with a flourish. "No, no, don't you bother; I'll splash the stuff into the glasses. . . . Be here all day, otherwise," he added, after Higgins had wandered off. Pitt pushed the soda syphon as if he were going to put out a fire. He handed Melrose his whisky. "What were we saying? Oh, yes. You see, what makes me see red is that there may be more real artists among us, but they can't manage, can't eke out an existence in a loft with a skylight and not enough money for a loaf."

This amused Melrose. Simeon Pitt's idea of unrecognized genius was quite stereotypically romantic.

"A few years back there was one, fellow named Jeremy Grey, whom you've never heard of because none of these damned gallery twerps would take him on. So reviewers like me, we never saw him. When I finally did, he was dead. And where I saw three of his paintings was in a pub. That's right, a pub. Some publican had traded drinks, probably, for the paintings. Remarkable work. I wrote a double column about Grey, wrote about him for a month."

It came to Melrose finally. Simeon Pitt! "You're *that* Pitt. The art critic for the *Times*. Before Fogg." Melrose seemed to recall this critic had been more than once referred to as "Pitt bull." "How could I have been so stupid not to put that together immediately?"

"Why, I don't know, man. How could you?"

Pitt was regarding Melrose over the rim of his glass. He looked so gleeful that Melrose had to laugh. Then he asked, "Do you know the Fabricant Gallery?"

"Oh, yes. I know most of them, though I don't get around much any more — aren't those the words of an old song?" He tapped his toe and hummed awhile. He stopped, continued. "When I had this job" — here he flicked a finger at the offending newspaper — "I was always making rounds; I felt it as a duty. Now I'd sooner save my time and my feet for a look round the Tate, the National, the Royal Academy. Old friends, old friends. I think of Matisse sometimes; I remember Vuillard and van Gogh, and it's a treat, a real treat, to know all I need do is heave myself out of this chair or my sofa at home and go. And there they all are again! Yes, there they are." Pitt sighed, as if in wonder that the paintings persisted, unchanged, dependable.

This flight of fancy was almost as much a transporting experience for Melrose as it clearly was for Simeon Pitt. *Old friends, old friends.* Matisse, Vuillard, van Gogh. Melrose could imagine the four of them — five if he himself were invited — the five of them here in Boring's deep leather arm-chairs, pouring the whisky, splashing the soda. The good stuff, the real art, gave you the shock of the familiar not the cold consort of the alien, the wretched stuff that left you outside in the snow. Real art invited you in.

Hell's bells, that was what was so enraging about that bogus white "series" of Ralph Rees! Just that: It *was* bogus.

"Mr. Pitt —"

"You were deep into something there, Mr. Plant."

"I was. We were talking about the Fabricant Gallery."

"Place in Mayfair, yes."

"Have you been there lately?"

"No."

"Would you care to go?"

"What? You mean today?"

"I mean right now."

"But we've just settled in with our whiskies, man!" Pitt raised his in proof of this.

"I'd deem it a personal favor, Mr. Pitt, and when we return we'll settle again and have a double." Melrose smiled his special smile, the one he was not wholly conscious he had, but it was as fetching as the smile of a very young child. It was, like the work of Matisse, Vuillard, and van Gogh, the real thing on offer. It invited you in.

"Excellent! I'll hold you to it. And here's to a good long stay in Boring's!" They raised their glasses. "How long are you staying, Mr. Plant?"

"I'm not quite sure, actually, Mr. Pitt. A few days, I'd guess."

"Well, it's pleasant, and, God knows, it's quiet here. Actually, I don't miss the noise and grind of the newspaper business, not at all. I have my digs in Chelsea, on my own, except for my dog and cat. Sounds lonely, I expect, but it isn't. To tell the truth, I enjoy being on my own."

Melrose smiled. It was as he'd suspected. Simeon Pitt was good company, not only to others but to himself, which was more important. "You don't have a large family, I take it?"

"No, not at all. A few cousins who live in the West Country. Barbara, my niece, who I have to lunch occasionally, usually at the

Ivy. She's coming here, actually, on Tuesday. That's Ladies' Day." He chortled. "Can you imagine? Ladies' Days in these times? But it's probably the only concession Boring's has made over the years to change." He drank the last of his whisky, brought the glass down heavily, and said, "I'm ready if you are, Mr. Plant."

"Ready, Mr. Pitt!"

Sebastian was the only one in attendance at the gallery when Pitt and Melrose turned up there a half hour later. Oh, yes, he most certainly knew Simeon Pitt: Sebastian fawned, and Melrose wondered why, given that Pitt was no longer writing reviews of gallery showings. Perhaps Pitt's was the sort of power that was never abrogated, or perhaps he was one of those whose good opinion was always sought, even after he could do one no harm.

There was small talk which Pitt cut short, and Melrose led him into the room where the *Siberian Snow* paintings were displayed.

Pitt took a quick look and a step backward. "What in hell's this?"

"A series of paintings called *Siberian Snow*. Ralph Rees is the artist."

Pitt managed a snow-blinded blink.

"You're kidding, Mr. Plant. It isn't Siberia and, hell, it isn't even snow. What's this supposed to be, minimal art? Like Reinhardt and Robert Ryman?"

"I'm not familiar with that school. If it is one."

"Well, those artists favor white, especially Ryman. It's pure, it's a non-color. But you can see variation in his paint surfaces. The idea behind it is an expression of pure art. I don't really understand it either, but I think I can safely say this ain't it!"

"The Fabricant Gallery seems to think it's — well, *something*."

"It's bloody *nothing*. Nil. *Nada.* Zilch. Zero."

Pitt pulled what looked like an eyepiece from his waistcoat pocket. It was a magnifying glass, which he now applied to the third painting, moving it around. "Funny texture. What's it painted on, do you know?"

"Sandpaper, I think he said." The squares ghosted through.

"This painter's a friend of yours?" Pitt appeared discomfited. "Sorry, didn't mean to —"

Melrose shook his head. "No, no, not a friend. I know him only slightly. How do you explain the fact that this has got at least one good review?"

"I'd explain by noting the reviewer is his mother. Please."

"The word, I believe, was *audacious*."

"Good word. I'd go along with that. Such as in, How would anyone have the *audacity* to fob this off on the public?"

Melrose moved closer to the fifth painting. "At first, you think they're all the same white. But then the white does change in this last one of the series."

"Why do you insist on calling it a series?" However, to humor Melrose, Pitt applied his glass to the last picture. "I suppose it's a slight variation. That's hardly enough to explain all five." Pitt shook his head. "I don't get it. I don't get it," he repeated.

It hadn't occurred to Melrose that there was anything to get. He said, "Let's look around. There's some good stuff here." There was only one example of "good stuff" as far as Melrose was concerned, and he wanted Pitt's comment on it.

They moved into the next small room, Sebastian looking up from his paperwork, tracing their progress with his eyes. He was crafty enough to know a person like Pitt wouldn't want to be accompanied by the dealer. They were standing now in the room where Bea's third painting hung, a North London view similar to the Catchcoach Street one. This was the one Melrose hadn't bought. He did not single it out now; he merely hoped Pitt would be caught by it and would approve.

Pitt commented on a big blaring geometric canvas that Melrose couldn't decipher, saying it wasn't bad, if a little crude, a little too obviously bearing the influence of Picasso. Then, upon seeing Bea Slocum's painting next to it, he said, "Now, *here's* a treat!"

Melrose let out his breath. "I like that one too. As a matter of fact, I bought one of hers."

"Good man! I forgive you for that white lot!"

Melrose's reply came on a laugh. "*I* didn't paint them!"

"*Nobody* painted them!'"

Melrose thought that a bit harsh. He also thought he wouldn't want to tell Simeon Pitt he owned one.

21

"Another twenty-four hours, and we're going to have to charge her, Jury." Chilten was clearly uncomfortable. "What surprises me is she hasn't got herself lawyered up by now. Says she doesn't need one, since she hasn't done anything. How naive. But she's been here since Thursday night; you'd've thought she'd be screaming the bloody station down."

"Unless she's extremely clever."

"Especially with the old lady punching holes in her alibi."

"That's what I mean. Kate McBride hasn't been pressing it."

Chilten expelled a long sigh. "You might be mistaken about that bus ride. It happens."

Jury smiled. "It does. Only it hasn't happened here."

Chilten shrugged, started banging desk drawers in and out.

"I'll talk to her again, Ronnie."

She vanished. Jury had been carrying that

around all day; it was never far from his thoughts, even when he'd been in the Pastis woman's flat or in the Fabricant Gallery. What had happened to this child, Sophie?

When the constable brought her into the room, Jury was standing by the small window that looked out over the spindly tree and the square of frozen grass in which it sat. He turned to say hello to her, feeling all of this had happened before, probably because they were meeting in the same place: window, table, chairs exactly the same as they had been the morning before. Or was there something else to this sense of déjà vu?

She said hello, offered him a smile that looked worn-out, and sat down at the table.

Jury sat in the same chair, not that there was much of a choice. He asked, "Did you go there to meet someone?"

Her eyes widened. "Go where? What do you mean? Who would I meet?"

"The priest. Charles Noailles." He watched her face for a reaction, but the face remained as still as undisturbed lake water. "He keeps an office at the palace, for his writing."

She looked at him with a smile he supposed could be called resigned. "You didn't see me, Superintendent. You saw *her*."

Jury ignored this. "He said he knew your husband quite well when you lived in Paris. He didn't know you very well."

She bent her head, seemed to be studying her hands, and was silent for a few moments. "Michael, my husband — yes, he was friendly with this priest. I didn't really know him. Michael needed a measure of spiritual sustenance. He was dying of leukemia."

There was a silence.

"I'm sorry. Go on about your daughter, Sophie."

Sadly, she looked at him. "Do you want to hear about it?"

"Yes, of course."

She looked at him steadily. "It was in Paris. I stayed on there after Michael died."

"In Saint-Germain-des-Prés."

She nodded. "It happened one day in the Madeleine district. There's that famous grocery Fauchon; it's a swank market, food laid out like art, and every kind of fruit and vegetable you can imagine. The different kinds of food are sold in different buildings. It was Sophie's favorite place to go. We'd make a day of it. First to the Tuileries, and then Annebelle's in the rue de Rivoli for hot chocolate, then the Métro to the Madeleine and Fauchon's. There was an organ grinder, who had his spot always just outside the door of Fauchon's fruit and vegetable section. Sophie loved this. He had a pet dog and a cat and a baby pram in which the two slept — can you imagine? Sometimes they were awake and going through their round of tricks.

"Fauchon's is very large, very festive, and very expensive. We were in the part that sells fruits and vegetables and I was buying apricots and peaches; I told Sophie to get potatoes and she was doing that, putting small potatoes into a sack. She did this very carefully, inspecting each one. A few minutes later, I looked around and Sophie was gone. Well, I didn't really panic at first; I thought she'd wandered next door or to the candy and pastry shop across the street — she wasn't supposed to, but it was narrow and crowded far more with shoppers than with street traffic. We'd been to Fauchon's so many times, she knew what was in each building.

"I went across and into the patisserie, but she wasn't there either. Then, afraid I might have simply missed seeing her in the vegetable and fruit department, I went back there. I waited for five or ten minutes, and it was then real panic began to set in. I started canvassing all the different sections. I found a policeman, finally, and told him, and he got another policeman and they searched the marketplace for half an hour. She was gone — just like that — vanished. They told me then to fill out a report for the police and to go to the British Embassy.

"When I finally got back to the rue Servandoni I think I still expected Sophie to appear. I thought surely she must be at home; she couldn't have disappeared without a trace." Kate looked away. "But of course she wasn't there. It was the worst day of my life — the worst. For something like this to happen in a foreign country . . ."

"When was this? When did it happen?"

"A little over a year ago. The police did all they could — well, I took that on faith; how was I to know? When I went back to Paris a few months ago to see if they'd found out anything in all that time, I was told there was no record of a report on what happened."

"No record? Why not?"

"They said a lot of files had been destroyed in an office fire. I had the most dreadful feeling that Sophie had been expunged, obliterated.

"When it first happened, when she just disappeared, I tried to think why anyone would abduct her. I put out of my mind — I had to — that it was sexual, that it was some pedophile, but I couldn't come up with other possibilities. Had she been kidnapped? Would ransom be demanded? We were comfortably off; Michael's family had money. But we certainly weren't wealthy.

"I stayed in the flat all of the next two days, hoping the phone would ring. Then I went back to Fauchon's. It was a waste of time, but I expect one still holds out hope that the person is back where you lost them. That it has all been a dream.

"The police, I like to think, were doing their best. I didn't ask them what usually happens in the case of a lost child; I didn't want to know the answer. Or, rather, I knew what must be the most common scenario; I simply didn't want it confirmed. Though I expect police are very hesitant to speculate — Are you?" She rose and went to the window.

Her movement perhaps had stirred the air, for a breeze touched Jury's face. It could have had no other source, in this dreary room with its grimy windows.

"I was unable to settle on anything, unable to decide what course of action to take. But there really wasn't — was there? — an act of mine that could have changed things. It wasn't until two weeks later that I got the first letter."

"Letter?"

"Typed on a computer, or I assume so. It's very hard to trace something done on a computer, I was told. It was short. It told me that if I wanted to see Sophie again, I'd have to do what they told me to. They were all posted in Paris. Different arrondissements, but all in Paris."

"You mean there was more than one?"

She nodded. "The thought that Sophie was alive and well — the sudden shift from despair to hope — this so overshadowed the strangeness of the note that I didn't try to understand what in God's name the writer wanted. Or what *they* wanted. In subsequent messages it was always *we*.

"I guessed they were ransom notes, or so I was supposed to think. There were three of them. This first one told me to go to Zurich, that I would find Sophie in Zurich after I had turned over five hundred thousand francs. I had more than that; as I said, my husband's family had money and we were well off. So I wondered why the ransom was so modest. That's only a hundred thousand American dollars, isn't it? I was to go to a coffee house called Le Métro and sit outside with the money in a carrier bag from Fauchon's. That is, I had to take one of their bags with me. Well, I did that: sat at a little table outside Le Métro and had coffee. I sat there all afternoon, went back the next day, and the next, until it was obvious no one was ever going to turn up.

"I went back to Paris. Over the next eight months, two more letters arrived just like the first, written on a computer, or I assume so. The second was short, like the first, and said I was to go to St. Petersburg to a cafe on Nevsky Prospekt. It was called the Balkan."

When she stopped again, Jury prompted, "And did you?"

"Of course. What else was I to do?"

Jury spread his hands. "And the same thing happened?"

"Not quite. As before, I sat and waited for nearly two hours. Then someone came, an ordinary-looking woman. She took the next table and opened a book. I stared at her. Finally, she raised her eyes and rose. Well, I thought she was going to approach me, but she merely walked away. . . ." Her voice died out.

"So it could have been anybody."

"It could have been anybody, yes."

"The third one?"

"This time I was to go to Brussels. The directions were the same: to go to a cafe in the Grand' Place. I had never been to these places, Zurich, Brussels, Peter — St. Petersburg, I mean — so it was difficult. The note called for the same things: the Fauchon's bag, the money, the bag set down beside the table.

"I thought I must have an enemy, some very cruel person who was playing a game. But I discarded that notion. What was going on was too bizarre. What satisfaction could there be in doing this only once every three or four months? Each time, I returned to the flat in Paris because I was so afraid of missing the one letter that would bring back Sophie. For how could I afford not to do what they said, these letters? How could I take the chance?

"Anyway. Do you know Brussels? The Grand' Place is that beautifully lit square van Gogh painted. It's surrounded by lights, and the light simply melts toward the center. But light is deceptive, isn't it?" Then she said, "Well, I simply couldn't stand Paris and that flat any longer. So four months ago, I came here, came home. And there's the property: Michael's uncle left him some property, a big house in Wales." Now she seemed slightly anxious. "I'm to see a solicitor about it next week. Thursday. I'll be out of here by then, won't I?"

"That's up to Detective Inspector Chilten." It wasn't, of course. It was up to the law regarding detaining people without arresting them. "But I imagine you will." She seemed more worried about the property than about her plight. Which simply could mean that she wasn't *aware* of her plight.

"It's in the Black Mountains, near Abergavenny, if you know Wales. I love the Beacons, love to climb there. They're deceptive, though; they seem an easy climb but suddenly they can be surrounded by mist." She smiled at Jury. "A challenge."

Jury leaned forward. "Did you ever consider someone wanted to keep you in Paris? Or away from England, at least, and so kept giving you false hope about your daughter?"

"Good lord, no." Her voice caught in a laugh. But the laugh died, or snagged on something she appeared to have recalled.

"Unless it's got something to do with the will. Michael's uncle's will. I have to take possession of this house by Christmas. And I have to meet with the solicitor on November twenty-seventh. That's Thanksgiving in America. But I'll be out of here by then."

Then, as had happened the previous morning, sounds came from beyond the door. It opened, and the WPC entered. Jury rose and watched Kate McBride rise also and the constable take her arm — took it gently, Jury thought. She was a woman who merited the concern of others, he thought.

As she walked out, she turned and said, "Thanks for coming." She turned away and then back. "Would you bring me some cigarettes when you come again?"

Jury nodded. He imagined he would come again. Certainly, she did.

22

Melrose recognized her as soon as he saw her standing in the doorway: Mona Dresser might have stepped out of one of the huge posters that had decorated the facade of the film palace Melrose had gone to as a child. As far as he knew it was his first theater experience: at the end of Mona Dresser's career and the beginning of his. That theater! The gilded halls, the chandeliers, the red plush and velvet. A moviegoer familiar with only the little sterile box-shaped screening rooms of today could never picture it.

"Miss Dresser," he said, smiling broadly. "I'm Melrose Plant." When she looked merely puzzled, he wondered how Jury had identified him. "Superintendent Jury told you I was coming, didn't he? Lord Ardry, perhaps he said."

"And which are you?"

"Both, actually. Though I prefer Melrose Plant."

"Hm. Were you ever an actor?" They still stood in the dark doorway.

Melrose was enormously pleased by being thought an actor. "No, never. Why?"

"Because you have a sort of magnetism many actors have and that insinuating actor-y manner. Smooth talker, I'd bet. Also, you're good-looking."

Melrose wasn't sure, now, that he wanted to be thought an actor; he didn't care for that "insinuating" stuff. But he broadened his smile to one even more "magnetic" (he liked to think). "What I do ordinarily is nothing at all. I sit in my big house drinking port by the fireplace and watching my old dog sleep."

"Sounds like we're two of a kind, then. Come on." Her hand did a little pirouette as she motioned him into her parlor.

That's what she called it. To Melrose the word had always conjured up small gas fires, thriving cold, horsehair armchairs, and a cloth laid for tea, gaudy cups and plates inscribed with names of seaside resorts. This description most certainly did not fit the room in which they stood and which looked to him like a stage set. No, a film set, for he could imagine a camera panning over its walls, where the paintings hung so closely together (was that an original Matisse?) they virtually blotted out the plaster beneath; the flower-patterned slip-covers, shiny with firelight; the lamps spilling their dusty-gold light across the carpet; the dark velvet curtains enclosing in their folds an even greater darkness. The room was very long, furnished with chaises, sofas, armchairs, big ottomans, pillows on the floor — she could have held a slumber party.

It was a sumptuous and dazzling set that Mona Dresser did not fit, with her somewhat dumpy figure, her round, obliging face, her untamed gray hair, and her tan cardigan and dark blue pinafore with, yes, a bunny family stamped on its bib. Since she herself did not seem quite at home in this heady setting, her visitors, paradoxically, did and wanted her to be comfortable too.

"Well, Mr. Plant, do have a seat and tell me who you are. Or aren't. I like a bit of mystery. I think I have some port, but I don't have a dog. I could borrow the neighbor's, though."

Melrose had chosen a cloud of an armchair covered in crushed velvet. He stopped her from rising to see to his comforts. "No, no. You can get the dog later. Miss Dresser, I just want to say you're the first actress I ever saw, and I still remember it. I think I know the secret of your appeal —"

"Because I was brilliant?" She waggled her eyebrows.

"Not that, it's because you made absolute strangers feel they'd known you all their lives. And that's acting genius."

She blushed. She fidgeted with the sleeve of her tan cardigan. "Oh, this is so much nicer than talking to Fulham police." She thought for a moment. "Although that superintendent — our mutual acquaintance — did have a definite sort of charm."

Melrose sniffed. This was the aunt who was *your* aunt — yours, not his. "Sort of, yes, for a policeman. He wanted me to come here to see if you might have thought of anything else. And also to talk with your niece."

She looked a bit doubtful. "With Linda? Oh, I'm sorry, but I'm not absolutely sure where Linda went. That doesn't mean she won't be back; she could come racing in here any moment."

Racing in. Melrose did not like the sound of that. Adults don't generally "race." Had Jury been completely honest with him?

"Are you a private detective, then? A gumshoe?"

"No. No, I'm not."

"You're someone who's got nothing better to do?"

Melrose scratched his ear.

"Well, your friends, the real policemen, seem to think Linda might be wrong in what she saw." She held up her hand as if to ward off any objection. "If Linda says it, it's so."

Melrose smiled. "She's that dependable?"

"Oh, Linda's not at all dependable. What I mean is, if Linda reports something to you, if she describes a scene, something she saw, it's accurate down to the blades of grass around the burial site or the color of the handful of dirt tossed on the coffin."

(She went in for grim metaphors.)

"Her powers of observation are quite spectacular, better than that Fulham policeman who came round." She shrugged. "But I don't know what else there is to tell. You'd better go and ask the family about all this."

"I had dinner with them last night."

Mona was astonished. "You mean you *know* them? The Fabricants? That dreary Russian woman?"

Melrose burst out laughing. "Somehow I wouldn't refer to Madame Kuraukov as dreary. No, decidedly not."

"Oh, she's exquisite to look at, I daresay. But she has no conversation. None. That's what I meant. I can't think why Clive ever married her. For her looks, I expect. But I still don't know how you come to know them." She leaned forward, pulled her skirt down farther, clasped her hands around her knees like a schoolgirl waiting to be told a bit of gossip.

"I met the brothers — your nephews?"

"Nicholas and old Seb? None of *mine* I shouldn't think, unless by marriage. But I scarcely see them. Go on."

"I met them in their gallery. I'd gone there to have a look round."

"This was all accidental?"

Melrose pursed his lips. "Coincidental, perhaps. Anyway, I managed to get myself invited to dinner."

"But how? They might be peculiar, but surely they don't invite every Tom, Dick, and Harry who comes into the gallery back to their house for dinner."

"I had leverage: I bought three paintings. Gave them the impression there was more where that came from, obviously had them believing I had a good deal of money."

"Have you?"

"Yes. "

"What did you buy?"

"Do you know Ralph Rees? One of his."

"Not one of the *snow* contraptions? Not one of *those?*" She clamped her hand to her forehead in mock horror. "I can't believe you'd do that. You seem sensible enough."

"I am. I purchased it for a friend who favors white."

"He certainly must."

"She."

"She admires things virginal, does she?"

"Hardly."

"All this makes me thirsty. Would you like some tea? Or a drink?" Melrose declined, and she sat back and fingered a ball of yarn. "That poor boy," she said, sighing.

"I beg your pardon?"

"Ralph Rees. I do feel sorry for him." She shook her head.

"Why? Because he's not any good?"

"Oh, no. Because he *is*. You see that portrait of me? It was just a little while before Clive died that he said he wanted a portrait of me as the character I'd played in our last production." She sighed, remembering.

Melrose got up to look at the portrait on the opposite wall. "I can hardly believe it!"

"Understandable, seeing me now. I was younger then." Mona rose and joined him.

"No, no. I'm talking about Rees's painting."

"Oh. Yes, if all you've seen of his work is that ridiculous stuff in the gallery. It's just beyond me, it really is. I couldn't help it, I simply told him he'd taken a wrong turning."

"I don't understand why he would change so dramatically."

"He claims his portraits were facile. They're too representational."

"That's generally what portraits are supposed to be," said Melrose dryly. "What would he say about John Singer Sargent? Too facile? Too easy?"

"I said much the same thing. You see this small one, this scene in Surrey? That's Ralph's too."

It was a traditional sort of British landscape, sheep in a summertime meadow, a wagon filled with hay. "Yes, this is something I wouldn't mind hanging up at all. Do you know him well?"

"No, not really. I ran into him the first of the year and he told me he was doing something entirely different."

"If he was talking about his *Siberian Snow*, he was certainly telling the truth. Do the Fabricant brothers have much influence over him?"

"Certainly. They have a gallery, after all."

"Oh, but no decent painter is going to change his entire approach just to see his work displayed."

"Why not? Writers become hacks to sell books, don't they?"

Melrose shook his head. "Probably they were hacks to begin with." He leaned closer to the painting to look at the country scene. "Anyway, in this case, it would be the other way round, wouldn't it? Those white paintings aren't commercially viable; it's his other stuff that is. This agreeable little painting could find a buyer very quickly."

"I suppose so. His portraits were well regarded. And so young — in his mid-twenties — when he did mine."

They stood in silence for a few moments, contemplating the group of paintings. "Is this Matisse an original?"

"Yes. The Mary Cassatt isn't, though. It's a very good copy, a self-portrait."

Melrose nodded and inspected another Impressionist painting, Monet or Manet, possibly, which showed a large gathering of people in the open air. He was struck by the similarity of several of the subjects, such as the two little girls at the center. "Whose is this?"

"Manes. It's called — oh, something in

the Tuileries Gardens."

They were silent for a few moments. He was trying to think of some way to approach the subject of the murder, when she helped him.

"My sable coat on a murder victim." She shivered slightly. "Hard to believe."

"I imagine. But . . . why did you give it to Olivia Inge?"

"She needed money, but I couldn't simply give her money. I told her if she didn't much fancy fur she should go ahead and sell it. Olivia's not well-off financially, and I knew she wouldn't take any from me, but I thought that might be something she could convert to cash."

"So you weren't surprised when she sold it."

"Not at all. I don't think I'd have taken it to a consignment shop, though. That did surprise me. She got two or three thousand for it. And the shop, of course, got its commission. Still, it's hard to imagine a person with that kind of cash to spend would be *in* a consignment shop. That's what surprises me."

"You don't have much to do with the Fabricants, then?"

"No. I have no reason to. It would be strange for me to want to be around

Clive's second wife. Particularly when she's Ilona Kuraukov. But they are not as disinterested in me as they might appear to be. They like to put Pansy in my way."

Melrose frowned. "I'm sorry?"

"Money, dear boy, money. They seem to have some idea I'd settle a large part of it on Pansy. Because of Clive, you see. They seem to want me to regard Pansy as Clive's granddaughter, which she isn't. Seb took the Fabricant name when his mother married Clive. That does not make Pansy any sort of blood relation; she's nothing to me. She doesn't even like me." She was interrupted by a rather fearsome banging on a door somewhere out of sight. "That'll be a delivery from the grocer. His boy does like to make as much ruckus as possible. Please excuse me."

Melrose nodded and watched her go. He then fell to contemplating the people in the Tuileries painting. He was struck by its seeming to be a collective portrait and, again, how much these men in top hats and beards resembled one another, as the two little girls in their full sashed dresses seemed so alike.

But his thoughts were interrupted by the entrance of a girl of around nine or ten, who set about looking under the chair opposite. Then she made quite a production out of rising from her near-prone position, ignoring his presence, and getting down to look under the sofa.

"What are you doing?" Melrose decided to be direct.

"I'm looking for my cat. He's a ginger cat."

"There are plenty of charming surfaces for him to lie on. Why would he shove himself under a chair or a sofa?"

Still on her stomach, she said, "I don't know. I'm not a cat. His name's Horace." She got up and, with her hands on her hips, rotated her head slowly to take in the charming surfaces. Then she dropped down again to look under the other slip-covered chair.

Given her apparent disregard for him, Melrose could only assume she had come into the room to inspect him. "You wouldn't by any chance in the world, by the most incredible coincidence, by the longest shot imaginable, and in line with my usual great good luck, be Linda Pink?"

"Yes!" This word was shouted from under the chair, where her head was.

"I admire your enthusiasm for yourself, but would you get up off the floor?"

She did, and so quickly that the air

seemed jarred by her presence.

At that moment a really big, drab, scuffed-up cat, which had clearly gone the rounds with neighboring cats, came in and took up a position by her side.

"Horace, where've you been?"

"Having a kip in a dustbin, it looks like."

Horace, insulted, swayed off with his chin in the air.

"Why don't you sit down?" Melrose asked, sitting himself.

"I don't know."

Why were children always so literal? "It wasn't actually a question, Miss Pink. It was more of a request. So that I can ask you a few questions."

"Are you a policeman too?" she asked, without sitting down.

Melrose debated lying but, unable to see the consequences of this, either good or bad, decided not to. "No. But I'm best friends with one you've talked to already." He had always thought the "best friends" concept really packed a punch with children.

"With one of those Scotland Yard ones?"

"Yes."

"He's my favorite policeman."

"Mine too." Melrose looked over his

shoulder. "What happened to your aunt, anyway?"

"She's out in the kitchen talking to Billy. He's always got all these problems and talks a lot. What kind of questions?"

"Things about the herb garden, you know, where you saw this bod— ah, lady. There seems to be some question about when you saw her and where she was lying."

"In the lad's-love. It was around seven o'clock, I guess."

"Aren't we close to Fulham Palace here?"

"Yes, it's only over there." She pointed off in a vague direction. Was he worth the trouble?

"Listen: If it's all right with your aunt, would you like to take a walk there? And perhaps find an ice-cream vendor. I'm sure they must have a refreshment place, for all the tourists."

She stopped plumb in her tracks and stared at him.

Good heavens, he *was* worth it!

Melrose put his plan for a walk before Mona Dresser, who agreed to it. Melrose said he could perfectly understand if she thought it might not be good for Linda to return to the scene of the crime. He supposed there would still be tape around the place and they wouldn't be able to venture too near it.

Out of earshot, Mona said Linda had been questioned by so many policemen, and had of course been talking about little else, that she saw nothing against it. "But I don't think you'll learn anything new. She's very certain of her story; Linda can be quite stubborn."

Really? Melrose raised his eyebrows.

"You lead," said Melrose, once they were out.

Was there any doubt that Linda would do otherwise? She was already ten paces ahead of him.

"Wait at the curb!" he ordered.

This got him a look reserved for fools.

"Where are we?" He was casting glances about as if they'd left civilization behind.

"Bishops Park Road," she answered, half running ahead.

When had they left the Fulham Road? Melrose had always loved the way London streets simply left off being what they were and started being something else, as if naming streets were nothing but whim. The Fulham Road lay more or less between the King's Road and the Brompton Road. Fulham was in SW6, and just off most of the maps of Central London, as if it had nearly made it but not quite and so had been banished to the outback that tourists don't visit. It hadn't that chic Belgravia look to it, where the bright sun fell across the pavement in spatters of gold coins. Nor had it the élan of Chelsea, or even the bedraggled charm of flowery South Kensington, which it bordered.

"We're here!" called Linda, as if the imposing stone gate piers were invisible to him. Then, moving off in another direction, she called, "We can get ice cream!"

The refreshments were located just a short distance from the gates. Melrose asked, "Do you want your ice cream now or when we leave?" This caused her face to pinch up with such a look of pained indecision, he knew they'd be stopping here all day if he didn't say, "Or both?"

Happy with that solution, she gave her order for a chocolate ice-cream cone, all the while looking with such longing at a glass jar holding candy sticks that he bought her one of those too. They returned to the gates and the grounds. Licking her cone, Linda had on her face the mesmerized look that cats get when lapping up bowls of milk.

They walked through the gate piers, and Melrose felt immersed in that left-the-world-behind feeling that washes over one on the other side of gated grounds. Perhaps one thought of all gates as symbolic of a passage from one life zone to another. (*You are leaving SW3 for SW10, which has been freshly renovated for your pleasure.*) For one thing, the familiar noises of children yelling, traffic rushing, sirens, and bells were so diminished that they might have been part of the old frayed world unraveling.

Beside him, Linda carefully sculpted her cone as painstakingly as if she were Rodin. "The Palace Museum's right up that road a little."

"I don't —"

"We've got to get maps."

"Is this uncharted territory?" said Melrose. "Anyway, you know where everything is."

"Almost. But you want to know about how the herb garden's laid out, don't you?"

As if she hadn't got it memorized, he thought, as he followed her into the cool environs of the little museum, which was composed simply of two or three rooms in what had been one of the wings of the palace. That building was itself so utterly unimposing — just a large squarish brick building — that he hoped people didn't come here thinking they'd find another Hampton Court or Versailles. But of course they wouldn't visit Fulham for that; he believed the poster on the pillar one passed to go to the museum: LONDON'S BEST-KEPT SECRET.

They went inside and entered a room overseen by a pleasant-looking woman to whom (obviously) Linda was no stranger. She sat overseeing the guides, cards, booklets, and maps and greeted Linda as if she were family: *Hel-lo, dear, is this a friend of yours?*

Melrose should have brought along his hoop and stick. He wondered if the discovery of a body in the knot garden out there somewhere had put a damper on business. Increased it, probably. He asked her.

The lady seemed at one remove from them, as if she had one foot in the museum and one in a better world altogether. *Oh, for a day or two. But you know how things are so soon forgotten, how transitory and ephemeral they are.* And she went on with this sort of talk until Melrose wondered if the ghosts of all the bishops of London were using her as a sounding board. But she seemed content enough and looked on everything around her (including Time, including them), speaking of the comings and goings of seasons and people as if she had already left this vale of tears and found a vista far finer. Melrose thanked her and tightly folded a twenty-pound bill into a small square and pushed it down in the Fulham Palace fund collection box.

Outside again, their walk took them by trees of every imaginable sort. He wouldn't have known any of them except for the giant oak and — in a generic way only — the pines, if he hadn't had the botanical garden tree map. They passed cedars, oaks, several kinds of maple, a giant redwood, and a sweet gum, and off on the other side were probably a dozen others.

"It's around here," Linda said, walking backwards.

"There must be forty or fifty different kinds of trees," Melrose said.

"There are. Come on."

The tree question put to bed, he followed her inside a large walled garden, which looked now, in November, unkempt, stiff and stale, heavy with brush. The knot garden that figured so prominently in this odd case was before them. To its left was a long quarter-moon-shaped fence with wisteria vine climbing its entire length and breadth. The fragrance must be, in the spring, simply heavenly, especially overlain as it would be with the infusion of scent coming from the herb garden. On the right was a glass house that had, he supposed, been a greenhouse but was now fallen into a state of total decay, glass broken, walls listing or collapsing. No wonder there was a fund for raising money. There was also a vinery, the old vines looking as hard and old and unyielding as hemp.

The garden itself was a fish shape, pointed at either end, widest in the middle. Where the fish's head might have been was an herb called feverfew. (Melrose had never heard of it and made a mental note to speak to Sergeant Wiggins.) At the other end, the tail end, was a triangular patch of thyme. He held the drawing out, noticing how the various patches of herbs on the one side were repeated both in shape and kind on the other. There were two patches of each herb. Top and bottom, end and end, were mirror images of each other. He was brought out of contemplating the mechanics of the design by Linda.

"Look!"

He looked across a circular patch of tansy and saw her lying in brown brush.

He walked around and asked her what the devil she was doing.

"I'm being her, the dead body." She lay with arms outstretched and face up.

"You shouldn't be lying in the —" He consulted the herb map.

"Lad's-love. Wait," she said. "Her eyes were open. Like this." Linda opened hers wide, ghoulishly.

"You have a brilliant future ahead of you as a scene-of-crimes expert."

"They said it was the lavender patch, but it wasn't."

Melrose kneeled down and looked at the patch of lad's-love. "Look, the police are usually very exact, they take pictures and measurements and just about everything. Could you have made a mistake?"

"No." She brushed a few twiglets and dead leaves from her hair.

"I'm going in there for a moment." He nodded towards the vinery.

He walked around inside the decaying glass house — or, at least, as much of an "inside" as it had, for what there was now was almost completely exposed to the weather. There was a bothy and a small building that had served as a potting shed. He moved through shards of pottery, pieces of glass. He stood turning over half of a clay pot, knowing he wouldn't find anything, for the Fulham police would have scoured the place thoroughly.

The trouble with the Fulham police was that they were trusting no one but their own findings. Understandable, he supposed; they certainly weren't trusting the report of a ten-year-old.

Still. If she'd gone close enough to see that the eyes were open, if she'd been that free of confusion, Melrose was willing to believe she knew just where the body had lain and when it had lain there.

23

It didn't surprise Melrose that the Crippses weren't on the phone, or, on second thought, it did. Ashley Cripps by now should have figured out a way to ambush the neighbors' telephone service, as he had done their electric. He was very good with wires. But perhaps it would take climbing up a pole, and Ash wasn't one to exert himself.

Melrose had tried the Museum of Childhood, where Bea Slocum worked, and been told that Saturday was her half day. If Bea had a telephone in her Bethnal Green flat, it wasn't listed. The next stop in his search for her was the Cripps family — though "family" in this case was not to be taken as the unit social services had in mind — as Bea was some kind of distant cousin and (if her painting was any indication) had a fondness for Catchcoach Street.

At the moment, Melrose was in a sandwich bar in Canary Wharf, seated on a stool and staring at the Thames, which appeared to be standing still, in tune perhaps with Melrose's own mental state. (He was big on the pathetic fallacy; he took his sympathy where he could find it.) He had considered eating one of the tautly wrapped sandwiches perched behind the glass but decided tea was all he wanted. Anyway, why would one of these doughty office workers want sun-dried tomato in with his cheddar? This was apparently nouveau-plowman's fare.

So his tea was getting cold as he thought about his visit to Fulham Palace. He had thought a wander about the rejuvenated Docklands might revive his flagging mental processes, but no ideas had come. Nor had the Thames budged an inch. He wondered what Wordsworth had gotten so excited about. He left the sandwich bar and searched out a newsagent's and sweet shop to fill up his pockets with bags of candy.

The Cripps kiddies were in the front "garden" (a euphemism in this case), rampant as moles or gophers, even in the near-dark. Or perhaps especially so, since the habits of the Crippses might best be relegated to the dark. Moles and gophers, though, at least spent a lot of their time underground.

Stopping on the pavement some yards from the house, he watched them at their ghastly games. More than one was taking place. Given there were seven of them, there were enough kids to go around.

The baby pram had been placed near the front door and then forgotten by Mum, leaving the baby to its fate. Two of the kiddies, boy and girl, were rocking it — not by way of appeasing the baby (who was letting out a high, thin wail) but as a way of competing to see which side could topple the carriage first. Any non-Crippsians would have checked to see the pram was empty before embarking on such foolishness. The Crippses, however, would check to see it was full.

Melrose had forgotten most of their names (a mercy to himself), but he recalled that one of the girls was Amy and one Alice. He believed it was Alice on the pram, competing with her brother. It amazed Melrose that any baby could survive in the Cripps family. But, just look, six of them certainly had — seven, counting the baby. So far.

Another boy of five or six, twin of one of the girls, was easy to recognize as Piddlin' Pete. Right now he had his pants down and was pissing into the plastic birdbath. His sister Amy (or Alice) acted in counterpoint. Her favorite trick was to hold up her skirt and let anyone interested know that she wasn't wearing knickers. Another boy was tied to a tree, while the oldest of them marched round it with a flaming torch, throwing off eerie shadows in the encroaching dark. Good lord, what was all of that newspaper and kindling bunched at his feet?

The position of the carriage was becoming more and more precarious, and the baby's howl more frightening, which naturally made the two Crippses on it laugh all the louder. Melrose threw caution to the winds (though he made sure he had the candy spills before advancing) and walked towards the house.

It was the oldest one, as stout and pugnacious as his da, and with the Crippses' signature sandy hair and eyelashes and whey-colored skin, who saw Melrose first. He dropped the torch (fortunately not on the kindling, but into one of the many holes in the earth) and set up a yell. They all stopped what they were doing (except for the one tied to the tree) and stared.

"Elroy! *Elroy!*" He turned towards the house and yelled even louder, " 'Ey, Mum, Elroy's here!"

Then they all rushed him, all except Piddlin' Pete, who grabbed at his crotch, not in the way small boys sometimes do, betokening anxiety, but with the clear intention of pointing his sprig of a penis towards the visitor.

"Whatcha got, Elroy?" *"Give us some sweets, Elroy, go on!"* *"I ain't got n't'un underneath, see?"* *"Go on, Elroy, gi' us them sweets!"*

Melrose drew out the little bags and began dispensing them, negotiating for information. "Tell me, is Bea Slocum here?"

Having secured for himself the largest bag, full of lemon sherbets, the oldest, toughest one could afford to dispense with the formalities of welcome. "Mebbe she is, mebbe she ain't. Who wants t'know?"

"Me, obviously."

Having whisked the last little white bag, this one containing Gummy Bears, from Melrose's hand, Piddlin' Pete was now marching about singing, "Bea, Bea, pee, pee, pee."

"I shouldn't try it, were I you. Not if you want to live to see another urinal." It occurred to Melrose that lack of a urinal held no horror for Piddlin' Pete. Obviously, he had inherited this obsession with his private parts from his father, Ashley, long known in police circles as Ash the Flash.

Then the door was thrown open and White Ellie filled it with her huge, slack, aproned self, waving a spatula. "Look 'oo's 'ere! I was tellin' Ash t'other day, 'I do wish that Melrose'd not be makin' it so long between visits.' Put that skirt down, gurl!" This was directed at Alice (or Amy).

Melrose said, passing through the door, "Just call me Elroy."

White Ellie chuckled richly as she shoved the pram through and picked up the baby, out of harm's way for another few minutes. "Robespierre, 'ere, remember 'im?"

"I certainly do," he said, regarding the calm, un-Crippsian little face of the baby — bigger, fatter — he recalled having rocked in his arms. The Cripps household had a strange effect on people, at least on him it did.

As the six kiddies steamed into the parlor, White Ellie barked useless commands as to how they should comport themselves. Then she dumped the baby back into the pram, gave it a motherly jiggle as she squinched up her eyes in some sort of baby greeting, and turned back towards the kitchen. "I'm just doin' Ashley's tea; he'll be back soon, I expect. Bea's in there. I expect you remember Bea?"

Beatrice Slocum sat slumped all the way down on her spine on the sprung, cabbage-rose-covered sofa, watching a huge battered television. After loudly announcing to Bea that Elroy was here again, the kids settled in front of the telly and declared a time-out to eat their sweets. This deceptive calm would last only for two minutes, so Melrose hoped he could keep her attention.

"Well, I'll be a monkey's," said Bea. "Look who's 'ere. There been another murder, then?" At which she fixed her attention on the telly again.

Or pretended to. Melrose thought her try at indifference was taking some effort, for the ho-hum did not reach her eyes, which were ordinarily a cool green, lighter than his own, less dense, registering more delight when she was pleased. It was the delight she was unable to keep out of them now, even as one of the kiddies was pummeling the other with a sofa pillow, enough to revive all of their energy. Pillows were being tossed and pulled, which inspired them, somehow, to start marching in a ring and chanting.

"Yes, as a matter of fact, there has been another one."

Bea had witnessed the death of a woman in the Tate Gallery; she had been questioned by Jury and then by Melrose over a pleasant dinner in a French restaurant. He had been hoping she'd forget the murder, remember the dinner.

"Bloody 'ell!" she exclaimed. "So I expect you and that mate of yours'll be at me and at me." False yawn.

"Why should we? You weren't there this time. But you still might be able to help."

"Oh, well, I wouldn't ever want to miss a chance to do that, would I?" She reached out the TV remote and clicked through the channels, which the goblin gang on the floor loudly protested, even though they hadn't been watching.

"I thought perhaps we could have dinner again. We could dine at my club."

"Your *wot?*"

She'd got so much of North London into that syllable she might have been practicing. Bea's accent went up and down, like Alice's skirt.

"Stuffy old men's club? Not bloody likely, me." She slumped farther down in the sofa. "Anyway, those places don't admit women."

"All that's changed."

"Not for the likes of me, I'll bet." She

said this smugly, as if nonadmittance at his club would be a point of pride.

It amused Melrose that she took satisfaction in this. "Perhaps not the way you're got up right now —"

Bea tossed the remote control aside and looked at him in open-mouthed astonishment that he would take exception to her costume, then turned her gaze to her combat boots and cut-off jeans. She pinched up a bit of the black turtleneck top. "I'm stylish, me. I saw in the *Telegraph* t'other day a picture of a runway model wearing almost exactly the same thing, except her boots had studs and she had on a rhinestone belt. And great, dripping rhinestone earrings. Far as I'm concerned, that just cheapens a person." While delivering this flash from the world of fashion, she had pulled a copy of *Elle* from somewhere in the laundry beside her, wet a finger, and turned one of its slick pages.

"Suit yourself," said Melrose. It was what Bea always said to demonstrate her lack of interest.

Now, seeing she might have encouraged him to withdraw his invitation, she said, "Wait a tic; I can always borrow something from White Ellie."

That should be improvement on a global

scale, thought Melrose, as Bea leaned forward and yelled Ellie's name.

No one need shout, though, for White Ellie was coming in even now, bearing tea in thick white mugs. " 'Ere, wet yerselfs." She handed one mug to Melrose and one to Bea, and herself sat down in a cloud of dust sifting up from a nearby easy chair, holding her own mug aloft.

Bea said, "I just wondered could I borrow that sleeveless-top thing you bought at the Bring 'n' Buy?"

"That orangey one? Just see it don't get stained, is all."

Melrose was curious. " 'Bring 'n' Buy'? Around here? That's one of those booths you see at church fetes."

"Well, we got — you kids, get out now. Leave us grown-ups to talk." They all clattered (what did they have that would make such a noise?) to their feet. Piddlin' Pete was using a bucket strategically placed to catch water dripping from the ceiling, while Alice lifted her skirt. Ellie gave both of them a good slap on their behinds. Of course, this energized the other four into marching round in a ring, chanting:

"Piddlin' Pete, Piddlin' Pete
Piddlin' all over Elroy's feet!"

Quickly, Melrose looked down at his shoes. Just missed his, but hit Bea's boot.

"Bleedin' lil blighter!" yelled Bea, as she pulled a rag that might once have been a vest from the laundry pile and wiped the toe of her boot. "Be back in a tic," she announced, and took the steps two at a time.

White Ellie screamed after the chanting kids, all six marching single file from the parlor, "An' 'is name ain't *Elroy!* How many times 'ave I got to *tell* ya?"

The chant continued through the front door.

Answering Melrose's question, White Ellie said, "We 'ave them fetes every other Sunday. Right back there in St. Ignatius. It's Ash got the idea. Clever lad, is Ash." She clucked her tongue in appreciation. "If only he'd get outa 'is 'abit of goin' down into the public toilets." She sighed at this chink in the Ashley armor. "Anyways, it's just like one o' them marketplaces in Algiers. What with all them Pakis and wogs. Yeah, him and Eddie — you met Eddie — they got this sideline, you know, pickin' up stuff people don't want —"

(Out of their parked cars and empty houses, mused Melrose.)

"— and they gotta 'ave a place t' sell it."

Melrose frowned. "Isn't that just a bit

dangerous? Right out in the open?"

White Ellie thought this was rich and laughed and slapped her big thigh. "That's t' beauty of it, ain't it? Is the Bill goin' to go lookin' for merchandise at a Bring 'n' Buy? Out in plain view, that's what Ash says." She tapped her temple. "Bright lad, is Ashley. Bit o' a wide lad, but bright."

With this, Bea came running down the stairs, wearing Ellie's Bring 'n' Buy spoils.

Melrose was astonished. The so-called "orangey thing" wasn't really orange but a sort of burnt orange, a copper color. It was a long beltless velvet garment, a vest that reached nearly to the floor. It was quite transforming. The transformation was also owing to Bea's having toned down her makeup by replacing the purple eyeshadow with a pale brown and applying a bit of blusher. Her changed hair color, the autumnal, leafy shades, was enhanced by the copper vest. He would not have been too surprised to see this rather daring combination of copper coat, cut-off jeans, and boots in a designer's fall collection. Bea was right, it could take a run down the runway.

"You look very Boring's," said Melrose.

24

Boring's had indeed relaxed one or more of its stringent rules, and this included admitting women. The Committee had gone round and round on this one, for it was not so much the *admission* of women as it was what they were going to do with them once they got in. It was the view of at least one member that, having got in, the lady should stand no more than six feet from the door until the gentleman whose friend she was had readied himself for his exit from the reading room and, with the lady in tow, from the club itself.

There were dissenters here. One could hardly call this the spirit of letting them "in." One could not allow the woman to simply stand cooling her heels. They should at least provide a chair by the door so she could sit down.

And there were one or two who wanted to go whole hog and allow the dining room doors to be thrown open to these female "guests." This was the proposal advanced by the youngest Committee member, one

who would have been declined member-
ship had his name not been on the list
since birth, and who was the heir apparent
(or, as the wags called him, "heir rampant") to an earldom and himself a viscount. Naturally, the old earl was a
member but seldom was in good enough
shape to visit London. So they all compro-
mised and decided to allow women as
"guests" for a trial period of ten years,
and, the arrangement being found to be
satisfactory, would then implement this
new ruling. Ten years should be long
enough "to get the kinks out."

Melrose had been told all of this by the
viscount himself the evening before, while
he'd been waiting for Jury.

"Has it worked to the members' satisfaction, then?"

"Seems to've," said the viscount. "Of
course, there are very few who want the
company of the ladies anyway."

Here they both looked round at the gentlemen in various stages of decrepitude
who were occupying the leather armchairs
and sofas. Then the viscount sat back and
smoked his cheroot, and Melrose sipped
his well-chilled seven-to-one martini and
thought about Diane Demorney.

Thus Bea Slocum, in her boots and

velvet vest, would have created quite a stir, had anyone wanted to be stirred. She looked around her, said "blimey" a few dozen times, and added it looked just like what she'd've thought it would. She indicated a white-haired gent fallen asleep with his head sideways over papers and port. "I guess that'll be you one of these days."

"I'm sure. Would you care for an aperitif?"

"No, but I wouldn't say no to a drink. Whisky, I'll have."

Melrose raised a hand to Young Higgins, who tottered over with his silver tray pushed to his chest like a shield and took their drink orders. He raised a gray eyebrow slightly when Bea said to make sure it was a single malt, not because this bespoke a long acquaintance with drink, but with drink of a lesser quality than Boring's was used to. He then went weaving back.

"Okay, so what'd you want me to look at?"

Melrose got up, saying, "Wait here; I'll be back in a second."

As he made his way up the fine broad staircase, he thought of Bea in her Bring 'n' Buy vest and how she had changed on him again. She had changed the first time when he'd discovered she painted and was not the little North London chit she wanted to give the impression of being. Over steak and potatoes *frites,* she had talked about J.M.W. (as she called Turner). Bea was also a lover of light. Now she had changed again, from one who painted into a painter.

The painting he had purchased was leaning against the wall, where the amber light of a wall sconce fell across its upper part yet did nothing to enhance pigments already so lit from within that lamplight became irrelevant. He carried it downstairs.

Melrose propped the painting up against the chair he'd been sitting in and watched the astonishment register in Bea's face.

She looked from the painting to Melrose and back again, her fist balled on her breastbone. Her voice, when she finally spoke, was tiny. "I'll be a monkey's." She opened her mouth to say something but instead, playing for time, took a swig of the malt whisky that the old porter had brought while Melrose was upstairs.

"It's marvelous," said Melrose.

Bea gave a little disbelieving laugh. "I guess I never did think I'd even sell one. And you went and paid five hundred quid for it?"

"As a matter of fact, Bea, it's my opinion it was undervalued. This is the best thing in that gallery." He did not tell her he had also purchased *The Storm*. That might seem as if he were simply trying to patronize her.

Bea was leaning forward and studying her painting, all manner of expression ranging across her face. There was doubt, as if she saw even now things that should be put right; there was pleasure at the things that *were* right. She seemed to grow increasingly oblivious to her surroundings. Her look was consuming.

This, he was sure, was the real Beatrice Slocum.

The assumed one was quick to resurrect itself. As if pretending to disinherit the painting, she drew back and cocked her head, saying, "I've seen better."

"So have I; only they're not for sale."

She flapped her hand at him. "Ah, go on."

"Beatrice, your painting is *by far* the best thing the Fabricants have on offer."

Before she could reply, Young Higgins came to call them to dinner. He carried their drinks for them, on a tray. Bea carried the painting.

The menu pleased Bea because filet

mignon was one of the choices, that and chips — or *frites* — a particular favorite of hers. Bea pointed out that this was just what she'd had for dinner at Dotrice, the little French restaurant.

Young Higgins came to take their order and didn't blink an eye when Bea ordered "steak and chips," whereas the French waiter at Dotrice had cut her a look that could have sliced the steak all by itself. Well, thought Melrose, breeding shows. He was rather proud of Young Higgins and intended to leave him a very large tip.

Bea asked, "What'd you mean you hoped I was tight with the Fabricant brothers? All I know is I should be grateful they'd hang my stuff."

"No. They should be grateful you let them. What I can't understand is the incredible lapse of taste they've shown in hanging those paintings by Ralph Rees."

"That white lot?"

"That white lot, yes."

Other diners had come in while they were ordering. Melrose smiled and nodded a greeting to Major Champs and Colonel Neame. They looked at Bea in a sort of wonder, as if they hadn't truly expected things to come to this. Cutlery clattered, glassware tinkled, napkins snapped. Melrose always thought these to be comforting sounds. The dining room was richly lighted, and the chandelier cast a glare across the snow-white tables.

It brought Melrose back to his subject. "*Siberian Snow.*" He shook his head.

"Well, I expect it's because Ralph is Nick's you-know."

"The Fabricant Gallery hasn't built its reputation by indulging their you-knows. No. There's something else." Melrose talked about his visit of the day before until Young Higgins appeared with their wine, a Bordeaux he had advised against as being a bit too lively. With somber aspect, he awaited Melrose's judgment on the wine's "liveliness." Melrose told him he would make every effort not to dance on the table and to go ahead and pour the wine.

Bea's attention was easily drawn from wine to food when their soup arrived. "Pumpkin. I never had pumpkin soup before." She spooned it up. "Umm. It's good." She had several spoonfuls before she said, "Thing is, a person's got his blind spots." She looked at him.

"Don't look at me as if I'm one of yours, thank you."

She smiled and went back to her soup. "I

mean the gallery. There's no accounting for taste." She took a sip of her soup and lightly tapped the spoon on the bowl, as if summoning up the soup spirits.

"There had better be accounting for artistic taste, or they'll be out of jobs."

They ate in companionable silence for a while.

Young Higgins appeared with their steaks and Bea's potatoes *frites.* He removed the soup bowls, set down the platters, and asked Melrose if they required anything else at the moment. Melrose told him, no, they were fine.

He watched Bea cut her steak into mouse bites, which she then forked into her mouth — one, two, three — chewed, swallowed, and said, "Listen, maybe it's the old lady."

Melrose stopped cutting his own filet to give her a questioning look.

"The old lady. You know, Seb and Nick's mum."

"Ah! I'd hardly put Ilona Kuraukov in the category of old lady. But what about her?"

"Only that she puts up a lot of money, you know, for the gallery."

Melrose wondered. "How'd you discover that?"

"From Ralph. He took me down the pub to celebrate I got in the gallery. He's nice like that, Ralph is. Anyway, he went on about how much he liked my work, even if his own was more avant-garde, and how I was more of a realist, whatever people mean when they say that."

"Probably that we unartistic yobs can recognize things in your paintings."

Bea seemed to be thinking this over. She shrugged. "Anyway, Ralph was getting more and more boozed up and started going on about how generous this old — what's her name?"

"Kuraukov."

"He said she puts up more than half for that gallery."

That was interesting. Perhaps it explained the impression he'd received of Ilona's influence over the others, and not just Olivia Inge, who was there, possibly, at the older woman's sufferance. "And did he say if she dictates what art they hang on the walls?"

"No. I mean, he didn't say." Daintily, as one who had been made overconscious of poor table manners but was still uncertain as to what they were, she picked up one of the strawlike potatoes and put it in her mouth. After she'd swallowed, she said,

"Thing is, seeing we're not up on his school of art, well, how would we know if Ralph's stuff was good or not?"

"And with that assessment, she plunged a century of criticism into total darkness."

Bea screwed up her face. Her resemblance to a baby monkey was endearing. "Say what?"

"The 'school' doesn't precede the artwork, it follows it."

"Ain't you the expert, then."

"It's common sense. The paintings make the school, not the school the paintings. Do you imagine Monet woke up one morning and said, 'Maybe I'll just try something new; a pointillist style might be nice.'"

"Seurat, you mean."

He smiled. Her correction had been automatic, not pretentious. It was difficult for her to profess ignorance, though that seemed to be what she wanted to do.

"Listen, Bea, I could really use your help."

Bea looked up from her steak. "What you gone and done, then?"

"Nothing." He was surprised he was glad at the look of alarm on her face. "It's the Fabricants I'm talking about. And Ralph, in particular. You have more access than I to that gallery —"

"You want me to nick something, is that it?"

"Of course not." His self-righteous tone was largely owing to his having some vague plans of the nicking variety. "All I mean is that you've got a reason for hanging out there."

She chewed, looking at him in a noncomprehending, bovine way, which he was sure she knew annoyed him and enjoyed doing for that reason. "Well?" she finally said. "Hang about doing what?"

"Listening. I'm especially interested in Ralph's snow sequence."

"The white lot."

"Yes. You're a painter. Where's the art in it?"

"Dunno. Far as I'm concerned, there ain't none." She had finished and shoved her plate away. "That was good."

"It's hard to believe Sebastian Fabricant sees anything in them, either."

"Well, I guess maybe we're wrong and he's right. But somebody must believe it. There's at least one buyer interested in a couple of 'em; more money than I'll see this year if Ralph sells 'em all."

"Yes, I heard about that."

"Uh-huh. Ralph says it's a collector. An

American, I think."

"This is a man I'd like to meet."

"All I know is, old Ralph's ecstatic." Bea was craning her neck for a better look at the dessert trolley. "You want a sweet, then? That pud looks good." She watched the trolley making its slow circuit of the diners.

Melrose made a sign to the young waiter with the spiky hair who was overseeing it. "Since those paintings are welded together — supposedly — as a 'progression,' you'd think having them go their separate ways would disturb him." He did not mention that he himself had purchased one, perhaps because he was afraid it would make Bea think he had a hidden agenda in buying *hers*.

"Ralph says each one can stand on its own."

"I've never known such an accommodating artist." Melrose shook his head as the trolley rolled over.

"Um. I like the looks of that chocolate gâteau, too." She frowned over the choices. "What kind of pudding's that?" she asked, poking her finger towards a dome-shaped, whipped-cream laden, rich-looking pudding.

"Queen of Puddings, that one is." The

young waiter sounded a little breathless, as if he'd been waiting in the wings for just such a chance as this. "And here's a plum and hazelnut torte. This one's a Floating Island." His finger moved to the lower tier of the trolley. "This is a Lemon Semolina gâteau. And, of course, the chocolate, and also the Chocolate Mousse Boring's."

Melrose was unaware that Boring's had a signature dessert and asked for that, while Bea pondered and pondered. He only wished she'd devote as much loving attention to the Fabricant issue.

"I'll just have that." She pointed to the Queen of Puddings.

Happily, the waiter set about serving up generous portions of the desserts, took Melrose's order for coffee in the lounge, and left them.

Melrose asked her, "Now if you set about painting a series, wouldn't you feel it was like cutting up the baby to have them separated?"

"I never wanted to paint one. This is good; how's yours?" She poked her fork at Melrose's mousse.

"Divine. Worthy of the name Boring's." He hadn't yet tasted it. "Those paintings in the back room. Is it usual to keep a stash of paintings hanging about until you need them? I mean, until the gallery does?"

"I guess they keep them, so when they sell one, they have another to put up. They've got two of mine back there." She licked the pudding from her spoon and then put her hand on the frame of the picture, which she'd insisted they carry with them to the dining room, as if it, too, might be hungry.

Yet she'd said not a word about wanting him to see the two others "back there," as if he'd done so much already she would never expect him to do more. Watching her lovingly patting the frame, Melrose would have thought he'd adopted it, rather than purchased it.

25

She came in and sat down, and he slid the cigarettes across to her. She thanked him. After he had lighted a cigarette for her, he said, "Brussels. You were speaking of the light in the square. You said it was deceptive."

Kate McBride smiled. "You have a remarkable memory."

"So do you. And it's why I'm sure I saw you Saturday night."

She looked at him squarely. "And it's why I'm sure you didn't!"

Jury smiled. "The cafe. Go on."

After another moment she asked, "Do you mind my telling it this way? I mean, exactly the way it was?"

"That's the way I want to hear it."

Still, she needed to justify it. "Because it helps me deal with it, you see. If I can retell details."

Jury nodded, watched her tap ash from her cigarette into the flimsy tin ashtray.

She started to talk. "I sat in the cafe — outside, I mean, at one of the sidewalk tables. It really is quite dazzling, that square at night. I must admit I was able to let go of my anxiety for a few moments, just looking. There were so *many* stars, and the streetlamps. . . ." She smoked. "I sat at this small table, waiting. Feeling helpless." Her shrug seemed to mark another defeat.

"But then?"

"Then a man came, a perfectly ordinary-looking man in a brown overcoat and fedora. He wore steel-rimmed glasses, and his hair was thinning. He sat down at the next table, just as the ordinary-looking woman had done. They might have been brother and sister, they might have been twins. I wouldn't have looked at him twice except I was looking at everyone. He ordered a cassis and unfolded a newspaper. He said, 'Look across the square.' You can imagine how my head fairly snapped around to see him, I was so surprised. He didn't even look at me. I looked across the square. Over there." She raised a hand, pointed.

The strength of her emotion had Jury's eyes following the length of her outstretched arm.

"A dark woman stood there with a child. It was Sophie."

Jury was startled. "You were certain? How —"

She leaned across the table, arms folded on it, eyes burning. The mix of amber and orange and blue flecks made it appear as if they did just that. She asked, "Do you have any children?"

"No." He felt saddened by this answer, as if it were an admission of failure.

She added nothing, only looked at him and then sat back.

Jury said, "I'm sorry. When this person spoke, was he Belgian? French?"

"It's impossible to say. He had that sort of accent — that *non*-accent — that's ironed out, not a wrinkle in it to designate a country or a place. Flat, you know."

"But — Sophie? If you knew *her*, did she — ?"

"Know *me*? I don't know if she saw me. Had she, I think she'd have called out or done something." Kate's chair scraped back and she rose and walked, worrying the ring on her finger. "They did nothing; they gave no sign of seeing me. Then *he* said, and his voice was entirely devoid of emotion, 'We only wanted you to see she's quite all right, that's all.'

"I said, 'Take the money and let her go, for God's sake!' And he told me hysteria was a very bad idea. He actually smiled. It was a grim little smile from a grim little mouth. Then he said, 'It's not the money we want, Mrs. McBride.' I asked him why in God's name he'd told me to bring it, then. He said, 'To see if you'd do it, that's all; to see if you could be trusted.' *Trusted!* Good lord! He said, 'What we want is his papers.'

"Michael had a sensitive position, and he never talked about his work. I knew he'd kept papers in a safe in our living room, and I'd never opened it. That is what I told this strange person. He said, 'I mean the manuscript, Mrs. McBride. We want the manuscript.' " She ran her fingers through her hair, shook another cigarette from the package. "Michael had been writing a book, you see. A novel, he'd told me. I hadn't read any of it. I asked this man why on earth he wanted it. 'Why would you want that? Why would you want his novel?' He turned then and looked at me, and that smile was in place again. 'That's what he told you, was it?'

"I just stared at him. I felt utterly at sea. I thought I'd never understand anything again. What was happening? He studied me for a moment and then went on. 'Outside of Aix-en-Provence there is a château, the Château Noailles —' "

Jury straightened in his chair. "Noailles?"

"Please," she said, holding up her hand, asking him not to interrupt. "He said, 'This is a magnificent château set in some two hundred acres of the loveliest part of Provence. The family — or, to be more specific, Edouard Noailles — is one of the most powerful in France, certainly one of the wealthiest.' He smiled that sardonic smile again. 'As I said, Mrs. McBride, we've no interest in your money. Edouard Noailles, among many other things, is a collector. He has one of the biggest private collections in the world. You do not need to know the details. Only to know that your husband was very much aware of Noailles and his business.'

" 'What has Sophie to do — why are you putting us through this?' I was near to screaming. 'Why?'

" 'But of course it shouldn't have been necessary. It was you who went to the gendarme — for all the good it did you, Mrs. McBride.' He moved for perhaps the first time, leaned across the table and said, 'Now, I trust, you will not bother with police again? It's a simple request. We want only the manuscript and your silence.

That is, if you're rash enough to read it before handing it over.'

"And then he simply got up, said, 'We'll be in touch,' and walked away. He walked away," she repeated, shaking her head.

The cigarette, unsmoked, had burned nearly to the fingers that held it. Jury took it from her hand, flicked it into the ashtray.

When she raised her head and looked at him, it was almost as if she were waiting for him to explain this whole lurid episode. She looked desperate; she looked as if it would take very little to drive her round the bend.

"This priest —" He stopped. She looked up, waiting. "If you saw him —"

Immediately, she shook her head. "It wouldn't do any good. I was never around him, barely saw him after that time in the islands."

"When was this meeting in Brussels?"

She thought for a moment. "Over four months ago. Before I returned to England."

"And did you go back to the police?"

"No, not directly. I was afraid to. And I didn't think it would do any good. You remember I told you there'd been a fire, some of their records had been lost, mine — that is, Sophie's — among them." Ruefully, she looked at Jury. "They'd no record of what had happened." She sighed. "It seemed, somehow, inevitable. Fate, I suppose I mean."

Jury looked at her for a long moment but said nothing.

She shook her head. Then she said, "This woman who was murdered, if she looked that much like me —"

"Someone mistook her for you? It's possible."

"It could hardly be a coincidence, her being there."

"The point is, how did *both* of you come to be there?"

She rose, tiredly, and stood there looking at him. "You still think it was me you saw, don't you?"

Looking at her, seeing the strain she was under, he felt almost guilty for saying it. "I know it was you, Kate."

26

The scratching at the door to Jury's flat, rousing him from a hard-won three hours of sleep, was something like that pervasive dream image of his childhood — skeletal, scrabbling fingers whose owner he never saw. He'd always awakened (blessedly) before that particular detail floated upwards from his unconscious.

Jury lay in a bed that looked as if it had been tossed by a brace of cops with a warrant and wondered, sleepily, if he were still six years old and if everything that he thought had happened over the last several decades had been just that — a dream.

He extricated himself from his mangled bedclothes, and this depressed him further because the cast-off sheets could not be accounted for by the presence of a woman with whom he'd made furious love the night before.

The scratching came again, accompanied by a timpani of tappings. By now he was on his feet and into his boiled-wool dressing gown and was walking barefoot to the door. He knew who it was, of course. Why was she up at — he checked his clock — seven-thirty on a Sunday morning? Especially on a Sunday morning that found him feeling just as bleak as he had on the past Sunday morning. Bleaker, probably. He was no closer to answers to the Fulham Palace business than he'd been then.

He opened the door, and Stone — who'd done the scratching — lowered his paw and dipped his head with a shame-faced expression that wanted to say, It was her made me do it, guv.

"Her" being Carol-anne (who'd done the tapping). She stood there with a string bag in a pool of sunlight whose source Jury could not track and decided it had to be Carole-anne herself. Light must have flared from her incandescent honey-red hair and eyes that could change from cerulean blue to near-purple, reminding Jury of the gradations of color he'd once seen in a view of the sea off Floridian sands. She stood there glowing in a sunflower-yellow dress. Minidress. Very mini, even for Carole-anne.

He shook his head in a wondering way. "You look like a Key West sunrise."

True to her watery Key West origins,

Carole-anne sailed in, flags flying. "Back in February you said I looked like a Santa Fe sunset. Here." She held out the string bag. "I brought you breakfast."

Jury's eyebrows shot up. Not over the string bag but over the fact she had not only remembered the compliment but remembered exactly when it had been delivered. Then he said, "Since when did you ever eat breakfast at seven-thirty on a Sunday morning? And what shop is open at that hour?" He looked at Stone, still waiting patiently — even politely — at the door.

Carole-anne walked to the small kitchen. "It's that Pakistani, Mr. Mashead; you know, the shop on the corner. It's open all hours."

Jury opened a desk drawer and took out the rawhide bone he kept for Stone, though he felt Stone should have something much more upper class. "If we had the manners of Stone we'd all be welcome in the courts of kings."

Jury moved into the kitchen, where Carole-anne had plugged in the kettle and was depositing the contents of the string bag on the counter. "Since when was you ever in Key West?"

Jury yawned. "Never."

"Then how would you know I look like a sunrise?"

"Because of the applause. People see it and applaud. Or so I've heard. Hemingway lived there. In Key West."

"Had to live somewhere, I expect." She took the wrapping from the sausages. There was a half loaf, a carton of orange juice, six eggs.

Jury was starving. "God, I could do with a cuppa."

"Well, I can't make it boil any faster, now, can I?"

"Blow on it."

As if answering a command, the kettle whistled. Carole-anne poured hot water into his chipped teapot, emptied it, then measured in some loose leaves.

"Tea bags are quicker."

She just looked at him. Then she put a bit of butter and oil in the frying pan and turned up the flame.

"It must be ready." He looked longingly at the tea.

"Oh, for heaven's sakes. It ain't even wet hardly. You're in a mood this morning. And if you think I'm about to do this *every* morning, you're barking up the wrong tree, you."

Stone lifted his head from his bone; he

did not like dog metaphors. "And what tree should I be" — Jury regarded Stone — "bellowing up?"

"Where's my apron?" Carole-anne always kept one hanging on a hook in Jury's kitchen.

It made him smile; he found it touching. "Hmm? Can't imagine. In the wash, perhaps?"

"Wash? What would you know about that? I don't think I've once in my life seen you in the launderette. Mrs. W does that for you." She smoothed her hands over her dress. "I don't want to dirty this. It's new."

"It's nice." Did Carole-anne ever look anything but?

"An Armani knockdown."

Jury frowned. If there was one designer he knew, it was Armani. It came from hanging about Marshall Trueblood. "Armani doesn't do yellow, does he?"

"It was probably after he'd been to Key West."

"Ha." Jury opened a cupboard where Mrs. Wassermann liked to stack dishtowels and found the apron, neatly folded, among them. It was a fussy, flowered thing with flounces and ruffles. He shook it out and put the bib over Carole-anne's head.

"Thanks, Super. Tie it, will you?" She

shot out her arms like a child.

The sensation of such close proximity to Carole-anne, so close he could smell her hair, its faint scent of citrus, was far from unpleasant. Too quickly, he stepped back, and overturned the milk jug. Fortunately, it was not full, and Carole-anne swung around, grabbed up some paper towels, and started mopping. "I've got it, not to worry." Wiping the counter, she looked up at him. "You look knackered, Super. You ought to have a bit of a lie-down."

"A bit of a sit-down's what I'll have. Ah. Ta, very much." Carole-anne had poured tea into a mug already replete with milk and two sugars. It was nice having someone around who knew how you took your tea. That had never occurred to him before. He blinked at a sudden dazzlement of sun streaming now though his kitchen window and onto her hair. Real sun, this time, but no brighter.

"You okay?" She frowned slightly, looking up from the sausages she was turning with a fork.

"Huh? Yeah. Right. I'll go sit with Stone."

Stone was neither asleep nor awake, lying with his head on his bone in a sort of suspended dog state. Jury sat down in his

favorite chair, which was itself half suspended between offering some support
and none, its springs sorely tested over the
years.

He drank his tea, looking towards the
window but not through it. He felt he had
stepped back as one might from one of
those thresholds painted by Magritte,
where nothing lies beyond the open door
but the tall blue sky or bottomless sea —
unknown, unending blue.

Sausages spit in grease. Was there any
smell more seductive than the smell of sausages? Well, yes, perhaps that smell of
citrus that had sent him back into the milk
jug.

Stone must have smelled it too, for he
woofed as if the sausage smell had pene-
trated his suspended state and found it
wanting. He rose up and shook himself,
then went into the kitchen to watch
Carol-anne.

Within the shelter of this sun-and-sau-
sage-besotted milieu, Jury closed his eyes
and willed himself not to think, which only
had the effect of speeding up the thought
process, images of the past week cascading
through his mind as if a film had been
fast-forwarded.

He did not want to think about Kate

McBride, about the Fabricants, about lad's-love and lavender, about Linda Pink.

No. He smiled. No, he didn't mind thinking about Linda Pink at all. It was beginning to seem the answer to this whole conundrum rested on his and Linda's shoulders. They were the only defectors from the party line. She had stuck to her story and Jury had stuck to his, though there was a sense of foreboding, something like the apprehension he'd felt on the bus when he'd seen Kate McBride.

He rested his head on the back of the chair, closed his eyes, followed her movements in his mind. He had almost forgotten he was here in his digs and not on a Fulham Road bus, when he felt a hovering over him.

"Super. Were you asleep?" She held out a plate with his breakfast on it. "Here."

He took it. "Wonderful. This looks wonderful. These sausages are a perfect brown. Can I have a napkin? You should be a chef."

She handed him a paper napkin and, with her own plate in hand, sat down on the sofa.

"Why do you have more sausages than I do?" Even so, he handed one down to Stone, who took it with surprising delicacy.

Without looking up from hers, she said, "Because I been out jogging already this morning, as usual. I need a lot of fuel."

Jury nearly spilled his sausages when he laughed. "Carole-anne, if there's one thing you do not need, it's fuel. You're combustible enough. Jogging? Jogging *as always?* Since when did you ever jog? Since when did you ever exercise at all?"

Carole-anne inspected a sausage for the most succulent bite. "Of course you don't see me; you never do any yourself, so how could you? There's a new gym opened up just last week in Islington High Street. Thinking of joining, me. Wouldn't hurt you to do the same."

"Yes, I can just see me whiling away the odd hour on a treadmill. Thanks, but no thanks."

"Well, it's a hedge against losing your looks. I mean, you might be handsome right now but who knows how you'll look in another five years."

Jury was surprised. "Me? Handsome? Right now? Good lord, I'm flattered."

"Well, don't be. Just do something to keep yourself up."

"I do do something. I spend my off-hours at the Angel."

Jury heard a clattering on the staircase

and saw Stone jerk his head up, then his whole self. He walked over to the door and sat looking at it. He even barked once. Stone never barked. Stone barking was almost Stone out of control.

Carole-anne bounced up from the sofa. "It's Stan."

Stone's earlier woofing had probably been the Lab's reaction to Stan coming up from the Angel underground stop. Were both Stone and Carole-anne blessed with second sight he himself had been denied? Probably. He was having enough trouble with first sight. Nor did he especially like the enthusiasm Carole-anne had displayed in nearly dropping her plate and rushing to open the door.

It was indeed Stan Keeler. All five-eleven, molten-eyed, guitar-carrying, talented bit of him. Stan Keeler had enough intensity for ten men, and Jury sometimes wished he'd riff some of it Jury's way.

After roughing up Stone's fur, kissing Carole-anne on the cheek (Jury took note that it was only the cheek, for he had often wondered if Carol-anne and Keeler had a thing going) Stan saluted Jury as if he were the commander of this base. "Yo, RJ. Thanks for looking after Stone here."

Stan always said that, even though he'd

never made the request. It was just his inner laser beaming out his comings and goings. He never told C-A or RJ when and where he was going. It seemed to dribble back to the other three flats in the form of postcards and sometimes telegrams. (Jury didn't know of anyone who sent telegrams anymore. He thought it quite poignant of Mr. Guitar to trouble to do it.) Stan was simply a nice guy, unusual for one who was such a cult figure. Jury only wished he weren't quite so damned magical.

"Where were you in Germany?"

"Munich, Frankfurt, Berlin. Clubs, real small places. For some reason I'm popular there."

Jury laughed. "You're popular everywhere. You were a big hit in Prague, my sergeant told me. How long are you in London this time?"

"I got some gigs I promised to play at the Nine-One-Nine. I haven't seen the guys in a month." *The guys* were the three other musicians in Stan's little group. Sometimes they went with him, sometimes not. "I'm going over there after I drop my stuff. Stone, want to go for a walk?"

The word had Stone banging his tail on Jury's wooden floorboards like a beaver.

"How about you, C-A? Want to go with

us? Watch me practice?"

Jury loved the idea of that group's "practicing." As if they needed it.

Both Carole-anne and Stone were up and nearly out the door. Carole-anne turned and said, "See you, Super."

Stan saluted again. "Talk to you later, RJ."

They left and Jury felt a void, despite sunlight, despite sausages.

27

He tried to fool himself into believing it might jog his memory, taking another Fulham bus. He would have liked to tell himself that what he was doing was looking for clues. But he knew that was a lie. What he wanted was to relive it. It was a journey he wanted to retake, a night he wanted to reinhabit, though for the life of him he couldn't say why. Last Saturday night's ride certainly hadn't been a happy one; far from it, for his thoughts had been doleful, morose. He felt he was watching one of those desk calendars you see in films, where time is disposed of by the fluttering over of pages, the days gone by in seconds, a year gone in a minute.

Jury had boarded a number 14 a short distance from the South Kensington underground and the Brompton Road. He had gotten off at the stop in front of the hospital across the road from the Stargazey.

The pub was more crowded, heavier with smoke than before, but then pubs tended to get that way on Sundays, there being little else people could think of to do. Kitty was there this time. He sat on the same stool at the far end of the bar where she was doing the washing up, rinsing sudsy glasses, and, with a slight frown, studying them for prints that had escaped the soap and water. So intent was she on this, she didn't notice him sitting down.

"You'd make a good fingerprint expert, Kitty. It *is* Kitty, isn't it?"

"Oh, hello!" She said this with real enthusiasm, as if finally she'd recognized a friendly face in an otherwise hostile crowd.

"Quite a mob today."

She sighed. "Always is on Sundays. People just don't know how to fill up a day when they're not in their offices. Sad, that." Then she blushed as if suddenly aware she'd just numbered Jury among this sad lot. "What'd you like?" She wiped her hands.

"Nothing to drink, thanks. Just some information. And I never introduced myself." He showed Kitty his ID. "I'm Richard Jury."

Her eyes widened. "Scotland Yard, is it?"

"It is." He had not picked up before that Kitty was Irish and wondered how he could have missed that lilt, wondered at this musical turn of speech from a country of unending troubles, as if inflection of speech were born of joy or woe. Jury took the police photos from a brown envelope — one of the murdered woman, the other of the woman he'd followed. But he did not lay them side by side, feeling that would be too suggestive.

"Do you recognize this woman?" He turned the photo of the victim to face her.

Kitty braced her hands on the bar, squinted as if she could better call up some deeply entrenched memory, and said, "Looks like one of our customers, though she was never a regular. Comes in —" Kitty stared at him. "You mean she's dead? What happened?" Again, she looked at the photo. "She always seemed a bit — I dunno — a bit sad, as if she had the weight o' the world on her shoulders." Kitty closed her eyes, as if visualizing the world's weight. "She'd come in sometimes for a drink, other times to use the phone. She wasn't on the telephone, see. And she paid the fella owns the place for her calls. She never talked long. I'll tell you, my *sister* can talk —"

"When was the last time you saw her, Kitty?"

She frowned in concentration. "A week

ago, ten days, maybe. I only work part-time, so you might want to ask someone else."

"I have." He put the second photo on the bar. "What about her?"

Kitty looked from the photo to Jury and back again, puzzled. "But it's the same one, isn't it?"

"Is it?"

Kitty brought the photo closer to her eyes, squinted again. "Well . . . perhaps she *is* different. The shape of the face, maybe."

"You couldn't say if *both* of them had come in here."

"Only if they'd come in at the same time, probably. Or if I'd been looking for two different women." Kitty drew the dishtowel from over her shoulder, started wiping glasses. "I dunno. You sure it's not the same person, one alive, one dead?"

This time he was the only one waiting at the bus stop. He let one bus go by, feeling absurd as he did so. He let it pass him up because it was one of the newer buses, fare paid as you boarded, single-decker. He was waiting for a double-decker. He waited for a quarter of an hour. Stupid.

Night seemed to come on earlier, more swiftly, with each passing day. It had been dead dark by half-five and it was half-six by now. Jury turned up his jacket collar and dug his hands into the pockets. He turned and looked down the street to Redcliffe Gardens. He had called Chilten, and Chilten had told him Kate had been released, or soon would be. Jury wondered if she was at home by now, having a cup of tea with old Mrs. Laidlaw.

When a double-decker finally pulled up, Jury swung onto the platform, nodded to the conductor, and climbed the stairs. This time there were only four other passengers, sitting in the rear of the bus. He took the seat in the front that looked out over the street that swam in the reflected lights of shops and cafes, still damp with a late-afternoon rain.

The bus stopped at the corner where the flower vendor kept his big selection, a carpet of bright flowers. As the bus pulled away from the curb, Jury heard steps ascending and women's voices hurried and excited. They settled behind him. Jury wouldn't have been surprised to find it was the American lady and her friend, still talking about Thanksgiving.

When they pulled up across from the Fulham Broadway underground station, he had such an eerie sense of last Saturday night's reinventing itself that he looked down to see if a woman in a sable coat was descending from the bus.

He sat back, with an uneasy feeling he had been keeping at bay throughout the day. Why was he so certain he had seen Kate McBride and not the woman who lay dead in the herb garden? When the others, the conductor and the several people who had been seated near the door that night, had said, Yes, that's her, the woman who'd got on and off the bus.

He told himself it was because he had seen Kate McBride over a much longer period of time; he had (and they hadn't) been watching her ever since she'd boarded the bus, until he himself had left it and followed her. He had seen her, off and on, over a period of time the others hadn't. And he was convinced that what had drawn the others' attention, and held it, was the fabulous sable coat and not the woman herself. Not her face. Though they claimed to be making the identification on the basis of her face. But it was really the coat, wasn't it?

Jury believed they were wrong, or, more accurately, he'd believed it then. Now he was wavering. Pondering this, he almost missed the stop at Fulham Palace Road and had to go down the steps quickly and swing off the bus after it had started. The conductor admonished him, leaning from the platform to shout that people got their legs broken that way.

Jury waved back to him and walked up Fulham Palace Road to Bishops Avenue, then on to the grounds of Fulham Palace.

It was almost seven when he got to the palace entrance. It started to rain like a movie rain; veils of it, thunder claps, lightning close by. He hoped he'd make it to the courtyard and Noailles's room before the rain came.

What had he expected Charles Noailles to say, other than what he did say?

"I've no idea what you're talking about, Superintendent."

"You're quite sure," said Jury, who was seated in the same run-down leather chair. "You have no connection — no family connection — with this château outside of Aix-en-Provence?"

Noailles was standing against the wall, fingering a compass. He half laughed. "As I said. No."

"Did Michael McBride talk to you about this book he was writing?"

Noailles shook his head. "He didn't

mention it, no."

"Would he have?"

"Would — ?" Now the priest did laugh. "I'm not a mind reader, Superintendent."

"No, of course not. I'm asking if you think he felt that close to you, if you were on intimate enough terms, that he might've told you about something rather explosive, an exposé of sorts, that he mightn't have mentioned to anyone else."

He thought this over, putting his hand against the window ledge, still holding the compass in his other hand. "Yes, I honestly think he would. Although he told me next to nothing about his private life, his wife, his daughter — I wasn't even aware he had a child. It just didn't come up, which might seem strange."

Jury told him, briefly, about Sophie's abduction. "Of course, none of this started until after McBride died."

"That's one of the worst stories I think I've ever heard, Superintendent."

Jury felt him to be sincere. He got up. "Thanks for seeing me, Father. I'll be in touch." He turned at the door and asked, "What *did* you and Michael McBride talk about?"

"God."

"For me, that's two dead ends in one

day. Good-bye."

He breathed air made even colder by the rain, the storm having passed over this particular place by now. He looked up at the night sky, at the barely visible stars, wondering again why he had come here. He hadn't expected the priest to be of much help. There was nothing new to see; nothing was going to reveal itself in the next lightning flash. The only answer he could give himself was that he felt a sense of attachment, as if something or someone were reaching out to claim him. He leaned against the stone pillar and listened to the storm already changing its random course and gathering strength elsewhere.

One alive, one dead. You sure they're not the same person?

Why did that bother him?

He stepped back from the entrance. The feeling, of the place having some claim on him, he had felt before in other places and circumstances just as strange. What it felt like was the undertow of homesickness. What was it, a sense of loss? Of what, he didn't know, only that it was something he missed.

Jury stood there in the silence, these feelings beginning to pass away like the rain. And oddly enough, painful as they were, he didn't want them to. I'm losing it, he thought; it was as if over a telephone line one heard the voice waver and get farther and farther away and finally fade out.

What he seemed to want was to get into the experience, inside it, but was kept — by what he preferred to think of as chance (the fall of the cards, the roll of the dice, the gamble) but what he feared was really his own cowardice — out.

28

Simeon Pitt and Melrose Plant had been sitting in two of Boring's old cowhide club chairs, reading their papers, when Pitt drew Plant's attention to an item regarding the Fabricant Gallery's *Siberian Snow* paintings.

"*Alleged* paintings, I mean." Pitt directed this comment not at Melrose but at the article. "I can't imagine Sebastian Fabricant believes the stuff is art. Fabricant's always been a decent gallery. Dependable, you know, and not completely over-the-moon with their prices, either. And they've discovered more than one artist, like this Slocum. Strong influence of Turner there, but I expect that's obvious." Simeon Pitt adjusted his spectacles and shook his newspaper.

"Turner is her favorite painter."

"It's the light, the light. Listen to this, would you? Here's Jonathan Betts: 'The daring series on show at the Fabricant Gallery in Mayfair, Ralph Rees's *Siberian Snow*, is worth a visit, if you haven't already' — *blah blah blah blah;* get on with it, you idiot — 'a group of paintings reminiscent of the minimalism of Robert Ryman or Newman's abstract expressionism.' What's he talking about — abstract expressionism? The man's hardly forty and in his dotage. It takes him so long to make a point he could have been a barrister." Pitt shook the paper again, as if he might loosen the print in so doing, and continued. " 'It takes considerable nerve for an artist to retain the passionate blankness of a scene —' The what of a *what?*" Pitt stared at Melrose. "Have you ever been struck by 'passionate blankness,' Mr. Plant?"

"Yes, once, but I soon recovered."

Pitt tittered and continued. " '— blankness of a scene and offer such nuances of color, such metonymy of line, such purity of space.' " Pitt crackled the paper together in the middle. "If I didn't know the man had less humor in him than a bull around a red cape, I'd say he's writing all of this tongue-in-cheek. Fabricant must have friends at the paper."

"You people can be bought?"

"You're joking, of course. I've known a food critic the price of whose column was a decent meal, and a theater critic persuaded with a third-row-aisle seat."

"Ah." Melrose sighed. "How disappointing."

"Why? Do you need somebody to tell you what to like?"

Melrose smiled. "Oh, I've already someone to do that!" He spent a moment thinking about Agatha. "But you yourself, Mr. Pitt, are — or were — doing the same thing."

Pitt wobbled a reproving finger in Melrose's face. "Wrong. Wrong. I was telling you what *I* like. Long as I could pick up my check at week's end I didn't give a damn what *you* liked. Where's that old waiter? I need a drink."

"Higgins? Right over there with Colonel Neame."

"Let's get him over here; I'd like a whisky. As I remember, you owe me one."

Melrose caught the waiter's eye and motioned him over. "I do indeed."

Pitt was smoothing out his paper. "I'm so deep into this bilgewater, I could be going down with the *Titanic*." Pitt read silently, mouthing words, disturbed only by Higgins's creeping up between their chairs, unseen.

"Mr. Pitt, what will you have?"

"Whisky and soda."

When the old porter had slipped away like smoke, Pitt continued with his review. " 'One cannot conceive of any recent painting more daring than the flamboyant *Siberian Snow.'* Oh, for God's sake! Daring? Flamboyant?" Pitt dashed his paper to the floor.

Melrose rather envied Simeon Pitt. The man so enjoyed his own company. He seemed to be talking more to himself than to Melrose.

"Here's daring!" Pitt retrieved his paper. "Here's flamboyance, if that's what you're after!" Pitt was pointing a finger at Melrose as if the latter had challenged him to a flamboyance contest. The finger then took a dive to the bottom of the page. "The thief who cut this painting clean out of the frame and made off with it!"

Where had Melrose heard about this before?

"Here's an article on the Hermitage." Pitt waved the arts page. "Don't you remember? It created quite a stir last February, everybody was talking about it." He read: " '— the audacious theft of a recently acquired painting by Marc Chagall, *Wingless, Wingless Angels*, which has yet to be recovered. This is a double loss, as the painting was the only Chagall in the museum —' which is strange, isn't it, considering he's Russian for God's sake; don't they support their own artists?"

Oh, yes. Agatha. No wonder he hadn't remembered. It was so rare anything Agatha said would bear the fruit of further conversation. "Is this the Hermitage painting?"

Pitt nodded. He clearly enjoyed the theft of a painting more than he did the review of one. "This thief, they say, can appear and disappear like Higgins back there." He returned to the paper. "Goes by the name of Dana. Hmph! Is that a first name? Last name? Man? Woman?" Pitt shrugged. " 'Wanted in' — by God — 'Argentina, Spain, Cyprus, and Cairo for grand larceny and assassination —' note they put the larceny first, ha. Assassination's apparently his or her forte. Theft is a sideline." Pitt lowered the paper and heaved a sigh. "Wouldn't it be pleasant to be anonymous like that? Roving the world, picking up work locally as it comes your way for whoever'll pay the tariff? A few francs here, a few yen there, a couple of pesos, a hatful of rubles."

"Oh, I don't know. Assassination, that could be a tricky business."

"Hm. Wonder how much you have to

pay him. Or her. Be nifty to think it's a woman doing it. But she could only get in here on Ladies' Day!" Pitt laughed uproariously.

"How do they know it's this particular person? And as you said, it could be a woman? Dana's a pretty unisex name, isn't it? There's Richard Henry Dana, the writer. There are several film actors, both women and men, whose first name is Dana."

Pitt grunted. "As to its being one person, it seems the crimes have his — or her — signature all over them." His eye fell on another piece. "Now here's something interesting. . . . Ah, thank you, sir!"

Melrose placed money on the silver tray from which the waiter had removed two whiskies and a syphon.

Young Higgins smiled his signature wintry smile, thanked Melrose, and drifted off.

Pitt returned to his plundering of the news and what he had been about to report before the porter's appearance. "Listen: 'All Souls Church, located in Oake Holyoake, Cornwall —' " He frowned. "Where the hell's that? Never heard of it. Well, it's Cornwall, after all. That's so much another country I'm sure there are dozens of little places nobody's heard of. Anyway:

"Holyoake was the scene early Sunday morning of a strange event. The body of a man dressed in a tuxedo was discovered by Miss Principia Soames when she appeared as she always does early on Sunday to tidy the church and see to the flowers. 'This church ain't used much between one Sunday and t'other, and so I expect he coulda laid here for days. Don't think I wasn't half scared, seeing him face down over there.' Here Miss Soames pointed toward the altar.

" 'All Souls is a small Tudor church,' the pastor, Reverend Brinsley, told us, going on to say it was almost derelict but that he did like to try to keep it up because 'All Souls does have one or two interesting features. Note that window over there; it could be a signed Tiffany —' "

Simeon Pitt laughed and coughed. Melrose edged down in his wing chair. "Will they get round to the body again?" Pitt held up his hand and read on:

" '— and we've a fine example of

390

16th-century misericords [Pitt laughed again].' Mr Bertram Missingham, Sheriff of Oake Holyoake — the title is complimentary, there being no official police presence in the village — revealed: 'Crime in Oake Holyoake has never been lower in the time I've been sheriff, and that's going on to ten years now. We're a peaceful people round here, and we're twinned with a place of near the same name in south Germany called Holioke.' When asked his opinion of what had befallen the body in evening dress in the chancel, he announced that he was in no position to say. Miss Soames remarked, 'It's a job keeping drugs and such out of Oake Holioke, but we done our best. He's a Londoner, must be mixed up with the Mafia. All I know is he drove in in his Beamer and dropped down dead.' "

Both of them, Pitt and Melrose, were laughing, both slumped in their chairs.

Melrose said, "I have a detective friend at New Scotland Yard. I think he should go to the place and investigate, don't you?"

Pitt was mopping a tear-filled eye with his handkerchief. "After he does that, he ought to investigate those paintings. Collusion, I'll bet."

"Oh?" Melrose said, to this opaque comment.

"Well, of course, Mr. Plant —" Pitt stopped; then his brow furrowed in deep thought. The way Simeon Pitt was eyeing him, Melrose might himself have been one of the parties to this conspiracy to — to what?

"Sandpaper, he said?"

"Rees's medium for painting? I think so, yes."

"You know — no! Not another word until I get a friend of mine in on this. Where's the telephone?" Pitt looked almost wildly around, as if all the phones that had been to hand had been snatched from his grasp. "Higgins!" Pitt thumped the arm of the chair. The ancient waiter came as quickly as he could but not quickly enough. Pitt called to him to find a telephone and bring it.

"You bought one of those paintings."

"Guilty, yes."

"Could you get it?"

"You mean, have them take it down? Yes. I think Fabricant was going to take down the ones they'd sold and deliver mine here."

Higgins was back with the telephone, which he handed to Pitt, and then plugged the cord into the wall. Pitt rubbed his hands, punched in a number.

Melrose listened to one side of a cryptic conversation between Pitt and the person on the other end, someone named Jay. Pitt hung up, smiled that cat-and-cream smile, and said, "I might just go round and have a word with Fabricant."

29

The gallery was not open on Monday to customers, but this did not apply to Scotland Yard. Opening and closing hours seldom did.

It was Sebastian, sleeves rolled up, who had seen Jury and his sergeant at the door and opened it. "You've caught us actually working. Sorry about that." He smiled broadly.

Jury returned the smile, "You've caught us at it too."

With that reply, Sebastian's smile became a rather uncertain cough, but he recovered. "I see. Well, but you chaps always are."

"Not always, sir, we do go on holiday sometimes," put in Wiggins, taking everything literally, as usual. "That's a nasty dry cough you've got there, sir."

Wiggins was introduced, and Wiggins was anxiety's antidote. More immediately, a dry cough's.

Sebastian visibly relaxed. It was difficult to throw up a defensive wall when Sergeant Wiggins was on the scene; he could dismantle it brick by brick with his concern and advice. "Don't take any of your over-the-counter medications; it's a waste of good money. Only thing for a really dry cough is lemon juice, honey, and ginger, strong as you can take it, with a little hot water to dissolve it all. But the less water, the better. Works every time." Wiggins's free advice was actually an invaluable ally — many nuggets of information had been mined belowstairs when Wiggins took a cup of tea with the kitchen staff during an investigation. Jury could do much the same thing by trying. But Wiggins could do it merely by breathing.

Sebastian led them down the hall to one of the display rooms, where Nicholas was hanging a large painting in a heavy gold-leaf frame. It was a traditional drover-with-flock-of-sheep thing, and Jury was surprised to see it in this gallery, which seemed to lean more to the avant-garde and the abstract.

Ralph Rees was in the next room, dismantling his *Snow* series. Having met the artist, Wiggins watched this with a deadly earnestness. One arm across his chest, his chin resting on the upright hand of the other arm, Wiggins prepared to take it all seriously. For once, though, this probably wasn't owing to the Wiggins sensibilities but to Jury's suggestion: "Don't laugh when you see them. Be dead serious."

This injunction rather surprised Wiggins, who would have found it impossible to laugh at anyone's brave attempt to paint, write, or play a musical instrument. The command was superfluous.

Now, Wiggins's somber appraisal of Ralph's *Siberian Snow* was all Jury could have hoped for. Assuredly, it was all Rees could hope for. Wiggins moved back, moved in close, moved even farther back, made a half-frame of fingers and thumb and looked at the white paintings that way, nodded and nodded his head, and made one or two throaty noises of approval. "Well, I must say, Mr. Rees, this is an interesting group. Extremely daring, isn't it?"

(Jury hoped he wouldn't fall into Plant's habit of calling it "this white lot.")

When Ralph asked Wiggins, "In what way?" — a question that would have frightened the casual fraud straight off the premises — Wiggins answered, "To paint it the way it looks. Especially that one with the fallen branch —"

Jury was at a loss until he realized

Wiggins was pointing to the canvas with the thin black line down in the corner. Branch?

But Ralph was merely nodding. "Everyone seems to see something different there, Sergeant."

Wiggins gave a condescending little laugh. "Some as can't tell chalk from cheese. Never mind them. When were you there?"

Jury, who had turned away to hide a smile, turned back, rather astonished. In all of his and Plant's talk about these paintings, it hadn't occurred to Jury that Ralph had *been there*. In Russia. It could as easily have been snow in Montana or the North Yorkshire moors.

"Twice I was there, not in Siberia but in St. Petersburg. It's where I met the Fabricants."

Jury asked. "When were you there; that is, when last?"

Ralph calculated. "Um. Last spring. March, I think. We — Ilona — Seb —"

"Seb what?" asked Sebastian, who'd returned from the storerooms in back.

"I was just telling Mr. Jury that we'd gone to St. Petersburg. Ilona goes several times a year. Well, it's her home, isn't it?"

Sebastian agreed. "St. Petersburg's

where she lives, really. In her heart, in her mind."

Jury wondered about this, given Michel Kuraukov's execution by the Cheka.

Wiggins, still thinking he'd found something in these paintings, nodded to them. "Did you paint all these when you were there?"

"Two of them I did. The others — well, I've been doing this over the last year. As you can imagine."

It was fortunate he'd directed this comment to Wiggins, who, indeed, probably *could* imagine. Jury couldn't. "I wonder, Mr. Fabricant" — Jury had turned to Sebastian — "if I might have a word with you?" He wanted the same word with the rest of them, but individually.

Sebastian led him into the office, a smallish room that housed another computer and the fax machine, a desk, and two slick-looking Eames chairs opposite the leather swivel chair in which Sebastian sat down.

"Do you know a woman named Nancy Pastis?" He saw that Sebastian was at least appearing to think this over, and perhaps (thought Jury) he really was. Jury didn't quite trust him.

"No. No, I can't say I do." Sebastian

looked at his watch. "Sorry. I don't mean to cut you short; it's just that I'm expecting a client about now."

"Don't worry, you won't cut me short," Jury said, ambiguously. "But it's Monday. You're not open on Mondays."

Sebastian's pause was marginal and the blush faint, but just long enough and just red enough to suggest the "client" might be a fiction. Then he said, "Appointments I take if I have to. This one's a good client."

Jury went on. "Nancy Pastis lives in Curzon Street and has a wall full of paintings. I'd be surprised if she hadn't been into your gallery, given she lives so close to it."

"She might well have; I don't see everyone who comes in here and probably wouldn't remember them unless we'd sold them something. Who is this person? Why are you interested?"

"Let's just say that I am." Jury smiled. "You keep a record of sales, don't you? And a mailing list?"

"Yes, of course. But —"

"Look."

Sebastian pulled over one of the two Rolodexes sitting atop his desk. He thumbed through it, shook his head. "No one by that name." He looked up at Jury. "This is the mailing list; we try to put anyone on the mailing list who purchases from us."

"Sales? What about that record?"

It was clear Sebastian wasn't pleased to have to rise and drag down a heavy ledger from a shelf. He sat down again and opened the ledger. "Look, I can hardly go over this entire list. It goes back for fifteen years." He inclined his head toward the shelf and the other ledgers there.

"If the ledger you have there is this year's, let's start with that."

Sebastian sighed. "But it'll take time."

"I could take the ledgers with me." Jury smiled. Tantamount to producing a search warrant, at least in implication.

Seb shook his head. "I'll start at the end and take the latest purchase first."

Jury nodded, watched him run his finger down one page, turn, do it on another; he was one of those people who silently mouthed the words he was reading.

"Ah. You're right, Mr. Jury. Nancy Pastis . . . here it is. *St. Ives.* This was back in February. February twenty-ninth."

Jury asked, "Is this a very small painting, framed in ash?"

Seb thought for a moment. "Yes. Quite

small. Of St. Ives."

"That's in Cornwall." Jury smiled. "It looks more like a port in Paradise."

"Does this help you?"

"Yes, but more if you recalled waiting on her."

He tapped the page. "This is my brother's writing. Both of us make entries. Do you want to ask him?"

"Yes." Jury rose and followed Sebastian down a narrow hall to a room at the rear which was very large and well lighted.

"We had skylights put in," said Seb, who asked Nicholas about the Pastis sale.

Nicholas gave this some frowning thought. "I like to think I remember everyone who's ever bought from us." He smiled ruefully. "But I can't. I remember the painting, certainly. But not the patron. Sorry."

"Maybe I could jog your memory. Do you recall the photo I showed you at your house?" Jury had drawn one of the police photographs from the inside pocket of his raincoat.

"This isn't that murdered woman? The one you found in Fulham Palace?"

Jury said, "Yes."

"Good lord. Yes, I guess I did see her. If I'd seen the photo in this context the first time, maybe I'd have —" He looked apologetic. "It's possible she came in before she bought the painting. Probable, I should say. People don't ordinarily buy the first time around. They want to think about a painting. I just don't recall seeing her at another time, that's all."

"How did she pay? Check or plastic?"

"Cash, I think. Oh, it wasn't all that much. Five hundred pounds. People have put down cash in much greater amounts than that."

Jury handed Nicholas one of his cards. "If you think of anything else about her, would you get in touch?"

Nicholas nodded. "Certainly."

"Thanks for your trouble. I'll go look up my sergeant. He appeared to be fascinated by Mr. Rees's paintings."

"Everyone is," said Sebastian. "We're trying to decide what to put up on that wall and how best to display the remaining two. We've sold three, now."

Wiggins was actually seated in a wooden chair supplied him by Ralph, and both of them were studying the snow series; Ralph had lined up the ones he'd taken down so that there would be an uninterrupted progression. At least, that's what Jury supposed. What in heaven's name did Wiggins see in all this? Wiggins was a no-nonsense type when dealing with anything outside of his little world of allergies and anodynes.

Jury said to Ralph, "You've sold some of the series, then?"

"Yes, and I'm thrilled. These two" — he indicated the ones propped against the wall — "to an American. And one last week to a British peer."

Jury glanced at Wiggins, who, with a crimped little smile, was bending over to study God-only-knew-what at the bottom of one of the paintings. Jury said, "A peer? Well, you know the aristocracy. Always have to be first off the bat with . . . things."

But Ralph interpreted the comment in his favor. "I'm extremely encouraged by all this attention."

Ralph's smile was so candid, so ingenuous, Jury felt a stab of sorrow, even of shame, that he'd come so close to insulting his work. The poor chap must really believe in what he was doing. "He'll probably be back."

"Who?"

"Your British aristocrat. They're never satisfied with just one of anything, not if there's more to be had. I know one who drives a Rolls *and* a Bentley."

Ralph looked doubtful. "He didn't say."

Jury smiled. "Trust me."

30

Melrose Plant was making his way to the desk to settle his bill on Tuesday before lunch and was still debating the least unsavory mode of transport back to Long Piddleton. Trueblood had left several days before, saying he had to get back to his business.

There was the train to Sidbury and then to Long Piddleton by cab, or he could give Diane Demorney a ring and ask her to collect him at the Sidbury station. She was so often in the offices of the *Sidbury Star* these days that it wouldn't inconvenience her. Diane appeared to enjoy performing minor acts of mercy for Melrose, as he was, after all, eligible, rich, and even — the highest virtue in the Demorney canon — "amusing." She had finished with her fourth husband years before and was getting bored with being on her own.

It struck Melrose that Diane was the polar opposite of someone such as Simeon Pitt, for she was unable to find her own company tolerable; whereas Pitt found little tolerable in others' company and could amuse himself endlessly on his own.

Because of her lack of inward resources, Melrose was surprised that she was finding the content for her column exclusively within herself. She certainly wasn't finding it in the zodiac. She couldn't be bothered to do *research*. Perhaps Diane was a more layered person than he had given her credit for. He considered this on his way to the telephone. Well, at least as layered as the jam on yesterday's jam roll.

In the Members' Room he saw the usual fleet of faces — not faces, actually, but newspapers and the hands holding them, the legs stretched out from under them, elbows, feet, ankles. The Members' Room was more a collection of body parts than bodies. There was Neame behind his *Daily Mirror*; there were Pitt's highly polished shoes jutting from the wing chair whose back was to Melrose. It saddened him to think of saying good-bye.

When Diane's bored yet mellifluous voice came over the line, Melrose said, "Diane! Listen, be a sport and collect me at the Sidbury train station, will you? I'll take the three o'clock so I'll get in just in time to buy you a drink." That should do it!

"Train? Good God, Melrose! What happened to your Bentley?" If he'd announced a ten-car collision, she couldn't have been more appalled. Public transportation was intended only for the needy — that is, the non-Bentley, non-Roller crowd. She herself had two.

"Diane, you seem to have forgotten: Trueblood drove me to London last week. We used his van, remember? So will you pick me up?" He heard what sounded like papers crackling in his ear. "What're you doing?"

"Melrose, I've just realized you've missed your horoscopes."

Horoscopes? How many had there been?

"I'll read this to you."

"Please don't bother."

"Oh, but it's no bother at all. Now let me just find . . . Capricorn, Capricorn. . . ."

He was sorry he'd furnished her with his date of birth.

She read: *"Charm will get you nowhere in this mess. Although you are used to sailing through any difficulty, you will find you're up against a stronger adversary than even you can put down."*

"What in heaven's name are you predicting?"

Her sigh would have leveled a field of

poppies. "*Mel*-rose. Why can't you understand your Fate lies in the pattern of the stars? *I* can't tell you what's going to happen." She continued. *"Since you are generally self-sufficient, you are subject to egocentrism and —"*

"Ego*what?*"

"Cen—trism. It means you're altogether too pleased with yourself. Don't take it personally. It's Capricorns in general, and that's not your fault, is it?

"As the moon transits Venus, you will find old friendships are the best." She paused, then said, "I'll just fix this next bit: *Pack up and go home. And above everything, Watch out!"*

Since she fairly yelled this, Melrose nearly fell off his seat. Then he thought for a moment the line had gone dead until he heard the crackling of what might have been cellophane, topped off by a bark and a voice shouting.

"Just getting out a fresh cig. Sorry."

"Diane, I called your house. Did you get a dog?"

"No. I'm at the *Star* offices, of course. I've got a deadline."

"But the number I dialed was your house."

"I have call forwarding. And don't forget

my pager, if you ever need to get in touch with me quickly. Didn't I give you the number?" She read it off.

Melrose wasn't going to bother jotting it down, but then he did. It might be good for a few laughs. He recapped his pen.

"Incidentally, Melrose, why have you been in London a whole week?" Her voice was a little whiny, as if his absence were a slap in the face.

"No special reason. Going to Harrods, doing one or two things for Richard Jury."

"Ah, Richard *Jury!*"

Talk about eligible, thought Melrose. But unmoneyed, untitled, uncountrified.

Another brief pause while she did something. "He's a Leo."

"He is? How do you know?"

"Marshall told me. Marshall knows everything."

"We're talking about the same Marshall, are we?"

"I should send Richard a copy of this week's *Star.* What's his address?"

"Scotland Yard, as always."

"What street's it in?"

"I'm not sure the street is absolutely essential, but I think it's in Victoria Street."

"Um." Silence. Probably writing it

down. "Now, to continue with Capricorn," she said.

Ye gods, he might as well fire up a cigarette himself.

"Let's see, we were at the warning. Here: *If you aren't careful you might find yourself encountering something dire.*"

"That's a rather gloomy old forecast, isn't it?"

"If you think Capricorn's bad, you should see Jupiter. Well, I'm off. Deadline. Ta-ta."

Melrose replaced the receiver, shook his head to clear it, and wandered back to the Members' Room, nearly colliding with a heavyset woman with two silver-handled canes who stared down her nose at him as if she were a victim of road rage. She was used to getting the right-of-way, obviously, and Melrose stood aside, extended an arm, and bowed slightly to usher her out of the room. He remembered then it was Tuesday, Ladies' Day. He hoped this woman wasn't Pitt's relation. No, that was a niece, wasn't it?

They were still in place, Neame dropping his *Mirror* long enough to see Melrose and wave. Melrose smiled and nodded and walked over to the wing chair on the other side of Simeon Pitt's. With the arts section resting against his chest, Simeon Pitt was having one of his catnaps. Well, he'd soon wake up. Melrose signaled Young Higgins, who bobbed over as if a strong wind were at his back.

"Coffee, please, Higgins." Melrose noted the cup on the table beside Pitt. "And might as well bring enough for Mr. Pitt, too."

"Yes, sir. I'll bring a fresh cup for him."

Melrose watched Young Higgins with the usual anxiety of wondering whether he'd make it to the bar or not, then turned to his *Telegraph*. After reading yesterday's news, he decided Monday must have been a real bore for most people and set it aside.

He watched Simeon Pitt for a moment. The newspaper wasn't moving.

He bent his head so that he could see Pitt's downturned face. Melrose went cold. For Pitt's eyes were not peacefully closed in sleep, they were half open.

Without thinking, Melrose yanked the newspaper back and threw it to the floor. He stood there, utterly paralyzed, any sound he might make caught in his throat. He was not even aware that the old waiter had come up to him with his tray.

The cups and French press slid precariously as Higgins nearly dropped the lot.

411

"Oh, my! Oh, my!" said Higgins, his rasping voice gone up a register or two. "A stroke, oh, my, the gentlemen's had —"

"Fetch the doctor. Call the police." Melrose didn't recognize his own voice.

As much as Young Higgins could rush, he rushed. Melrose looked after him and then down at the body of Simeon Pitt, where the blood around the wound in his chest would be nearly invisible to a man with Higgins's vision. It had almost passed Melrose's inspection, given the dark brown plaid of Pitt's waistcoat. The bleeding must have been largely internal.

Melrose straightened up and saw his hands were shaking as badly as Young Higgins's.

For a moment, he heard Diane's voice: *Watch out!*

31

The Members' Room moved into something resembling wakefulness, if not into outright excitability, over the death of Simeon Pitt. It had not yet been bruited about that Mr. Pitt had died not of cardiac arrest but of stab wounds — wound, rather — a single one artfully delivered to a spot just over the sternum.

"Somebody knew how to do it," said Phyllis Nancy, stripping off her gloves. "The bleeding is almost exclusively internal; the lungs are full of blood."

Wiggins asked, "Why in God's name would someone do this in full view of these people?"

Jury just shook his head. "One stab wound. That's rather incredible."

"As I said, someone knew what weapon to use. Stiletto, it could have been. Long, thin. I can't be more precise than that."

Melrose had called Jury, who together with Sergeant Wiggins had arrived just before Detective Inspector Milderd and Sergeant Webber from police division C.

They in turn had been preceded by several uniforms who had been, handily enough, by a linen van at the curb, whose driver they appeared to be questioning. One of the Boring's staff had called to them frantically and they had come on the double.

Jury had brought not only Wiggins but his favorite medical examiner, Phyllis Nancy, aware he might be treading on the toes of C Division, and had explained to DI Milderd that since Dr. Nancy had been with him at the time he'd received the call, he had brought her along.

Dr. Nancy never missed a trick. Once, she had seen on a body what might be taken for a tiny pinprick as an entryway for a poison (later discovered to be ricin), after another doctor had set down cardiac failure as cause of death. Heart failure it certainly had been, but caused by the poison, introduced on a heavy embroidery needle discovered in the embroidery basket of the victim's cousin. Jury had always admired Dr. Nancy's imaginative grasp of factors that lesser medical examiners couldn't put together. She was also captivatingly feminine and didn't mind being told so, in one way or another.

No, Phyllis Nancy missed nothing; only, in the case of poor Pitt's chest, there was nothing that could be missed. She said death had occurred within the last three, possibly four, hours, and could anyone here pin it down better?

Melrose could help only by way of saying he'd seen Simeon Pitt at breakfast. That had been around nine-fifteen or nine-thirty, when Melrose had come down. Pitt seemed much as usual. It was his habit to sit in the Members' Room after breakfast, sometimes for the whole of the morning, reading various papers.

DI Milderd asked Melrose, "Did he have visitors usually?"

"No," said Melrose. "I mean, I never saw him with anyone, although, yes, he did mention a niece. This is the club's Ladies' Day. I believe he said she was to lunch with him."

Milderd asked, "Did he say anything else about her?"

"No, that was all."

Sergeant Webber said, "You were friendly with Mr. Pitt?"

"Well, yes. I certainly liked him. He was art critic for the —" Melrose stopped. In the wake of the morning's happenings, he had all but forgotten Pitt's telephone call yesterday.

"Yes, sir?"

"It's probably nothing, but Mr. Pitt made a phone call yesterday." Melrose told them about it.

"This Jay person, he never said a last name?"

Melrose was tired of these two sticking to his tweed jacket like burrs. "No. Look," said Melrose, "I met Simeon Pitt only last week. That's as well as I knew him."

"Yes, Lord Ardry, but —"

Aha! There's the problem, right here. The way he'd said it. Cops hated the aristocracy.

"— but three other gentlemen, who rarely did more than exchange a good-evening with Mr. Pitt, said you often sat with him and had lively conversation and drinks," Milderd said.

Webber added, as he slowly (and smugly) batted his eyelashes at Melrose, "And were out and about with him, some days."

"Three times! That's how often we had drinks and talk. As far as out and about goes, we went once to an art gallery not far from here." As Milderd was going on, Melrose stopped listening. He was instead thinking about Pitt's telephone call and the Fabricant Gallery. He came out of this daze to hear Milderd addressing him.

"Lord Ardry?"

"What?"

"As I *said* —"

(The aristocracy never pays attention.)

"— the waiter confirmed that you often joined Mr. Pitt for a drink. Mr. Higgins, that would be."

Melrose looked over to where Young Higgins seemed to have grown visibly more sprightly since the murder. Look at him! Over there in a huddle with Neame and Champs, demonstrating what he'd heard when he'd hovered near the medical examiner. Hands clasped, shoving an imaginary knife into his chest. God! Another murder would bring him tap-dancing out of the kitchen like Fred Astaire. Well, thank the Lord, here at last came Jury.

Seeing he was an acquaintance of Jury, Milderd and Webber both looked at Melrose afresh — and with far less interest. Webber pocketed his pen and flipped his notebook shut. Waste of time, talking to this yob.

Melrose said to Jury, watching their retreating backs, "Why in hell aren't they spending their time more resourcefully, instead of jamming me up between them?"

"You must admit," said Jury, "you're the best bet in the room at the moment." He swept his arm over the room to take in the stout woman with the two canes and two other older women who had come for the Ladies' Day luncheon. All three women had drawn themselves up and stayed that way throughout the police presence. Then there were the four elderly gentlemen (including Neame and Champs) gathered round Higgins, who now had clasped his spidery fingers about his throat to demonstrate the full range of his knowledge of murder methods.

"God, I knew Simeon Pitt for just a few days." Here Melrose's irritation — misplaced emotion — evaporated and gave way to real sadness. "We had coffee and drinks together. He was one of the most enjoyable souls I've ever met." Had that, indeed, been the scope of their friendship?

"I'm sorry," Jury said kindly.

"Your DI Milderd appeared to think I was about to be written out of his will." He added, "I told them he was expecting his niece — Barbara something. Damn, I don't believe he gave me the last name. Anyway, she's from around Oxford, or near it. . . . There's the porter!"

Mr. Budding, who had gone out for forty-five minutes to run some errands, looked white as a ghost. He seemed to take it personally that a murder had been committed in his absence. Yes, he'd said there was a young lady (at Boring's that could be any woman between fifteen and fifty) visited Mr. Pitt noonish — no, 'twas earlier; elevenish, it was — as Mr. Pitt ordered morning coffee for her. Budding was now behind the desk opening the register.

Jury frowned. "But neither Mr. Higgins nor your young porter remembered a visitor."

"They wouldn't, see, as I served them coffee. Here we are!" He twirled the guest book on its carrousel so that Jury could read it: *Mrs. Amons for Mr. Pitt.* "I remember saying to her he was expecting his niece and was she Mrs. Amons? She said yes and signed the guest book." He tapped it with a shaky finger.

"Describe her, would you?" said Wiggins, his notebook out.

"Let's see. Attractive, she was, and well dressed. Tallish, light hair. I do recall she was only here for twenty minutes, if that."

"You watched her leave?"

"Certainly. She said her uncle had fallen asleep and she didn't want to disturb him. If you'll excuse me, sir, I believe I'm wanted." Mr. Budding scurried off to answer the young porter's signal.

Melrose said, "Fell asleep? That's ridiculous. The man would never have fallen asleep in the middle of a visit from a relation. He was too aware of things."

Mr. Budding was back, looking paler than when he left. "I've just been informed of something very odd. Our Mr. Neal, there" — and he nodded toward the young porter with the spiky hair — "has just told me that whilst I was gone a Mrs. Amons called and left a message for Mr. Pitt. Said she was having a bit of car trouble and waiting for the RAC." Mr. Budding removed a large handkerchief from his back pocket and wiped it across his forehead. "I don't see how this is possible, sir, as the woman who was here at eleven o'clock said *she* was Mrs. Amons, and I must say I'm very much upset by this."

Jury nodded. "I can understand, Mr. Budding. But you'd never seen Mrs. Amons, I take it, so how were you to know?"

Mr. Budding, somewhat reassured, left them.

"Am I surprised? I don't think so. I'll tell Milderd."

Jury walked over to confer with Milderd, leaving Melrose to his own thoughts. They weren't pleasant. Melrose sat down heavily and tried to bring back the whole of Pitt's conversation. Who was the "expert" he was going to call? What was he "expert" in? Something to do with fraud in the art world? He had referred to "Jay."

Having reminded himself he must call Diane and tell her not to meet the train, Melrose was distracted momentarily by the sight of Pitt's body, enclosed in a black body bag, being loaded onto a gurney. He walked over to where Jury was standing.

"Listen." He drew Jury aside. "There's something that may or may not be important." He told him about Pitt's telephone call and his intention to "go round and have a word with Fabricant."

Jury thought for a moment. "So did Fabricant send someone round to have a word with Pitt?"

32

Jury stood outside the gate and watched Olivia Inge trimming back the rosebush with shears that cut like butter through the tough stems. He stood there for a few moments, wondering about her, wondering why such a woman would see herself as the needy poor relation. Olivia mystified him. Her brief and early marriage had availed her little, apparently, in terms of either financial or moral support. But she was Olive Fabricant's daughter, with as much right to whatever Clive had left as Nicholas, and surely more than Sebastian, Jury would have thought. Yet she seemed to have relegated herself to the role of hanger-on. Stepdaughter to Ilona Kuraukov. Not an enviable relationship.

"Mrs. Inge."

She had been focusing so completely on her task that the sound of her own name appeared to frighten her. She looked behind her.

"Olivia," said Jury. The first name had slipped out unbidden. He was not quite as easy with first names as Sergeant Wiggins.

"Oh!" She pressed her gloved hand across her breast. "You startled me."

He smiled. "Sorry."

"The rest of them aren't here. Did you want — ?"

"You, actually. Could we talk?"

"Of course. Let's go inside. It's too cold out here and it's getting dark. And as far as my name's concerned, I much prefer the first. It doesn't sound so suspect-like."

"Suspect? Did I say you were?"

"You don't have to."

She stripped off her gloves, and Jury was reminded of Phyllis Nancy. The thought of an autopsy made him feel somber. His expression must have reflected this, for Olivia asked, "Is something wrong?"

He held the gate for her. "Something's always wrong. It comes with the job."

The warmth was welcome inside. And it appeared that tea had been laid (probably by Hedda). "This is wonderful! Hedda's timing is always perfect. That, or she's a mind reader." She took his coat, asked if he'd like tea.

"Yes, I would."

Jury sat down in the sofa Ilona Kuraukov had stood behind. He could almost feel her presence at his back. As he settled into it, Olivia handed him his tea in a delicate cup, china that looked thin as a veil.

She sat opposite him, in the armchair, and raised her own cup. "Cheers."

"Cheers." He took a drink of tea, felt better. "Why would I suspect you?"

She shrugged. "I've no idea, since I haven't done anything."

"Where were you late morning, early afternoon?"

"Here it comes." Her voice grew theatrical. *"And where were you at the time old Chalmers was shot?"*

Jury smiled. "Not Chalmers; not shot."

She regarded him quizzically.

"His name wasn't Chalmers."

"Are you saying someone else was murdered?"

He nodded.

Looking round the room as if for something to come to her aid, she said. "I've been here all day. By myself, doing some gardening."

"Do you get the *Times*?" When she nodded, seeming even more confused, he said, "Read the arts section?"

"Of course. It's usually the first thing I read."

"Ever hear of Simeon Pitt?"

Her contemplative frown seemed genuine enough. "No . . . wait, yes. Yes. He used to write a column, didn't he?"

"Highly regarded in the art world. Your world."

"You mean my brothers', Superintendent. Just before Ralph's show, I heard Seb laughing about something in a review he was reading and saying, 'Just thank God Pitt's gone.'" Then she quickly put her hand to a cheek that had flushed. "Oh, good lord. You mean it was he? This Simeon Pitt?"

"Yes."

She looked down at her cup. "That's —" She shrugged.

"This review. Your brother knew Pitt's review would be negative. Pitt had written negative reviews before about shows at the Fabricant Gallery?"

"Once or twice. But it's my understanding that Mr. Pitt is — was — usually hard on new painters."

"What about Rees's reviews? Were they good? Bad?"

"One or two have been good. I'd hardly think a bad review a motive for murder."

Jury said nothing to that. He set his cup and saucer back on the silver tray, got up, and walked close to one wall where a large canvas hung. It was a still life: flowers, fruit, and a triangular guitarlike instrument. "What is this instrument?"

"A balalaika. I've always liked that music."

"I don't believe I've ever heard one."

She laughed. "Well, if you went to Russia, you would. There's something nostalgic about the sound of a balalaika. Rather like the zither in that Orson Welles film. Haunting."

He drank his tea and looked at her. "Do you go with the others? To Russia, I mean." He was still looking at the still life.

"I have done a couple of times."

He turned. "St. Petersburg?"

Now it was her turn to regard him over the rim of her cup. "Is this germane to your investigation, Mr. Jury?" Her smile was slightly ironic. "Our holidays?"

"Yes." He said it easily and smiled.

Her smile was quickly lost to him. "Why?"

With a shrug, Jury turned back to the painting. "I'm not sure."

"You're not sure, but you seem quite serious."

He said nothing and turned and looked from wall to wall. There were perhaps a dozen or more paintings. "Who chose this art?"

"They did — Sebastian, Nicholas, Ilona, of course. That's one of hers. I mean, she painted it." Olivia indicated the one he'd been studying.

"Really?" Jury looked at it again. "It's lovely."

"Don't let Ilona hear you say that."

"What's wrong with loveliness?"

"To her it means decorative."

"Shallow?"

"Yes, I expect she'd say that."

Jury still looked at the painting. "What I've been wondering is why Madame Kuraukov can still have such — well, generous feelings about Russia after what happened to her husband." He turned to regard Olivia. "Michel — was that his name?" When Olivia merely nodded, he went on. "His execution wasn't, of course, an isolated case, but that's cold comfort."

"I agree. I certainly agree. Communism was murderous. But, you know, St. Petersburg was her home for most of her life."

Jury nodded. He was still up and turning to take in every painting in the room. "There's not a bad painting here." He accepted the cup she had refilled.

She laughed. "Would you expect there to be?"

"In view of the Rees exhibition, yes, I expect I would. I find it strange there'd be only that one example of highly questionable art. I don't think it's just me and my failure to appreciate it to think Rees's paintings are non-art —"

She interrupted him. "Non–subject matter, perhaps, but then people have said the same thing about Mark Rothko."

"Surely you're not telling me there's a similarity between the two."

Olivia smiled slightly, almost apologetically. "I suppose not."

"Rothko's stuff intimidates me. Rees's simply makes me feel duped." He returned to his seat and took a sip of cold tea. "What's really strange is that Rees's work would garner favor with not just one of them — Nicholas, say, which would be understandable — but all three of them. Nicholas might be soft on Ralph, but the other two would have to be soft in the head. Which they so clearly aren't."

"But perhaps they're just humoring one another. They are family, after all."

Jury shook his head. "No. Sebastian is too good a dealer and has a reputation for taste. Why would he risk it to humor his brother and his brother's boyfriend? And you'll never make me believe Madame Kuraukov would humor anybody. There has to be another reason." He looked into her eyes, their sheen softly fuzzed by firelight. "Why don't we have lunch?"

Olivia laughed. "That's a quick change of topic."

"There's a great little Indian restaurant in the Old Brompton Road."

"Well — yes, that would be very pleasant." She rose. "What about the other reason you say there has to be?"

"What?"

"For the Fabricants' supporting Ralph's work."

Jury had wondered if she'd prompt him on this. "I wish I knew. Come on."

33

It was the afternoon for the palace tour and Linda insisted on taking it. "You'll learn a lot."

Melrose was not sure he liked the implication that he came up wanting in the knowledge department. And he had just bought her an ice-cream cone, which he had depended on to make her less mobile. That was a joke. For a few moments, he'd lost her, couldn't see where she'd gone. And then he picked her out, running across the grass, heading for a clutch of visitors who were making their way around to the main entrance and the courtyard.

Melrose sighed and followed her.

The palace guide was talking about Tudor brickwork. She pointed out that the black triangles of brick on three sides of the courtyard were formed by the actual ends of the bricks themselves. On the fourth side, the black design had actually been painted on to match; hence it was slowly wearing away from exposure to the elements. Satisfied with her prologue, the guide was shepherding them toward the front door when Linda said, "Aren't you going to tell them about the wicked gate?"

The guide frowned. "I'm not sure I —" Then, understanding, she smiled. "Oh, yes. The wick'd gate. Not *wicked*, dear. Yes, as you can see the gate is made so that the small door there will accommodate only one person at a time. That's to see if the person is friend or enemy and to avoid opening the entire gate and letting a battalion of men on horseback through." Sunlight touched the guide's glasses. The lenses gave off a blind glare that made the woman look sinister. As she turned towards the big front door again, she looked back and said to Linda, "We won't eat that inside, dear, will we?"

We will if we want to, thought Melrose, watching Linda lick her ice-cream cone, just as we will continue to think of the gate as "wicked."

After a few comments about the wide hallway's woodwork and ceiling, the guide led them into a large, empty, and very chilly room. To the stragglers in their group (Melrose being straggler number one), she said, "we all want to keep together now."

No, we don't. Melrose loathed touring

houses. He looked at Linda, who was listening raptly to the guide's description of the architecture of this room, of the big fireplace adorned with tiles and with carvings of bowls of fruit on the overmantel.

Having polished off her ice cream, Linda's hands were now clasped almost reverently at her waist, and her mouth was partly open, as if she had trouble breathing through her nose. Why, wondered Melrose, was she listening so intensely, her lips moving as if taking the words in through her mouth? Why was she listening when she apparently knew more than the guide? She knew, he imagined, what the gardener knew, what the guide knew, what the museum keeper knew, and possibly what even the bishops of London knew. It occurred to him (and it saddened him to think so) that Fulham Palace was Linda's home-away-from home. The roads, walks, borders, and boundaries were as familiar to her as the layout of her aunt's house. It was for this reason that Linda wanted to hear about the palace; it was like hearing one's favorite story again and again at bedtime. And the storyteller better look sharp! Any discrepancy or any hole in the narrative would be brought swiftly to that person's attention.

Which was what she was doing now, upon hearing a list of contributions made to this room — the Great Hall — by various bishops of London. Linda piped up: "Tell us about the tortures. The ones Bishop Bonner did." A few chuckles could be heard from the visitors, and the guide's face reddened a little, drew in like a knot.

It was clear the guide meant to skip Bishop Bonner's doings — why, Melrose couldn't say, as it was much the most interesting news yet — for she was leading them through the door, across the hall, and down a narrower hallway. The building had the cold feeling of one not much used to pilgrims. Nonetheless, Melrose kept up. They were taken into a small and quite beautiful chapel. Melrose moved to the front of the little group to stand beside Linda, ostensibly to monitor her behavior but more (he suspected) to be on the winning side. They were given details about the east window and the quatrefoil and, when one of the pilgrims asked about the use the chapel was put to, were told that the rector of All Saints had to give permission for anything taking place here, such as weddings and christenings.

"Which he won't," Linda told the assembly, with a sigh that might have been heartfelt, suggesting her own baptism hung in the balance.

"Perhaps," said Melrose, as they were filing down the hall again, "we could go see the rector of All Saints about the jeopardy in which he's placing your soul."

Linda peered up at him, her face screwed up in a knot, like a big carbuncle. "What're you talking about?"

"I have no idea."

The next room was light and airy but also without furniture, or at least period furniture. Melrose spent the few moments not listening (he could always ask Linda) but, instead, thinking of Simeon Pitt. His death was too unexpected; his murder, too bold and too brazen. Why hadn't the killer waited until Pitt was outside the club? And this was, apparently, a woman's work, to boot. She had stabbed Pitt with surgical precision; there had been no aborted or exploratory cuts, no evidence that Pitt had raised his hands and arms in self-defense. Melrose had an image of this woman rising from her chair to go to Pitt's, leaning over him, ostensibly to look at something in the paper or to hand him something. The woman was undoubtedly *not* the niece, Barbara Amons, so how had she explained her presence?

Was it someone Pitt knew? (For there was no reason it couldn't have been a total stranger.) What about the artists he was so tough on? This line of thought was fruitless, since Melrose did not know who Pitt knew, or the artists Pitt took down. Who was the person Pitt had called — Jay? This could have been a man or a woman. Melrose squeezed the bridge of his nose. Why couldn't he have been more like Linda, absorbing Pitt's every word?

He still couldn't get over the audacity of the whole thing, more audacious, even, than the murder in the public grounds of Fulham Palace.

Melrose stood there, eyes blind to the moldings, ears deaf to the guide's description, thinking about the killer's moving the body. If Jury believed Linda, he did too. He wanted to go back to the herb garden and was glad that this room was the last thing on the agenda. He whispered, "We've got to go."

"It's not finished yet. We get tea and biscuits now. You have to wait."

Exasperated, Melrose said, "I'll get you tea and biscuits later."

Unmoving, she demanded, "Where?"

"At the Ritz. Only come along now; we're going back to the gardens."

Seeing it had something to do with the dead body, Linda didn't offer more argument, and they left the palace proper.

Outside, Melrose turned to her and said, as sternly as possible, "Linda, do not—I repeat, do *not* — get separated from me again! Do not run off the way you did."

She scratched her neck and said, "It was *you* that got separated from *me*. You weren't keeping up." She looked around as if she might go back in and get a few witnesses to this careless behavior of his.

"You know what I mean. Here, you must hold my hand."

"I don't want to. Then I can't do anything on my own."

"That's the point; you're not supposed to be doing things on your own. At least, not when I'm with you." Was that circular reasoning? "All right, you don't have to hold my hand if you promise not to go running off. The same thing might happen to you as happened to poor Sophie." They were walking past the giant redwood tree.

"Who's poor Sophie?"

"You don't know her. When she was younger than you are now, she got separated from her mum in a shop —"

"What kind of shop?"

"A market. A fancy one in Paris."

"I've never been to Paris."

"That's beside the point."

"What did she look like?"

Melrose frowned. "I don't know. It doesn't make any difference."

Linda sighed as if adults didn't know what was important and what not. "What happened to her?"

He was angry with himself for letting the Sophie predicament leak out; it had shown very poor judgment and he knew Linda would be relentless in her demand to know what happencd. "Well, she got taken while she was putting potatoes in a bag."

Linda was dumbfounded. Not because Sophie was taken, but because of what had occupied her at the time. "Why would she put potatoes in a bag?"

There was nothing for it, he guessed, but to tell her at least the beginning of the Sophie tale. His story was interrupted more than once by demands to know more about the organ grinder's cat and dog and baby carriage. That Sophie had met such a dire fate didn't appear to concern her. It was all the violence on television, he supposed. Desensitization, that was it.

Linda's one hundredth (and, prayerfully, final) question was not about Sophie's lost mother, not about the kidnappers, not about the imagined dangers of the child's plight, but about the potatoes.

"What kind were they?"

"What earthly difference does it make? Must you know every single detail? Good God, it's like talking to Proust. *N'allez pas trop vite.*"

"What's that mean?"

"It means . . . they were Rose (Clouds and Yukon Golds." He was pleased with himself; he had pulled *those* potatoes out of a hat!

"I never heard of them. Where'd they take Sophie when they kidnapped her?"

Melrose was now concerned that perhaps she *was* worried. "To a film."

Linda licked the candy stick she had held him up for again and seemed to be thinking. "Well, I'm glad Sophie doesn't live around me."

What an odd thing to say. "Why?"

"Because she sounds so boring."

"Boring? What do you mean?"

"Well, if you were Sophie, would you pick out potatoes when there was an organ grinder and a trick cat and dog right outside?"

Melrose frowned and stopped as they rounded the wall on which wisteria would grow in rich profusion in the spring. As

438

Linda raced to the herb garden, his frown deepened.

He stood looking down at the triangular patch identified as lad's-love and the one across from it marked lavender. He asked Linda again if she was certain the body had lain here — he pointed to the lad's-love.

"I've told everybody a thousand times, yes."

"Perhaps, but you haven't told me a thousand."

"I guess you want me to lie down in it again."

"Certainly not. I didn't want you to lie down in it in the first place." Children were such ghouls.

Two things, he decided, had gone wrong for the killer: Jury should not have been on that bus, and Linda should not have been in this garden. He pondered this while watching her go into the ruined green-house.

If the body had been hidden in there, why?

To delay discovery. But he kept coming up with *why?* no matter which road he took.

He sat down on a small stone bench in front of the wisteria vines, thinking about

Kate McBride and Sophie and, most of all, Simeon Pitt. Melrose leaned over, arms on knees, and looked at the dark earth at his feet. Under which Simeon Pitt would soon be buried. Melrose truly mourned him. It was so rare to find someone who didn't talk balderdash or berate your ears with inconsequential conversation.

He looked up, didn't see Linda, and rose quickly. He called her. "Linda!"

No answer. *"Linda!"*

An answer came back. *"Wha-at?"*

"Nothing." He sat again and continued to think about Pitt. Artists whose armor he'd put a dent in, columnists not so successful as he — but surely not possessed of the large-scale passion it would take to kill a man.

"Linda!" he shouted again.

"What?" came the reply again.

"What are you doing?"

"Nothing."

Had he expected any other answer? Did he think she was in there translating *Paradise Lost* into Slovakian or discovering a billfold full of identification left by the killer?

Pitt had come to some conclusion about the Fabricant Gallery and was about to do something — it must have to do with a future act and not a past one. At least, Melrose was working under that assumption. It must be those damned white paintings of Rees's.

"Linda!"

"*Whaaaaat?*"

"I think you should come out of there now." He searched his mind for some greenhouse horror. "There might be snakes. And spiders."

"Okay."

He watched the door. Did he really think she'd appear?

"Linda!" He got up.

"What?"

Oh, for pity's sake! He went to the ruined glass house and through the door, or what was left of it. She was just standing there, looking at something she held that she quickly made a fist around when she saw him.

"What's that?"

"What?"

"That." He nodded towards her closed hand.

"Nothing."

"No, it isn't."

"It's a *secret*. Have you got to know *everything?*" She turned away, but not before looking at him as if he'd gone loopy.

Well, he knew better than to push her for information. "If you found something related to this crime, you realize you're obstructing justice and the police will have you for it," he said, testily and stuffily. "I'll wait for you outside."

In another breathless moment she was out the door, walking right past him. When he just stood there, she turned and said, "Well, come *on*," as if justice-obstructing were all on his side and the police would know where to look.

34

When she came to the door of the Redcliffe Gardens flat, Kate looked different, a little younger, more relaxed, and, if possible, more vulnerable. Of course she would be more relaxed, probably relieved as hell to be shut of Chilten and the Fulham police station. That would bring the color back to her cheeks, or perhaps it was the rose of the silk blouse she was wearing.

When she had hung up Jury's coat, she led him into her sitting room, which was suffused with the warmth of the fire. The room was pleasantly furnished, very English with its floral prints in slipcovers and curtains. It was on the small side, but generous for one person. There was only one bedroom.

She offered him coffee. "With a shot of brandy, how's that sound?"

"You must be reading my mind."

She hesitated in the doorway. "I doubt that I could."

While she went off to fetch the brandy, Jury stood and looked around. Framed posters in German and French. Jury didn't know if this reflected taste or travel. No photographs, a couple of shelves of books. Quite a CD collection, one of which was already playing. Mozart, he thought, reminding himself for the hundredth time he should know, not guess. He sat down in an armchair, felt the relief in his back. He hadn't known how tired he was until he sat down. He looked across the room at a large painting, some forest scene, he thought, and got up to view it more closely. It was actually of a house. Only part of the house could be seen; the rest was obscured by the woodland in front and mountains rising behind. But what woods and what mountains! The light coming through the trees might have been the painter's idealization of the scene, but perhaps not. *Blaen-y-glyn* was written on a small brass plaque at the bottom.

"Beautiful, isn't it? The house and the land — there's a hundred acres of it — are so beautiful it makes you want to weep."

He hadn't heard her come up behind him. "This is the place in the Black Mountains?" When she nodded, he asked, "Why did your husband's uncle make moving in by Christmas a condition of inheritance?"

"I don't know. Perhaps he didn't want

the place to go untenanted for a long period of time. Or didn't want it sold. Michael's mother was American, and I think he felt Michael should come home. 'Home' being upstate New York."

"Then why would he leave your husband property in Wales if he wanted you to live in the States?"

"I've no idea. He died not long ago, poor man. The first Thanksgiving after his death we were to sign papers at a solicitor's office at the Inns of Court."

"That's day after tomorrow."

"Yes. Perhaps he wanted to remind Michael of his American origins. He was a little wacky, I expect. Let's sit down."

She had brought coffee and a cut-glass decanter and two snifters on a black enameled tray painted with a bowl of roses. He accepted a cup from her. He leaned forward, the glass between his hands, the lush aroma of a superior cognac making him vaguely dizzy. Jury remembered that it was she who had asked him to come here. "Why did you want to see me, Kate?"

Hesitating, she fingered the decanter. "First: are you still so determined to believe you saw me that night?"

Jury didn't answer immediately. Then he said, "Determined isn't the way to put it. It

445

makes it seem I want it to be true. But it's the other way round: I *don't* want it to be true, and I'd sooner believe you weren't within a mile of the bloody place."

She dropped the glass stopper back into the bottle. The clink reverberated in the still room. She sat down opposite him on the sofa. "You were right."

He was not tempted to say, I know. Instead, he felt that coldness in the pit of his stomach, the way one feels when one hears a diagnosis confirmed, as if he hadn't all along been sure and needed the confirmation. He held his cup in both hands, seeking any fresh source of warmth, and waited.

"There was another" — she looked across at Jury, straight across the distance between them — "another letter. I was to go to Fulham Palace. I was even told to get off the bus at the Fulham Broadway station and walk and then reboard the bus, if I could, or board another. When it got to Fulham Palace Road, I was to get off and — well, the rest is obvious. There was a little map of the grounds and the walled garden. I haven't the least idea why this place was chosen, any more than the other places."

"And when you got there?"

She cocked her head and smiled slightly. "You're certainly cool, Superintendent; you don't seem surprised."

"It's Richard, and I'm totally un-cool, and I am surprised. Although the possibility did occur to me that this was another attempt — but go on."

When she said it, her voice was dry, as if she were parched, emotionally. "This woman was just — lying there, in that sable coat. You were right about the coat, too. I was wearing one — mink." She shook her head in both disbelief and wonder that she could have come upon this scene. "That was all. That was absolutely *all*." Her terrible position in this whole business must have struck her suddenly and terribly, like a blow to the chest, for now there was a burst of tears as she fell back against the sofa.

"Kate." Jury moved to the sofa, laid his arm atop her own outstretched arm, laid his cheek against her hair. It smelled of lavender. "Kate," he said again, the word muffled by her hair, and twined his fingers within hers.

When he did this, she twisted around and laid her head on his chest. She said, "There are times I think I can't stand it anymore, being alone."

"I know the feeling."

She moved away from him, and he let her go. She stood up and drank the rest of her cognac. Then she started moving about the room, tidying pillows that didn't need tidying.

He sat back and watched her. "So it wasn't like the others, this meeting place. What about the message itself. Did you keep it?"

"Yes." She moved to the back of the room to a small kneehole desk and slid open a drawer. She came back to the sofa, handed the paper to him, and sat down again. "It's shorter than the others; there's a different —" She looked around, as if words hung in the air from which she might take the right one. "A different tone, I guess you'd say."

It was a half page of white paper, thicker than the ordinary typing or printer paper Jury was used to seeing. The message was brief; *Your meeting place is Fulham Palace, the herb garden.* Then the time and date and where she was to leave and reboard the bus.

Jury said, "All of the others mentioned Sophie."

She nodded. Her elbow on her knee, her mouth was pressed against her fisted hand.

Jury held the note up to the light. "This wasn't done on a computer; it was typed."

She turned around, read it again. "I didn't notice. How stupid of me. I knew something was different. The whole thing is different."

Jury put it in an envelope and said, "It looks as if you were set up, Kate."

She stared at him, her mouth opening and closing. "But — *why*, Richard? And how could anyone know about Sophie — I mean about the other places, the meetings in Brussels and Petersburg?"

"Who did you tell?"

"No one. I mean, except for the Paris police, of course."

Now Jury was looking at the map, done on a piece of flimsy paper. It showed the way to the knot garden from the stone pillars. "This map is traced." It looked familiar to him. He folded it and put it in the envelope, too, and put the envelope in his pocket. "Kate, you must have told someone; you could have done that and forgotten, or without meaning to —"

"For God's sake, Richard, how could I tell someone my child's been kidnapped, without meaning to?"

"Sorry. You're right . . . but what about that awful day when it happened?"

She thought for a moment. "Yes, of course, I asked a lot of people if they'd seen Sophie. I was hysterical."

Jury thought of the priest. "What about Charles Noailles?"

She frowned as she turned to him again. "But that was before it happened, I mean when Michael knew him. And you told me he didn't even know Michael had a daughter."

"His church was right there, near the rue Servandoni. St. Sulpice. You said you could see the spire from your flat. It's a hell of a coincidence, don't you think? This person out of your past who knew your husband so well turns up in one of the offices of Fulham Palace. I don't trust coincidences." She said nothing, and he took her silence for sorrow. "I'm sorry, Kate. I'm so sorry."

She came to sit beside him again and he pulled her over, pulled her head down against his chest. "Look, Scotland Yard has tremendous resources. We'll get her back." Jury didn't believe that, but it was an easy lie. It was always an easy lie, and he felt slightly ashamed. He rubbed her back and wished he knew something both true and comforting to say.

"There's something I've been wondering

about all week," she said, without moving her position and looking at him. "Why, when you followed me all that way from the pub, didn't you then follow me into the palace grounds? Why didn't you come in?"

Now he turned his mind to this again, this time wondering about what might have happened, what potential tragedy might have been averted — or brought about — if he had done so. Would his presence have rearranged everything? From the dead woman's position, to Kate sitting at that table in the station, down to that vase of roses, the magazines in that rack, the books, the light spilling from beneath a frosted glass lampshade — would it all have been changed? Over her shoulder he looked almost coldly and clinically around the room, despite the great upheaval in his heart. And he wondered that the room itself didn't fly apart: paintings and posters drop from the walls, books fly from the shelves, lamps overturn. He felt divided and began to see some faint glimmer of an answer to her question in this: that even if he had gone in it would be as if he hadn't, that he could not have left foot- or finger-prints or anything behind to show he had been there. When he finally answered, he imagined the question had already been forgotten.

Because I wasn't invited. But that sounded so strange that he didn't say it. He settled for, "Fate, I guess. It wasn't in the stars."

The awful paradox of something he refused, refusing him.

35

"Is your medical examiner absolutely certain that it was an exit wound?" Melrose asked. They were sitting in the Members' Room having morning coffee.

"Dr. Nancy? No. It's not as easy as you might think to say whether a person was shot in the front or the back. The bullet can tell you what it passed through and, often, the order of the passing. According to the position of the body in the lavender, and the blood and residue pattern, Nancy Pastis was shot at close range in the chest."

Melrose fell to contemplating the stag over the mantel and wondering about blood sports. "But you've said you believe Linda really *did* see the body in the lad's-love, so what about that?"

"You know what-about-that. The killer moved the body."

"Yes, yes," said Melrose, irritated that Jury wasn't reading his mind, "but why?"

"My assumption is, to hide it. But you're trying to get at something. Why don't you just tell me? Want another coffee?"

"I suppose so."

"Don't do it on my account." Jury motioned to the porter.

"It's not really a theory, not anything so grand as all that. I'm just wondering if the body was moved to suggest the bullet's coming from another direction. Such as the palace itself." Melrose was pleased with himself. Sounded rather good, that.

"Ah. Are you thinking of the priest, Noailles?"

Melrose frowned. "Well, yes. Kate McBride knew him, didn't you say?"

"I did. But I'm not sure what you're getting at. Did Nancy Pastis know him? Anyway, according to him, it was Michael McBride, not his wife, that he knew."

"But there's got to be some connection with the Pastis woman. Both of them showing up in the unlikely venue of Fulham Palace at night — that's a bit of a stretch, you must admit."

"You think it's something to do with Noailles."

"I didn't know until now that Pastis was shot at close range. I thought she might have been shot from a distance, you know, such as from the palace."

"I considered that when I was in Noailles's room. You can't see the herb garden from his window. Even assuming he had a rifle with a scope." Jury smiled. "Sorry."

Melrose sighed. "Here I've been doing all this thinking. . . ."

"You need the practice."

"Oh, ha. If I do well enough, are you going to hand me a metal badge and a six-shooter?"

"Maybe."

"Then let's move on to another point. The conductor of the Fulham Road bus and several others mistakenly identified the woman they saw. If the person on the bus was actually this Pastis woman —"

"She wasn't. It was Kate McBride."

"You're still so sure?"

"I saw her that night, remember? I mean, over a long period of time." Jury shrugged, trying to play it off. "And, also, she told me."

"Told you? When? Why?" Melrose tossed down his napkin as if it were a glove inviting Jury to duel. "I'll be a monkey's. After all that denying and denying. . . . Why didn't she admit it before?"

"Because it puts her at the scene of the crime, a place none of us wants to be put." Jury spooned sugar into his cup, glad Wiggins wasn't here to remind him of his teeth. "We've found no one else who was there. It looks bad, don't you see?"

"Of course I can see. I can see this case is getting away from yours truly. What made her tell you, finally?"

Jury smiled. "To clear her conscience, something like that."

"Something like that, indeed!" Melrose picked up one of the biscuits that had been served with the coffee, studied it as if a runic message might be imprinted there, and said, "You said, *I saw her,* meaning that you'd never believed she *wasn't* there. You always knew it was she. Correct?"

"I suppose so."

Melrose put down the biscuit, having learned all he could from it. "She knew you knew it and wouldn't stop knowing it." His look at Jury was prodigious. "*That* was why she admitted it, old bean, old Super." Melrose could claim at least that point.

Jury didn't want him to claim it. "What difference does it make?"

"What difference? The difference is whether you're being manipulated or not."

"I think her reason makes sense. Now she's a suspect, after all. A role no one wants to play."

"You don't say *she's a suspect* with anything like conviction. All right, why in

God's name was she going to Fulham Palace at night? Was it to see this priest? The chap she claims not to know very well?"

Jury shook his head. "To meet someone. Someone who didn't turn up." He told Melrose about the note.

"You mean another aborted meeting?" When Jury nodded, Melrose asked, "But why in hell didn't she tell the police or you this before?"

"She didn't think we'd believe her."

Melrose ran his hand over his forehead. "Ye gods, everything seems to be getting more mucked up than cleared up. And it's almost back to square one with the victim — Nancy Pastis."

"Not quite. Her flat's in Shepherd Market — in Mayfair — pricey flat and walls full of pricey paintings."

"Uh-huh. Then she didn't live far from the Fabricant Gallery and might even have bought something there?"

"She did."

"She *did?* And did they wine her and dine her, as they did me?"

"No. They don't treat everybody as they did you."

"I have a certain magnetic charm."

"Oh, it's not that. It's because you

457

bought one of Rees's paintings. They must be pretty hard to unload. Not to mention two by Bea. You purchased three paintings at one clip." Jury sipped the strong coffee. "They knew Nancy Pastis. Nicholas recalled her, finally. Frankly, I can't imagine forgetting anyone who buys in there, the prices, my God. Month's salary, it'd cost me."

"The only connection between your Kate McBride and the Fabricants and Nancy Pastis *and* Mona Dresser is the very tenuous one of a sable coat that keeps getting passed around. . . . Wait a minute! That coat! What about *that?* If Ms. McBride was wearing it, how in hell did it turn up on Ms. Pastis?"

"It didn't."

"Didn't? *Didn't?*"

Jury shook his head. "There were — are — two coats."

Melrose slid his stool back from the bar as if this proximity to impossible coincidence were too much to take. He held up his hands, palms out, to push it away. "Oh, no, oh, no. That both of these women were wearing Russian sable — oh, please."

"They weren't. Kate McBride's is mink. Maybe someone who knew fur could have told the difference in the dark; me, I wouldn't know the difference in the light. My only experience with fur is what these protesters paint on their placards. Or what my tongue feels like after a night at the Angel."

"Then it was the Pastis woman who was wearing Mona Dresser's coat?"

"Yes. Presumably came by it through this consignment shop."

"Then what happened after Kate McBride got to Fulham Palace? Who was the contact?"

"No one. What she found was a dead body, and it scared the hell out of her. Not just because the woman was dead, but because she looked like Kate herself and was wearing fur."

Melrose frowned. "Then is it possible this is a case of mistaken identity?"

"Yes. But I think she was being set up for the murder."

Melrose picked up his coffee, held it as if toasting someone or something. After a few moments, he said, "There are all of these people — the Fabricant clan, Ralph, the late Simeon Pitt, Mona Dresser, McBride, and Pastis — and not a blessed thing do they have in common. The fur coat connects Pastis and Mona Dresser and Olivia Inge. But not the Fabricants.

The brothers are connected to Nancy Pastis by virtue of the painting she bought. But they've nothing to do with Kate McBride. Simeon Pitt is connected to the Fabricant Gallery because of his past reviews of openings, perhaps to Ralph, though he was gone from the art scene before Ralph came along — or there would have been a review I'd love to have read!" Melrose felt a sudden onslaught of sorrow and stopped. He drank his coffee in silence.

"You really liked him, didn't you?"

Melrose cleared his throat. "I did." He turned to look at Jury. "When I think about Pitt, I have two reactions, sadness and rage. It simply makes me furious that a man can't sit in the peace and quiet of his own club chair and be safe. It enrages me that a killer can just walk in off the street and put a knife in you. In him."

"I know. I'm sorry."

After another moment of silence, Melrose asked, "Could I have a look at this Pastis woman's flat?"

"I don't see why not. Something particular you're looking for?"

"No. I'd just like to see if I can hit on something that connects all of them. At this point, nothing I can see does." He set down his cup.

"Yes, there is." Jury looked across at the chair where Simeon Pitt had last sat.

"What?"

"St. Petersburg."

36

The police had removed the yellow crime-scene tape and Boring's was back in business — if one could call catering for Colonel Neame and Major Champs and two old fellows Melrose didn't recall having seen before, snoozing over their books and papers, "business." There had been the mutual exchange of clumsily framed condolences from Neame and Champs. It was as if Melrose were the last of the Pitts. Perhaps it was morbid sitting here across from Pitt's empty chair, sitting beside the one Jury had just vacated, but Melrose still sat.

Not a single living soul, Simeon Pitt had said, about his lack of intimate companions. He had said it as if he'd won a victory, as if being unencumbered with family, and even friends, were a height all should aspire to. Yes, Simeon Pitt had been the most self-reliant person Melrose had ever known.

St. Petersburg. They had all been there. The Hermitage.

Pitt had read the item to him about this

stolen painting. What was it? What was it named? Melrose looked at the table between the two club chairs for the paper Pitt had been quoting from. It had been cleared away, yesterday's paper being an anachronism in a men's club where the chief order of business was the daily paper. Melrose looked around for a porter. He gestured to Young Higgins, who had reverted from the lively raconteur persona brought on by murder back to his snail-paced self. When Higgins arrived, Melrose asked him if Monday's *Times* and *Telegraph* were still around somewhere and to please bring him coffee also.

Higgins found the *Telegraph*, expressing consternation that he couldn't find the *Times*. He went off to get the coffee.

Melrose scoured the paper. Here was the article about Oake Holyoake, which had been the mise-en-scène for the murder of some fool in a tux and a Beamer, he who had stopped in the village church (for what reason Melrose couldn't even guess at) and gotten shot for his troubles. The vicar had been far more intent upon talking about his quoins and tiles than about somebody dropping dead in the chancel. The villagers were more interested in promotion than in murder. In Oake Holyoake the

Saint Valentine's Day massacre would have gone unnoticed except as an advertisement for garage space.

Melrose went to the arts section. Here it was, the bit Simeon Pitt had read him: the painting stolen from the Hermitage, cut from its frame so smoothly and quickly one would have supposed the frame had never held it. *Wingless, Wingless Angels*, it was called. The only Chagall in the museum.

St. Petersburg. How many incarnations had it had? Leningrad, Stalingrad. For nearly three-quarters of a century, caught in the grip of Lenin and Stalin.

Pitt's friend, Jay. Had he talked to him finally? Trying to trace this person would be impossible. Perhaps Jury could set the British Telecom dogs on the heels of Boring's outgoing calls or could himself run down everyone Pitt knew, but the task seemed daunting.

Young Higgins, coming up behind him, made him jump.

"Done with Monday, are you, sir? Ready for Wednesday?"

Neither, Melrose wanted to tell him, as he looked at his dead friend's chair. He asked Higgins to bring him a telephone. He felt the need to talk to Bea Slocum, which surprised him, since he rarely felt it as a need to share his thoughts with others.

Perhaps he should think about that when he had time to think about it.

The phone in her flat rang ten, a dozen times before he put down the receiver. Bea hadn't an answering machine. Good girl. Long buried were those images of black telephones in empty houses, ringing hopefully and going unanswered. Oh, it was all so easy now! Horribly easy, and together with the ease came the emptiness, as it very often does. No more anticipation, no dreaming on the event, no ring of telephones echoing down hallways. Melrose sighed. It was, perhaps, melancholy, but it was at least a fantasy, and fantasy was getting buried under efficiency these days.

Melrose called the Museum of Childhood and was told she'd just left. "Said she was going to some church sale where her friends live. E Five or Six, I think she said."

Melrose thanked the woman and replaced the receiver. This must be the church White Ellie had been talking about, the one where Ashley and his friend flogged their wares. Or somebody's wares.

Later, he might try to find her. Right now, he intended to venture forth to Shepherd Market. He hove himself from his chair and informed Young Higgins that he wouldn't be having lunch.

Jury had sent the page bearing the message to Kate McBride to the Fulham headquarters right after he'd passed the context of its turning up to Ron Chilten. There was little chance that the paper itself would be traceable. Chilten said he would have her picked up again. Jury had asked him to what end, after she'd told them what she'd seen?

"Because she just told you she was there, man."

"As far as you were concerned, she was there before."

"You mean as far as *you* were, Jury."

"Hindsight would save us all, Ron. You still treated her as if she were there."

The first time she had given them nothing. Chilten had questioned her on the assumption she'd been at Fulham Palace on that fatal Saturday night. They had assumed she was present and therefore a suspect — the only suspect they had.

He sat at his desk, restlessly turning pages, deep in Kate McBride's past. He brooded. What bothered him was not her admission, finally (for he hadn't needed to be told), but the hell she must have been put through and was still going through. (And in this respect he had put in a call to the Paris police even before he had called Chilten, had made his inquiry, had been told finally — after a half hour of being switched back and forth — that all records housed in that particular part of the building had been destroyed in a fire, as Kate had said. The case was utterly cold; they sounded neither hopeful of a successful outcome nor enthusiastic.)

Jury could not remember a case that had dead-ended at so many places, as in a stroll through a maze, one is sent off through another green channel and then another until one is stopped again.

The rattle of the *Daily Mirror*'s pages kept pace with Jury's thoughts, like dead leaves skidding across the cobbles of some little street in Paris. He thought it again — that none of this disturbing business about Kate was the cause of his present dark mood. What disturbed him really was what he himself, had he been in Kate's shoes, and little Sophie been *his* child, what he would finally have done. He'd have killed for her.

And that, in the end, was the blank green hedge he was left to face.

37

He did not know what he expected to find or even what he was looking for. But Melrose was sure he had never seen so many exotic pieces collected in so small a space. He picked up a Chinese jade horse from a sofa table inlaid with turquoise with jade and jet in its center.

The objects here spoke not only of money but of travel. Melrose doubted anyone would find that warrior's spear or that *makishi* mask at Harrods. Both were hanging on the wall to the right of the fireplace. If she had been to someplace like Zambia (probably the origin of the mask), then she had traveled widely.

Melrose started to look at other artifacts with an eye to their origins. He could not assign a provenance to the rug beneath his feet; that she could have obtained at Harrods, but it would have cost her. In the glass-fronted cabinet against the wall was a collection of porcelain and jade figurines that looked as if they would furnish the owner with income for the rest of her life.

On the other side of the fireplace was a Russian triptych icon featuring several saints, who looked grimly out from under emblazoned haloes.

Everywhere there were photographs, not of people but of places. Here were a cluster of snapshots of a tropical place, black sand suggesting Tahiti. Others of groups of natives, three wearing elaborate masks, probably Polynesian. Another was of a wide river, with two figures as black silhouettes against a sun that cut a wide swath on the water, making its surface appear to be smoking. Melrose could almost hear the oars *whish* and the water break and the wind comb the palm fronds.

Still wearing his coat, Melrose sat down on the sofa, running his hand over the supple leather. It looked old but was probably just distressed. Nevertheless, it was as fluid as velvet.

He got up to look at the wall of paintings. Jury was right; she must have loved art to have arranged so many across one wall. His eye trailed over a row of paintings of various periods and styles and stopped at a gorgeous rendering of a city muffled in snow. Russia, or perhaps Czechoslovakia. The onion domes floated above the snow-laden buildings, glowing like pearls.

Framed in dark wood against a darker matting, the ice and snow seemed to rush out at him and he felt an actual chill. He looked at the bottom to see what was written there: *Nevsky Prospekt*. St. Petersburg.

Jury was right; it seemed to be everywhere.

He was assailed by the strong fragrance of vetiver. It smelled like ashes; it would be difficult to describe to someone else how the smell of ashes could be so seductive.

"Oh, hello."

He jumped when he heard the voice behind him, coming from the open doorway. The woman who stood there was holding a bag full of groceries that looked much too heavy for her. She was one of those elderly ladies who reminded him of paper valentines, the old kind one comes across in antique shops: hearts glued to doilies, lacy, gold-fringed, and faded.

Melrose immediately stepped to the doorway and took the heavy burden of groceries from her. "Let me help with this."

"Oh. Well, thank you. I only live just next door." She looked around the hall. "Where's Constable Beane gone?"

"I don't know; I saw the policeman outside, that's all."

She seemed amused and Melrose hoped

he hadn't sounded patronizing with his offer to help; after all, she'd carried the bag this far, hadn't she? But she also seemed pleased, so there might yet be a place in the world for gallantry.

He followed her into her flat and took the bag into the kitchen, where she asked him if he would stay to tea.

"I'd love a cup of tea," he answered, suddenly thirsty.

She said it would just be a minute and for him to make himself at home. Given her flat, it seemed the right instruction, for it was a place where one could make oneself at home. This flat was in sharp contrast to Nancy Pastis's. The furnishings and fittings here were not luxurious, though by no means were they poor. The slipcovered sofa and easy chairs, the corner shelves that held not Chinese porcelain but souvenirs — *A present from Brighton* scrolled across a saucer, enameled boxes declaring love and friendship, several old fairings — all so trenchantly English that Melrose grew almost sodden with sentiment.

He sat down. He knew what the tea tray would look like and for some reason felt comforted. A flowered teapot with matching cups and saucers, a plate of biscuits and one of seed cake. (He had seen the cake poking out of the top of the bag.) Nancy Pastis, had she asked one to tea, would probably have used the samovar and glasses in metal holders.

The tea tray appeared, a large silver one, and he was pleased he had been dead on about its contents. Again, he rose to help. He set the tray on the oval table — which he was sure was the right place for it — and said, "This is awfully kind of you. I was on the edge of perishing."

She tucked a strand of hair back in the bun at her neck. "I hope the cake is all right. I've never used this particular pastry shop before, and I thought I'd just try it." She was pouring the tea. "Would you like some toast? At least that's dependable." She sliced the cake.

"No. This is fine. Wonderful."

She sat back from the tray with a little lurch. "I forgot to introduce myself. I'm Vera Landseer. Are you a policeman too?"

He laughed. "Lord, no. I'm Melrose Plant, the friend of one. He's already been here."

"That nice man, the handsome one? Superintendent, I believe. Drury or —"

"Jury. You've a good memory. He says people are always demoting him to

472

Inspector status."

"I didn't."

"You made a hit, then. Yes, he told me about you."

She seemed to delight in this. "I only wish I could be more help in this awful business. Even though I lived next door, I saw little of Nancy. Once or twice she had me over to tea —"

Melrose almost asked if Miss Pastis had used the Russian samovar.

"— and once I had her here. The thing is, she was seldom around. She did a great deal of traveling. To the most exotic places! Places most people only dream about seeing. What struck me as strange was that she did this on her own. It seemed to me she was *always* on her own. That's quite brave and unusual, isn't it? Women do not like doing things on their own, do they? How often do you see a woman alone in a restaurant or the theater? Well, I expect I'm setting women's rights — or whatever it's called — back by decades."

Melrose chewed a biscuit, as he thought he didn't often go anywhere himself except to the Jack and Hammer or, sometimes, to places where Jury felt his presence could help. He rarely had occasion to dine alone in a restaurant and never occasion to go to the theater alone, as theater in his area was noticeably absent. But he did not say this, as he thought it might strike Vera Landseer as lacking bravery. "No, you're quite right. Hardly ever do I see women doing those things on their own. Miss Pastis didn't have many callers, I take it."

Vera shook her head. "Not that I was aware of. It feels strange talking about her like this. . . . I mean, when she's dead." A brief shudder gripped her.

Melrose frowned. It struck him that the police had turned up neither relations nor friends, not to mention lovers, of Nancy Pastis. Vera Landseer might be the only person who knew her on even remotely intimate terms. She had at least had tea with the Pastis woman. He found this lack of acquaintance strange. No matter how one kept oneself to oneself, it was unlikely one could get through life without leaving a trace, a trail of family and friends behind. How could it be otherwise? Even the resourceful Simeon Pitt had a relation of whom he was very fond, and numerous acquaintances, even though he rarely kept their company.

"Is something the matter, Mr. Plant?"

"What?" Melrose came out of his brown study. "No. No, I was just thinking."

"Deeply, apparently. May I ask, what of?"

"Yes. Nancy Pastis's lack of acquaintance. As you said, she did all this on her own, yet she clearly wasn't a recluse, not with all the traveling she did. You did talk to her, even if only in a superficial way." Melrose put down his teacup, picked up his plate of seed cake. "Did you form any opinion of her?"

Vera looked past him, out of the window at the failing light. "One does, I suppose, form opinions; one can't help it. But of her — I can only say she was remote. Hard to reach. I mean, one doesn't want to intrude or pry, so one senses — as with you, as with that pleasant Scotland Yard superintendent — one senses an invitation. Or not. I'm not talking, understand, about the overfamiliarity we're subjected to today. The new nurse in my doctor's surgery called me Vera the other day, when even the doctor still calls me Mrs. Landseer. Well, at least we haven't given ourselves over to the vulgar familiarity of that American habit of tacking on 'Have a nice day.' I'm not talking about that sort of thing. By invitation I think I mean accessibility. I'm being vague; do you understand?"

Melrose nodded.

"I found her to be superficially friendly but chilly. Cold."

"Was she misanthropic, do you think?"

Vera Landseer's gaze returned to the window, the tarnished sky beyond it. "That, or —" She shrugged, as at a loss to explain. "It's as if some faculty were missing. When we talked, I got the strange impression that she wasn't."

Melrose waited. When she didn't explain, he said, "Wasn't what?"

"Talking. Wasn't participating, even though she asked me in to tea. It was as if this whole tea thing" — she waved her arm over the tray — "were a meaningless ritual — no, more of an anachronism. As if she weren't, as they say, on the other person's wavelength. Misanthropic, perhaps, or perhaps running. You know, fugitive."

An odd thing to say, thought Melrose, once he was back in Nancy Pastis's flat. He was in the room she apparently used as a study. As Wiggins had said, there were no clues here as to her movements. Circulars, bank statements, catalogs from Harrods and Liberty's, but no letters. And most of all, "no jumble, sir," the sergeant had said. No jumble — that was quite true. It was the most orderly place he had ever been in, short of a museum.

Something was missing. He looked from bookcases to desk to shelves back to the desk. That was it: a computer. Could one walk into anyone's study or look at anyone's desk these days and not see a computer? Perhaps there was a laptop. Melrose looked at all the shelves but didn't find one.

He stood there looking round for some moments, thinking about what Vera Landseer had said about Nancy Pastis.

He felt there was something else missing. She was.

38

"Nancy Pastis," said Ronnie Chilten, "died in 1960."

Jury waited, knowing Chilten was waiting too on his end of the telephone in the Fulham station. He was waiting for a reaction, a "what?" or "meaning what?" Jury, Chilten knew, was waiting for an explanation.

Silence. Without too many pauses, caesuras, enjambments, Jury said, "Okay, Ronnie, I'm mystified. Tell me." He pulled out the bottom drawer of his desk and stuck his feet up.

"She was four years old when she died."

Jury moved the receiver away from his ear the way one does who's had confounding news. He brought it back, wishing Chilten weren't so fond of these fucking mind games. Blood out of a stone, getting information out of him. "You going to explain this, Ron, or should I come over to Fulham and beat it the hell out of you?"

Wiggins, concocting something across

478

the room that looked like blue mouthwash, raised his eyebrows at his boss's tone. He was too used to Jury's infinite (it sometimes seemed) patience.

"In other words, Rich, Nancy is not who Nancy says — pardon, said — she is. Or was."

"Go on."

Chilten didn't like to go on without teasing at least one gasp of surprise out of whoever he was talking to, particularly a higher-up. But he did. "Our background check turned up the usual records: bank, credit card records, mortgage — there isn't one, she paid cash — British Telecom, utilities, et cetera, et cetera. You'd be amazed what we can do."

(Jury himself not being a policeman.)

"But then ran up against a brick wall. Dead. We couldn't take her back further than three years ago."

"Which was when she got the flat in Mayfair."

"Nothing. Zero. Zilch. *Nada, nada, nada.*"

Jury sat, rocking back and forth in his swivel chair, one foot scraping the edge of the drawer. He watched Wiggins tapping his teaspoon against the viscous blue mixture. "The little girl who died: Nancy

Pastis. . . . There must be a few other women by that name, Ronnie."

"There are. We found three, actually. Histories all present and accounted for back to birth."

"You're saying —"

"I'm saying our Fulham Palace lady isn't Nancy Pastis. She's someone else."

This time, Jury didn't think Chilten paused for effect. "Someone who needed a birth certificate to —"

"— to get a passport, documents. You're right with me."

"That far, anyway." Jury leaned over his desk, watched Wiggins drop another ingredient into his glass that blossomed into white froth; at the same time, Wiggins was absorbing Jury's phone conversation. "How about forward? I mean, what else did you find out about her in the three years? She needed a passport; she was traveling, obviously. Russia, France — where else?"

"Argentina, Russia again, French Polynesia — Papua New Guinea —"

"That's Melanesia."

"Yeah, okay. Anyway, those were on the passport you saw. The visits were brief. Few days, week at the most."

Jury said, "You've been in her flat. The

woman must have traveled most of the time. In the three-year period covered by that passport, I'd think she must have been in other places. Didn't the Landseer woman say she was just back from Northern Ireland?" Something bothered him now; he drew a hand over his forehead. He looked over at Wiggins and motioned for him to pick up the phone on his desk. "I'm having Wiggins listen to this."

"Okay with me. Does this suggest anything to you?"

"Come on, Ronnie, don't play games. What it suggests is that Nancy Pastis was traveling under a false name with an illegal passport, for purposes we don't know but won't like when we do know. What else have you got?"

"Thing is, she must have had other passports, so I'm assuming she might have been issued them in the same way. So we're running a check, a cross-check. It's a big job for our equipment."

Fulham police had as easy access to the Yard's computer system as any other branch of the Metropolitan police. But Jury didn't say that. Chilten was, after all, being extremely forthcoming with information.

Jury thought for a moment. "You're

trying to check what birth certificates have been applied for — kids, babies who've died — to see if you come up with the same thing? But, my God, that would take one hell of a search, Ron. Do you have any parameters?"

"Women born in the sixties — more or less — who would have been her age now, if they'd lived. Her age being forty-one, according to the passport."

"Check on stolen passports."

"Am doing even as we speak. I don't get it. Say she had managed to get herself another passport, maybe several. Why was this one left in her desk?" When Jury didn't answer, Chilten said, "There must be another passport."

"Another name. Maybe the real one."

39

"Come on," said White Ellie, waving Melrose through the front door. "Tea's up." She motioned for him to follow her into the kitchen.

The house was almost funereal in its quiet. Glancing into the parlor (ordinarily the site of revel and carouse), Melrose thought he glimpsed a baby crawling out from under a great pile of laundry. He had approached the house guardedly and weighed down by the usual little screws of sweets. He'd been stunned to find the front garden empty of all but the signs of the last battle (clubs, stones, broken glass).

He sat down on a broken-legged wooden chair at the kitchen table as Ellie tossed a teabag into a mug, filled it with hot water, doused it with milk from a pint on the counter, and set it before him. A bit of ash from the end of her cigarette had dribbled down the side of the mug. She said, " 'Ere's sugar."

How can one improve on perfection? thought Melrose, shoving the bowl away from him with the tip of his finger. Not that he didn't take sugar; he was merely suspicious of some tiny thing he thought he had seen nose-diving into its center.

"So I sez t' 'im, 'Frankie, don't be takin' the piss out, and don't be gettin' Ashley into yer lockup.' Them rozzers do Frankie's garage ev'ry week, seems like." This last comment was to quicken Melrose's understanding of what Frankie got up to, whoever he was. White Ellie continued the story, begun, as usual, in medias res. "Why, last month, 'e come back wi' a t'ousand quids' worth o' them li'l enamel boxes when he visited one of them stately 'omes. You know 'im?" she asked, not really waiting on an answer, pretty much certain that any friend of hers must by now be a friend of Melrose. "Wide lad, our Frankie." As if Ash Cripps weren't wide enough himself to keep him out of anybody's garage. "But 'ere's what 'e does — keeps the good stuff in back covered up so Blind Ollie — 'e's the Bill round where Frankie lives — so 'e's so taken with the stuff up front like these 'ere li'l box things that 'e don't look in the back. I gotta gi' Frankie credit for usin' the old bean-o. Anyways —"

While White Ellie rambled on, the

thick-limbed baby-in-the-laundry had crawled into the kitchen and was paid no mind by Ellie, deep into her glutinous tale of Ash and Frankie. Considering the traps that awaited the child — de-limbings by that cleaver on the floor, scaldings by the kettle perched precariously on the hob, electrocutions by the several wires running into that dish of water (Ash Cripps's unpatented mousetrap), poisonings unlimited by the stuff in various containers easily grasped by little fingers and straightaway ingested — considering all this, Melrose was in awe of the child's having lived this long.

Ellie yelled — when the tot went for the lye — "Robespierre, get outa there!" The baby gurgled and headed for the cleaver.

Melrose commented on the wonder of Robespierre's having grown.

"Growin', ihn't 'e? 'E's nine, ten months. The spit o' Ashley, ain't 'e?"

Robespierre was the spit of everyone in the Cripps clan — they all had those gin-pale and lashless eyes, that yeasty skin, that compact, stubby, fireplug build — except for White Ellie, whose own build had earned her the sobriquet of Elephant (Ellie merely the shortening of same, and not her real name. Melrose had no idea what that was). Yes, it was definitely a signature look, even more than an Armani or Ralph Lauren or Issey Miyake. Yes, one could have picked out "the Cripps look" walking down the runway faster than one could a Versace.

"Indeed," said Melrose, "the very spit. But if you don't grab that knife away he won't have Ashley's nose."

" 'Ey! 'Ere, ya li'l bleeder!" Ellie reached out and grabbed the knife Robespierre was trying to get his fat little fingers around. She tossed it on the counter. "You want to see Beatrice, I expect. So we'll walk over to St. Iggy's. Be a nice stroll, it would. I'll just take off me strides, put on a skirt." She was out of her chair, tea poured down the drain, and through the door before Melrose could finish saying, "What about Robespierre, here?"

She shouted back, " 'E's got 'is stroller!"

As he waited, he regarded Robespierre, wondering how such a young tough, ten months old or not, could be contained in a stroller. He was presently chewing a crust of bread he must have wrestled from that adamantine-looking loaf. Melrose gazed round the kitchen, lit a cigarette, and enjoyed his afternoon. Unlike Sergeant Wiggins, for whom the ambience of the

Cripps kitchen was surpassed only by Bosnia's, Melrose rather liked it, as he liked all things that were barely describable. He was a natural candidate for a guided tour of Woburn Abbey, surrounded by a dozen old ladies; for a week in Ibiza in a no-stars hotel; for one of those unmentionable holiday camps where you had to use tokens for money.

When she returned, Ellie was wearing a voluminous flowered frock, the flowers similar to the pattern on the wallpaper (whose flowers had been improved upon by the family Cripps, who had seen the similarity to genitalia), and a straw hat with bouncing wax berries. In her hand she held a small camera.

"If you wouldn't mind just droppin' Robbie into 'is stroller. And put this 'ere in your pocket." She handed him the camera.

Melrose had also brought a camera. Clearly, Ellie and he were on the same wavelength. Now, he commandeered both cameras and the burly baby and set him in the candy-striped stroller. Robbie bounced and pounded and howled, not caring for his little canvas prison. Ellie just gave him a smack and he stopped and smiled.

Once out of the door and down the walk, Melrose was put in charge of the stroller and Ellie hooked her hand through his arm and pointed them all in the direction of St. Ignatius. A late afternoon sun washed the sidewalk, striking Robespierre's light hair and turning it to filaments like dandelion weed. It lit the berries on Ellie's hat. It polished the brown leather buttons of Melrose's cashmere coat, its pockets bulging with sweets bags and cameras.

They turned a corner, and White Ellie said, "It'd be ever so nice if you could 'ave a word with the kiddies, as you know 'ow much they respect you."

Respect? *Respect?* Melrose lifted his chin, wreathed himself in smiles, and inhaled the bright, chill November air. White Ellie was hardly one of those mums who sentimentalized her brood, but every parent goes blind sometimes. The only things the Cripps kids respected was money up front and a kick from behind.

Lowering her voice to a whisper, looking anxiously at the terraced houses, as if they had eyes and ears and gave a tinker's damn what this trio was up to, White Ellie said, "An' I wish you could 'ave a wee talk wi' young Alice. It ain't good the way she lifts 'er skirt up an' 'er wi' no knickers on. Where'd she learn that, I ast ya?"

Where indeed, what with her father getting nicked on a regular basis for showing himself in the public toilets? Melrose assured White Ellie he'd do what he could, patted the arm hooked so sedately in his, and determined that someone had to take a picture of the three of them, before the camera got started on its life of pornography.

Ah, Alice!

The "social," which was held every month, according to the big sign in the courtyard of St. Ignatius, was surprisingly well attended, and not only by the multinational sector (it looked like a meeting of the United Nations), their screaming kiddies wanting ice cream and cotton candy. There were some well-heeled types here, too, and Melrose wondered if word had really got around to the dealers. White Ellie waddled off to locate Ashley, leaving Melrose with the stroller and Robespierre.

There were "stalls," in this case largely tables, some with an impromptu tentlike affair set around them. Melrose caught a glimpse of what really looked like his own Derbyware and was surprised upon closer examination to see that it was — not his, at least he hoped not, but the real thing. The old pensioner — or not, considering his prices — talked the stuff up, and when Melrose asked where he had acquired it, said, "Belonged to me old auntie. She left it to me, bless 'er soul." Melrose purchased a cup and saucer for an outrageous sum — though no more than Trueblood would have asked, he supposed — to replace the one broken by his cook, Martha, who still shook her head over the gap in the dinner set. He put it in the carryall attached to the stroller, and Robespierre howled briefly.

The next little booth sold bits and bobs of jewelry, spoons, war medals, and other small items. Then came several stands of antiques: bureaus, clocks, chairs, marble statuary, paintings. The providers of these estimable pieces all talked like Ashley Cripps or racing touts. Finally, he found Ash's own "stall," which he was running with another fellow who, Melrose assumed, must be Frankie. Ash was delighted to see him and wrung his hand nearly off the arm in his enthusiasm.

"See ya got little Robbie wit' ya. Ain't he a chip off, then?" Introducing "me friend, Mel" to Frankie, he gave Mel a clap across his back that nearly sent him over the stroller and into a stall of lace and linen.

Frankie struck Melrose as a rather surprising companion for Ashley Cripps, given his military bearing and his waxed mustache, waistcoat, and spats. Frankie apparently specialized in gemstones. Melrose assayed this lot of jewelry and decided that not all of it was of the costume variety, nor were all the stones semiprecious. His brief excursion into the value of antiques, a subject taught him remorselessly earlier in the year by Marshall Trueblood, had touched on old stones and things like Victorian lockets and rings sporting small locks of braided hair and cameo or jet brooches. There had also been a brief lecture on precious stones: diamonds and emeralds. It was the last two in the list that Melrose was curious about now: surely, that ring in the middle of the line was set with a diamond of at least one carat, possibly more. It was surrounded, however, by pieces of far less, if any, intrinsic value. Melrose picked up a rather heavy, ugly aquamarine.

"Superior quality, that," said Frankie. "My elderly aunt, a woman of uncommonly fine taste, left it to me. I believe it was the dear lady's engagement ring. It's a pity I have to sell it at a mere fraction of its value."

Ash said, "We're lettin' that lot go for twenty-five quid."

Melrose gave him a look. It wasn't even worth five, and he said so.

Ash shrugged. "Seein' as how you're one o' me mates, 'ow about ten? Can't do fairer'n that."

"Oh, I believe you could." Melrose returned the ring, this time plucking up the diamond. "Twenty-five for this? I'd pay twenty-five."

Frankie adroitly plucked the ring from Melrose's fingers. "I fear that one is already spoken for."

"Then this one, perhaps?" Melrose picked up the emerald.

Ash said, nervously, "That 'un too, mate."

"Then why are they on display?"

Ashley didn't answer. He looked off across the schoolyard and motioned to Frankie. "Damn rozzers won't leave a body be. Blind Ollie, it's 'im, all right."

Melrose gazed over the tops of heads to see a tallish policeman strolling amongst the stalls. He had just turned away from the Bring 'n' Buy and appeared to be coming their way.

Frankie nudged Ash, and Ash, in turn, nudged Melrose into a sort of musketeerish mood, all for one and one for all.

"What you got to do," said Ash, "is just

stand 'ere, like you was thinkin' a buyin' one o' these 'ere." Ash grabbed up the diamond and put it in Melrose's hand. In much fuller and fruitier tones, Ash and Frankie greeted their policeman — for Melrose had no doubt he'd been following their escapades so long that he had truly become "theirs."

"Well, now, if it ain't our Constable Ryland. 'Ow are ya, Ollie?"

The constable nodded, hands behind his back, looked for a moment at the black velvet–covered display without much interest, and said, "Been over to your house, Frank. Your missus let me have a look in that lockup you got."

"You're welcome any time, Mr. Ryland. Any particular reason for this visit? Or is my garage merely your home-away-from-home?" Frankie ran a forefinger under his mustache, rather like an old-time villain might do.

"Another house was hit over in Highgate. Winnington. That's kinda your patch, right, Frank?"

"I've no idea what you're talking about, Constable. My patch, as you put it, hardly extends beyond my front garden."

"Well, there was a lot of stuff went missing from the Highgate place. China, silver, jewelry, even a dinner jacket. Odd, that." Ryland looked from one to the other, not forgetting to take a dekko at Melrose. He nodded. "Friend of yours, boys?"

"Not a bit of it," said Frankie. "A customer. And if you wouldn't mind, we'd like to go back to our business."

Ryland grunted, looking extremely irritated that he couldn't slap the cuffs on them then and there (including, Melrose felt, on himself) and push them into a van. Instead, he walked away.

When he was out of sight and hearing distance, Ash and Frankie went about boxing each other (and Melrose) on the shoulder, laughing fit to kill. Ash had to wipe his eyes with his handkerchief. Then he took the diamond from Melrose's hand and amidst his weepy laughter said, "Didn't I tell ya, best place to hide it, put it out. Like Frankie here says, 'You want to hide a diamond, put it in a tiara.'" Then he gave Melrose another smart clout on the shoulder.

Knowing the C:ripps kids' desire for quick results in everything, Melrose had had the foresight to bring a Polaroid. First he had Frankie take one of White Ellie, Robespierre, and him, posed like a little family. Then several of the kids, with Alice refusing to mind her manners. Next, one of Bea and Melrose (Bee mugging for the camera); last, one of the whole lot of them. The results were immediate and charming. Melrose had never seen himself looking quite so blithe. Bea, seeing how silly she looked in the one with Melrose, made Ash take another, with her sitting on a low stone wall, showing plenty of leg, while Melrose leaned against it.

"Oh, ain't that luv'ly," said White Ellie, as if they were all in a wedding party. "You do look sweet together." She was looking at the freshly developed Polaroid shot of Melrose and Bea sitting on the wall.

To Melrose they didn't even look together. "Look, she's pulling the corners of her mouth back. You call that sweet?"

But Ellie would have none of that, said she would take it home straightaway and hang it up, "soon as my Ashley packs up his clobber."

In his mind's eye, Melrose saw himself in Nancy Pastis's apartment, looking at that wall of paintings. It was then the penny dropped.

40

Jury drank what was left in his pint and set it on the counter, with a wink at Kitty and a nod to refill both his and Kate's glasses.

He had called Melrose Plant on the Stargazey's phone to tell him he wouldn't be having dinner with him at Boring's and listened in turn to Plant saying he was going back to Northants to look for an art restorer. Jury asked him what he was talking about, but Plant didn't explain and instead began a brief argument about searching the Fabricant Gallery.

"You and your mates go into the gallery and have a look round, if that's what you euphemistically call it."

"Can't do that. We don't have reasonable grounds."

"What? One of them murdered Simeon Pitt!"

"Even if that's true —"

"Damn it, of course it's true! He guessed what they were up to."

"Can you see one of them killing in that way? It would take a measure of flamboyance, at the least, to walk into that club and stick a knife in somebody while other people were in the room. All I can do at this point is go back and question them again. And don't forget the other murder."

He must have forgotten; Plant's mind wasn't on Nancy Pastis. Jury replaced the receiver and collected the two glasses Kitty had filled.

She looked across the room to where Kate was seated at a bench and said, "I see you found her."

Jury smiled. "I did indeed, Kitty."

All the way across the room, he was jostled to within an inch of spilling the beer.

"Thanks," said Kate, as he set down the drinks. After he sat down himself, she put her hand through his arm and got closer. "This place is blue with smoke. Doesn't that get to you?"

"Oh, it gets to me all right, but it's good for the soul — resisting temptation." He looked at her, smiled. "Well, some of it, anyway." He picked up his glass. "What's an art restorer do?"

"I'll take a wild swing at the answer and say he restores art. Why?"

"Oh, just this friend of mine who helps me out, unofficially. The one from Northants. I mentioned him to you."

"The ex-earl in that little village?" .

"That's the chap. I was just talking to him. Says he wants an art restorer."

Kate thought for a moment. "Ah." Then she asked, "He's the one who gave up his title?"

"Titles. Had a whole raft of them: Earl of Caverness, Viscount something-and-something, Marquess of Glengarry and Glen Ross. On and on."

Kate laughed. "*Glengarry Glen Ross* is a play by David Mamet."

Jury shrugged. "Well, there're a couple of Scottish titles in there somewhere."

"Was it politics? Did he want to be a commoner so he could run for the House of Commons?"

Jury laughed. "Lord, no, not him. Political is the last thing he is." Jury drank his beer. Plant had disquieted him; he felt uncomfortable.

"Are you all right?" She put her hand on his face.

He looked at her, smiled. "Absolutely. Only" — he drank down nearly half of his beer — "I've got to get somewhere. I'll see you tonight? Your place? Or are you tired of your place? Want to go to the cinema?"

"You've got to be kidding." Kate laughed.

41

Melrose sat in his club chair, letting his late-morning coffee go cold, chewing the side of his thumb. This was a habit he had indulged in since childhood, which neither his mother nor his nanny had been able to break him of. The habit was one he resorted to when he was in deep thought. Here the thought included a rerun of the conversation with Jury he'd just had. Melrose should have been more forthcoming, more specific in telling his friend what was taking shape in his mind. But perhaps that was the problem; it was still amorphous, not yet jelled.

They had been there, the Fabricants had, in St. Petersburg at the same time Ralph was. *Flamboyant.* Pitt had used that word in speaking of the theft of the Chagall.

Melrose did not want the murder of Simeon Pitt eclipsed by this Nancy Pastis murder.

What the devil constituted "reasonable grounds," anyway? He was absolutely sure that the Fabricants were responsible for Pitt's death.

Melrose went back to chewing the side of his thumb. Well, it wasn't Jury's fault; after all, they couldn't go in and toss the place. To get a warrant Melrose imagined one had to satisfy stringent conditions, and there were no visible ones insofar as the gallery or the Fabricants themselves were concerned.

This was why Melrose was chewing his thumb, in deep thought. The damned paintings would be gone if he didn't act immediately. Probably being wrapped and crated in that storage room at the gallery this very min—

Storage room.

Bea. Of course.

She was as silent on the other end of the phone as Jury had been, until she finally said, "Where did you get this idea?"

"Yesterday, at the fete. Frankie lobbed it over the net, or whatever they do to tennis balls. 'If you want to hide a diamond, put it in a tiara.' "

"Of course. It's really clever. Even if they didn't do it, you are for thinking it."

Melrose couldn't quite sort through that syntax and didn't try. "You know they're getting the paintings ready to ship. Have they crated them yet?"

"A couple, I think. See, each one has its own separate wooden box."

"Okay, how are they wrapped?"

"What do you mean?"

"Just that. Did they wrap them in brown paper, tie them with string? Twine?"

"Yes. Brown paper, twine."

Melrose beat his head with his fist, as if this might speed up the thought process.

"Hey? Hey? You there?"

"Sorry, I'm trying to figure out — listen, have you a painting there you could wrap up" — Melrose's eye fell on the copy of the *Telegraph* he'd meant to read — "wrap up in newspaper and lug it along here?"

"I'm in Bethnal *Green,* love."

"I know. But couldn't you get a couple of hours off from your job? I mean, it's not going to take more than a half hour once you get here. The gallery's only ten minutes away."

"Yeah, I expect they'll let me."

"And, Bea, listen. What we're doing is undoubtedly larcenous. But I'm working it out that if we're caught you'll be an innocent participant, manipulated by me, Fingers Plant."

"You are a caution. Manipulate *me?*

Don't make me laugh, Fingers." She hung up.

Melrose was less than a minute getting up the stairs with the newspaper. He wasn't more than five minutes using it to cover his already gallery-wrapped snow painting. He carted it downstairs, returned to his club chair, and signaled Young Higgins, pointing to his cold coffee. When the steaming pot arrived, he told the porter to watch out for a guest; he was expecting a young lady within the next half hour.

It was difficult to tell if this request sent Young Higgins into cardiac arrest, for that was what he looked to be in most of the time. Finally, but frostily, he said, "Certainly, sir."

It wasn't, after all, Ladies' Day.

While he waited for Bea, he wandered into the saloon, once a gaming room, now a library filled with dark leather volumes and dim lamps, room of permanent twilight. On a bulletin was a notice from the Managers announcing a candidate for election. Melrose remembered his father, the old Earl of Claverness, saying that one's name would be down in the book a decade or even two before coming up for election.

He wondered if a candidate could still be blackballed by one vote. He enjoyed the image of members filing up and dropping a white or black ball in the box. He turned to see a portrait of Wellington on the far wall, regarding him coldly.

The shelves contained tooled-leather volumes of various histories of Europe, all under a layering of dust that spoke sadly of their lack of use. On a lower shelf, gaudily jacketed guidebooks sat beside leather-bound ones that looked to be somewhere around a hundred years old, but that didn't matter. Greece and Turkey — the one he pulled out — never changed much. It was quite interesting. He could take a ferry to Delos and visit a flea market in Athens if he wanted.

Melrose disliked shopping — really, what had he to shop *for*, what with Mr. Beaton making his clothes and Ruthven and Martha buying the food? — but he liked reading about it.

From Rhodes he could hop up to Turkey and shop at the Grand Bazaar in Istanbul — my lord, three thousand shops on sixty streets! . . . Here was a title for you: *Grand Vizier of Suleyman the Magnificent* (that was one he would divest himself of in a New York minute). He wondered if he'd get elected to Boring's.

He wandered around Turkey for a while, looking for bargains, and then skipped over to Morocco. Marrakech. He could walk through Djemaa el Fna square and see jugglers and acrobats and snake charmers — Covent Garden, in other words. He could bargain in the souk for copper and carpets. Look at those rugs! And then up to Casablanca, where he pictured himself in Rick's club behind a veil of smoke, with Claude Rains behind another demanding to see his passport. Thence to Tangier — how the very air thickened with romance! — where he could buy a carpet or a camel for a pittance. Well, a camel would certainly spiff up the Blue Parrot, Trevor Sly's pub. He saw himself in a fez, babbling in tongues, bargaining with the vendors for silver and leather.

It was a mere hop, skip, and a jump across the Straits of Gibraltar to southern Spain, but he'd have to search out another guidebook for that. He reshelved Turkey and found garishly covered Fodor's and Nicholson's guides for Paris, remembered that swank marketplace beloved by Sophie McBride, and looked it up in the Fodor's index.

Fauchon's . . . grocery to billionaires . . .

famous for the artistic arrangement of its fruits and vegetables . . . smiling salespeople. . . . He read on, and his frown deepened. He checked the Nicholson guide also. He looked at the far wall, as if some explanation might come from the portrait of the Iron Duke, and read it again, and jumped when Higgins slid up to him out of seeming nowhere to tell him his guest had arrived.

Melrose took it as a good omen that Nicholas was in charge, Sebastian having taken a client to lunch at the Ivy. The fellow, said Nick, was an old bore and he himself hadn't wanted to go. To Beatrice he said, "Wonderful to see you, darling."

Melrose thought that if it was at the "darling" stage, Bea was becoming a valuable commodity.

"I think we've sold him your Limehouse painting, sweetie. Seb's client."

"The old bore? Sounds likely for one of my lot, right?"

Despite this careless-seeming soignée attitude, Melrose could feel her excitement.

"And what do you mean, you think?" said Bea.

"I'm fairly sure. He'll be back after lunch, and he told me quite firmly to take it down. See?" Nick pulled Bea's painting out from under the counter.

Melrose was again struck by its freshness. There was something about Bea's paintings that made the viewer think he was seeing a place for the first time.

"D'ya mind if he takes these two back to the storage room? I just want to set them up against the ones I brought in yesterday and see if they got a prayer. I'm not really sure about them, especially the big one." She tapped the one Melrose was carrying and handed over the smaller of the two, also wrapped in newspaper. "Can he just take them to where my others are?"

Nicholas graciously waved Melrose along to the rear of the building, and he started down the hall with both paintings.

When Beatrice saw Nicholas start to follow after, she said, "Wait just a tic, Nicholas, will you? I want to talk to you about frames. I don't much like the one you used."

As Melrose went into the storage room he could hear them arguing amiably in the background. He saw the individual crates immediately. Two of the paintings were inside wooden crates, but they were as yet not nailed shut. Inside each was a brown-paper-wrapped painting. The other two —

and, Melrose bet, the poor cousins — were leaning against the stone wall. He knew all he could do was guess, but he worked it out that he had better than a fifty-fifty chance, if he was reasoning correctly. All he had to do was pull one out, remove the newspaper from the one he'd brought with him, and slip it in the crate instead. He positioned the one he'd removed by a lone painting of a water spaniel in its declining years — what was *that* doing with the Fabricant brothers? — took the newspaper from around Bea's own painting, only half the size of Ralph's, and set that against the other. He left the room. The operation had taken only a minute. Nicholas would have no sense of his malingering back here.

As he walked up to them, he said, "I'd certainly say the small one's wonderful, Beatrice. As good as, if not better. Go back and have a look. Cigarette?" Melrose snapped open his gold case and shoved it in front of Nick's face.

Beatrice excused herself. When she was halfway down the hall, Melrose called, "Oh, wait a tic, *darling*" (he was fast picking up the lingo). He quickly reached her, said, "It's by the dying dog," and as quickly returned in time to light Nicholas's cigarette. "What on earth's the problem with this river scene of hers? It's gorgeous." Melrose had picked it up and was holding it at arm's length.

Exhaling a thin stream of smoke that turned lavender against Bea's sun-drenched water, Nicholas agreed. "God, these people are such perfectionists."

Melrose laughed, was laughing still when Bea came trotting along with a newspaper-wrapped painting and her own smaller one, now unwrapped. She handed the larger over to Melrose and directed Nicholas to study the smaller. "I like this one, but I got to do more work on the big one, Nicky love."

Nicky love? Ye gods, he wouldn't last for a moment in the art world. Melrose had to give Nicholas credit for a quiet study of the painting before he broke out in compliments. The Fabricants were, after all, serious lovers of art. Too serious, probably. It occurred to Melrose that Nicholas might not even be in on it. Melrose even doubted that Ralph himself was in on it, although he couldn't explain to himself how they'd managed the trick if he weren't. If, indeed, they had managed a "trick." He could be dead wrong.

"We'd better be going if we're going," said Melrose, "if we're to catch that show at Bingham's." A showing of avant-garde work was being advertised in the arts section wrapped around the painting he was holding.

Nicholas screwed up his face in distaste. "You going to that thing? I can guarantee you won't see anything worth the visit."

Melrose laughed as his glance slipped down the ad again. "He's one of my dear aunt's favorite people. Shamus Neeley."

Nick looked at him uncertainly. "Neeley's the owner, not the artist."

"I know." Idiot, stop trying to be clever. "My aunt always goes to his shows. She's a big supporter of the gallery."

Nicholas smiled. "Well, if she's that sort, tell her we're here, won't you?"

"Will do. Come on, Beazy."

Bea squinted up at him. *Beazy?*

Outside, Melrose stopped for a moment and leaned against a shopfront. He took out his handkerchief, surprised that he'd been furiously perspiring. "Ye gods."

"That dog wasn't dying. I could have missed it."

Melrose gave her a look. "Oh, certainly. Anyway, you were sublime. *Sub-lime.* I just wanted to grab you!"

She sidled up to him. "Well, give old Beazy a kiss, there's a good lad." He did.

They were leaning against the wall, locked together, until they both had to stop for air. "We'll miss gingham's," said Melrose.

"I've better art at my place."

"I'll be a monkey's." He kissed her again.

"She's been moping about ever since she got home from school."

Jury tried to picture Linda "moping about" and couldn't quite manage it. He smiled.

"I don't know what she wants to see you about, Superintendent."

Mona Dresser waved him into the living room.

It was, as before, a pleasantly disheveled room. Like a none-too-young demimondaine, the room tried to keep itself up but never quite managed. Pieces of clothing, scarves, silk throws were tossed across all available surfaces. Still, it gave Jury a pleasant shock to find the room exactly as he'd left it. Not even the shadows on the walls had shifted. Before he sat down in the chair he'd occupied before, he picked a silk scarf and a handbag from the seat.

"Oh, just toss those things aside, Superintendent. We're not very good housekeepers here, as you already know."

Jury smiled. That he "already knew" apparently released Mona Dresser from the bother of citing particulars. "Where's Linda, then?"

"She wants you to go to the palace with her. Don't ask me why."

"Okay, I won't. But I will ask you one or two questions."

"Of course."

"There's been another murder. It's been in the papers, so I expect you've read —"

"Simeon Pitt, you mean. I knew him."

"You did?"

"Not terribly well, but he must've stood in for whoever covered the theater for a short while. Or perhaps it was just the one occasion. *She Stoops to Conquer*, the one we took on tour, you know."

"The one you took to St. Petersburg."

"Yes. Petersburg was only one of the cities."

"Why would he have been covering a play touring the Continent?"

"I don't know. Some loony idea his paper had. He was quite generous in his praise, and I don't think people realized this — I mean, the sort of person he really was. I thanked him for that review; I got to know him a little, in the way of things. He did *not* set out to savage paintings or plays — well, he could hardly have savaged

Goldsmith, could he? He was not trying to sell himself or prove how clever he was." She sighed. "So if you're going to ask me, did rage drive me to kill the poor man —" Mona reached for the shell cigarette box.

"No, I actually didn't hit on you as the killer."

She wiggled her eyebrows at him as she struck a match to light her cigarette faster than he could reach over with the table lighter. "You don't think I've got the balls to walk into that men's club and stick a knife in someone?"

"I don't think you're foolish enough to do it." Jury smiled. "It's taking one hell of a chance."

Concentrating, she bunched her lips around her cigarette, turned it, said, "So it must be someone who enjoys that — taking chances, I mean. Have you anyone on your list with a flare for melodrama? I mean, other than me?" She smiled broadly.

She was waiting for him by the stone pillars, and he had to credit her with a serious intention in this meeting, for he felt she would otherwise have been waiting in the little building that dispensed tea, biscuits, and ice cream.

"Hello, Linda," he said, and, matching

her serious turn, kept the smile out of his face and voice. "You wanted to see me?"

She had a hard rubber ball that looked as if dogs had been chewing it, which she tossed and caught, tossed and caught. "I found something in the herb garden. Come on!"

She led him through the grounds, keeping her silence and tossing her ball, led him into the walled garden and thence to the herb garden. In the ruined greenhouse she plucked an object from the worn sill. "I left it here because I know you're not supposed to move stuff. It's this necklace." It was a locket, corroded with age. "I sprang it open. Look."

It had been pried open, and the little monochrome portraits inside of two children, a girl and a boy, in Victorian dress seemed to shrink within the tiny frames. A circle of glass still covered the boy's face; the girl's was stuck to the metal through the glue of time. They both looked serious and sad, as children always seemed to in those old days. Maybe they still do.

"It's probably her children."

Jury shook his head. "No, they can't be. This locket's been here for decades, Linda. It's nearly green from oxidizing."

Linda looked at him carefully, inspecting

him almost, as if a mark would appear on his skin betokening a break in the chain of truth. Jury wondered whether she wanted to believe or didn't want to believe the children were those of the woman she'd found dead. He didn't know. Did she look relieved? He didn't know that, either.

Then she spun away like a pile of leaves, with the chewed-up ball, which she started bouncing. But it was too damaged to bounce, so she tossed it up in the air. She was gearing up for something, Jury thought.

"I found it when I was here with that man that knows you."

Jury frowned. "You mean Mr. Plant?"

"We went on the tour. He didn't know anything about the palace at all."

"Neither do most people. It's one of London's secrets, they say."

"Well, it'll stay that way if they don't get a tour person who knows more." She caught the ball, threw it up again.

Jury smiled. "In a couple of years, you can apply for the job."

Compliments were of no interest to her at the moment. "He made me lie down in that lad's-love where the body was."

"Mr. Plant made you do that?" Jury doubted it.

"Almost. He would've if I didn't do it anyway." The ball landed on Jury's leg.

"Ah. But you did."

"I guess you think I'm wrong too."

"No, I don't think you're wrong, Linda. I just can't explain it, that's all."

There was a silence. "If I'm the only person that knows it, I guess somebody'll come and get me like he said they got Sophie."

Jury was totally surprised. "Sophie? Where did you hear about her?"

Linda told him what Melrose had said. "I'm not as dumb as Sophie, though. So I'll get away."

This was the issue, then. That she'd be stolen away, kidnapped like unhappy Sophie.

Jury knelt down in front of her, grabbed her hands down from the air. "Linda, *nobody* — understand, *nobody* — is going to get you. We won't let them. I won't. And remember: You might have been the only person *at first* who knew the woman was moved, but all the police know it now. So somebody would have to steal all of us away and that would be a job, wouldn't it? The whole Fulham police force and part of Scotland Yard, and one person trying to manage all of them. Can you picture it?"

First Linda looked serious, then her mouth twitched, then she started to laugh. Jury let go of her hands, and she clapped both of them across her mouth.

Jury got up, and her eyes followed him. Then he remembered what she had said and asked, "Why was Sophie dumb?"

"She acted really stupid." Linda went back and picked up the locket again. "If it was me and there was an organ grinder and a trick dog and cat right outside I wouldn't pick out potatoes. I'd be out there. Even you would, I bet."

Jury smiled. He had for some reason been permitted to join the legion of children.

"What'd she look like?"

"Who?"

"Sophie." She held up the locket. "Are you sure this isn't her?"

"I'm sure. It's much too old. Much. Those pictures go back to Queen Victoria." Jury blew on his hands. The temperature must have dropped fifteen degrees. He turned his collar up. "I think we'd better be getting back. It's cold and getting dark."

Linda looked down at the locket again. "Maybe it was Queen Victoria's children." Doubtfully, she looked at him. But he did not need to confirm or deny it. It was a shot, her expression said, fallen wide. She ran off down the path, turned, and called back to him. "Well, it was *somebody's* children!"

Her voice rang out frostily, and Jury was aware both of her anxiety and his own and a coming rain.

After getting Linda back to Bishops Park Road, Jury caught a bus along Fulham Palace Road. He felt (absurdly) as if the increase in Linda's cheerfulness had been proportionate to a decrease in his own.

He could not explain this; he knew only that the gathering dusk had gathered him into it, and he felt, as he watched the shoppers and the people going home from work, a steady erosion of spirit.

He sat on the top deck, looking down, and when a double-decker came from the other direction, he could look straight across where a man sat alone, in a coat much like his own and with a weary expression he imagined was also much like his own. It gave him the eerie feeling of seeing himself as he had been riding almost two weeks ago on that other bus.

Before any of this had happened. And he almost expected, after the bus had pulled out from another stop, that the feet and the voices moving clumsily up the half-circle of stair would turn out to belong to the American and her friend. He would have welcomed the loud, brash American right now; she might have prevented him from thinking.

He thought about Linda, and about Sophie. As the bus stopped and started and passengers clambered up and down the stairs, Jury thought about travel. *Zurich, Brussels, Paris, St. Petersburg. Petersburg. Peter.* He got off the bus two stops before the Stargazey. He wanted to walk, needed, now that the train of thought had been started, to end it, conclude it.

Walking along, he realized that today, in America, it was Thanksgiving.

When he sat down at the bar, not as crowded as before, everyone home, he supposed, having dinner, he took comfort in the rows of bottles, in their gleam and shine. It simply made him feel that care was being taken.

Kitty came down the bar, running her cloth along the inner edge as she did. She missed no chance to beautify. The bar shimmered in the reflection of the overhead lights. "Hel-lo! Back again, are you?"

Jury nodded, asked for a whisky. "It's

getting cold as hell, Kitty."

"It's been pretty warm for November, so I guess we've been lucky so far." As she took down the whisky and set up a glass for him, she rubbed at the bottle.

Jury smiled. "Pour me a double."

She did. "One of those days, is it?"

He sat there quietly, not making conversation, and she seemed to tune in to this mood. She started picking bottles from the shelves, giving them a careful rubdown. There were only a half dozen others at the bar and they were well along in their drinks, nursing them. Jury looked up at the pillar — he was sitting in the same place — at the postcards there. He thought about the one he'd sent to Plant. Forgot to ask him about the recipe. He downed his drink. Still, he didn't leave. But he didn't want another drink. He sat that way for a moment, watching Kitty give that extra bit of polish to the Sapphire gin bottle.

"Kitty."

She turned, smiling. "Want another?"

He shook his head. "Do you have children?"

"Me? Why, yes." She looked around as if searching for their pictures. "Two, I have. Boy and a girl."

"What do they look like?"

It surprised her that anyone would ask, much less a Scotland Yard superintendent.

Alfie and Annie, her children, got described in almost interminable detail.

Jury put more than enough money on the bar and said, "That's what I thought."

Her look, as he walked to the door, was puzzled.

43

The following morning found Jury sitting in his office, thinking about what Kitty had said and watching the clock, as if surcease of trouble would come from pushing back the hour he was to appear in Redcliffe Gardens. Depressed by this line of thought, Jury fell to deciphering a message that Wiggins had taken down, a message from Carole-anne.

It was actually a message Melrose Plant had left at Jury's digs, where Carole-anne often answered the telephone. Carole-anne would never be mistaken for Mercury, and Jury would sooner read a message washed up in a bottle on a beach.

LOOK UP FUTONS IN FODOR. OR MAYBE HARVEY NICHOLS.

Jury stared at the wall. Harvey Nichols? Did they sell futons?

Then the phone had rung and dragged him back through the looking-glass.

It turned out to be Ron Chilten. He wasn't looking for Chilten to further rend the fragile fabric of his beliefs.

"Argentina," said Chilten, and waited.

Although something would clearly lead away from "Argentina," nothing had led up to it, and Jury really was not up to a Chilten cliffhanger this morning. He shut his eyes tightly, cursed under his breath, said, "I've heard of the place, yes."

"How about the Muerte del Sol? Familiar to you?"

The next time he saw Chilten he just might make *muerte* more familiar to *him*. "I'll tell you something, Ron; we could probably save time if you'd just tell me, straight out; see if I can take it."

"Muerte del Sol, if you recall, is — or was — that guerrilla bunch that split off from the military, say, four years ago, and a year later, when it tried for a coup, went down because its leader, name of" — Chilten rattled through papers — "Juan Ascension, got murdered. Assassinated, it went round. By somebody with a sniper's rifle and a steady hand."

Jury waited. "This lesson in South American politics is interesting but, unfortunately, lost on me. What the hell's it got to do with —"

"Patience, patience, I'm just filling you in."

"That's swell, but filling me in on *what,*

exactly?" Jury watched the slow rhythm of Wiggins's measuring out some kind of orange glop from a squat bottle. He'd sooner drink that than listen to Chilten.

"What we were talking about, Ricardo. You've forgotten already? Passports, other passports."

Jury sat back, interested in the context. "Nancy Pastis went to Argentina, you mean?"

"Or, say, Justine Cordova? Another dead baby, Jury. Who applies for a passport six years ago. Just as I hit the Argentina police, surprise, surprise, I discover they're coming at her from another end, been trying to get a lead on her for years."

Jury swallowed as if he were indeed swallowing orange glop. "Nancy Pastis, you're saying? This Cordova woman is also — was also Nancy Pastis."

"Um. Yes and no."

Jury could almost hear Chilten smiling. "Then how, Ron?"

Unfortunately, this only begat another stop on the Chilten questionnaire. "Remember reading about the killing of that British executive, world, I think, for IBM? Couple of years ago in Moscow?"

"No."

"Another dead kid, apparently, was in

Russia — just like Nancy Pastis — this one named Amanda Walker, Irish lass. Irish dead lass, I mean."

Chilten paused and Jury prompted him. "Go on."

"Now we're up to dead child number three: Eve Fellowes. Eve was in France when a Frenchman named Jules Pointier was killed, another sniper's bullet."

"Wait a minute, Ron. Even if Nancy Pastis was traveling in those countries, the other three you've named would be using the passports named, not the Nancy Pastis passport."

"Jury," Chilten paused. "The point is all these targets were murdered by dead kids. I mean, don't you think that's kind of strange?"

Jury said nothing, sat there staring at nothing.

So Chilten said it again. "They were all assassinated by dead people. And who's to say that this woman with at least three fake passports — three names — might not have gone in at other times as Nancy Pastis?"

"What about the Papua New Guinea entry?"

"Nothing there. Maybe Nancy was just taking a holiday from murder. Hell, she earned it."

"If there's a connection."

"It sure as hell cranks up the motive, doesn't it? Imagine the heat with half a dozen police forces on your sorry arse."

"I missed a beat, there."

"Oh, I thought you were with me. Dana. You know, the one nobody's been able to fit a face to. The one they think pulled off the theft of that Chagall in St. Petersburg. The thief, the professional assassin. Dana."

44

Melrose opened that eye that was not crushed into the several goose-down pillows and looked toward the window. He hoped he was looking at day, not dawn. He'd finally got back to Long Piddleton at 2 A.M. and had convinced himself he'd hardly had a wink of sleep until he remembered he'd woken himself up several times during the night, snoring.

With one side of his face pushed against his pillows, only one ear was available to him for hearing what sounded like laughter floating up the staircase. He frowned. He recognized that laughter: Trueblood. Trueblood's cackle cutting across Ruthven's rumble. What in God's name had they to laugh about this early, and why was Trueblood at Ardry End?

He was afraid he was about to find out when he heard ascending footsteps and then a pounding on his door.

"Melrose!" Trueblood yelled.

"Go away."

"Come on, old trout. Things to do!"

"I don't want to do things. Go away."

Far from going away, Trueblood opened the door and walked in. "Thought you'd lapsed into a coma." He pulled a walnut side chair over to the bed, regarded the chair's worn and intricately embroidered seat before he sat down, and said, "Nice piece, this; you should get it recovered. This burled wood looks —"

Melrose did turn over then. "Do I have to have a lecture on burled wood first thing this morning? I'd sooner duel. It's dawn, after all." He turned his back again and closed his eyes.

He heard a match strike. "It's not dawn. Cigarette?"

"No, *thank* you. I'm not one who has to smoke first thing in the morning."

"It's afternoon. Get garbed."

Hearing it was afternoon, Melrose felt less sleepy. "Where's my tea?"

"One of those who can't move without your cuppa? I'll tell Ruthven."

Ruthven, however, needn't be told. He was already at the door, which was open. He sailed into the room, silver tray before him like a ship's figurehead. From the squat silver pot, a ribbon of steam issued and threaded its way past Melrose's nose. "Ah!" said Melrose, as Ruthven poured.

Bowing slightly to Trueblood, as if they hadn't been hooting down there in the hall for God knows how long, Ruthven asked, "Sugar, sir?"

"Oh, about fifteen lumps, thanks," said Trueblood.

"Sir," Ruthven answered, beginning to measure it out.

"Just kidding, Ruthven. Two's fine."

"Sir." Possibly the last and certainly the best proponent of the his-not-to-reason-why school, Ruthven would not have shown surprise if Trueblood had asked for fifteen lumps of coal. He'd have measured it out. Finished with pouring both of these helpless creatures their cups of tea, Ruthven bowed again, turned on his heel, and sailed out.

"God, but if you ever want to reduce staff, give me him, will you? He's remarkable."

"*Staff* at Ardry End consists of three people, that's all. There's Ruthven and Martha and Wyatt Earp. You may have Momaday any time you want." Melrose yawned widely.

"Get your skates on, man. Don't you want to see what I've been up to for the last ten days?"

Melrose finished his tea and pulled his

legs from the warm coverings. He did not think anything Trueblood could have been up to could match what he himself had been up to, but he didn't say so.

He checked to make sure the brown-wrapped painting was where he'd left it against the wall.

Shaved, dressed and full of toast and more tea, Melrose stood and surveyed the banner across the door of the Long Piddleton library: REST READ AND LATTE AT THE LIBRARY!

"Bloody marvelous!" he said.

When they walked in, Una Twinny, the librarian, literally had her hands full. There were half a dozen customers waiting to have their books checked out and as many more wandering through the stacks. For this little library, that was a crowd.

"Come on," said Trueblood, leading him into the library's other room.

The new Latte at the Library coffee shop opened promptly at nine, with the library itself. "How in God's name did you get all of this done in ten days?"

"With a lot of help from Ada Crisp, for one. She donated all the chairs and three tables."

Ada Crisp thought Marshall Trueblood

walked on water, ever since he had served as her defending solicitor in the infamous chamber-pot incident.

"We acquisitioned two more tables from the rectory, and Betty Ball supplied a fifth from the bakery, to say nothing of donating all these pastries." Trueblood swept an arm over the plates of scones, croissants, hot-cross buns, and a beautiful vanilla-iced gâteau decorated with violets. "I found an espresso machine in London and brought back a crate of not-very-good china and that delftware. Which is good. The other pieces in here come from the shop, and the Sidbury Ladies' Club donated the checked tablecloths and napkins. Really, the place has quite a bit of tone. Several chaps from here gave their time to paint and redo the fireplace tiles. The florist in Sidbury insisted on donating those gorgeous flowers."

On a highly polished bureau (donated by Trueblood's Antiques) sat a large display of roses, larkspur, and snowdrops. In front of the electric logs a big dog slept. "Where'd you get the — wait a minute! What's my dog doing here?"

"Mindy? Oh, we're just borrowing her for a while. You know, until we're firmly established. Every shop needs a cat or a dog. All the pubs have them —"

"But that's *my* dog. Mindy!" Melrose called out, sharpish.

The dog didn't respond, beyond turning its face toward the warm logs, reminding Melrose of himself that morning. They sat down at the table near the dog, and Trueblood went to the counter for latte. He returned in a moment with cups brimming with foam. "Delicious," said Melrose, licking the foam from his upper lip. "I don't know some of these people in here. Has Mr. Browne's reputation traveled beyond Long Piddleton? Has his infamy reached Sidbury or even Northampton?"

"He is not, let's say, a popular player. And you can imagine how he likes the idea of this, can't you? All of the Piddletonians who have been renting their new books from Browne are taking their business elsewhere. In other words, here. Theo is threatening a lawsuit."

Melrose brightened. "Another legal battle?"

"He's making all sorts of claims. For one, he says we can't get a clearance certificate because of infestation. Says he saw three mice"

"Were they blind?"

"— running through here. Well, I called

Rent-to-Kill and they came straightaway. They said there was no problem. Then Browne claimed the bylaws say the library isn't zoned for retail business purposes."

"*Zoned?* Good lord, if there were zoning laws Mrs. Withersby wouldn't be living in one of those almshouses."

"If there were zoning laws, Withersby wouldn't be living anywhere."

It was speak-of-the-devil time, for Melrose looked around to see Mrs. Withersby, of Indolents Anonymous, coming through the door with a pail and mop, and a cigarette dangling from the corner of her mouth.

"Ah, here's Withers, good girl."

"Good girl? What's that supposed to signify?"

"Why, that Withers has kindly donated her time to char for the coffee shop."

Melrose had just taken a drink of coffee and gasped and sputtered, sending a brief rain of droplets into the air. "Donating her *time?* That's like saying a Franciscan monk is donating his Lou Reed collection. Withersby doesn't do anything with her time. What she sees in the deal is free coffee and fags from anyone who's got them." At this, Melrose pulled out his cigarette case. "I'm counting to ten. . . .

Six . . . seven . . ."

"Well, if it ain't the Cray brothers come to collect their protection money. Got an extry fag there, Lord of the Manor?"

Melrose got up, all polite solicitation, and offered his case. Mrs. Withersby helped herself to five or six. Who was counting? "My pleasure." He reseated himself.

Mop and pail by her side, still with her old coat and flowered kerchief on, Mrs. Withersby got down to business. "I'll have an espresso, me."

"Absolutely," said Trueblood, all charm. He raised a hand to get the coffee tender's attention and pointed to Mrs. Withersby, who, having got fags and free coffee, left them. Trueblood went on. "People were almost begging to help. Little Sally McVittie's mum is the lady over there working the espresso machine. She's a first-rate cappuccino maker. I heard her uttering dire prognostications as to the fate of 'the moneylender and child abuser' — her way of referring to Mr. Browne."

"Oh, I know young Sally, all right." Melrose laughed. He looked across the room at a tall cherrywood bookcase, which housed some thirty or forty of the very newest books. "Where'd Miss Twinny get all those new books? Has the library system finally improved?"

"I brought them back from London. Just went into a bookstore and said I wanted several dozen new works of fiction and would they give me a discount? Those new ones are loaned out at five per day, at least seventy-five percent cheaper than Theo's. Of course the library drove his stupid book rentals out of business."

"Marvelous! Trueblood, what can I say?"

"You can say two more cappuccinos. A pound a cup, which is cheaper than the Emporium Espresso in Sidbury."

After Melrose had gone to get refills and spent a sunny few moments chatting with Sally's mum about Sally's and Bub's reading habits — Miss Twinny being far more accepting of Bub's spilling things on books than Theo Wrenn Browne ever was or would be — she told him, "My Sally, she thinks the world of you, Mr. Plant."

This pleased and ruffled him. He went through a series of protestations (oh, my, no . . . I didn't do all that . . . giving me too much credit) before he collected the cappuccino and two hot-cross buns and returned to their table.

Trueblood was smoking one of his

crayon-colored cigarettes and fiddling with a small printed sign that said, SMOKING SECTION. "I put this there," he said, sheepishly. "Now, what's all this about an art restorer?"

"Do you know one? You must, in your line of work."

"Hmm. Several, as a matter of fact. There's a woman in Northampton, actually. But you still haven't told me for what. I'm all ears. What went on in London?"

Melrose told him about Simeon Pitt. "Stabbed, right there in clear view of several of the members."

"My lord. My lord," he said again. When Melrose didn't elaborate, Trueblood said, "Well, come on, old trout. *Why? What's your theory?*"

Melrose was silent for a moment. "D'you mind if we just wait before I tell you that? I'd rather have a specialist looking at it first. Right away, because —" *because Seb or one of them might discover the missing painting,* he didn't add. "So if you know someone as close as Northampton —"

"Good as done, old sweat. I'll call soon as I get back to the shop." There was a bright beep and everyone looked around, including Melrose. "It's just this." Trueblood had reached into his waistcoat pocket and pulled out a pager. He checked the number, returned the thing to his pocket.

"You? You got a pager too? Diane has one of those."

"Right, old sweat. You should get one. It's loads of fun. Diane and I page each other all the time. Our office numbers, of course; that's where we're busiest."

"Busy? Diane Demorney, busy?"

"Well, it's that newspaper job."

"For God's sake, it's not like she's hauling a camera around in Algeria. I mean, how many Milky Way emergencies can there be? Here, give me your number. I've got hers." Melrose extracted his address book. "I'm going to call her up and drive her crazy."

"All you have to do, see, is call the number and then it shows up on the pager and she rings you back immediately . . . more or less. Diane doesn't do anything immediately."

"I *know* how it works."

"You should get one. Withersby has one."

"*Withers* has one? Oh, please." He looked across the room where Mrs. Withersby was leaning on her mop, talking with Sally's mum, drinking her espresso with her little finger hooked out. "You might as well give a pager to the Hunchback of Notre Dame."

Trueblood snorted a laugh. "You should get one."

Melrose snorted back to indicate his disdain of such frippery. "Over my dead body."

45

"Richard! I thought you were coming hours ago." There was no recrimination in Kate's tone, only concern and surprise.

"Got held up. I often do. The job, as we say, the job." He looked round the living room. "This room" — he turned to face her with a smile — "doesn't suit you."

Her look was puzzled. "You never criticized it before."

"I'm not criticizing it. I never really looked at it before."

Across the back of the sofa she had tossed the jacket of her gray suit, the one she had been wearing when she'd been "detained." He lifted it off, read the label: "Max Mara. Very handsome, very Upper Sloane Street." He replaced it. "Max Mara and this room don't go together."

Now she really seemed disturbed. "What on earth's wrong?"

"Nothing," he said, tossing his coat across the sofa. "There's some good news, really." He looked at her for a long and sinking moment as if something within him were slowly falling away, descending to the riverbed, seeking bottom.

"Good news? Well, go on, tell me. Fulham police are not going to take me in again? That would be very good news."

"It's not that, no. I was just talking to an Inspector LeGrande in Paris. Despite the records having burned up, we've got a fresh lead on Sophie. But he's not really clear as to what she looked like. What did she look like?"

Kate sat back with an involuntary shake of the head. It was the silence, that fractional pause, that got to him even before the answer. "Oh." Kate shrugged. "She was blond. Like me."

As she rose from the sofa and started for a small bureau that held the whisky and sherry, Jury thought of Kitty, the stream of details about her kids. He did not think that "Oh, blond" and a shrug were part and parcel of a mother's lexicon.

"There are no pictures of her here. Is the memory too painful?" He turned on the sofa. "The entire story was a lie, wasn't it?"

Ice cubes tinkled into glasses. When she didn't answer, he went on. "It was a brilliant fabrication, but it lacked a couple of things. You never described her — how she looked, what she wore, what she was like — and yet you could go into the most minute detail about your surroundings: Fauchon's, the organ grinder, the animals. The second thing — which I had pointed out to me — was that a little kid wouldn't act the way Sophie was acting. I should have realized all of this when Charles Noailles said that Michael McBride had never mentioned a daughter. He was close to Noailles. It would be almost impossible not to say something about a daughter he was 'besotted with.' That's how you put it, wasn't it?"

"You're fantasizing. Why on earth would I make all of that up?" She walked over and put the glass of whisky in his hand.

But he did not turn to face her; he wished he would never have to again because she would have taken on the same hard lines as had the furniture, the silver, the china. He would be seeing someone else. "Very good reasons, I should think. Most important, I was the only one who could place you at the crime scene. Everybody else thought I was wrong, given the two of you look so much alike. It was to gain my sympathy, to make me want to believe you. Besides that, all of that convoluted story with its meetings and its queer directions to foreign places — well, in case you didn't get me to cave in, and you finally had to admit I was right, then you'd have a reason for going to Fulham Palace. It would have been one more weird meeting demanded by your persecutors. You even explained the absence of any record of Sophie's 'abduction' with a fire, a fire that really did happen. And if right now you showed me Kate McBride's passport, I'd find she'd been to Zurich, Belgium, and St. Petersburg at just the times you said you were there. Even that eventuality you covered. The only slip was your calling it 'Peter.' Only someone intimate with the city would call it that."

Jury stood up as he said this, drank some more of the whisky that was bringing him no relief at all, and turned to face her. As he did so he heard a familiar metallic *snick*. The gun surprised him no more than he was surprised to see she looked like a different woman. It was a big handgun, a Walther, and she held it professionally, one hand propping the wrist, as if she knew how to use it, as indeed she had.

Many times, he imagined. "This is her flat, isn't it? Kate McBride's? The one in Mayfair, as I was about to say, suits you far better. Why did you kill her?"

Her smile was a mere movement of the lips, not a smile; it didn't touch the voice, the eyes. The laugh was short and breathless. "Why? For someone as clever as you, I should think it obvious."

"I'm not that clever, clearly."

"I wanted an identity. Not one cooked up with phony passports and licenses, but one that honestly *existed*. I happened on that pub by accident a few months ago. Someone there took me for Kate McBride. It was then I began to get the idea. I watched her for a long time, where she went, what she did, how she looked. I got into her flat, looked around, found her life in journals and letters. Everything I needed to know. I saw Mrs. Laidlaw once when I was locking the door. She thought I was Kate, too." She smiled again. The gun didn't waver. "That house in Wales. I would have loved to live there; I really would."

"How did you know about it?"

"The silly woman used the telephone in the pub. I was sitting right there. It's amazing how much information people give away without one's even asking for it. And that property is of course why I had to make her disappear right away. She was setting up an appointment. If *she'd* gone to the solicitor, *I* couldn't very well turn up and be Kate, could I? I'm tired; I've got enough money for several lifetimes; I want to stop, live in Great Britain, be just another Brit."

"You can hardly be that. You can never be just another anything. You're not even Nancy Pastis."

"That was my second reason for killing her. I wanted to get rid of Nancy. That's what made it a little complicated. I could, of course, have just left, after that little girl found the body. But since nothing happened and she showed no sign of doing anything, I simply followed my original plan and went back. Mrs. Laidlaw is a sweet old thing, but not very sharp."

"You wanted Nancy Pastis's body identified. Why didn't you leave the passport with it?"

"Come on, Richard. Your police are smarter than that. It would have looked planted."

"Noailles," he said, puzzled. "You didn't even know him. How —"

"Of course I didn't know him. You were the one who brought him up, remember? You told me about him. I said that the information people give away is quite amazing."

"And you even managed to make me suspicious of him. That cock-and-bull story about the Château Noailles. God, I'm stupid."

"Oh, there is a Château Noailles near Aix-en-Provence. I try to stay as close to the truth as I can. And you're far from stupid, Richard. I think your trouble is you look at glass and see diamonds. Too many facets, too many layers, too many possibilities. Too many to act. The Hamlet syndrome, maybe?"

"Nancy Pastis, I take it, was not just another Brit? Who are you?"

She shrugged. "What difference does it make?"

"Simeon Pitt was murdered two days after Fulham police let you go. My friend —" He stopped himself. The less said about Melrose Plant, the better. "What have you to do with the Fabricants?"

She said nothing; she had moved one hand to put on her Max Mara suit jacket, switched the gun to the other as she gathered up her coat. The gun had never left him, nor did it as she moved over to the desk, opened the top drawer, collected papers, and stuffed them in her deep coat pocket. A few more steps and she hitched her bag over her shoulder.

Jury felt a strange calm; he couldn't understand this. The adrenaline should be pumping like crazy. "You could answer the question."

"Was there one?"

"Simeon Pitt."

"I didn't know him."

"Did you kill him? Because whoever the hell did it is just too damned bloody cool."

"There was only one question. I answered it."

"You're going to shoot me; I won't be able to tell anyone."

"What makes you think I'd shoot you, Richard?"

"Somehow it's the impression I've been getting," Jury said dryly. Literally, dryly. His mouth felt as if it had never known saliva.

She smiled. "I don't think I could. You're too —" She glanced away for a moment, almost as if looking at him were painful.

"You're not going to shoot me?" Jury couldn't help it; he laughed. "My God, you put something in that drink, didn't you?"

"Nothing much. Just enough to keep you quiet for a few hours. It'll hit you hard, fast. Wait."

"Someone who takes the kind of chances

you take, love, is bound to be brought down."

"Then it should be by you, don't you think?"

For some reason, the voice of Caroleanne came to him: *Is that one of your compliments, then?*

He smiled, had to sit down before he fell. "Is that a compliment?"

Her hand was on the doorknob, the gun lowered, but fractionally. "Perhaps. I don't give many."

"You wouldn't have much bloody chance to. To walk into a men's club, simply pull out a stiletto, and stab one of the members. You must be handsomely paid, Kate."

"I don't do it for the money, not anymore."

"What then?"

"For the rush."

She was gone.

It hit him. Hard.

46

Melrose was considering getting out a knife and attacking the top layer himself — sandpaper, Rees had said. His curiosity was killing him. But the damage he might inflict made him too nervous to try. He wished he hadn't given Ruthven and Martha the evening off; he had no one to cajole or complain to. He couldn't get hold of Richard Jury — talk about somebody who should have a pager. Remembering Diane's, he leafed through his little address book and found the number and dialed. When he'd called her from London, he'd told her he was hiring a car, and she had sympathized with him for having to drive a cheaper Mercedes.

The doorbell sounded its soothing treble note, and Melrose would almost have been glad to see Agatha at the moment. Indeed, he opened the door with the expectation he'd see her and took an involuntary (and he imagined unfriendly) step back when he saw the woman standing there.

She smiled. "Mr. Plant?" She removed

her wallet from her purse and held it out so that he could see — he supposed — some identification. "I'm Posy."

While he stood there staring, she smiled and cocked her head, as if waiting for the penny to drop.

Light dawned. "Oh, Trueblood! I completely forgot he told me he knew someone who could help me with a painting."

She nodded. "Mr. Trueblood rang me up."

"Come in, come in! You're from Northampton, then?"

"That's right. No, thanks, I'll keep my coat on — I've been getting chills all day. Hope it's not flu. What an absolutely gorgeous house." She stood in the center of the big marble hallway, turning slowly around. "You have some lovely paintings here. Is that a Stubbs?" She nodded toward a study of mares and foals.

Melrose wasn't even sure. "More or less. Listen, the painting I want you to look at, it's in here, in the living room." He showed her the way. "What I need isn't precisely art restoration, but more getting the top layer off."

"That's quite a tricky operation. There are solvents, of course, but one has to be quite a good technician to do that."

Melrose had moved to the armoire, behind which he'd set the painting. "Are you?"

"Good? Oh, yes." She laughed.

He smiled and pulled out the painting, which he lugged over to a wooden settee against which he leaned it. "I don't think it's a case for solvents."

"This is the candidate for restoration?" She regarded it silently. Then she said, trying not to laugh, "Can't understand why you want to get the top layer off."

Trueblood was supposed to have sent him an art restorer, not a stand-up comedienne. "Neither can I." They both laughed.

She asked, "Well, but what is it?"

"Snow. Russia. Siberia, according to the artist. Run your hand over the surface." As she did so, he said, "Sandpaper. The chap who painted this has a technique of putting a thin layer of sandpaper over the canvas underneath."

She nodded. "I've heard of that. Makes for interesting texture." She had been kneeling in front of the painting and now rose to her feet. "So it's not removing the white paint, but the sandpaper, right?"

"Isn't that easier?"

"Decidedly." She opened the leather

satchel she'd placed on the wooden bench and removed what looked like a jeweler's loupe. This she positioned in her right eye and bent her head close to the painting, again running her hand over it.

Melrose couldn't think why she'd want it magnified. "It's nothing but a solid square of white; what detail do you think you'll see that way?"

"Um. It's not the paint I'm examining, but the texture and the thickness." She opened her eye wide and let the loupe fall into her hand, then turned the painting and ran her fingers down the side. "It's whatever's under the sandpaper you're interested in?"

He nodded. "Another painting. Although I'm not really certain."

"Let's have a look." Out of the satchel this time she pulled what looked like a scraping knife, the sort house painters use. She applied this to the lower corner and very carefully pried off the layer of sandpaper, about two square inches of it.

Melrose knelt down beside her and looked. "Yes. I don't see anything. Take off some more."

"I'll have to do this slowly; I'm afraid of damaging the canvas. Do you think it's valuable?"

"It's caused enough trouble to be price-less."

She smiled. Very carefully, she continued to remove the upper layer until she'd freed over a quarter of the painting's surface. She stopped. "Why would anyone do this?" She rose from her crouch and looked at him curiously.

Melrose did not want to tell her, so he settled for, "It's my Uncle Soames. He's quite addled these days."

"Really?" She reached into the satchel again.

Melrose, trying to make out what looked like a signature, said, "Couldn't that be the name of the original painter?"

"I'd say so."

"How did you —" He turned and saw the gun pointed at him. He was speechless.

"Sorry, Mr. Plant." Quite pleasant she was about this, adding, "Now, if you'll just stand back there" — she motioned with the gun — "I'll simply pack up everything and be off."

Melrose had backed away and was more shocked than frightened. "Who in hell are you?"

"It's not important." She was dropping things back into the satchel.

"How did you know I had the painting?"

"Well, *somebody* took it from the Fabricant Gallery. And you're really the only possibility as far as we knew."

" 'We'?"

"Ilona and Sebastian. You and your painter friend —"

Melrose forgot the gun. "Listen, leave Bea Slocum alone; she's straight out of this." The ringing of the telephone, which sounded to Melrose's ears more like a shriek, cut him off.

"Answer it!" she hissed. "Before it wakes your staff."

Thank the lord Ruthven and Martha had gone out. Why didn't she realize he was staffless? He'd opened his own door, after all. The gun was jammed against his ribs. "Pick it up; hold the receiver so I can hear."

Oh, wonderful, was his fleeting thought. If she listens to the other person, how do I get a message through? It's Jury! Make it Richard Jury, please God! Let it be Jury! He can read minds.

"Melrose? Melrose? What did you want?"

Diane! Hell's bells. How can I get a message through? "Diane . . . darling! Thanks for calling, love."

A brief pause while Diane must have

been trying to work out endearments he'd never used with her. Then she spoke, rather tentatively. "Yes, I —"

Don't let her talk. *Don't talk, Diane!* Melrose could feel the warm breath of the executioner on his cheek. He could also feel the gun. "Listen, Diane. Dear. I knew you'd want to hear right away about Mildred." Diane was stony silent. Dear God, was it *possible* that Diane could pick up on something from his side? "She's not doing well, darling, not at all."

Silence. And then Diane responded. "Oh, dear. I'm so sorry, darling. What's wrong this time?"

My God! Diane Demorney was *thinking*, thinking on her feet! "I'm really afraid it's near the end, Diane."

"How dreadful, dear."

"Yes. I wondered if you could possibly go round to her place. You know, it's on the Northampton Road. Go round and see to her, poor old soul."

"Yes, of course. I'll start straightaway."

"Remember, though, how skittish she is. Don't let her hear your car or she'll have another attack."

The gun dug. "Diane, I have to ring off."

Melrose hung up. Where was she? At the Jack and Hammer? At home? As long as she wasn't in Sidbury, she could get here in minutes.

The gun directed him back to the living room. "I asked about Beatrice Slocum. Is she all right?"

"Presumably. I haven't seen her." She had removed plastic wrapping paper from the satchel and began the awkward process of covering the painting with one hand.

"How did you find me?"

"Your friend Superintendent Jury mentioned a friend of his wanting an art renovator. His friend the ex-earl, he said. It was only the work of a moment finding an aristocrat who lived in Northants who had surrendered his titles."

"But Trueblood. How did you know *him?*"

"I never heard of him. You're the one who brought him up."

In silence he watched, feeling helpless, as she slowly covered the painting and then, with only the occasional glance away from him, taped up the protective covering. "The Fabricants paid you to get this painting back? Why would you bother? Hadn't you already been paid for the original theft?"

"You don't understand. Now the painting's mine."

Melrose was amazed. "This was your fee?"

She hoisted the painting under her arm. "Not originally, no. I'm recompensing myself for having to steal it once again and, of course, for taking care of Mr. Pitt. Sebastian said the man was about to expose him."

It was one of the few times in his life he had ever felt blind with rage. He took a step toward her and heard a small, sharp *click*, like a twig breaking.

But it wasn't her gun.

"I hope I'm not interrupting anything."

Diane's voice stopped both of them. Dana whirled toward the French door. Diane fired, holding the gun straight out, single-handed and tilted like some teenage shooter. She missed and hit the drinks table, splintering the Stoli vodka.

"Shit!" she said.

The woman fired twice, shattering the wall sconce and the Tiffany lamp. The room went black.

"Diane!" yelled Melrose, amidst the rush of rain and running footsteps. "Are you all right?"

It took only a few seconds for his eyes to adjust to the dark and to find a working lamp. He pulled the cord, and mellow light flooded that part of the room. Where the woman had stood, she no longer was.

"She rushed right by me!" said Diane.

Melrose had come up beside her, and both of them stood staring out into the rain. Diane stood now with one arm across her breast, the other, elbow bent and gun pointed at the stars.

"You're holding that gun like a martini. Put it down."

"Speaking of which" — she looked towards the broken bottles — "if that was the *last* of your vodka, I'll shoot myself. Just a figure of speech, Mildred." She dropped the revolver into Melrose's hand and made for the sideboard where the bottles were. "Who was that dreadful woman, anyway?" she asked, in a tone that was much less interested in the person than turning up another bottle of vodka. She was kneeling and rooting in the bottom of the sideboard, shoving bottles around. "Melrose, you *don't* try and get by with only one *bottle?*"

There were times, thought a dazzled Melrose, Diane's languor was a blessing. He was astonished that she'd moved so quickly. "My God, Diane!" Melrose went to her, pulled her up, and gave her a huge hug. "How did you manage to figure out that obscure message about Mildred?"

Diane raised a polished eyebrow. "Mildred? Oh, it wasn't that, exactly. No, it's in your horoscope, Melrose: *Danger awaits in the guise of a new friendship. Don't answer the door.* Well, I knew it wasn't *Mildred* you'd let in. Ah, here's one at the back! And the vermouth. Good. Care for a drink?" She measured vodka and a whisper of vermouth into a pitcher and stirred. "Where's the ice?" She found some in a bucket and put cubes in a squat glass. "I expect I'll have to take it on the rocks. Ugh."

"Just make yourself at home, Diane."

"Thank you," she said, sitting down in Melrose's favorite wing chair, martini and cigarette as firmly in place as her gun had been. "You never told me who she was. I must say, though, that she's got good taste in clothes."

"I don't know who she is. I'm calling the Northants police."

"Bit late for that. But what was she *doing* here? Honestly, Melrose." It was as if he'd been awfully careless in forgetting to screen the people he let in.

"Collecting a painting."

Diane's painted eyebrow rose fractionally. "Painting?" Her eyes roved the room in something like meditation and then snapped back to Melrose, standing with the telephone. "Not my painting, don't tell me!"

" 'Fraid, so. Hello, hello?" He spoke into the receiver. "Listen, there's been an accident — well, more an incident here." He gave the constable the information, hung up, and dialed New Scotland Yard. Jury wasn't there, nor did they know where he was. Melrose got Wiggins, told him what had happened in short, succinct sentences, dropped the receiver back in the cradle. "A drink, a drink." He splashed three fingers of whisky into a glass and plopped down on the sofa. "My God." He was going for the cigarette box when he remembered. "Diane. Why'd you call me, anyway?"

Both her eyebrows went up now. "The pager. You called my pager, remember?"

Melrose slid down on his spine. "Thank God I did." He flashed her a smile. "You were brilliant."

"Yes, but *next* time, Melrose, be first through the door, will *you?*"

It was his eyebrows that rose now. "I thought I was."

47

Jury fought his way upwards through currents that beat him back, would not relinquish their hold. As he drifted back and down, he felt he didn't want them to. Drifting beneath the surface was better, was, indeed, pleasant.

He had a dream; he was at a fun fair. Wiggins was astride a yellow horse on the merry-go-round. Chief Superintendent Racer was at the top of the big wheel, stuck against a black and starless sky. Melrose Plant had rushed Jury's dodgem car, given it a good crack, and knocked Jury out onto the floor. He was lying there with the cars wheeling around him, but in no danger. The cars came close, then receded like waves. He lay there until the cat Cyril jumped on his chest and put its paws over his eyes. He could not shake Cyril off.

Jury woke in the Redcliffe Gardens flat, saw that it was dark, and turned his head to look at his watch. He'd been out for nearly seven hours. It was morning — black morning, but morning nevertheless.

He had a pulsing headache but seemed to have suffered no other ill effects.

She'd left the phone in working order, thank God. He called New Scotland Yard and told them to issue an All Points. He hadn't much hope of her turning up at Heathrow or Victoria, not after seven hours, but who knew for certain? She'd had plenty of time to leave the country. God knows she certainly had a passport.

He called Fulham headquarters and got Ron Chilten, who told him he and Wiggins had tried every number they could think of to get hold of him and where in hell had he been?

Wiggins got on the line and told him that Mr. Plant had called several hours ago and told Wiggins about the woman. He was all right, now. No damage done except the painting was gone.

Ilona Kuraukov had been wearing her fur and a long string of Russian amber beads when she opened the door of the Chelsea house to Jury and Wiggins. It was as if she'd expected them. Now, Ilona Kuraukov sat in the Fulham station smoking a cigarette, Wiggins and Jury sitting across from and beside her, the tape running. Sebastian Fabricant was in another room with Chilten and his sergeant.

"Neither Nikolai nor Ralph knew anything about this," she said.

"How could Rees not know? He painted them," said Jury.

"He painted four of them and only thought he'd painted the fifth. For heaven's sake, I'm a painter too. Do you really think it would be difficult to mimic Ralph's 'style' in those paintings? Sebastian, of course, would be able to tell, but not Nicky. So leave him alone. Please."

Please, yes, but it sounded more like a soft-spoken order than a plea.

She went on. "I will certainly say this for your country — before you kill a king, you try him. But in Russia? The czars were murdered by gangsters. Nicholas, Alexandra, their children were executed by the Cheka, nothing but gangsters. Russia was always run by gangsters until Stalin died."

She sat there talking Russian history. She had made no move to deny that it was she who had instigated the theft of the Chagall and that it was she who had paid the woman called Dana. As far as the murder of Kate McBride was concerned, she'd had nothing to do with that. "That Dana did on her own. Quite a remarkable woman." Ilona had smiled.

Jury had not returned the smile. "Simeon Pitt?"

She shrugged. "He threatened to expose Sebastian and the gallery." She paused. "It was the October uprising and its aftermath that murdered the men in my family. These revolts are usually carried out, and quite stupidly, by fanatics. Lenin, going around in disguise, could never keep his wig on; he kept dropping it, and on the night of the uprising he forgot his makeup. Trotsky, Lenin, Stalin, and that utterly mad policeman, Dzerzhinsky — that's what it needs for a revolution: craziness and fanaticism and sadism. The storming of the Winter Palace?"

As if they had asked. They let the tape run. Jury was in no hurry. Wiggins kept getting up and sitting down, but he didn't interrupt.

"It was completely haphazard. The ministers thought it laughable and did nothing; the Bolsheviks didn't know what they were doing. My husband, Michel, was there. He was a young man then. Much later, when he was one of the curators of the museum, he participated in crating and sending off all these works of art to save them from destruction during the siege. He was taken from the Winter Palace and executed. Do you know why? Because he knew these paintings so well and could describe them so vividly he could make you see them. Art was his life.

"The revolutionaries replaced murder, plunder, looting, rape, pillage, and riot with murder, plunder, looting, rape, pillage, and riot. Rioting by mobs, who are on no side but their own. The Reds committed atrocities; the counterrevolutionaries — the Whites — committed atrocities, perpetrated pogroms. Russia has spawned generations of ignoramuses. In the Great War, my father was a cryptographer. Telephone wires were scarce, so orders were passed by radio. Code books were also scarce, so the orders were sent in clear. Russians by the thousands, the army, had no weapons and had to wait until one of their comrades died to pick up his.

"There were massacres and more massacres. Lenin loathed the kulaks, the peasants; Stalin loathed everybody. He had anyone executed whom he perceived as a threat. Kirov, the Leningrad Party boss — his murder was of course ordered by Stalin, who then wept publicly over what he called an atrocious act. It was the excuse for the purges that began then. My uncle was one of Kirov's bodyguards. He was mysteriously killed in an unexplained crash.

"My brother was convicted in one of Stalin's show trials, the Shakty trial. There were a dozen others with him, all innocent. Confessions extracted under torture. Those trials! When you want to deflect the blame from your own failure — and it was certainly Stalin's failure — stage a trial."

Wiggins interrupted. "This Dana. How did you get hold of her?"

Ilona Kuraukov looked at Wiggins as if he were a simpleton. "I knew her. I didn't know her as Dana, of course, but I'd known her as a girl."

"What's her name?"

"I imagine you mean her real name? Anna Kerensky. I don't expect it will do you any good to know that, though."

"She's Russian?"

"Belorussian. She was orphaned when her father was publicly interrogated and whipped and shot by the NKVD as a spy. Her whole village was exterminated. Her uncle was a priest who gathered his parishioners inside this small church. Sanctuary? He must have been simpleminded. The Bolsheviks took everything we had, all our furnishings, certainly our art. I steal one painting and think it's hardly recompense.

"Try them, beat them, torture them, murder them. My father, my husband, my brother, my uncle: all murdered." Ilona Kuraukov inhaled deeply of the cigarette she had twisted into the long ebony holder, exhaled a thin stream of smoke.

"The trouble with such plans is that they often involve more than was intended. Kate McBride. Simeon Pitt. An old Russian cleaning woman. Justice begins with one person, doesn't it?"

Her eyes slid away from his face and back again. "Ah, that *sounds* good, Mr. Jury." She shook her head.

"Mother Russia." And she fell silent.

48

"I can't believe it," said Jury, who had pulled up the same chair that Trueblood had pulled up only two mornings before. He had not, however, commented on its provenance.

"Everybody seems to be visiting me in bed these days. Can't even wait until I've had my tea," said Melrose testily.

Jury had appeared early this morning. Good lord, *eight?* Surely the clock had stopped. Melrose picked it up and banged it down a couple of times to get it running. "You must've left London at dawn."

"I did. Would have been here sooner if I'd got the message."

"Where in hell were you? Nobody knew where you were."

"I was . . . out cold, you could say." Jury studied the ceiling molding.

"Ha! At least you're getting your sleep. More than I can say." Melrose made a production of yawning and then neatened the sheet and blanket across his chest. He felt a little like royalty, felt as if supplicants were paying obeisance to him in his bed-chamber as he couldn't himself be both-ered to rise.

"You look like Wiggins."

That was not the effect he was striving for. Even more testily, he said, "All I can say is, where are the police when you need them?"

"Believe me, I'm really sorry." Jury put his hand on Melrose's shoulder. "If there'd been any way —" He dropped his hand.

Jury's tone was so totally heartfelt and sincere that Melrose felt ashamed. He dropped the act and swung his legs out of bed. *"Aargh."* He dropped his head in his hands. "Diane and I had a drink or two. One Demorney martini is the equivalent of a year's worth of Absolut ads."

"Well, it's obvious she wasn't aiming at the vodka. Too bad she missed."

"Want some tea?" Melrose tugged at the tapestry bellpull beside his bed.

Jury nodded. "Breakfast, too. I didn't get any."

"Oh, Martha will be cooking up a repast for both of us, make no mistake." Melrose was up and tying his robe.

Jury regarded its texture. "Cashmere?"

"Isn't everything? I've got to wash." Melrose padded into his bathroom.

"If we dawdle, it'll be time to go to the Jack and Hammer."

"It's only a little after nine," answered Jury, tucking into his second plate of eggs and bacon. He looked over at Melrose, who was tap-tap-tapping his boiled egg. "You're not going to do soldiers again?" Jury pointed his fork at the oblongs of toast Melrose had cut.

"I always do. Now that we're settled down, answer my questions."

"Answer one for me first. You left me a message —"

"Ah, yes. Did it help?"

"It might've done, except you gave it to Carole-anne. This is tantamount to not calling in the first place. It was something about futons. I was to look them up in Fodor's. According to Carole-anne, that is."

Melrose dropped his head in his hands and moaned gently. He sat up. "Not *futons*, for God's sake, *Fauchon's*."

Jury studied his eggs for a moment. "I should have been able to work that out, really."

"You shouldn't have *had* to work it out." Melrose picked up a soldier.

Jury looked at him. "Well?"

Melrose crunched his toast, swallowed. "Oh. According to this travel guide, Fauchon's is one of those swank stores whose policy is 'Hands off the goods!' You know, it's like squeezing pears or something at Fortnum. The customer does not help himself."

"And so Sophie . . ."

Melrose nodded. "And so *Sophie*. Little Sophie couldn't have been —"

Jury leaned back, shook his head. "— bagging potatoes."

"Now, tell me: What about the coat? What about the body? Being moved, I mean."

"The reason she wore the sable was the same reason she got off and on the bus. She wanted to be remembered. But she didn't want her *face* engraved on anyone's memory, so that ankle-length, swanky, and highly controversial fur would be what stuck in people's minds. She was right, too. That's what the witnesses recalled. And the two of them certainly looked enough alike that there'd be no jarring note there. As for the body, she hid it for a couple of hours so that she could establish an alibi, *if* Kate McBride — that is, herself — ever came under suspicion. She wouldn't have, not if I hadn't been on that bus."

"You remembered the face as well as the coat." Melrose dipped an oblong of toast in his egg and regarded Jury keenly.

Jury nodded but said nothing.

"You knew it was she." Melrose prompted him.

"Say I knew it was *someone*."

"You know what I mean."

Jury spoke then as if he hadn't heard. "But not Kate McBride. Not her because she was dead."

Melrose paused. "This woman — what does she call herself?"

"Dana."

"She *wanted* the police to work out that she was the dead woman, that the dead woman was Nancy Pastis, and that Nancy Pastis was actually Dana. That way she could go her merry way and not be hunted. Why, then, did she make it difficult for you to discover this? I mean, why not leave ID on the body — like Nancy Pastis's passport? Did the dead Kate McBride not resemble the passport picture enough?"

"Oh, she did. Amazing what a few tricks with hair and makeup will do to blur the line between one woman and another, if the fundamental similarity in looks is there to begin with. No. It's a good question. I'd say the answer is because identification on the body would be too obvious. This woman has a super-subtle mind. She likes to play games. And she is very, very cool." Jury rose and went to the sideboard, where he removed a silver dome and plunked a rasher of bacon on his plate. "Also, I think she was bored."

Melrose swung around to regard Jury. "Bored? Am I to suppose she murdered my friend Pitt out of *boredom?*"

"No." Jury reseated himself. "Because Pitt knew and told Fabricant he knew. The Fabricants — Seb or Ilona Kuraukov — got in touch with Dana." The name was as foreign to his tongue as the taste of some exotic honeyed melon on one of those Pacific islands. He shook his head as if to loosen the name. "I'd say it was Ilona Kuraukov's idea; she got it when she saw what Rees was doing in St. Petersburg."

"You know, I find it hard to think of Ralph Rees as doing this. His conscience, misguided as it is, just seemed unsullied."

"Oh, he wasn't in on it."

"How could he *not* be?"

"Tack the sandpaper over the stolen painting, then paint it. Ilona is a painter. She could have done it with no trouble. Unless, of course, one believes that white lot a work of genius. I don't think Nicholas was in on it either. Not if his pal Rees wasn't."

Melrose was cracking the top of another egg with his spoon. "But how in God's name did she get it out of the Hermitage?"

"They still don't know. It was cut from the frame —"

"Good lord, they have guards! They have a security system."

"Seems a few moments before the damage was discovered, the guards were distracted by something going on elsewhere. As far as getting it out goes, it wasn't a large painting. The Hermitage people think it might have been rolled and stuck in something like a hollow cane."

"They make you park things like that — canes, walking sticks — by the door before you go in, don't they?"

Jury shrugged. "I would think so, but given the cops got there so quickly and nobody left and everyone was searched —" He shrugged again.

Melrose dipped another bit of toast. "So it's still missing. And so is she."

"It is, and she is. Yes."

When Jury and Plant walked into the Jack and Hammer a little after eleven,

Trueblood jumped up from where he'd been sitting between Diane Demorney and Agatha and wrung Melrose's hand, saying to them that this was the most excitement they'd had since the body in the *secrétaire à abattant* days.

"Or the Man with a Load of Mischief days."

Jury smiled at Diane. "You were brilliant, only —"

Diane rolled her eyes as if suffering an onset of terminal boredom. "Now you're going to ask if I have a license to carry the thing, Superintendent."

"No. I was going to say what you did was very dangerous —"

"A violation of the 'reckless disregard for life and limb' statute?"

Jury laughed. "Okay, okay."

"I *mean*," said Diane, leaning very close to him and tilting her head so that her crow-black razor-cut hair fell across a well-turned cheekbone, "given *some people* weren't available for protection, one has to improvise." Diane sat back, plugged a cigarette into the ivory holder, and wiggled it for a light. She might brandish a revolver about, but certainly not a match. Trueblood lit it. Then she said, "Are we having a drink or has everyone taken the oath?"

"We're just trying to decide who's in the chair."

Without any hesitation, three pairs of eyes fastened on Jury.

"I get the point," he said, and called over to Dick Scroggs, who came, for once, as if he'd grown wings. He liked Jury.

Hands under his apron, Dick said, "Oh, you needn't order, sir, as I know just what everyone wants. Martini with a twist . . . half pint of Old Peculiar . . . Campari and absent. . . ."

"*Absinth,* old trout. Lord, you're a publican and you don't even know what you're selling?"

Diane regarded him as she might have an alien. "Dick, you know I don't drink martinis until the sun is over the garden."

"Yardarm," said Melrose.

"Whatever. When it gets where it's going at noon."

"Okay, miss, then what'll you have?"

Diane raised her arm to examine her diamond and pearl watch. "Twenty-eight minutes."

"Listen," said Trueblood. "Let's all go over to the library until then. We'll have a coffee." He was out of his chair.

"*Coffee?* At *this* hour?" inquired Diane.

"The new coffee shop." Melrose got up

too, pulled at Jury. "You've got to see it."

"What coffee shop?" Jury asked.

Nobody answered as they all got up.

"But it's Sunday!"

Nobody answered and they all trooped out.

"It's quite illegal, you know," said Theo Wrenn Browne, who was sitting at one of the tables in the coffee room, Agatha beside him like a seal in her slick dark fur jacket, looking ready to take on any protesters.

The party of four sat down at the only vacant table, unhappily next to Melrose's aunt and Browne.

"And this espresso," said Browne, making a face after a sip, "isn't even good. Tastes bitter."

Bitter? Melrose glanced across the room at Sally and Bub's mum. One can always hope.

Said Agatha, finding it fertile ground for attacking her nephew, "This woman, Melrose, who nearly shot you —"

(Talk about hope.)

"— what on earth were you doing with her? You never did have the good sense to keep out of harm's way."

His fault, naturally, that he'd been

robbed and nearly murdered.

"Where's Vivian?" asked Jury. "I haven't seen her in a long time." He looked into the library, as if she might be hiding out in the stacks.

"What we've come up with is," said Agatha, danger to her nephew already pushed aside, "Theo and I have found this 'coffee shop' is breaking all sorts of laws. You haven't council permission for this. And it's in the bylaws that the library *cannot* be used as a place of trade for food and drink, nor has it passed a hygiene inspection."

"Yet I see you're eating some of Betty Ball's uninspected scones," said Melrose.

"You've done Una Twinny no favor here," said Browne, trying to look concerned but only managing to look pleased as punch. "She'll no doubt be fired when her superiors hear of this."

"Over my dead body," chimed in Trueblood.

Agatha adjusted her seal collar and said, "Oh, well, we all know your penchant for peculiar arrangements, Mr. Trueblood. I'm not at all surprised."

Her surprise took a backseat to everyone else's when, suddenly, Vivian rushed through the door, looking wild and exclaiming, "Melrose!"

And, to everyone's astonishment (except Diane's, who was having to light her own cigarette), Vivian quite literally threw herself at Melrose after he'd risen to greet her. "Oh, heavens, oh, God, you could have been *killed!*" She stepped back, eyes wet, face mottled red, and shook him a little. "Why do you *do* these things!"

His fault, as usual.

"You!"

Ah, not his but Jury's fault.

One hand on her hip, Vivian was shaking a finger in Jury's face so instructively he reared back in his chair. "Why do you keep on involving him in your police business?"

Jury shrugged. "Because he's good."

That was, God only knew, no answer (though Melrose liked it), and, shuddering from the senseless danger of it all, Vivian fell into one of the chairs just vacated by three elderly women who seemed to find the goings-on next to them less than restful.

Melrose was delighted that he'd called up ungovernable emotion in Vivian. That she was bawling out Richard Jury was an unforeseen treat.

"Who was this — this *person* who very nearly shot you?"

"Oh, we went to school together donkey's years ago."

Vivian was up and pummeling him, then just as quickly sobered up and merely sat there blushing.

"I can tell you one thing about her," said Diane, ratcheting the flint of her silver cigarette lighter.

Five pairs of eyes swiveled in Diane's direction, waiting.

"That suit was a Chanel."

They all blinked, lost on the Demorney sea of inconsequence.

"No."

The five pairs of eyes swiveled round to regard Jury, who'd spoken.

"Max Mara."

Melrose thought he said it awfully sadly, as if Max, once among them, would never come again.